MARY, QUEEN OF FRANCE

JEAN PLAIDY

First published in Great Britain 1964
by Robert Hale Ltd

Published in Large Print 2008 by ISIS Publishing Ltd.,
7 Centremead, Osney Mead, Oxford OX2 0ES
by arrangement with
Arrow Books, one of the publishers
in The Random House Group Limited

British Library Cataloguing in Publication Data

Plaidy, Jean, 1906–1993

Mary, Queen of France. – Large print ed.

1. Mary, Queen, consort of Louis XII, King of France, 1496–1533 – Fiction
2. Henry, VIII, King of England, 1491–1547 – Fiction
3. Louis, XII, King of France, 1462–1515 – Fiction
4. Suffolk, Charles Brandon, Duke of, d. 1545 – Fiction
5. Great Britain – History – Henry VIII, 1509–1547 – Fiction
6. France – History – Louis XII, 1498–1515 – Fiction
7. Historical fiction
8. Large type books

I. Title

823.9'12 [F]

ISBN 978–0–7531–8158–4 (hb)
ISBN 978–0–7531–8159–1 (pb)

Printed and bound in Great Britain by
T. J. International Ltd., Padstow, Cornwall

Contents

Part One: The English

CHAPTER ONE

The Betrothal of Mary

Although the wind blew from the northeast, whipping the cold waters of the Thames, bending the rushes and long grasses on the banks and throwing itself, as though in anger, against the Palace walls, the barges continued to arrive, and great personages alighted at the privy steps.

The young girl kneeling in a window seat watched them with satisfaction.

"Why, Katharine," she said, without turning to look at her sister-in-law, who sat sewing on her stool near the window, "my lord Dudley and my lord Empson are arriving now. Who next, I wonder." She pulled at her plentiful red-gold curls. "And to think, Katharine, that they are coming to honour *me*!"

"Nay, Mary, you are over-vain. You should remember that it is not you they honour, but your father's crown."

"By God's Holy Mother," retorted Mary, "is it my father's crown then who is going to solemnise its nuptials tomorrow in this Palace?"

"We know it is yourself who is going to do that. But the honour these men do is not for an eleven-year-old girl, but because she is the daughter of the King of England."

"I am twelve, I would have you know," retorted Mary. "Twelve and . . ." She began to count on her fingers. "Twelve years and nine months. Almost thirteen. So there!"

"That is not so very old, and it is unseemly that you should use such oaths, which are in truth blasphemy."

"Oh, Katharine, you are such a *dull* creature."

She jumped from the window seat and, running to Katharine, put her arms about her. "There, I did not mean that. But you are so *good* . . . and I can never be good. At least I don't intend to be until I am so old that I must think of repentance. But you are not of that age yet, Katharine. Why don't you stop thinking about what is right, and think more about what is amusing?"

She put her head on one side and regarded Katharine. Poor Kate! A widow already — and of some years' standing. It must be . . . she tried to count again . . . six years since Arthur had died, and poor Katharine had been growing older and sadder ever since.

"We are not put on earth to amuse ourselves, Mary," said Katharine quietly.

"But *I* was," persisted Mary.

"You are young, and you are not as serious as you should be; but as a Princess you have your duty, and that is something you should never forget."

"Duty!" cried Mary, and she swung round so that her tawny, damask petticoats showed beneath her green velvet gown. She pointed her toe and went on: "Oh, Katharine, have you tried the new dance? It goes like this. Henry showed me." She danced awhile, her hair streaming out behind her, her round face pink with the exertion, her blue eyes brilliant. Katharine said a prayer for her. She was so beautiful, so passionate, so self-willed, so spoiled; for even the King, who thought of little but enlarging his exchequer, softened at the sight of his youngest child.

"And," went on Mary, coming to a sudden halt, "I should like to remind you that Henry uses that oath, and if Henry does, then so shall I."

"You should not imitate his bad habits."

"Henry's bad habits! He has none. He is my wonderful brother. Do you know, Katharine, I love him better than anyone in the world." Her face darkened suddenly. "I should love Charles, I suppose, but he is not like Henry." She ran to the picture which she had propped up on the window seat, and coming back, sat at Katharine's feet holding it out before her. It showed the Prince of Castile, a boy with sleepy eyes and a heavy jaw; his mouth was slightly open, and it was scarcely a prepossessing face. "Now can you imagine anyone *less* like Henry?" went on Mary. "And that is Charles, my bridegroom. Oh, what a wonderful thing it would be if Henry were not my brother. Then I might marry him."

"You are very frivolous and talk a great deal of nonsense," said Katharine primly; but in spite of herself she was smiling. She thought: it is the same with us all. We tremble for her; we deplore her frivolity; and yet there is not one of us who is unaffected by her charm. After all, she is but a child. She will grow up. "Dear sister," she went on, "tomorrow is a very solemn occasion for you. If you would like to pray with me . . ."

Mary shook her head emphatically. "I have said my prayers for the day, and you are quite wrong, Katharine. It is a joyous occasion. Did you not hear the bells ringing out this morning? There will be music in the streets and the people will make bonfires and dance round them. They are all so pleased because I am going to marry Prince Charles. There is nothing solemn about it. My father says it is a good marriage. So do all the old men from Flanders. They say that trade will flourish because of me . . . and that in marrying Charles I shall be doing my duty to England and my father's House. So if I am doing all that, I'll not be solemn too. How the wind howls! They say it is hot in Spain. Is it? You know, because it was once your home. Katharine, one day I shall be *Queen* of Spain."

Katharine shook her head resignedly.

"My poor, poor Katharine," Mary rushed on. "All this talk of marriage makes you sad. You remember your own marriage and poor Arthur. Oh, Katharine, I am sorry. But smile. You shall dance tomorrow. Did you know that there is going to be bull-fighting and bear-baiting? There'll be hunting and hawking, and I'll swear there'll be jousting. It is going to be so exciting. Henry says that we do not have enough gaiety at Court, and when he is King . . ." She stopped and put her fingers to her lips. "But it really will be a very fine ceremony, Katharine, and you should enjoy it, with the rest of us."

She heard the sound of laughter from below, and running to the window, she knelt once more on the seat.

"It is Henry," she cried. "He is returning from the hunt. Henry! Henry . . ."

She was tapping vigorously on the window, and the group of young men below looked upward. In their centre was her brother Henry, already, although not yet eighteen, over six feet tall. He stood, legs apart, hands on hips, for the groom had taken his horse. He was soberly dressed, but only because his father deplored extravagance, and he managed to wear his clothes with a jaunty air; and indeed their very sobriety accentuated his dazzlingly healthy looks.

"Hey, sister," he called; then he turned and spoke to his attendants who immediately burst into laughter, implying that his wit was irresistible.

He entered the Palace and in a few minutes had flung open the door of the room and was striding toward his sister.

She leaped up at him, putting her arm about his neck; he swung her round and she shrieked with delight. Katharine, quietly watching, thought how much they resembled each other and how pleasant it was to observe the affection between a brother and sister. It was particularly comforting to realise that Henry was capable of such deep feeling, because she hoped that one day she might be the object of his devotion. She saw in this young man her chance of regaining her lost dignity, and the humiliation of the last years had been almost beyond bearing. Had she not made a great effort to suppress her feelings, she could have hated the King of England, who had treated her with such cold indifference since the death of her mother had reduced her value in the eyes of the world. But now her father, Ferdinand of Aragon, was no longer merely King of Aragon. He had enjoyed great successes in Europe and therefore his daughter had ceased to be as insignificant as she once had been. She knew it was solely for this reason that she was allowed to be the companion of the Princess Mary — still humble, it was true, yet no longer completely banished from Court.

When her mother was alive, this dazzling young Prince had been promised as her second husband; she still hoped that he might remember that promise. So in his presence she was nervous, eager to please and yet afraid that she would betray her anxiety to do so.

"I can scarce wait for tomorrow," Mary was saying.

"Are you so eager to leave us then?" demanded her brother.

"Henry, I never want to leave *you*!"

His smile was sparkling. He loved praise and could never have enough of it.

"And you know," went on Mary, "it is only a ceremony. I am not to go away for years and years . . ."

"Let us hope not," cried Henry.

"Then you would have no sisters near you. You have already lost Margaret. Oh, Henry, I wonder what it is like in Scotland. Do you think Margaret ever misses *us*?"

"She has a husband to think of now, but they say Scotland is a dour country. I'd rather be here in Richmond."

"Henry, perhaps Charles will come and live here, and I needn't go away."

"Is that what you would like, little sister?"

"Will you command him to do so?"

"I . . . command the Prince of Castile!"

"Indeed you must, because you will be able to command the whole world when . . . when . . ."

The sister and brother looked at each other for a few seconds, then Henry remembered the presence of Katharine. He turned to her and said: "My sister prattles, does she not, Madam?"

"Indeed, she does, Your Highness."

"Katharine has been telling me I should pray more and talk less. I won't, Henry. I won't. I *won't*."

"You are a bold creature," said Henry. "Now listen to me. When the ceremony is over there will be a banquet and afterward a great masque. We will show these Flemings how we can dance and sing. You and I . . . with a few of my friends . . . will slip away and disguise ourselves. Then we will return and dance before the Court. They will be enchanted with us and, when they are asking each other who we can be, we will throw off our disguises and show them."

Mary clasped her hands together and looked up at the ceiling. "Oh, Henry, you think of the most wonderful things. I wish . . . oh, how I wish . . ."

"Tell me what you wish."

She regarded him solemnly. "That I need never go away from you and, because being a Princess I must marry, I wish there was one who looked as you do, who spoke as you do, and was so like you in all ways that people could not tell you apart."

Henry gave a bellow of laughter. He looked at Katharine as though to say, what do you think of my sister? Is she not ridiculous?

But he was contented that she should be so. He was indeed a contented young man. He believed that everything he wished for would soon be his. Every direction in which he turned he found adulation, and very soon — it could not be long because the old man was coughing and spitting blood regularly now — he would be the King of this country.

His friends paid him all the homage he could wish for; when he rode through the streets of his father's cities he was cheered more loudly than any. He knew that the whole of England was eagerly awaiting that day when they could call him their King. He would have everything — good looks, good health, charm, gaiety . . . and all that great wealth which his father had accumulated so single-mindedly over the years.

Yet nothing pleased him quite so much as the adoration of this little sister because, knowing her well, he knew too that when she expressed her love she spoke from the very depth of her heart. Young Mary had never attempted to hide her love or her hatred; had he been a beggar she would have loved him.

He sensed too the yearning tenderness in the demeanor of the other woman, and he felt some regard for her.

This was a happy day for, although on the morrow Mary's nuptials were being solemnised, it was only by proxy and she would be with him for some time to come. So he had not to think of parting with her yet.

Mary smoothed her skirts and tried to look demure. Katharine, who had been selected as her guardian for the occasion, was well pleased with her. In spite of her exuberance, thought Katharine, she was a Princess and could be relied upon to act with dignity whenever the occasion demanded that she should.

The girl looked beautiful and it was certain that the Sieur de Bergues, who had come as proxy for the eight-year-old Prince, would go back and report what a charming creature she was. Not that the bridegroom would be very interested at this stage. How lucky Mary was! It would be years before Charles was old enough to claim her.

Mary smiled at Katharine. "Dear Charles!" she said. "He is so much younger than I am. I expect I shall have to take care of him." She sighed. "He looks delicate. That's a pity."

"When you were younger *you* were delicate and you grew out of it, so perhaps he will."

"Assuredly he will; and he'll grow as tall as Henry."

"Few men grow as tall."

She looked wistful. "I know. Henry's bride will be so lucky, won't she? Imagine being Henry's bride *and* Queen of England."

Katharine, who never ceased to imagine such an eventuality, did not answer; but Mary leapt up and kissed her suddenly because she knew exactly what was going on in her sister-in-law's mind. Mary had always kept her eyes and ears wide open for Court gossip, and she coerced and bullied her attendants into keeping her informed. Secretly she wished Katharine luck, for she was very fond of her, although she was often irritated by all the piety and somewhat melancholy outlook. If she would but laugh more and pray less, thought Mary, Henry would be more inclined to view her with favour. Although of course royal princes and princesses could not choose their spouses and it would not rest with Henry whether he married her, unless . . .

She stopped her thoughts running in that direction. Hers was an affectionate nature and her father had never been unkind to her; but he had never been effusively loving as she would have liked him to be; it was simply not in his nature to be so. Yet he had shown that he was not entirely able to resist her, and it was exhilarating to know that she alone could make his lips quirk in amusement, could bring a note of softness into his usually harsh voice. But his Court was so dull, and Henry was always saying how different it might be.

She thought of her sister Margaret who some six years before had taken part in a similar ceremony when the proxy of King James IV of Scotland had come to Richmond and had married her in his master's name.

She could scarcely remember Margaret now, except that she had quarrelled often with Henry. They had missed her though, because she was like they were — full of vitality, eager to enjoy life.

Arthur had not been like that; he had been more like their parents. Poor Arthur — such a sickly boy, and she certainly could not remember what *he* looked like. If he had lived Henry would not have been Prince of Wales but a member of the Church. Imagining Henry as Archbishop of Canterbury made the laughter come bubbling up. So perhaps it was all for the best . . . for Henry was surely meant to be King.

"Are you ready?" asked Katharine.

"Yes."

"Then let us go, for they will be waiting for you."

Mary looked about the reception room, which had been her mother's and which had been draped with hangings of cloth of gold for this occasion, thinking: when next *I* see this room I shall be betrothed. I shall have a new title — Princess of Castile — and that rather vacant-looking little boy will be almost my husband. Poor Charles, I shall have to take care of him, I can see.

Thinking of him thus she felt tender towards him and was not at all displeased that he was to be her husband.

Katharine took her hand and led her into the great hall, which was hung with silk and decorated with ornaments and gold and silver plate. She saw her father standing with the Sieur de Bergues and, beside him, the Archbishop of Canterbury.

Henry was there too. He was excited because all such ceremonies delighted him; he loved grandeur and it was his continual complaint that there was too little of it at the English Court.

He gave his sister a smile as their eyes met; this she acknowledged briefly because she knew many eyes were upon her, among them her father's.

How ill he looked! His skin was growing more yellow, his eyes more sunken; and Mary felt a pang of remorse because she had been looking forward to the time when the Court would be gay, knowing that it could mean only one thing.

She smiled at him tenderly and the King, watching his lovely daughter, was unable for a second or so to control his features.

Now she was standing before the Archbishop of Canterbury and he was addressing the assembly. The dull old man! She could not concentrate on what he was saying. She was thinking of a long ago day, before Margaret went to Scotland and they had all been in Richmond watching the barges coming from the Tower. She remembered hearing that her mother was dead. There had been a baby sister who had died too; they had called her Katharine. Life could be sad . . . for some people. She did not believe it ever could be for her, but that did not prevent her from being sorry for those who suffered.

"Repeat after me." The Archbishop's voice sounded stern. How did he guess she had not been attending?

"I, Mary, by you John, Lord of Bergues, commissary and procurator of the most high and puissant Prince

Charles by Grace of God Prince of Spain, Archduke of Austria, Duke of Burgundy . . .

She was smiling at the Sieur de Bergues, who was looking at her with the utmost seriousness.

". . . take the said Charles to be my husband and spouse . . ."

It was the turn of the Sieur de Bergues, but she was wondering what disguises she and Henry would put on after the banquet. Would they dance together? She hoped so. No one could leap so high and so effortlessly as Henry.

The Sieur de Bergues had taken her hand and was pushing the bridal ring onto her finger; then he stooped and, putting his lips to hers, gave her the nuptial kiss.

It was really a very simple matter — giving a solemn promise to marry.

From the Palace windows she could see the light of the bonfires, she could hear the sound of rejoicing. The people were going wild this day, and all because their little Princess had gone through a ceremony solemnising the nuptials between herself and the Prince of Castile.

Inside the Palace the merriment was even greater. It was not often that Henry VII gave his courtiers an opportunity to be extravagantly gay. For this occasion noblemen and their wives had brought out their richest jewels. It was folly to do so because the King would note their wealth and set his cunning ministers, Dudley and Empson, to find means of transferring some of his subjects' goods to the royal exchequer. But they did not care. They were starved of pleasure; they wanted to dance and masque, joust and hunt; they wanted to wear fine clothes and dazzle each other with their splendour; they wanted to vie with each other; and this was their chance to do so.

Mary was surrounded by a group of her women. They were all talking at once, so it was impossible to hear what they were saying, but she understood that they were to wrap themselves in gauzy veils, which would give them an oriental look, and there were masks to hide their faces, that they might mingle with the dancers and remain unrecognised. This was Henry's idea and she thought it a good one.

Her women were exclaiming as she stood before them. "But I declare I should never have guessed! The Lady Mary is tall for her age. Why, no one would believe she was not yet a woman . . ."

"Hurry!" cried Mary. "I can scarce wait to be among the dancers."

In the hall, with her ladies, she joined other masked dancers whom she knew to be Henry and his friends.

She heard whispers: "But who are these masked ladies and gentlemen?"

"I have heard they come from far off places to see the English Court."

She laughed to herself as she picked out a tall figure. She was certain who he was and, going up to him, touched his arm.

"I pray you, sir," she said, "tell me how you came here this night?"

He was trying to disguise his voice, she guessed, and she had to admit that he did it admirably. "Might I not ask the same question of you, Madam?"

"You might, but you would get no answer."

"Then let us agree to curb our curiosity until the unmasking. Would you dance with me?"

"I will do so."

So they danced and she thought: I have never been so happy. "This is the most wonderful ball I have ever attended," she told him.

"And you must have attended so many!"

She laughed. "Are you suggesting, sir, that this is my first ball?"

"My lady, you put thoughts into my head which were not there before."

"You speak in riddles, sir."

"Then let me offer one plain truth. I'll swear there is not a lovelier lady at the ball than my partner."

"And I'll swear there's not a more handsome gentleman than mine."

He pressed her hand. "Now we are pledged to stay together that we may prove our words."

She sighed. "Indeed, it is a duty."

And so it was, for even when the ritual of the dance parted them temporarily they came back to each other.

She wanted to tell him that he had put up a very good disguise, that the change in his voice was miraculous; even so he could never hide himself from her. But to have done this would have spoiled the masque. He would want her to express surprise when they unmasked — and so she would. It was all part of the game.

What a wonderful brother she had, who could remain at her side through the ball, for he was a young man and, she had heard, fond of women. He would be a little disturbed on her account perhaps, for she was over-young to move disguised among the dancers; so he was determined to stay at her side to protect her. Dear Henry! Beloved brother.

She delighted in his skill in the dance. None leaped higher, none could turn and twirl so gracefully. When they unmasked she would tell him how proud she was of him, how dearly she loved him.

When the time came for unmasking she stood before him, her eyes alight with pleasure, and as she took off her mask he cried: "By my faith, it is the Princess Mary."

With a deft movement he removed his mask. She stared, for the man who stood before her was not her brother.

"But," she began, "I thought . . ."

"I please Your Highness less unmasked?" he asked.

"You were so like . . ."

"His Highness the Prince? He swears he gives me an inch . . . but I am not so sure."

"You must be the two tallest men at Court, so it is no small wonder that I was misled. But you danced as he dances . . . your voice is even a little like his."

"I crave Your Highness's pardon, but may I say this: Charles Brandon is as eager to serve you as he is to serve your brother."

She began to laugh suddenly for she guessed that this man had known all the time that she believed him to be her brother and had done his best to impersonate Henry. She could always enjoy a joke, even against herself.

He laughed with her while she studied him carefully — large, blond, handsome, vital. In truth a man; a little older than Henry, a little more experienced of the world.

"I never saw a man to remind me more of my brother," she said. "My mistake was excusable."

He bowed low. "A gracious compliment from a gracious lady," he murmured.

Later Mary thought: that night was the most important of my life up to that time because it was then I first became aware of Charles Brandon.

The merrymaking over, the Sieur de Bergues with his followers went back to Flanders, and the Princess had to return to the schoolroom. It was true she had a dignified establishment with her own suite of waiting women, and the fact that she was known as the Princess of Castile did add somewhat to her dignity, but there were still lessons to be learned; there were Latin and French exercises to be completed and she had to sit over her embroidery.

The Court too had returned to normal. The King was disturbed by the cost of entertaining the Flemish embassy and was more parsimonious than ever. He was often irritable because he was in great bodily discomfort and, knowing he could not live long, he could not stop himself wondering what sort of king his brilliant and vital heir would make. Young Henry was vain, too fond of fine clothes and gaiety; these cost good money and he was not sure now whether, in his attempts to imbue the boy with a reverence for gold, he had not given him an urge to exchange it for worthless baubles. He was eager to arrange a match for his son; it was a matter of great relief that his daughters were satisfactorily placed — Margaret was Queen of Scotland, and that was a match which pleased him; while Mary as wife of the Prince of Spain would marry even more advantageously. No, it was not his daughters who worried him. It was his son. As for himself he did not despair of getting more children, although he was aware that as he was no longer in his prime he should act promptly. His thoughts were now on the Emperor Maximilian's daughter, Margaret of Savoy, who was aunt to Charles, Mary's affianced. But each day he felt a little weaker and because he was shrewd he knew that his courtiers were looking more and more to the Prince of Wales than to the old King.

One of his greatest pleasures was to watch his daughter as she went about the Court. He would study her when she did not know that she was observed; she was a wild and lovely creature and he often wondered how he could have sired her. She had a look of her maternal grandfather, Edward IV — all his surviving children had that look. It was a grief to him that out of a family of seven only three were left. But what a joy to think that his two daughters would be queens, and his son a king. When he looked back to the days of his youth he could congratulate himself; and that reminded him that there was one to whom he should be forever grateful. She was at the Court now, for whenever possible they were together and during those months since the nuptial ceremony they were often in each other's company. This was his mother, the Countess of Richmond and Derby.

It was she who supervised the education of young Mary and did much to impress on her the importance of her position.

One March day, a few months after the nuptial ceremony, Mary sat over her embroidery, cobbling it a little, for she was impatient with the needle and preferred to dance and play sweet music; and while she worked she was thinking of the new song she would play on her lute or clavichord and of which she would ask Henry's opinion. It was such pleasure to be with Henry and his closest friend, Charles Brandon, with whom she now shared a secret joke because she had mistaken him for her brother. Neither of them told Henry that; they sensed he would not be pleased that someone could really be mistaken for him, and that his own sister should fall into such an error might be wounding.

Sitting staring into space Mary did not notice the approach of her grandmother until the Countess was beside her, taking the piece of embroidery from her hands.

She started guiltily, and was sorry that her embroidery was so poor since it displeased her grandmother.

"This is not good," said the old lady.

"I fear not, my lady."

"You should work harder, my child."

"Yes, my lady."

Mary looked at the stern face before her, thinking how sad it was to be old, and that her grandmother was really ancient, because the King seemed an old man and he was her son.

"It would please your father if you showed more diligence. What will your husband think of a bride who cobbles with her needle?"

"He is but a boy, my lady," replied Mary, "and as he is the heir of Spain and Flanders, I doubt he will weep over a piece of embroidery."

"You are too pert, child."

"Nay, my lady, I did not mean to be, for it is my opinion that Charles would as lief I had a strong healthy body to bear him sons than nimble fingers to embroider. There will be women enough for that."

"And it may well be to perform both services."

Mary looked startled. "Nay, Grandmother, I should never stomach a faithless husband."

"That which could not be prevented would have to be endured. My child, you have much to learn. You remind me of your brother."

"I am pleased to do so."

"That is good. Tudors should stand together."

"Have no fear, my lady. I should always stand with Henry."

The Countess patted Mary's hand. "It rejoices me to see this love between you. Always remember it, and when you are in a strange land do not forget that you are a Tudor and owe loyalty to your own."

"I shall always be loyal to Henry."

Margaret Beaufort, Countess of Richmond and Derby, took the needlework from her granddaughter's hands and began to unpick the stitches. She was not particularly interested in the work but she did not wish those sharp bright eyes to read the emotion she feared she might betray. She was anxious on behalf of her son for whom she had lived since that day, over fifty years ago, when he had been born, a posthumous child; she had schemed for him, and the great goal of her life had been to see him on the throne of England. Few women could have seen such an ambitious dream come true; for it had been a great struggle and at one time it had seemed well-nigh impossible of achievement.

But there he was on the throne of England — her beloved son; and never would she forget the day when the news of what had happened on Bosworth Field was brought to her.

"Glory be to God," she had cried; and often she asked herself, for she was a pious woman, whether then and on other occasions she had been guilty of idolatry; for never had a woman adored a son as she had her Henry.

He was well aware of it, being shrewd enough to know who was his best friend; and the woman who had been nearest and dearest to him during his years of struggle and of glory was his mother.

Now she was frightened, for she could see death creeping nearer and nearer; it had already set a shadow on those features, so cold and unprepossessing to others, so dear and beautiful to her.

How could she bear to go on living if her beloved son should be taken from her? What purpose would there be in life when for so long she had had only one ambition — to serve him?

He had shown her that she could still serve him, when he had read the thoughts in her melancholy eyes.

"Mother," he had said, "you must stay close to the children to guide them, for they are young yet."

"My beloved," she had cried out in alarm, "they have the best of fathers to guide them."

"They need their granddame. Henry is headstrong. I know full well that he approaches his eighteenth birthday but he is as yet a boy." The King had sighed deeply. "I sometimes think that being so full of bodily vigour has made him over fond of useless pastimes. He is not as serious as I could wish. Margaret is in the care of her husband. And Mary . . ."

"Mary is like her brother — headstrong and greatly indulged by all."

"She needs a strong hand. I have tried to wean her from her frivolity."

"You love her too dearly, my beloved. She is sharp and knows well how to play on your feelings."

"But, Mother, I have never been a tender father. At times I have watched children and their parents and I have said to myself: mine never run to me in that fashion. Mine never laugh with me like that."

"You are King and no child ever had a better father."

"I have heard my wife tell her children stories of her childhood, of the gaiety of her father . . . and he was a king."

"You have been a good father to your children, Henry."

But he was sad. A sign that he was growing more and more infirm. He was remembering certain acts which had taken place during his reign, and was wishing they had not. He even regretted some of the methods by which he had extorted money from his subjects. As if it had not been important to build up a rich exchequer! thought his mother. As if he had not taken all for the glory of his country and never for himself! How much had he ever spent on fine raiment? Had he ever frittered away one golden crown on senseless pleasure?

She was thinking of this now as she picked at the stitches in Mary's woeful work. Mary watched her in silence, sensing her mood and half understanding what had inspired it; but she could not help thinking: if my father dies there will still be a king of England. And it was so much more pleasant to picture young Henry, resplendent in purple velvet and ermine, than old Henry, withered with disease.

"Mary, my child."

"Yes, my lady."

"The King suffers much in health."

Mary nodded.

"He loves you dearly. Why do you not go to him and show a little tenderness?"

Mary's lovely blue eyes were wide with astonishment. "Go to the King!" she cried.

"Forget he is the King for a while. Remember only that he is your father. Go to him, and when you have knelt and kissed his hand, put your arms about his neck, tell him that you have ever loved him dearly and that he has been a good father to you."

Mary shrank away. Was her grandmother serious? Was she raving? One did not go to the King and put one's arms about his neck. Even his favourite daughter could not do that.

"He would be a little startled at first," went on her grandmother, "and then he would be so happy. Mary, your father is a great king; he took this bankrupt kingdom — which was his by right — he took it from the usurper Richard, and he made it rich and strong. Such a task was a great tax on his energies and he had little time to laugh and frolic. Perhaps this has made you feel that he is over-stern. But go to him and tell him how much you love him."

Mary was pensive. It would not be easy, for she, who was always spontaneous, would find it difficult to play a part, and in truth she had no great love for her father.

Her grandmother put the embroidery into her lap and rising, kissed her. Then she went away as though in a great hurry.

Mary paused outside her father's apartments.

"My lady," said the page, "His Grace is with his ministers."

Mary turned away relieved. She had been rehearsing what she would say, and it sounded false to her; she was glad the need to say it was postponed.

The King asked who was at the door, and when told it was the Lady Mary he smiled.

She had some request to make, he thought. What does she wish? Some new bauble? She grows more like her brother every day.

Yet he had a yearning to see the pretty creature; and if it were a new gown or even a jewel she wanted he would perhaps grant her her wish; but he must impress upon her the need for sobriety and explain that all the extravagant display, which had accompanied her nuptial celebrations, had not been for personal vainglory but to show to foreigners that England was wealthy, because wealth meant power.

He turned back to the task before him. He had decided that all those who had been imprisoned in London for debts of under forty shillings should be discharged.

He was beginning to be tormented by remorse when he contemplated the extortions which Dudley and Empson had committed in his name; and now that his conscience was beginning to worry him on this score, he realised that he was a very sick man indeed.

There were cowslips in the meadows near Richmond and the blackthorn was in blossom. The air was enlivened by birdsong, and all this meant that it was the month of April and spring had come.

But in the Palace the old era was ending and the new one had not yet begun.

The fifty-two-year-old King lay on his bed and thought of his subjects; he wondered ruefully how many of them would shed a real tear at his passing.

Fifty-two. It was not really old; yet he had lived a full life and there was so much of it that he wished he had lived differently. He had recently pilgrimaged to Our Lady of Walsingham and to Saint Thomas of Canterbury, and there he had sworn to build a hospital for the sick poor.

Time! he thought. I need time. He hoarded time as once he had hoarded gold; he was fighting with all his strength to hold off death a little longer until such time as he could make peace with himself.

But death would not wait.

Mary came to his apartments, planning what she would do and say. She would go to his bed and put her arms about his neck. "I will not call you Your Highness, but Father," she would tell him. "Oh, Father, we do love you . . . Henry and I. We understand that it was necessary for you to be stern with us. We love to dance and play and we often forget our duty . . . but we want to be good. We want to be the sort of children of whom you can be proud."

Did that sound false? For false it was. Neither she nor Henry wanted to be anything but what they were.

"It is the Lady Mary," said one of the pages to another.

"I have come to see my father."

"My lady, the priests are with him."

Holy Mother, thought Mary, is it then too late?

His body had been taken from Richmond to Westminster, but not with any speed for, although he died on the 21st day of April, he was not moved until the 9th of May.

There was reason for the delay. An image of him in wax must be made ready to be clad in his robes of state and placed in the coffin, and remain there during the funeral, holding the ball and sceptre in its hands. The chariot which would hold the coffin had to be covered in black cloth of gold; and all those noblemen who lived far from Court must be given time to arrive for the ceremony.

It was to be a grand funeral. The King had left money to pay for masses which were to be said for his soul, as he asked, for as long as the world should endure. He had become very uneasy during his last days on earth when he had realised that he would not have time to make all the amends he had planned.

The new King had already left Richmond for the Palace of the Tower. That was well, because he found it difficult to hide his elation. His father was dead and he had been a good father; but what a stern one! And had he not treated his son as though he were a child?

Freedom! thought Henry VIII, dreaming of his future.

And Mary, while she prayed for the soul of her father, could not prevent her thoughts wandering as she considered what a change this was going to make to all their lives.

It was a great occasion when the funeral cortege passed through the capital. At London Bridge the Mayor and the City Companies received it and merchants mingled with apprentices in the crowds which followed it to St Paul's.

As was the custom with the dead, people remembered virtues rather than failings.

And when all was considered, his epitaph was as good as any king could hope to achieve.

"He brought us peace," said the people.

Yet never had they cried: "The King is dead. Long live the King!" with more hope, more exultation than they did in those spring days of 1509.

The sorrowing Countess of Richmond sat with her grandchildren. She had an arm about the girl but her eyes were on the boy.

"It was your father's wish that I should continue to guide you, Henry," she explained. "My dear grandson, you will find the task before you not always a glorious one. There is more to kingship than riding through streets and listening to the cheers of the crowd."

"I know it well," answered Henry, not as coolly as he would wish, for he was still in awe of his grandmother.

"So I shall always be at hand to give you my counsel and, remembering your father's wish, I trust you will consider it."

Henry took her hand and kissed it.

He would always remember, he assured her.

And Mary, seeing the shine in his eyes, knew that his thoughts were far away in the future. He was looking at freedom stretching out before him — glorious, dazzling freedom. He was eighteen and King of England. At this moment he was too much intoxicated by the joy of being alive himself to think of anything else.

Oh, thought Mary, it will be wonderful now he is King! England will be merry, as she was meant to be, and all the country will be in love with such a sovereign.

A cold fear crept into her mind. And where shall I be? How much longer can I hope to remain in England? Am I forgetting that, over the sea, a bridegroom is waiting for me? But not yet . . . not yet.

She was too much of a Tudor not to live in the moment.

Mourning for King Henry VII could not be expected to last long when there was a young handsome man waiting to put on the crown.

Hope was high throughout London and the country. There would be joy such as had never been known before; gone were the days of high taxation. He had shown his intentions by throwing Empson and Dudley — those notorious extortioners — into the Tower; he had proclaimed that many debtors to the crown would be excused. He made it clear that he wanted the old days of anxiety to be forgotten, that the merry era might begin without delay.

He rode through the streets, this golden boy, and often the Princess of Castile rode with him; he so handsome, she so lovely; and the crowds cheered themselves hoarse for these charming young people.

There was another who rode with the King, for he had decided after all to marry his brother's widow, and this was a match which found favour with the people, for Katharine was known to be meek and serious by nature; the fact that she was a few years older than her bridegroom seemed favourable too. She will steady him, said the people. For he is gay and over merry, bless him. It will be good for him to have a serious wife.

So the days of mourning were quickly over, for how could the people mourn when they were about to see their King and Queen crowned?

On the eleventh of June — less than two months after his father's death — Henry married Katharine and the coronation of the pair was arranged for the twenty-fourth of that month.

Mary, who was then three months past her thirteenth birthday, must of course take a prominent part in the celebrations.

What a joy it was to ride in the procession from the Tower to Westminster, to see Archbishop Warham anoint the head of her beloved brother.

His open face shining with delight, he looked magnificent in his robe of crimson velvet edged with white ermine which fell away from his massive shoulders. Beneath it his coat of cloth of gold was visible and he looked even bigger than usual because he sparkled with diamonds, emeralds and rubies. Katharine was beautiful too in her gown of white satin, and her lovely hair loose about her shoulders.

"Did you ever see one so handsome as the King?" asked Mary.

Then she saw who it was who was standing beside her. In his fine garments, worn in honour of the occasion, he was strikingly handsome himself.

"Never," murmured Charles Brandon, smiling down at her.

She studied him speculatively, and pictured him in crimson velvet and ermine, and she thought: there *is* one to equal Henry, and that is Charles Brandon.

And she was suddenly very happy to be in a world which contained those two.

A coronation must be celebrated with appropriate entertainments, and Henry assured his subjects that because he must mourn his father he was not going to cheat them of their pleasures. They must look forward not back; and the glittering pageants they would witness should be symbols of the future.

At the banquets Mary found herself seated close to her brother and his wife; and where Henry was, there was his good friend Charles Brandon. In the dances which followed the feasting Mary often found herself partnered by this man, and was dissatisfied when he was not at her side; she was sure that he knew this and endeavoured to remain with her.

When she was alone with her women she would do her best to bring his name into the conversation, for the next best thing to being with him was to talk of him.

"Charles Brandon," said one of her women, "why, there is a man to avoid."

"Why so?" demanded Mary.

"Because, my lady, he is one of the biggest rakes at Court."

"Doubtless he is much pursued."

"That is likely so. What a handsome fellow! And what a roving eye! I've heard it said there are secrets he would rather not have brought to Court."

"There will always be slander against one so attractive."

The woman raised her eyebrows and looked knowledgeable. Mary understood such looks and knew that she must curb her tongue lest in a short time the rumour went through the Court that the Lady Mary, who was no longer a child, was over-interested in Charles Brandon.

When she next danced with Charles she said to him: "Is it true that you are a rake and a philanderer?"

He laughed, and she laughed with him because she was always so happy in his company that everything seemed a matter for laughter.

"My lady," he replied, "I never intended to live the life of a monk; although, by some accounts, it would seem that monks are not all we believe them to be."

"And if the tongue of slander can touch them," said Mary, "how much readily will it busy itself over one so . . . so . . ."

He stopped in the dance; it was only for a few seconds but to Mary it seemed for a long time, because that was the moment of understanding. She had betrayed her feeling, not only to him but to herself. A great exultation took possession of her and it was immediately followed by a terrible frustration; for how could that for which she longed ever be hers?

She loved Charles Brandon. More than any other person in the world, she loved him and she could only be completely happy in his company; but across the water a boy with a heavy jaw and sloppy mouth, heir to great dominions, was waiting until the time when he should be old enough to send for her as his bride.

In the ballroom, with this knowledge bursting upon her, she understood the tragedy which befell so many royal princes and princesses, and knew that it was hers.

Margaret Beaufort, Countess of Richmond and Derby, was very tired, for the coronation celebrations, following so quickly on the funeral, had exhausted her, and from the moment she had looked upon the dead face of her son she had known that life had lost all zest for her.

Her beloved son was dead; what reason had she for living? The children? He had wished her to take care of them; but they would answer only to themselves. She had known that for a long time. Neither of them resembled their careful father, and would go their own way, no matter what advice was given them by their grandmother.

She had lived for sixty-six years, which was a goodly span; and it was because she had been only fourteen years old when she had borne her beloved son that she had been able to take such a prominent part in his counsels; there was no great difference in their ages, and Henry had always been old for his years.

Now she could say: "Lord, I am ready. Let thy servant depart in peace." She could look back on a life of piety. The universities of Oxford and Cambridge would remember her generosity for as long as they were in existence; nor were they the only beneficiaries of her good works.

She took to her bed before the coronation festivities were over and when she died peacefully, bringing the celebrations to an end, John Fisher, Bishop of Rochester, declared: "All England for her death had cause for weeping"; and it was true that the news was received with sorrow throughout the land.

The old King and his mother dead! A new way of life was certainly opening out before the country.

Perhaps the new King was not quite so grief-stricken as he declared himself to be. Perhaps he felt the last of his bonds breaking. He was no longer in leading strings. Absolute freedom was his, and that was a state for which he had always longed.

And the young Princess? She wept for her grandmother, but the old lady was a figure of the past, and at this time of exultation and apprehension Mary could only look to the future, could only ask herself whether it was possible, if one were determined to have one's will, to flout the whole Court, the whole world, to get it.

One could not deeply mourn the passing of a woman who had lived her life, when one's own was opening out before one.

There was no room in Mary's heart and mind for other thoughts or emotion.

She loved with all the force of a passionate nature. It was no use telling herself that she was not yet fourteen years of age. Her grandmother had borne a son at that age. She was a woman now, understanding a woman's emotions; and because she had always had her way she did not believe she could fail to get it now.

Charles Brandon was the man she had chosen for her husband. She cared nothing for ceremonies which joined her to a boy whom she had never seen.

"I must marry Charles," she told herself. And she added: "I will."

CHAPTER TWO

The Rise of Charles

Charles Brandon was well aware of the effect he was having on the Princess Mary. He was amused and flattered, for she was a charming creature and he — who prided himself on his knowledge in such matters — would have been ready to wager that not only would she in a very short time become one of the most beautiful young women at the Court, but also one of the most passionate.

It was a pleasant situation, therefore, to be the object of the child's adoration.

Had she been anyone else he would have been impatient to exploit his advantage; but the King's sister must be treated with caution; for the King's sake, or perhaps more truthfully for his own.

He knew Henry well, as they had been together for years; there was a certain primness in Henry's character which could make a man's dalliance with his sister a dangerous occupation. Henry was as sensation-loving as his friends; he was not averse to a flirtation here and there; indeed he was just discovering the full delights of the flesh and, if Brandon was not mistaken, would gradually become a more and more eager participant in what they had to offer. But he had quickly discovered that, in dealing with the King, an element of caution must always be employed; and knowing Henry's great regard for young Mary, it was obvious that he, Brandon, must enter with the utmost caution any situation involving her.

It was a pity. He was thinking of her constantly; and strangely enough he was becoming critical of his mistresses. They were not fresh and young enough. Naturally. How could they hope to compete with a virgin whom he knew to be but fourteen years old? He was as certain of the first fact as of the second. And there she was, as deeply enamored of him as any woman had ever been; and he must remain aloof, constantly reminding himself who she was.

A fascinating situation, yet one he must resist.

If she were not affianced to young Charles, would it be possible . . .?

Oh no, he was allowing the King's friendship toward him to put preposterous ideas into his head. He had been very fortunate; it was up to him to see that he remained so.

So, during the weeks which followed that moment of revelation, Charles Brandon often thought back over the past and saw how luck had brought him to his present position and that he must not run any risk of jeopardising his good fortune.

Yet what harm was there in seeking the company of this charming girl? A touch of the hand, an eloquent look, could mean so much; and even a cynical adventurer could not but be moved by the love of a young girl.

In her impetuous fashion Mary was falling deeply in love with Charles Brandon; and he, in his way (though it was not artless as hers was, for it was not without calculation and reservation), was following her lead.

Charles could remember the day he first came to Court. He had been very young indeed, but not so young that he could not understand what a great honour was being bestowed upon him. His mother had often told him the story of Bosworth Field.

"Your father," she had said, "was standard-bearer to Henry of Richmond, and had been a faithful follower of his, sharing his exile in Brittany."

It was a wonderful story, young Charles had always thought, and he could never hear it too often. As his mother told it he could clearly see Henry Tudor embarking at Harfleur and arriving at Milford Haven with only two thousand men.

"But my father was one of them," Charles always said at this point.

"But when he landed, Welshmen rallied to his banner, for he was a Welshman himself."

"But it was my father who was his standard-bearer," young Charles would cry. "Tell how he rode into battle holding the standard high."

And she would tell him how Richard III had challenged him to combat and how the brave standard-bearer had fallen at the hand of that King.

"So we shall always be for the Tudor," Charles had announced. "Because it was the usurper Richard who killed my father."

And when Henry, Earl of Richmond, became Henry VII of England he did not forget the brave standard-bearer's family.

There are certain occasions which stand out in a lifetime and will never be forgotten. For Charles, the first of these was that day when the messenger came from the King.

"You have a son," ran the King's message. "If you care to send him to Court a place shall be found for him."

What rejoicing there had been when that message came! "This is the great opportunity," he was told; "it is for you to see what can be made of it."

In his own home he was an important personage; he was possessed of exceptionally good looks; he had strong limbs and already was tall for his age. His nurses and servants had said of him: "*There* goes one who knows what he wants from life and how to get it."

He had been taught jousting and fencing and had excelled at these sports; it had been the same with wrestling and pole-jumping. There seemed to be none who could equal him. True, Latin, Greek, and literature were not much to his taste; he was the reluctant scholar, grudging every moment that was not spent out of doors.

He could remember clearly the night before he had left for the Court, how he had knelt with his mother and their confessor and had prayed for his future. They had asked that he should be courageous and humble, that he should always serve God and the King. His thoughts had wandered because he was picturing what the King would say when he came face to face with Charles Brandon.

He had been a little hurt when, arriving at Court, he had not seen the King for weeks, and then only glimpsed him; it seemed at that time an astonishing thing that Charles Brandon should be at Court and the King appear neither to know nor care.

But soon he was given his place in the household of the young Duke of York, and it was not long before he made his presence known there. He was glad that he had been assigned to the household of the younger brother, although it would have been a greater honour to have been in the household of the Prince of Wales. Arthur would never have been his friend as Henry was, for he and Henry were two of a kind. Henry was some six years younger than himself but they had not known each other long when both recognised the affinity between them. It was Charles Brandon who was selected to fence with the Prince and when they practised archery and pole-jumping together, Henry was put out because Charles always beat him.

"I am bigger and older than you," Charles pointed out, "so it is but natural that I should beat you."

Henry's eyes had narrowed as he had retorted: "It is never natural for a commoner to beat a Prince."

Charles was young but he was shrewd. After that he let Henry win now and then; not every time; he did not wish the Prince to be suspicious that his vanity was being humoured; and the occasional win pleased him better than if he had always scored. Charles was becoming a diplomat. He decided that the Prince should win more and more frequently as time passed, for then he would always want to play with his friend Charles Brandon.

He was beloved of Fortune, he knew it. Having been born a few years before his Prince, he was that much wiser, that much stronger in the early days of their relationship. They grew side by side, until the Prince was as tall as he was — blond giants, of a size, and not dissimilar in appearance, both ruddy, both with that hint of corpulence to come in later life, two sportsmen, so perfectly matched that all Charles had to do was make certain Henry appeared to be that fraction more skillful in their games; but only a fraction so that Charles might be the worthiest of opponents; he need only bend forward a little to give his Prince that extra inch; all he had to do was please his Prince and his fortune was made. He was indeed blessed, for when the Prince of Wales died, Charles was the devoted friend of the new holder of that significant title: the King-to-be.

It was small wonder that he found life an exhilarating adventure.

He remembered the occasion of his betrothal to Anne Browne. He had been attracted to Anne the moment he saw her, and because of his precocity, he longed to be married; but Anne was considered too young as yet. He thought of her standing beside him while they were ceremoniously betrothed; a fragile girl, her long hair falling over her shoulders, her eyes meek — half eager, half frightened, he thought; she looked at the handsome boy beside her and her emotions were easy to read. She thought herself the luckiest girl alive, being betrothed to Charles Brandon.

It was not, of course, a brilliant match, for Anne's father, Sir Anthony Browne, was merely Lieutenant of Calais; but the Brandons had not known at that time how Charles's friendship with the heir to the throne would advance his fortunes.

Back at Court he continued to be that friend whom the Prince of Wales kept most often at his side. Sometimes when he and Henry rode out hunting together they would break away from the main party, tether their horses and stretch themselves out on the grass, talking of the future.

Henry said: "When I am King, my first task shall be to conquer France."

"I shall be beside you," Charles told him.

"We will go together. None shall stand in our way. You'll be a good soldier, Charles."

"At Your Grace's right hand."

"Yes," Henry agreed, "you shall be at my right hand."

"Your standard-bearer . . . as my father was to your father."

Henry liked that; he was inclined to sentimentality.

Then they would talk of the balls they would give when they returned to England as conquerors.

"Fair women to wait on us," murmured Henry, his little eyes shining.

"The fairest in all England to serve Your Grace, and the next fairest for me."

Henry liked Charles to forecast the masques and entertainments and this Charles did, for his imagination was a trifle more vivid than his master's, although not much more so. That was why they were in such accord. Charles only had to remember to be one step behind his master, and all was well.

When he told of his betrothal to Anne Browne, Henry was a trifle envious because he was longing to be married.

"But when I marry it will be to a princess, an heiress to great dominions."

That was true, and in comparison little Anne Browne, for all her delicacy, for all her charm, seemed unworthy of the greatest friend of the Prince of Wales.

He began to picture Anne at the balls and tourneys. It was difficult to imagine her in cloth of gold and scarlet velvet. He could see her clearly in a quiet country mansion, at his table, in his bed. But at Court? Scarcely.

It then occurred to him that the delectable Anne Browne, disturber of his dreams, was no worthy wife for Charles Brandon.

It was in his grandfather's house that he first met Margaret Mortymer. Margaret was a widow, ripe and luscious, resentful of her state. Her dark, smoldering eyes were ready to rest on any young and personable man, and when they discovered Charles Brandon her desire for him was immediate.

His grandfather lived quietly in the country not far from London, where Margaret had her home; the two young people were much together while they stayed under the roof of Sir William Brandon.

Margaret's late husband, Charles discovered, was his grandfather's brother, so there was a connection, while Margaret herself was distantly related to Anne Browne.

Margaret was well connected, being the daughter of Neville, Marquis of Montacute, and widow of Sir John Mortymer, but in the first weeks of their friendship Charles was more aware of her physical charms than of her family background.

She was older than he was, an experienced widow; and although he was no virgin he learned that he was as yet a novice in the art of lovemaking.

Afterward, those hot summer days lived on in his memory like a dream that would have been best forgotten, but from which he believed he would never quite escape.

His erotic nature was titillated to such a pitch that he was ready to attempt any act which might satisfy it.

"Soon," she told him, "you will return to Court; and how shall I see you then?"

He did not know, but he assured her that he would find some means of reaching her bed.

"But what of my reputation?" she demanded. "Here it is easy. We are both guests of your grandfather. How can you, a young man, come frequently to my house. How can you stay the night? Only if you were my husband could we be happy."

He told her of his betrothal to Anne Browne, adding: "If I were free, I would not hesitate to marry you. Why did we not meet years ago?"

Margaret knew the solution, which was that he must obtain a dispensation, which need not be difficult because she had friends in the right quarter who would arrange that it should be procured with speed.

Margaret was a forceful woman. She was not going to let him escape. He thought now and then of Anne with the gazelle eyes and the adoring smile; he knew that she would be bitterly hurt, and he did not want to hurt Anne. He began to suspect that in his way he was in love with Anne, the virgin, more than he could ever be with the flamboyant widow, although his physical need of the latter was greater.

He knew Margaret was a match for him; he knew that she would never allow him to evade her; so he consoled himself that the daughter of the Marquis of Montacute was a better match than that of the Lieutenant of Calais.

Anne's gentle eyes continued to haunt him until he and Margaret were married, but for the first months he found his life with her all that he could wish, so that he rarely gave a thought to the girl whom he had jilted.

He could not, however, stay away from Court indefinitely and the Prince was commanding his friend to return. It had been amusing to go back, the married man, to confide in the Prince, to bask in the royal and avid curiosity concerning his life with a woman.

But when he returned to her, some of the magic had gone for it was inconceivable that one so lusty could remain a faithful husband and he had discovered that there were girls at Court who could give all that Margaret gave and not demand marriage in exchange. He began to wonder whether he had been a little impulsive, particularly when he saw Anne again, grown taller and no less fragile, reminding him of a pale daffodil. Poor Anne! Her eyes were tragic when they met his, though not reproachful.

His conscience worried him a little, for he feared she might die of a broken heart.

Once more he confided in his Prince. Henry's response was vehement, for the sentimentality of his nature was touched by the thought of little Anne Browne.

"You should have the marriage pronounced invalid and marry Anne," he told his friend.

"But how so?"

"How so? Marriages *are* pronounced invalid. Why not yours? If Anne dies of a broken heart you will be her murderer."

The more Charles thought of Anne the more he desired to marry her and rid himself of Margaret. He was weary of erotic and passionate women for a while; he wanted a pure virgin. He no longer wanted to be instructed, being ready now to act as instructor.

"Anne, Anne, how could I have done this?" he asked himself. "I was led astray. I was young and foolish . . ."

"There must be means of ending that marriage," Henry told him. "There are always means of ending marriages which have become distasteful."

Charles, gratified by the royal interest and setting himself to work on his problem, discovered that the Prince was right. There were always ways. Margaret's first husband was the brother of Charles's grandfather. Surely that placed them in the second or third degree of affinity? Then Charles had been betrothed to Anne Browne who was related to Margaret. He was certain that with a little help he could arrange that his marriage should be pronounced invalid on the grounds of consanguinity.

At this time he had another of those brilliant strokes of good fortune which were a feature of his life; Margaret discovered that she was as weary of the union as he was. She wanted a husband who was with her all the time and Charles's place at Court made this impossible. She therefore would put nothing in the way of having the marriage dissolved.

When he was free, Charles at once sought out his first love and without hesitation married her.

Here was a different kind of wife! Here he had nothing to regret! Anne was meek and loving; she made no demands; she was thankful for any scrap of affection he gave her; and almost immediately she became pregnant.

Like his royal master Charles loved children and the thought of having a child of his own made him very happy. Moreover, Henry was interested in the coming child, and growing more and more impatient to marry and have children. Sometimes Charles feared that his master's envy might in some way turn him against him; but it did not, and when Charles's daughter — whom he called Anne after her mother — was born, Henry sent as rich a present as he could afford. Not that it was a handsome gift, as his father kept him very short, but it gave Charles and Anne great pleasure to bask thus in the favour of the man who would one day be King.

For a while Charles was content; he lived his life between the Court and his home where Anne and her little namesake were always waiting for him. There were several light love affairs at Court which was quite natural, he consoled himself, since he must in the course of his duty spend so much time away from the marital bed; and he placated his conscience with the thought that even had Anne known of these she would have understood.

In the course of time she again became pregnant, and little Mary was born.

Henry followed his friend's married adventures with the utmost interest and chafed more and more at his own bonds which would not allow him to act as freely as Brandon did.

Anne died soon after Mary was born; Charles mourned, but not deeply; he had already begun to wish that he had married a more spirited wife, for life with Anne had been becoming rather dull. Charles began to think then that the humdrum life was not for him; he wanted adventure all the time. Here again he asked himself whether he was Fortune's favourite, for Anne's early death had saved him from the discomfort of discovering he had made a second mistake.

He was now free — a widower. It was true he had two little daughters, but he was fond of them and they presented no difficulty. They were well looked after and he visited them from time to time; his visits were the highlights in their lives and they adored him.

Life had taken a very pleasant turn. The old King had died and his friend was now in the supreme position; Henry had a wife of his own and was no longer envious of Charles's married state. The friendship had not slackened in any way; in fact it grew stronger. At all the coronation jousts and tourneys it was Charles Brandon who was closest to the King. He had a rival in Sir William Compton, but there was nothing new in this because Compton had been a page of Henry's when he was Duke of York, for the boy had been a ward of Henry VII. Compton was a kindred spirit and Henry was drawn to him, but he was no Brandon; he was neither as tall, handsome, nor as skilled in the joust. Compton had been a butt for them both. "Come on, Compton, you try now," Henry would say; and he and Charles would look on, mildly contemptuous of the other boy. But Henry had a great affection for him all the same, and Charles had at times wondered whether the Prince might not feel more tender towards one who was far behind him than another who was his equal.

Henry did not forget his friends, and those who had been close to the Prince of Wales were now as close to the King. He at once appointed Compton Groom of the Bedchamber, and shortly afterward he was Chief Gentleman of the Bedchamber, then Groom of the Stole and Constable of Sudeley and Gloucester Castles. But there were equal honours for Charles. Immediately on his accession Henry made his friend Squire of the Royal Body and Chamberlain of the Principality of North Wales; later he became Marshal of the King's Bench and the office of Marshal of the Royal Household was promised him.

It became clear that King Henry VIII was not going to keep those solemn old men, appointed by his father, in office; he was going to surround himself with the young and the merry. So Charles could look forward to great honours and a successful life at Court.

It was at this stage that Charles became aware that he had attracted the attention of the King's young sister.

Charles knew that he must act with the utmost care. To be the chosen companion of the Prince of Wales was pleasant and diverting; to be King's favourite could be dangerous. In those early days of kingship, Henry was a careless giant scattering handfuls of gifts on those he favoured, but there were many ambitious men ready to scramble for the treasures he threw so lightheartedly, ready to kick aside those for whom they were intended. And for all his ready *bonhomie*, temper could spring up suddenly behind those merry blue eyes, turning a smile to a scowl in a matter of seconds.

And at every ball and banquet Charles was thrown into the company of the Princess Mary. She herself arranged this.

There was little of the Tudor caution in Mary; she belonged completely to the Plantagenet House of York.

Thus recklessly must her maternal grandfather have conducted himself when he defied his counsellors and married the beautiful Elizabeth Woodville, scorning political advantage for the sake of love.

She fired his imagination and his senses; he was certain that if he did not take care she would lead him to such great disaster against which he would be powerless to defend himself. He realised that in all his affairs with women he had never been so close to danger as he was at this time. He knew he should avoid her company. But how could the King's favourite courtier and the King's favourite sister, both of whom he loved to have beside him, keep apart?

Whenever Henry wanted to plan some entertainment — and in these early years of his reign he was continually planning them — he would cry: "Brandon! Mary! Come here. Now I would plan a masque."

And the three of them would sit together whispering in a window seat, Mary between them, slipping her arms through theirs with a childlike gesture which completely deceived her brother.

Charles understood how very near he was to danger on an occasion when Henry summoned them both, with Compton, to his bedchamber.

Henry's eyes were alight with pleasure. "News, my friends," he said, "and I tell you before it becomes known to any others. My hopes are about to be fulfilled. The Queen is with child."

Mary impulsively went to her brother and, putting her arms solemnly about his neck, kissed him. Henry held her tightly against him, tears glittering in his eyes.

"Dearest, I am so happy for you," said Mary.

"God bless you, little sister. I told Kate you should be the first — outside ourselves — to know it."

Charles took the King's hand and kissed it. Then he cried: "God bless the Prince of Wales."

"Your Grace," murmured Compton, "there is no news I would rather have heard."

"Yes, yes," said Henry. "This is a happy day. You know how I long for a son. My heir . . . the first of them. Kate and I intend to have a quiver-full."

"It is a good sign," Mary told him. "So soon after your marriage."

Henry pinched her cheek. "You talk like an old beldame. What do you know of such matters?"

"What I learn at your Court, brother," murmured Mary with a curtsy.

Henry burst into loud laughter. "Listen to this sister of mine! She's a pert wench and not chary of making this known to her King."

"She is sure of the King's love," answered Compton.

Henry's eyes were very sentimental as he put an arm about Mary. "Aye," he said, "and she is right to be. Pert she is, and I fancy somewhat wayward, yet she is my sister and I love her dearly."

Mary stood on tiptoe and kissed him again.

"You see," said Henry, "she would use her wiles on me. It is because she is going to ask me for something, depend upon it. What is it, sister?"

Mary looked from Compton to Brandon and her eyes rested a second or so on the latter.

"I shall not abuse your generosity by asking for small favours," she replied. "When I ask it shall be for some great boon."

"Hark to her!" cried Henry delightedly. "And what think you? When she asks, shall I grant it, eh, Compton? Eh, Brandon?"

"Of a certainty," answered Compton.

"Our friend Charles is silent," said Henry. "He is not sure."

"I am sure of this," Charles answered, "that if it is in your Grace's power to grant it, grant it you will. But the Lady Mary may ask for the moon, and that, even the greatest King in Christendom could not grant."

"If I wanted the moon, I should find some means of getting it," replied Mary.

"You see, our sister is not like us mortals." Henry was tired of the conversation. "We shall have the foreign ambassadors to entertain this Shrovetide, and I shall give them a banquet in the Parliament Chamber of Westminster; afterward there shall be a masque. We shall dance before the Queen and it shall be in her honour. She herself will not dance. We have to think of her condition. When the banquet is over I shall disappear and you, Brandon and Compton, will slip away with me."

"And I shall too?" asked Mary.

"But of course. You will choose certain ladies. Some of us will dress ourselves in the Turkish fashion — not all though. Edward Howard and Thomas Parr are good dancers; they shall be dressed as Persians, and others shall wear the costume of Russia. The ambassadors, with Kate and the rest of the spectators, will think we are travellers from a foreign land . . ."

"Oh," cried Mary, "it is to be that kind of masque! I tell you this, I shall take the part of an Ethiopian queen. There will be veils over my face, and perhaps I shall darken my skin . . . yes, and wear a black wig."

"Perfect!" cried the King. "None will recognise you. Charles, have Howard and Parr brought here. Fitzwater too. And let me consider . . . who else? . . ."

Mary was not listening. She was looking at Charles, and her blue eyes reminded him of her brother's. She was thinking of herself disguised as an Ethiopian queen; in the dance she would insist on dancing with one of the two tallest Turks.

Charles shared her excitement.

How long, he wondered, could they go on in this way?

It was hot in the hall; the torch bearers, their faces blackened, that they might be mistaken for Moors, had ushered in the party, and the dance had begun. There was one among them who leaped higher and danced with more vigour than all the others, which excited cries of wonder from all who beheld him.

The Queen on her dais was indulgent. When the masque was over she would express great surprise that the Turk who danced so miraculously was her husband, the King. What a boy he was! How guileless! She, who carried their child in her womb, loved him with greater tenderness than he would understand.

Now the "foreigners" were mingling with the dancers and the Queen of Ethiopia had selected a tall Turk for her partner.

"Why, Charles," she said, "you are much too tall for a Turk, you know. And so is Henry."

"I fear so."

"It is of no moment. Everyone is happy pretending they do not know who you are and who the King is. Do you think Henry believes he is deceiving them?"

"He wants to believe it, so he *does*. If he did not, the masque would have no meaning."

"I am like my brother, Charles. I too believe that which I want to." Her fingers dug into his flesh and the light pain was exquisite; he wished it were stronger. "But," she went on, "I would not waste my energy pretending about a masque."

"You would choose more serious subjects?"

"Charles, I tell you this: I do not believe I shall ever go to Flanders as the Princess of Castile."

"It is a great match."

"It is a hateful match. I loathe that boy."

"It was once said that you loved him dearly."

"My women used to put his picture by my bed so that it was the first thing I saw on waking; they used to tell me I was in love with him, that I could not wait for the day when we would be husband and wife."

"And was it not so?"

"Charles, do not be foolish! How could it be? What did I know of love? I had never seen the boy. Have you seen his picture? He looks like a drooling idiot."

"The grandson of Maximilian and Ferdinand could scarcely be that."

"Why could he not be so? His mother is mad."

"My lady, have a care. People are wondering what causes your vehemence."

"Have I not reason for vehemence? To be given in marriage to a boy younger than myself . . . a boy whom I know I shall hate! If I could choose the man I would marry he would be a *man*. Tall, strong, excelling in the jousts. I have a fancy for an Englishman, Charles. Not an idiot foreigner."

"Alas, matches are made for princesses."

"I would I were not a princess."

"Nay, you are proud. You are like your brother. Your rank delights you."

"That is true, but there are things that delight me more. Oh, have done with talking round this matter. I know my own mind. I know what I want. Shall I tell you?"

"No, my Princess. It would not be wise."

"Since when has Charles Brandon become such a sobersides?"

"Since his emotions became engaged where he knows they should not."

"Charles! Are you a puppet, then, to be jerked on strings, to be told: Do this! Do that? Or are you a man who has a will of his own?"

"My lady, I should ask you to give me permission to leave your side."

"Charles, you are a coward!"

"Yes, my lady; and if you have any regard for me, you must see how misplaced it is, for how could you feel friendship for a coward?"

"Friendship!" He heard the tremor in her voice and he knew that she was near to tears. "I am not a child any more, Charles. Let us at least be frank with one another."

He was silent and she stamped her foot. "Let us be frank," she repeated.

He gripped her wrist and heard her catch her breath at the pain. In a moment, he thought, she would attract attention to them and the first rumours would start.

He drew her closer to him and said roughly: "Yes, let us be frank. You imagine that you love me."

"Imagine!" she cried scornfully. "I imagine nothing. I know. And if you are going to say you don't love me, you're a liar, Charles Brandon, as well as a coward."

"And you, a proud Tudor, find you love a liar and coward?"

"One does not love people for their virtues. I know you have been married . . . twice. I know that you cast off your first wife. I should not love you because you were a virtuous husband to another woman, should I? What care I, how many wives you have had, how many mistresses you have? All I know is this, that one day I shall command you to cast them all aside because . . ."

"My love," he murmured tenderly, "you are attracting attention to us. That is not the way."

"No," she retorted, "that is not the way. You called me your love."

"Did you doubt that I love you?"

"No, no. Love such as mine must meet with response. Charles, what shall we do? How can I marry that boy? Is it not a touch of irony that he should be Charles, too. I think of him as *that* Charles and you as *my* Charles. What shall we do?"

"My dearest Princess," he said soberly, "you are the King's sister. You are affianced to the Prince of Castile. The match has been made and cannot be broken simply because you love a commoner."

"It must be, Charles. I refuse to marry him. I shall *die* if they send me away."

He pressed her hand tightly and she laughed. "How strong you are, Charles. My rings are cutting into my fingers and it is very painful, but I'd rather have pain from you than all the gentleness in the world from any other. What shall I do? Tell me that. What shall I do?"

"First, say nothing of this mad passion of yours to anyone."

"I have told no one, not even Guildford, though I believe she guesses. She has been with me so long and she knows me so well. She said: 'My little Princess has changed of late. I could almost wonder whether she was in love.' Then, Charles, *my* Charles, she put up the picture of *that* Charles. But I think she meant to remind me, to warn me. Oh Charles, how I wish I were one of the serving maids . . . any kind of maid who has her freedom, for freedom to love and marry where one wills are the greatest gifts in the world."

She was a child, he thought; a vehement, passionate child. This devotion of hers which she was thrusting at him would likely pass. It might well be that in a few weeks' time she would develop a passion for one of the other young men of the Court, someone younger than himself, for he was more than ten years her senior.

The thought of her youth comforted him. It was pleasant enough to be so favoured by the King's sister. He was at ease. None would take this passion seriously, and certainly he was not to blame for its existence.

If he attempted to seduce her as she was so earnestly inviting him to do, there would be danger. Henry might not respect the virginity of other young women, but he most certainly would his sister's.

Charles knew that he was being lured into a dangerous — though fascinating — situation, but he believed he was wise enough to steer clear of disaster.

She was pressing close to him in the dance.

"Charles, tell me, what shall we do?"

He whispered: "Wait. Be cautious. Tell no one of this. Who knows what is in store for us?"

She was exultant. They had declared their love. She had the sort of faith which would enable her to believe the movement of mountains was a possibility.

She had already made up her mind: one day I shall be the wife of Charles Brandon.

When Henry's son was born there was more merrymaking. The boy made his appearance on the first of January; he was a feeble child who struggled for existence for a few weeks, and by the twenty-second of the following month had died.

This was Henry's first setback, his first warning that what he urgently desired was not always going to be his.

He was plunged into deepest melancholy; and that was the end of one phase of his life. He had spent almost the whole of the first two years of his kingly state in masking, jousting, and feasting; but with the death of his son his feelings had undergone a change; he would never be quite the same lighthearted boy again.

He wanted to give himself to more serious matters. His father-in-law, Ferdinand of Aragon, had persuaded him to join him, with Pope Julius II and the Venetians, against France; and because Henry saw in war a vast and colourful joust in which, on account of his youth, riches, and strength, he was bound to succeed, he was ready to follow his father-in-law's advice and promised to send troops into France.

War now occupied Henry's mind; he was constantly closeted with his statesmen and generals; and while he planned a campaign he dreamed of himself as the all-conquering hero who would one day win France back for the English crown.

He was impatient because he could not collect an army without delay and go into battle; he had thought a war was as quickly organised as a joust. His ministers had a hard time persuading him that this was not so, and gradually he began to see that they were right.

The Court was at Greenwich, the King much preoccupied with thoughts of conquest; and one day when he was walking with some of his courtiers in the gardens there, Mary saw him and went to him.

She signed to the courtiers to leave them together and, because Henry was always more indulgent to his sister than to anyone else, he did not countermand her order but allowed Mary to slip her arm through his.

"Oh, Henry," she said, "how dull is all this talk of war! The Court is not so merry as it used to be."

"Matters of state, sweetheart," he answered, with an indulgent smile. "They are part of a king's life, you should know."

"But why go to war when you can stay here and have so much pleasure?"

"You, a daughter of a king and sister of one, should understand. I shall not rest until I am crowned in Rheims."

"Do you hate the French so much?"

"Of course I hate our enemies. And now I have good friends in Europe. Between us we shall crush the French. You shall see, sister."

"Henry, there is one matter which gives me great cause for sorrow. You could ease my pain if you would."

"Sorrow! What is this? I was of the opinion that life used you very well."

"I do not wish to leave you ever, Henry."

"Oh come, my dearest sister, that is child's talk."

"It is not child's talk. It is woman's talk, for I am a woman now, Henry."

"What! Are you so old then?"

"Henry, as you love me, stop treating me as a child. I am sixteen years old, and I am begging you not to send me to that odious Charles."

"What's this?"

"You know full well. Against my wishes I was affianced to him. I am asking you to break off this match."

"Sister, you are being foolish. How could I break off this match? The Emperor Maximilian is a good friend to England. He would not be, I do assure you, if I said to him, 'There shall be no match between your grandson and my sister . . . because she has taken a sudden dislike to the boy.' "

"Henry, this is *my* life. I am to be sent away from home . . . to a strange land . . . to marry this boy who looks like an idiot . . . and his mother is mad, we know. So is he. I will not go."

"Listen, little sister. We of royal blood cannot choose our brides and bridegrooms. We must remember always our duty to the State. We have to be brave and patient, and in good time we grow to love those chosen for us because we know it is our duty to do so."

"You married whom you wished."

"Kate is the daughter of a king and queen. Had she not been I should not have been able to marry her . . . however much I wished for the match. Nor should I have done so, because I have always known that to consider the advantages to the State is the first duty of princes."

"Henry, something must happen. I cannot go to that boy. He is but a boy . . . and I thank God for that, otherwise I should have been cruelly sent away from my home and all I love, ere this. He is about twelve years old now. When he is fourteen they will say he is old enough to have a wife and then . . . then . . . unless you save me . . ."

"It is two years away, sister. Dismiss it from your mind. In two years' time you will understand more than you do now. You will be reconciled to our fate. Believe me, a great deal can happen in two years. Why, at one time I repudiated Kate . . . then, when I was King, I married her."

Mary stamped her foot. "Henry, stop treating me as a child."

He smiled at her as indulgently as ever, but there was a sharp note in his voice. "Remember to whom you speak, sister."

"Henry," she said vehemently, "it is because I never want to leave England. Let me marry in England. Greenwich . . . Richmond . . . this river . . . this King . . . these I love."

He patted her hand. "Methinks," he said, "that I am over-soft with you, sister. It is because of the great love I bear you. I no more want you to leave us than you wish to. But I can no more keep you back than I could have kept Margaret."

"You did not care that Margaret went."

"I had no wish for her to go to Scotland. I love not the Scots."

"And you love these Flemings, these Spaniards?"

"My wife is a Spaniard, sister, remember. Oh come, smile. Do not grieve about tomorrow when there is so much to make you smile today. I will tell you something. We will have a masque to beguile the time. You shall help me plan it, eh? And it shall be in your honour. How is that?" He turned and called: "Brandon! Compton!"

And it was when they were joined by these two that he noticed the look which Mary bestowed on Charles

Brandon. She was too young to disguise her feelings and Henry believed he knew why she had suddenly become so eager to avoid the marriage with Charles of Castile.

So she had cast her eyes on Brandon. Well, Brandon was one of the most attractive men in his Court . . . *the* most attractive, with one exception. They were so much alike that when they wore masks one was often mistaken for the other. They could have some good sport with this resemblance.

Oh yes, he could quite understand the effect a man like Brandon would have on an impressionable girl.

It was nothing, though. A passing fancy. This happened with young girls now and then.

Brandon at the moment was unattached. It might be well to deal with that matter. When he had time he would remember. In the meantime he must keep Mary amused, for he was too fond of the child to be able to look on unmoved when she was unhappy.

She would have to go to Flanders or Spain at some time, but that time was not yet. He had to remember that she was a young girl with a young girl's fancies.

All the same he would do something about Brandon.

Henry's friendship with Charles was greater than ever during that year, and the King appointed his friend Keeper of the Royal Manor and Park of Wanstead and Ranger of the New Forest. Instead of Squire of the Royal Body he was now Knight of the same, and they were rarely out of each other's company.

One winter's day when they were returning from the hunt together Henry said to Charles: "I should like to bestow some title on you, Charles, and I have been turning this matter over in my mind for some time."

"Your Grace has been so good to me already . . ."

"It gives me pleasure to honour my friends. But you who are so often in the company of your King should have a title. It has been brought to my notice that Elizabeth Grey is the sole heiress of her father, John Grey, Viscount Lisle. I propose to make the girl your ward. Then it is up to you, Charles; marry her and you will take over the title. Viscount Lisle! What think you?"

"I thank Your Grace."

Henry slapped his friend's arm. "Go to," he said. "You have our leave to visit the girl. She has more than a title to offer you, Charles. There's a fortune to go with it. Now go, and come back and tell me you have become Lord Lisle. It grieves me to see you without a wife."

Charles renewed his thanks to the King and left Court, wondering whether Henry was more astute than he had imagined. But perhaps no great shrewdness was necessary. Mary, with her passionate vehemence, could so easily betray her feelings. Doubtless she had already done so to her chief lady-in-waiting, Lady Guildford, who had been her governess since her childhood; could it be that Lady Guildford had thought it her duty to inform the King?

If he were to prove that he was not to blame for the Princess's passion, he must obey Henry's command with speed. If there had been a hope of marrying Mary he would have worked with all his might to bring about that desirable end; but there was not. Why, he thought, even if she were not affianced to Prince Charles, she would never be allowed to marry plain Charles Brandon; and if Henry thought he had raised his eyes so high he would feel it imperative to slap him down. Who knew, that could be the end of the brilliant career which was opening out before him.

He arrived at the home of Elizabeth Grey to find a mansion which was an appropriate setting for a rich heiress. All this land would be mine, he thought. This house, a fortune, a great title. I trust she is beautiful.

He waited in the long hall for her servants to tell her of his arrival, but while he paced up and down he was thinking of Mary, picturing her fury when she heard that he was married. He murmured: "Mary, my Princess, it is useless. You would have had us both in the Tower." She would answer: "Willingly would I endure imprisonment in the Tower, for I would rather be dead than married to Charles."

She was a wild creature; she had escaped the discipline which had been enforced during the lifetime of her father; the restrictions Henry VII had imposed on his children could only make them more eager for freedom. The same was true of Henry, and, he was sure, of Margaret. They were headstrong people by nature; they called themselves Tudors but they had inherited none of the caution of Henry Tudor; they were Plantagenets, every one of them — adventurers who would demand of life what they wanted, and use all their tremendous willpower to acquire it.

He would have to explain to her that it was at the King's command that he had married Elizabeth Grey. She would despise him, stop loving him; and perhaps that would be as well for her peace and his.

There was a commotion at the head of the great staircase, and he heard a shrill, imperious voice saying: "*Must* I see this man?"

"My lady, you must. It is the order of the King."

Then she was coming down the stairs, lifting her skirts almost disdainfully; her little head high, as she looked straight ahead, walking regally like a queen in her palace. Brandon was astonished, for she could not be more than eight years old.

She stood before him and held out a hand. He bowed his tall figure a very long way and looked into her face. She was no beauty and her expression at this time was far from agreeable. Her governesses stood a few paces behind her.

Charles straightened up. "I would speak with the Lady Elizabeth in private," he said.

For a moment the child's face betrayed her fear; then she said: "Very well." And to her attendants: "You may wait in the winter parlor."

She was both imperious and apprehensive, as though she recognised that she was a very rich little girl, and that riches could mean power in some ways, disaster in others; Charles, who was fond of children, felt a little sorry for her.

When they were alone he said: "You know the King has commanded me to come here?"

"I know it," she answered.

He took her hand and led her to a chair on which she sat while he drew up a stool and placed it opposite her, before seating himself.

"You should not be afraid of me," he assured her.

"I trust not," she answered.

"Then why does my presence worry you?"

"Because I know why you have come. The King has chosen you to be my husband."

"And you like me not?"

"You are very old, and I do not want a husband."

"It is because you are so young that you think me old. It is also because you are so young that you do not want a husband."

"And it is because I have a large fortune that you want me for a wife."

"My dear child, the King commanded me to come here. I did not seek this any more than you did. Shall we say we are victims of circumstances?"

"I am happy here. I have many people to care for me. My father is dead." Her lips trembled. "But I have others to love me."

"Do not be downcast. You are over-young to marry. You could not have a husband for at least five years."

She looked relieved, and suddenly laughed in a merry fashion. "In five years," she said incredulously, "why, by then . . ."

"I shall be quite ancient and beyond being a husband!" He laughed. "Not quite, my lady. But it may well be that in five years' time you will have a different opinion of me from that which you have today."

She was unconvinced, but clearly she did not find him such an ogre as she had feared he might be.

"The King has made you my ward," he told her; "and as your guardian I must stay here awhile and make sure that you are being well cared for. It is the King's wish that we should become betrothed to each other. But do not be alarmed. I do assure you that this will be only a simple ceremony; and we shall not be married until you are at least thirteen years old, which must be quite five years' away. Come, show me the house and introduce me to your attendants. I promise you that in a few days you will recognise me as your friend."

The little girl rose and put her hand uncertainly in his.

She said: "And if, when the time comes, I do not want to marry you . . .

"Then I shall not force you to do so."

Elizabeth Grey was clearly happier than she had been since she had heard that by the King's command she was to become the ward of Charles Brandon whom Henry had chosen to be her husband.

As he learned the extent of Elizabeth's wealth, Charles could not but feel gratified. Henry must indeed think highly of him to place such a prize in his hands. He was glad that the child was too young for marriage, because he would have time to prepare her for it; and since he could not have Mary, she would be a very good substitute.

She was an ungracious little creature whose confidence was not easily won, but he was sorry for her. Poor child! To lose her father and then suddenly find herself, on account of her position and wealth, offered to a stranger!

She would find that he was no brute. But how to convince her of this?

An incident occurred a few days after his arrival which made the little girl change her mind.

She and Charles were riding together through the countryside with a few of their attendants when, passing a river, they heard cries and, pulling up, saw a child of about three or four years struggling in the water.

Charles was the first out of his saddle and, striding into the river, grasped the child and brought her to the bank.

His handsome clothes were ruined by the water and the child was so still that she appeared to be dead.

"She is not dead," cried Charles. "We must take her back to the house as quickly as possible. Give me your cloak, Elizabeth, and we'll wrap it about her. Everything I have on is saturated."

When the child was wrapped in the cloak, Charles remounted, and, holding her in his arms, took her back to the house. There he and Elizabeth looked after the little girl, who was suffering from shock and chill; but apart from this no harm had come to her and in a few days she was well.

When they questioned her she was able to tell them that she had neither father nor mother. Charles made inquiries in the village, where he learned that she was an orphan only tolerated by an aunt who had a brood of her own and did not want her. It was clear that this callous woman was far from grateful to Charles for saving the child.

"What shall we do with her?" asked Elizabeth.

Charles laughed. "I'll not have made such an effort in vain. I came here to find one ward. It seems I have found two. I also have two daughters. I am going to send this child to be brought up with them."

So Elizabeth found clothes for the child, who followed Charles wherever he went, rather to his amusement.

Elizabeth, who was not demonstrative and did not win the child's affection as Charles had done, watched solemnly. She knew that Charles took pleasure in the child's devotion, largely because he had saved her life.

Elizabeth said: "You are a kind man, but I think a vain one."

"At least," he answered with a laugh, "I have won some small approval."

Before he left for Court he had persuaded her to make a contract of marriage with him, assuring her that this contract could be broken if, by the time she was of a marriageable age, she had no desire to continue with it.

He took with him the child he had rescued, and placed her with his own daughters, where she was to be cared for as one of them.

He was not displeased with that adventure. Now that he had the marriage contract he knew that Henry would create him Viscount Lisle; he would have the title in advance, and he had not to think of marriage for another five years.

When he returned to Court Mary demanded that he meet her secretly in the gardens of Greenwich Palace.

She turned on him angrily when he came to her. "So you are affianced to Elizabeth Grey!"

"At the King's command."

"Is it fitting that a man should have a wife found for him? I should have thought any worthy of the name would have chosen for himself."

"I am not yet married."

"But affianced . . . for the sake of her money and title, I understand."

"For the sake of the King's pleasure," he retorted.

"And when does this marriage take place?"

He took her by the shoulders and shook her a little. "My Princess," he said, "I am affianced to a girl of eight. It will be five years before we can marry. A great deal can happen in five years. When I entered into this contract I was playing for safety."

She began to laugh suddenly, holding up her face to his. He kissed her and the passion in her delighted and alarmed him.

"Five years' grace for you," she said when at last he released her. "About two for me. Much can happen in five years . . . even two years. Charles, my mind is quite made up."

"My dearest, do not allow your impetuosity to destroy us both."

She threw her arms about him once more.

"Nay, Charles," she said. "I'll not destroy us. But I will find a way . . . and so must you."

He wondered afterward whether his position had not in fact become more dangerous since his betrothal to little Elizabeth Grey.

The King was angry. His first foray into France had been a dismal failure, and the English were a laughing stock on the Continent of Europe. It was true Henry himself had not crossed the Channel but he was very put out because his soldiers had, as he said, failed him. His force, under the Marquis of Dorset, had landed in Biscay where they were to attack France while Ferdinand took Navarre. Ferdinand, however, had proved himself a questionable ally; he had promised the English Guienne, that region of southwest France which had come to England with the marriage of Henry II, and which the present Henry was eager to bring back to the crown. Ferdinand, however, had no intention of helping the English; all he wanted was for them to engage part of the French army so that he might be relieved of their attentions while pursuing his own goal. Consequently the English had lain at San Sebastian without provisions or arms and, because they drank too freely of the Basque wine, which they found a poor substitute for English ale, they contracted dysentery and, in spite of Henry's orders that they were to remain at their posts, mutinied and came back to England.

It seemed to Henry then that God no longer favoured him. He had lost his son; and now his own men had disobeyed him. He knew that Ferdinand was treacherous, and the fact that he was his own father-in-law did not soften that blow.

There was one way in which he could win back his self-respect. He himself was going to France.

Thus it was that in the May of the year 1513 he decided to lead his own army against the French.

The great *cortège* was on its way to Dover. An army of fourteen thousand men had already crossed the Channel and were awaiting the arrival of the King; and now Henry was setting out on the first great adventure of his reign.

He was determined that this should be a glorious occasion. He rode at the head of the cavalcade, his coat of gold brocade, his breeches of cloth of gold, his hose scarlet, and about his neck, on a chain of gold, a huge gold whistle encrusted with gems of great value. On this he blew from time to time.

The Queen and her ladies accompanied the party to Dover; and among this party was the Princess Mary, uneasy because Charles was going to war; and, although she loved the dazzling ceremonies before the departure, she hated the thought of the two men she loved so dearly going into danger.

The night before they sailed the four of them were alone together. Henry and his wife, herself and Charles; and she was envious of her sister-in-law who, like herself, was apprehensive, yet at the same time deeply content, because Katharine was pregnant and Henry was very affectionate toward her and had greatly honoured her by making her Regent in his absence.

Lucky Katharine! thought Mary, who need make no secret of her fear and love.

Mary threw herself on her knees before her brother that night. "Henry," she said, "you must take care, and not go into danger."

Henry laughed aloud. "My dear sister, we are going to war. Would you have me hide behind the lines?"

"Why must there be this war?" demanded Mary.

"Come, come, that's women's talk. There must always be wars. We have a country to subdue. I promise you this: when I am crowned, you shall come to see the deed done."

Mary murmured, her voice shaking with emotion: "Take care of each other."

Then she turned away and stood at the window, staring out to sea.

Henry was studying Charles shrewdly. "Well, my Lord Lisle," he said, stressing the title to remind Charles and Mary how the former had come by it, "my sister is deeply concerned for us. Methinks she loves us well."

Then he smiled fondly at his meek wife who gave him no cause for anxiety. She would take charge of the realm while he was away, and on his return she might be holding their son in her arms.

Henry was delighted with his campaign. He joined his armies at Thérouanne where he found a timber-house with an iron chimney waiting to house him; and many tents were at his disposal, some of them as long as one hundred and twenty-five feet. It seemed possible to wage war in the utmost comfort, and when the Emperor Maximilian joined him, soberly clad in black frieze (for he was in mourning for his second wife), he came, he said, to serve under Henry as a common soldier. This delighted Henry and it did not strike him as strange that the seasoned old warrior should place himself in such a position. Inexperienced as he was, Henry believed himself to be godlike, as those surrounding him had been telling him he was, for as long as he could remember. So Maximilian, receiving a hundred thousand crowns in advance for the services of himself and his Lanzknechts, accepted pay (provided by Henry) like any soldier serving under his commander. Henry did not know yet that the Emperor wanted the capture of the twin towns, Thérouanne and Tournay, to facilitate trade for the Netherlands, and that he was ready to play the humble subordinate that they might be won at Henry's expense.

And when the towns were taken — an easy conquest, for the French put up little resistance — and Henry wanted to go in triumph to Paris, Maximilian persuaded him to go with him to Lille and the court of his daughter, the Duchess of Savoy, where he could make the acquaintance of the Emperor's grandson, Charles, who was betrothed to his sister Mary.

Henry was disappointed, and grumbled to his friends — Charles, Compton, Thomas Boleyn.

"Why," he growled, "I had thought to go on to Paris, but it seems the Emperor does not advise it."

Compton suggested that the French might put up more resistance for Paris than they had for those two border towns, and they had to remember that the autumn was almost upon them, and that the Emperor had warned them of the discomfort of Flanders's mud.

Charles was overcome with a desire to see the boy who was betrothed to Mary and was not eager to continue with the war because, unlike Henry, he was beginning to see that Maximilian was not the friend the King so artlessly believed him to be; and it seemed that those two wily adventurers, Maximilian and Ferdinand, were of a kind, and their plan was to use Henry's wealth to get what they wanted.

So he joined his voice to Compton's, and Henry was not loath to be persuaded.

"I hear," said Henry, "that the Lady Margaret is comely and eager to entertain us."

The matter was settled. They would abandon war for the time being and give themselves up to pleasure in the Court at Lille.

The company was in high spirits. News had come from England that the Scots had been defeated at Flodden by what was left at home of the English army, and that James IV of Scotland had been slain.

Henry was jubilant even though James had become his brother-in-law by marrying his sister, Margaret Tudor.

"Never did trust a Scotsman," he had often commented; and he was not displeased to have his doubts of them confirmed. For as soon as he had left England they had started to march against England. Well, they had learned their lesson. Conquests abroad; conquests at home; what better time for revelry?

And Margaret of Savoy had determined that there should be revels.

Margaret, twice widowed, was still young; being devoted to her nephew, the fourteen-year-old Prince Charles, who had spent much of his childhood with her, she was eager to learn something of the boy's bride-to-be; and in any case it was always a pleasure to have an excuse for revelry.

When her father with his guests rode to the Palace she was waiting to greet them, her somewhat plump figure attired in regal velvet, her smile kindly; and with her was her nephew and the Emperor's grandson, Prince Charles.

The boy was embraced with affection by his grandfather, then presented to Henry. Charles Brandon, standing behind his master, wondered if Henry was thinking the same as he was: Poor, brilliant, lovely Mary, to be given to such a weakling!

The boy's picture, which Mary had come to loathe, had not lied; and he had changed little since it was painted. There were the prominent eyes and the heavy jaw, the mouth which did not close easily; there was the lank yellow hair, and the boy certainly seemed to have to concentrate with effort in order to follow the conversation.

And this was the greatest heir in Europe, the boy who would inherit the dominions of his Imperial grandfather Maximilian and his Spanish grandfather Ferdinand! The son of mad Juana!

Brandon's indignation rose at the thought of Mary's marriage.

Then he noticed that their hostess was smiling at him.

"My lord, Lisle," she was saying in a soft and gentle voice, "it gives me great pleasure to welcome you to my Court."

He took her hand and kissed it, and he fancied she lingered at his side just a little longer than was consistent with etiquette.

In the private apartment allotted to the King, Charles, with Compton, Parr and Boleyn, assisted at his toilet.

"The lady is not without charm," commented Henry. "But the boy . . . It's past my understanding how Max can feel so pleased with him."

"He looks to be an oaf, Sire," said Compton.

"Looks, man! He is. Did you notice how he stammered?"

"He has a great affection for his aunt and a respect for his grandfather," added Thomas Boleyn.

"The boy's in fear of his future, I'll warrant," said Henry. "He clings to auntie's skirts, wanting to stay the baby forever. Ah! Has it occurred to you that Max won't last long? He's getting old. Ferdinand's getting old. Then that boy will be one of the greatest rulers in Europe. Louis is no longer young; I hear he suffers from the gout and diverse ailments. But he'll be of no account because France will be ours. That'll put the long nose of that Dauphin of his out of joint. Dauphin! I tell you this, Francis of Angoulême will never mount the throne of France. There'll be two monarchs standing astride the continent. The oaf and myself. I tell you, my friends, that gives me cause for great pleasure."

"Your Highness will do with him what you will," cooed Compton.

"So this is a happy day for me to see that young fellow with no more brains than an ass."

"I am sorry for the Princess Mary." Charles realised that he should not have spoken.

He had broken in on Henry's pleasant reverie because he had reminded him of the Princess's passionate pleas; and as Henry was fond of Mary, his pleasure in the apparent stupidity of Charles was spoiled by the reminder that his sister must marry the boy.

He frowned. "'Tis the fate of princesses to marry for reasons of State." Then his jaw jutted out and he continued coldly:

"Methinks, my lord Lisle, you concern yourself overmuch with this matter."

It was a warning.

Margaret of Savoy, having been twice widowed, was no coy virgin and she was young enough to think now and then of another marriage, although her experiences of matrimony had scarcely been comforting. When she was three she had been betrothed to Charles VIII and sent to Amboise to be brought up to be Queen of France. But in order to link France with Brittany the marriage had been repudiated and Margaret sent back to Maximilian while Charles made a match with Anne of Brittany.

Later she had married the Infante of Spain, only to lose him and their child within a short time of their wedding. And after that she had married the Duke of Savoy, uncle of François, who was now Dauphin of France.

Her marriages seemed doomed not to last, for he too was dead and she once more a widow.

But she assured herself that did not mean that one day she might not find a husband with whom she could live in peace and pleasure. I have married for political reasons, she told herself; why should I not now marry to please myself?

When had this thought come to her? Was it when she had welcomed the King of England to her Court and found that his close friend was one of the most handsome men she had ever set eyes on? Before his coming she had been eager to meet him because her agent at the camp of Thérouanne, Philippe de Brégilles, had written to her of Charles Brandon. "Lord Lisle," he had written, "is a man who should interest Your Grace, for he is at the right hand of the King; and it is clear that Henry listens to what he has to say."

And now he had come to her Court she found him the most interesting member of the party.

It was not difficult to arrange that she should be next to him at table or in the dance; she began by pretending that she wanted to question him about the Princess Mary.

"I ask *you*, my lord Lisle," she said, as he sat beside her while the minstrels played and the food was served, "because I see how fond the King is of his sister and I feel his account of her might be affectionately prejudiced."

"The Princess Mary is deemed to be the loveliest lady at the English Court, and reports do not lie," Brandon told her.

"Then I am glad. But tell me, is she gentle and kind? You have seen my Charles? He will be gentle and a little shy at first. I hope the Princess will be ready to discover his excellent qualities which are not apparent to all at first."

"I am sure the Princess will be patient."

"Tell me, is she eager to come to him?"

Charles hesitated. "She is young . . . she is uncertain. She loves her home and her brother."

"Poor child! Life is difficult for royal princesses. I remember my own fate."

"It has made Your Highness tolerant?"

"I try to be. I am so anxious for the boy to be happy. He is a good boy and he will be a great prince. You do not believe me? Why, Lord Lisle, I had thought you would be a man to look below the surface. Charles is slow of speech because he does not speak without thought. Have you noticed that when he does say something it is worth saying? Do not underestimate

Charles, Lord Lisle. And you should warn the King of England not to."

"I will do so, Your Highness."

"I am sure you will. Tell me of England. I long to hear what the Court is like. I have heard it is quite brilliant since the young King came to power."

He talked to her of the jousts and entertainments while she listened avidly.

And when he and the King's gentlemen were in Henry's bedchamber that night the King said: "Did you notice that the Archduchess seems mightily taken with our friend Charles Brandon?"

Compton had noticed it; he tittered, while Henry's laughter burst out.

"Well, well, he's a handsome fellow, *our* Charles. A little different from *theirs*. The lady noticed it, I'll swear. Why, my lord Lisle, 'twould be a goodly match for you if you could marry Margaret of Savoy!"

"Your Grace is joking. The lady was asking me about *your* Court."

"She had her eyes on me, but she said to herself 'He's well and truly married.' So she turns to you. You know you are a little like me, Charles."

"I have heard that said, Your Grace, and it has given me great pleasure. I fear I grow a little more vain every time it is repeated."

Henry smiled affectionately at his friend. "Well, 'tis true enough. We might well be brothers, and I'd suspect we might be, but for the fact that my father was a man who never strayed from the marriage bed."

"As was meet and fitting in so great a king," murmured Charles.

Henry's lip jutted out; he had found some of the women of this country tempting and, because he had assured himself that what he called a little gallantry was an essential part of a soldier's life, he had succumbed to temptation. He did not like to be reminded of this.

"'Tis true," he murmured, "that my father was a great king . . . in some ways."

"He never had the people with him as Your Grace has," Charles said quickly, realising his mistake a few seconds before, and Henry's expression was sunny again.

"The people like a king who is a man also," he said. "They have a fancy for you, Charles . . . particularly the women. So 'tis small wonder that Margaret looks on you with favour."

Henry changed the subject then, but he was thoughtful. His friends did not take Margaret of Savoy's interest in Charles Brandon very seriously. The daughter of the mighty Emperor could scarcely marry an English nobleman whose only title was that which he had taken from his ward whom he had contracted to marry.

But why not? Henry asked himself. He could with the aid of a pen give his friend a title which would make him worthy . . . or almost. An earldom? A dukedom?

Henry was uneasy now that he had cast his eyes on the young Prince Charles, for reports would be quickly carried back to Mary of his unattractive looks; she might even rebel. He did not want trouble there. He loved that girl; she was like himself in so many ways and she had always been his favourite sister. She and he had stood together against Margaret, that elder sister who had often been critical of her bombastic brother. Mary had never been critical. She had always been the adoring child looking up to one who seemed all that a big brother should be. No, if Mary shed tears and pleaded with him, she'd unnerve him. He liked to see her merry. He had noticed the looks she had cast at Brandon. Why did the fellow have to have this attraction for women? Even Margaret of Savoy was not unmoved.

If he himself were not known as such a virtuous husband it would be the same with him. Charles had not that reputation. It was well known that he had been married twice already and was on the way to marrying again; and only he knew how many women there had been between, and doubtless he had lost count. It was a pity Elizabeth Grey was only a child. He would like to see Charles married, because he believed that if he were, Mary might come to her senses. While he remained free she could be capable of anything.

Why should not Margaret of Savoy marry a man who was well known as the King's best friend and right hand man?

He sought an opportunity of speaking to Charles when they were alone together. As they strolled in the gardens he made it clear that he wished to be alone with Brandon, and putting his arm about Charles's shoulders affectionately, said to him: "I did not joke when I spoke of you and Margaret, Charles. If you could persuade the lady, I'd put nothing in your way."

"Your Grace!"

"I see no reason why there should not be a match between you. I have a fancy that when she marries again it will be to please herself. Max can't dictate to a woman of her stature; and she has married for political reasons already. By God, she has an eye for you. Methought she could scarce keep her hands off you." The King burst into loud laughter. "Why Charles, it would suit us well to have an Englishman like yourself become the son-in-law of his Imperial Highness."

"What thinks, Your Grace," His Imperial Highness would say to such a match?"

"Let the lady win *his* approval, Charles. I tell you you have mine."

Henry slackened his pace and others joined them. Charles felt bemused. Ambitious as he was he had never looked as high as this.

Those were weeks of feverish excitement. He had no doubt that Margaret was in love with him. And he? Margaret was a comfortable woman, genial, friendly, worldly-wise; she had much to attract him. He knew though that he would never cease to think of Mary. If he were a simple country gentleman and Mary his neighbor's daughter, there would be no hesitation at all; they would be married by now. If she were a village girl, a serving maid, she would be his and he hers, for his passion, although not matching hers because he held it in check so much more easily than she could hers, was for her. But she was a princess and to love her could mean death to ambition, perhaps death itself.

On the other hand Margaret was personable, charming, eager to be loved.

So they danced together and much conversation passed between them; and he told himself, If I can win her hand I shall be almost a king. He would take his stand beside her in the governing of the Netherlands; and he would work whole-heartedly for the advancement of English affairs.

"Have you ever thought of marriage?" he asked Margaret as they danced together.

"Often."

"And would you marry again?"

"I married twice and I was singularly unlucky. Such misfortunes make a woman think a great deal before taking the step again."

"Perhaps it should make her very hopeful. No one continues in such ill luck."

He took her hand then and drew off one of her rings.

"See," he said, "it fits my finger."

She laughed and then said: "You must give it back to me."

He did so at once and he thought: that is her answer. She enjoys playing this game of flirtation but she is not seriously contemplating marriage with me.

His manner was a little aloof and noticing this, she said: "My lord Lisle, I could not allow you to have a ring which many people would recognise as mine . . . not yet."

He looked at her quickly: "Then I may hope?"

"It is never harmful to hope," she answered. "For even if one's desires are not realised one has had the pleasure of imagining that they will be."

"It is not easy to live on imaginings."

"In some matters patience is a necessity."

He was very hopeful that night.

Henry wanted to know how his courtship was progressing and when he told him everything, he was delighted. "When we return to England," he said, "which we must do ere long, I shall bestow a title on you; then you can return to the Low Countries and continue with your courtship of the lady in a manner commensurate with your rank."

"Your Grace is good to me."

"When you share the Regency of the Netherlands, my friend, I shall look to you to be good to me."

When next Charles was with Margaret he talked of his marriage to Anne Browne and his two little daughters.

"I should like to see them," Margaret told him. "I greatly desire children of my own."

"I would I might send my eldest daughter to be brought up in your excellent Court."

"I pray you send her, for I should have great pleasure in receiving her."

He told her then about the child whom he had rescued from the river, and she said: "Poor mite. Send her to me with your daughter. I promise you that I shall myself make certain that they are brought up in a fitting manner. You see, soon I shall be losing Charles and I shall miss him greatly."

It was a bond between them. While she had his daughter and his protégée at her Court she would not forget him, Charles was sure.

Henry was making preparations to return to England. He had completed a treaty, before leaving Lille, in which it was arranged that the following May he should bring his sister Mary to Calais where they would be met by the Emperor, Margaret and Prince Charles; then the nuptials should be solemnised, because the boy was fourteen and the Princess would be eighteen, and there was no need to delay longer. The Emperor was eager for heirs, and an early marriage should solve this problem.

Margaret asked then that, if the King should fail to have heirs, the crown of England should go to Mary.

Henry scarcely considered this. Not have heirs! Of course he would have heirs. Katharine was pregnant now. Simply because they had lost their first, that was no reason to suppose they would not have a large and healthy family.

One of his favourite reveries was to see himself, a little older than he was now, but as strong and vigorous, with his children round him — pink-cheeked boys bursting with vitality, excelling in all sports, idolising their father; beautiful girl children, looking rather like Mary, twining their arms about his neck. Of course there would be children.

But he had no objection to agreeing to this condition. Moreover, in view of what was happening in Scotland, he had no intention of letting the throne pass to his sister Margaret and her son — whose father was that enemy who had attacked England while he, Henry, was in France, stabbing him in the back. Glory to God, the fellow had received the reward of such treachery on Flodden Field!

And so they returned to England.

The people had assembled to cheer their King who came as a conqueror. It was true he had only those two towns of which to boast but he planned to return the following year, and then it would be on to Paris.

Beside the King rode the Duc de Longueville, a very high ranking French nobleman of royal blood, whom he had taken prisoner at the Battle of the Spurs. The crowds stared at this disdainful and elegant personage, whom the King insisted on treating almost as an equal. Henry had become very fond of Longueville, largely because he believed that such a high nobleman, being his prisoner, added greatly to his prestige.

There must be balls and banquets to celebrate the return, but in spite of the splendour it was not a happy homecoming.

Katharine, who as Regent had used all her energies in organising the defeat of the invading Scots, had exhausted herself in the process and consequently had had a miscarriage. This threw the King into a mood of deep depression, particularly when he remembered Margaret's request that, should he die without heirs of his body, the crown should be settled on Mary; moreover Katharine had Flodden Field to offer him while he could only boast of Thérouanne and Tournay, and reluctantly he faced the fact that the greater glory had been won unostentatiously at home.

Then there was Mary to be faced. The truth could not be kept from her. Charles was present when the King told her that she must be ready to leave for Calais the following May.

She looked from her brother to the man she loved with stony reproach; her lips quivered, her eyes blazed; then she turned and, forgetting the respect due to the King, walked hurriedly from his presence.

Henry — and Charles — would have been less alarmed had she shouted her protest at them.

The situation needed careful handling, thought the King. Mary was sullen; she never ceased to reproach him. There were occasions when she refused to continue with preparations for her marriage.

It is Brandon, of a certainty, Henry told himself. She still hopes for Brandon. If he were out of the way she would be more inclined to reason.

He sent for Charles.

"My friend," he said, "I propose sending you as my ambassador to the Netherlands. You should make your preparations without delay."

Charles bowed. Now that he was back, now that he had seen her again, he had no wish to go. He felt himself being caught up in her wild hopes. He dared not be alone with her. She would be arrogant in her desire; and how could he be sure that he could persuade her that they could so easily destroy themselves?

In her opinion, all should be tossed away for the sake of love; but that was because she was an inexperienced girl. She had been pampered all her life; she did not believe that the world would ever cease to cosset her. Brandon was older; he had seen beyond the glittering Court; he remembered men who had been sent to the Tower for smaller offenses, and only walked out to the block.

It would be well if he escaped before he were drawn into that conflagration about which she did not seem to understand they were dancing like two moths round a candle flame.

"And, Charles," went on Henry, "you shall go in such a manner as will add to your dignity. Lord Lisle will be no more. Elizabeth Grey is not for you. I fancy Margaret will smile more kindly on the Duke of Suffolk."

Here was honour indeed; but his first thought was: If the Duke of Suffolk can aspire to the hand of an Archduchess, why not to that of a princess?

But he saw the purpose in his King's eyes and made ready to leave for the Netherlands.

CHAPTER THREE

The French Proposal

Before the Princess Mary were laid out the treasures which had been brought for her inspection. There were rich fabrics, velvets and cloth of gold, and miniver and martin with which to fur her garments; there were necklaces, coronals and girdles all sparkling with priceless gems.

She stared at them stonily.

Lady Guildford held up a chain of gold set with rubies. "But look at this, my lady. Try it on. Is it not exquisite?"

Mary turned her head away.

"Please allow me, my lady. There! Oh, but it is so becoming and you have always loved such beautiful ornaments!"

Mary snatched the trinket from her neck and threw it onto her bed, where Lady Guildford had set out the other treasures.

"Do not bother me," said Mary.

"But the King has asked to be told your opinion of these gifts."

"Gifts!" cried Mary. "They are not gifts, for gifts are given freely. These are bribes."

Lady Guildford trembled, because the King had come into the room smiling, certain of the pleasure the jewels must give his sister.

"Ha!" he cried. "So there is my little sister. Decking herself out with jewels, eh? And how does she like them?"

Mary turned her face to him and he was startled by her pallor. Her blue eyes seemed enormous. Could it be that she had lost flesh and that was why she looked so?

"She likes them not," snapped Mary.

Henry's face crumpled in disappointment, and Lady Guildford held her breath in dismay. He would be angry, and like everyone else at Court, she dreaded the King's outbursts of anger. But because this was his sister whom he loved so deeply he was only filled with sorrow.

"And I had taken such care in choosing what I thought would please you."

She turned to him and threw her arms about his neck. "You know well how to please me. You do not have to buy costly jewels. All you have to do is stop this marriage."

"Sister . . . little Mary . . . you do not understand what you ask."

"Do I not? It is I who have to make this marriage, is it not? I assure you I understand more than any."

He stroked her hair and Lady Guildford was amazed because she was sure that was a glint of tears she saw in his eyes. He forgave his sister her boldness; he suffered with her; it must be true that Henry loved nobody — not even his wife — as he loved his beautiful sister.

"Mary," he said gently, "if we broke off this marriage it would mean our friendship with the Emperor was broken. He is our ally against the French. If I wrote to him and said there shall be no marriage because my sister has no stomach for it, there might even be war between our countries."

"Oh Henry, Henry, help me."

He held her against him. "Why, little one, if I could, I would, but even you must fulfill your destiny. We cannot choose whom we would marry. We marry for state reasons, and alas this is your fate. Do not be downhearted, little one. Why, you will charm your husband and all his Court as you charm us here. I doubt not that in a few months, when you are as loved and honoured over there as you are here, you will laugh at this foolish child you once were. And you will not be far off. You shall visit us and we shall visit you. And, dearest, when you come to our Court we will have such a masque, such a banquet, as I never gave for any other . . ."

She jerked herself from his embrace, her eyes dark with passion.

"Masques! Banquets!" she cried. "Is that all the balm you have to offer for a broken heart!"

Then she ran from the apartment, leaving him standing there, bewildered — but miraculously not angry, only sad because he could see no way of helping her.

There was a further check to his plans. Charles Brandon, now the Duke of Suffolk, was ready to set out for the Netherlands where he would fill the post of Henry's ambassador. And once he is out of England I shall feel easier in my mind, thought Henry, for it is because she sees him constantly at Court that she has become so intractable.

Before the newly created Duke set out, however, a courier arrived with a letter from Margaret to Henry.

She was deeply embarrassed. A rumour had reached her father that she proposed marrying Charles Brandon, and the Emperor was extremely angry. She therefore thought it advisable that before he set out for the Netherlands, Brandon should marry Elizabeth Grey to whom she knew he was affianced. This she believed was the only way in which her father could be appeased.

Henry stared moodily before him. Clearly Margaret regretted that piece of romantic folly, and when Brandon was no longer at her side she realised that marriage with him would be incongruous. She was telling him and Charles that that little episode was over.

He sent for Charles and showed him the letter, and the manner in which his friend received the news was in itself disconcerting, because it seemed to Henry that the fellow was relieved.

"What of marrying Elizabeth Grey?" he asked.

"She is but nine years old, Your Grace; a little young for marriage."

Henry grunted.

"Then," he said, "you must perforce leave for the Netherlands without delay." He brightened a little. "It may be that when Margaret has you at her side once more she will be ready to snap her fingers at the Emperor."

Charles bowed his head. He did not want the King to read his thoughts.

Henry said: "Then begone, Charles. Leave at once. There is no time to say your farewells to . . . anyone. I expect you to have left by tomorrow."

So Charles left for Flanders, and the Princess Mary was more and more melancholy as the days passed.

The Duc de Longueville, guest, rather than prisoner, at the Court of England, found means of writing to his master Louis XII.

He did not regret his capture, he wrote, because it was so amusing and interesting to watch the young King of England in his Court. At the moment there was a great bustle of preparation for the Princess Mary's marriage to young Prince Charles. The Princess was not eager; in fact, he heard on good authority that she was imploring her brother to stop the match. Not that her pleas were of much avail, although Henry was made very anxious by the importunings of his sister.

"He loves this girl," wrote the Duke, "as, to my mind, he loves no other; and it does not surprise me. If my gracious liege could see her, he would understand. For she is of a truth the loveliest creature in the Court. Her hair, which is the colour of gold, is abundant and falls in thick shining curls to her waist; she has a healthy complexion like her brother's, and her eyes are large and blue — though at this moment somewhat melancholy. She is well formed and graceful, high spirited by nature, though downcast at the prospect of her marriage, seeming a little younger than her eighteen years. A delightful girl."

Henry liked to ride out to the chase, the French Duke beside him, for the man was an elegant and witty companion and Henry enjoyed his company; in addition it was so delightful to contemplate that he had taken the Duke prisoner in battle.

Once as they rode back to Greenwich after a pleasurable but exhausting day, Longueville said to Henry: "Your Grace, do you trust the Emperor?"

"Trust him!" cried Henry. "Indeed I trust him. We fought together in Flanders and he served under my command."

"A strange gesture from his Imperial Highness."

"Oh, he is a simple man. He told me that he was old and I was young; and that it was a mistake for youth to serve age. It should be the other way about."

"And he was paid highly for those sentiments, I'll swear."

"I paid him as I would pay any generals serving under me."

"And won for him the two towns he wanted?"

Henry flushed scarlet. "You forget, sir, that you are my prisoner."

"I forget it not," answered Longueville, "although the gracious manner in which you have always treated me might make me do so."

"I forget not your rank."

"Then, Your Highness will perhaps listen to my opinions, for I was a confidant of the King of France, my master, and I could be of use to you."

"How so?"

"Your Highness discovered the perfidy of Ferdinand of Aragon."

"That is so."

"Would it surprise you to learn that the Emperor and Ferdinand are now making a treaty with my King, while professing friendship with you?"

"I perceive," retorted Henry, "that you believe yourself to be the ambassador of the King of France. I must perforce remind you that you occupy no such post. You are the prisoner of the King of England."

Longueville bowed his head, but a sly smile played about his mouth. He knew that he made Henry very uneasy.

As he was given the freedom of the Palace, Longueville did not find it difficult to speak a few words to the Princess Mary, and one day he presented himself at her apartments to ask for an audience.

Lady Guildford was inclined to forbid it, but Mary heard the Frenchman talking to her lady-mistress and idly asked what he wanted.

He begged to be allowed to speak to her, and Mary told him he might. Lady Guildford hovered in the background while he did so.

"My lady," said Longueville, "I have news which I think you should know. As you will guess, I receive letters from France and I know what plots are afoot.

Prince Charles, who is betrothed to you, is now being offered a French Princess, and his grandfather, Ferdinand, has actually declared that if he does not take her and abandon you, he will leave his Spanish dominions to Charles's younger brother, Prince Ferdinand."

Her eyes widened and lost a little of their melancholy.

"Is this so?" she said thoughtfully.

"I thought you would wish to know, for you are too proud a lady to think of marriage where you are not wanted."

"My lord Duke," answered Mary, "I thank you, and I beg of you, keep me informed, for you are right when you say I have no wish for such a marriage."

He left her, satisfied; and when he had gone she ran to Lady Guildford and began to shake the startled woman.

"Did you hear that?" she demanded. "Charles is being offered to a French Princess, and his grandfather Ferdinand wants him to abandon me. This is a happy day."

"You must not excite yourself."

"Not excite myself! Are you mad? Of course I shall excite myself. This is the best news I have heard since they betrothed me to that idiot. I'll not marry a boy who does not want me." She was laughing hysterically. Then she stopped and said: "Poor French Princess!"

Henry tried to shut his ears to the rumours. It was too humiliating. He had been duped by Ferdinand; could it be that he had met the same fate at the hands of the Emperor?

He refused to believe it. He thought of the man humbling himself before him, coming to him in black frieze, a widower mourning for his wife. "I will serve under you . . . and I must be paid as you would pay your generals. We will take these two towns . . ."

He had not said that they were the towns *he* wanted. And what good were they to England? Had the Emperor been laughing at the King of England, as Ferdinand had, exploiting his vanity?

Henry would want absolute proof before he believed it.

Charles Brandon returned from the Netherlands where Margaret had been friendly, but cool. Clearly there could never be a question of marriage between them.

"All my plans are coming to naught," grumbled Henry.

Mary sent for the Duke of Suffolk.

"Have a care, my lady," warned Lady Guildford. "Remember the Duke's reputation. He is not a man to be lightly invited to a lady's private apartments."

"You may leave this to me," Mary retorted imperiously. "And when he comes I wish to be alone with him."

"But my lady . . ."

"Those are my orders."

He came and stood before her, and when Mary had dismissed Lady Guildford, who went most reluctantly, she put her arms about his neck and they stood for some seconds in a close embrace.

It was he who took her hands and withdrew them from his neck; they stood looking at each other.

"Charles," cried Mary, "Margaret has refused you and Charles is going to refuse me. Was there ever such great good fortune?"

He looked at her sadly, and she shook her head in exasperation.

"You despair too easily."

"Tell me for what you think we may hope," he asked.

"I am eighteen and marriageable. I must be given a husband from somewhere. And if a Duke is worthy of Margaret of Savoy, why not of the Princess Mary? That is what I shall ask my brother."

"He thinks you far more precious than Margaret of Savoy."

"He must be made to see reason."

"I beg of you, be cautious for both our sakes."

She threw herself against him: "Oh Charles, Charles, who ever was cautious in love?"

"We must be . . . if we wish to survive."

Her eyes sparked. "Do not think I spend my days sitting and dreaming. I have made a plan."

He looked alarmed; she saw this and burst into laughter. "You will soon discover what it is. Very shortly you will receive an order to appear at the Manor of Wanstead. Then you shall hear all about it."

"Mary . . ."

She stood on tiptoe and put her lips against his.

"Kiss me," she said. "That makes me happier than talk. By the Holy Mother, there is so little time when we may be alone; Mother Guildford will find some pretext soon to come and disturb us. Oh, you are back . . . miraculously free . . . as I am! Charles, Charles, do not ever think that I will allow them to take you from me."

He abandoned himself. How could he do otherwise? She was irresistible; he could even ask himself: what did it matter if this was the end of ambition? At moments like this he could believe he would willingly barter all he had achieved for an hour with her.

Charles was not the only one who was summoned to the Manor of Wanstead. Thomas Wolsey, Bishop of Lincoln, received a command to attend, as did the Bishops of Winchester and Durham.

When they arrived they found Sir Ralph Verney, the Princess's Chamberlain, already there; with him was the Earl of Worcester who told them that, on the instructions of the Princess Mary, he was to take them with him into the great hall.

There Mary was waiting to receive them. She looked more than beautiful on that day; she was regal; she had put on a purple cloak which was lined with ermine, and standing on the dais she greeted them with the utmost formality.

When she had spoken to each singly, she begged them to be seated, while she addressed them.

She spoke in her high clear voice and, although now and then during her discourse her eyes fell on Charles, she gave no suggestion that she regarded him in any special light; and the impression she gave was that he was there because he was the Duke of Suffolk and for no other reason.

"My lords," she said, "I have assembled you here to speak of a matter which touches my royal dignity, and I look to your loyalty to the Crown to support me. I know I can rely on you. It has been brought to my ears that the Prince of Castile and his family continually conspire against my brother and this realm. I am, therefore, resolved never to fulfill my contract with him."

There was silence among the assembly, but there was one among them whose eyes gleamed with satisfaction. Wolsey had risen high in the King's favour since the war, and he saw himself rising still higher. He had long doubted the sincerity of the Emperor, and that the alliance with the Prince of Castile should be abandoned suited his plans.

Mary continued: "I beg of you all to plead my cause with the King, my brother, who may well be displeased with me for summoning you hither."

Charles, watching her, thought: how wonderful she is! There is no one like her. Who else, but eighteen years old, would have dared summon her brother's ministers to her presence and make her will known?

He was exultant because he was beginning to believe that she must achieve her desires — and hers were his.

When Mary rode back with her attendants to Greenwich, the people came out to cheer her; they marvelled at her appearance for, on this occasion with the certainty of victory in her eyes, she was so beautiful.

She had not been so happy since she had realised the difficulties which stood between her and the man she so ardently loved, and one of the reasons for her elation was that Thomas Wolsey had spoken to her when taking his leave.

"My lady," he had said, "you may rely on me to do my utmost with the King to have you released from this match which is repugnant to you."

Mary recognised in that man a spirit similar to her own.

"Wolsey is on my side," she told herself.

Henry no longer had any doubt of the perfidy of the Emperor.

Envoys from France had arrived at Greenwich, ostensibly to make terms for the return of the Duc de Longueville and other prisoners whom Henry had taken at Thérouanne; in fact they came to bring a message from the King of France which was for Henry's ears alone, and as he listened to it the veins stood out at his temples. Not only had Ferdinand renewed his alliance with France but the Emperor Maximilian was his ally in this and — behind the back of his comrade-in-arms, Henry of England — had made his peace with the French. It was, however, the wish of the King of France to make friends with England; and if His Grace would summon the Duc de Longueville to his presence, the Duke would lay before him a proposition from the King of France.

Henry summoned the Duke to his presence, and with him that minister on whom he had come to rely, Thomas Wolsey; and when the King heard what the Duc de Longueville had to say his eyes glistened with something like delight. By God, he thought, here is a way of avenging myself on that pair of rascals. Foxy Ferdinand and Imperial Perfidy will dance with rage when they hear of this.

The matter was settled and it only remained for the principal person concerned to be informed. Henry sent for his sister, the Princess Mary.

When she came to his presence Thomas Wolsey was with the King, and her warm smile included them both, for she believed Wolsey to be her friend.

Henry embraced her.

"News, sister, which will be most welcome to you."

Her smile was dazzling in its satisfaction.

"We are breaking off relations with Maximilian, and a marriage between you and his grandson is now impossible."

She clasped her hands together. Gratitude filled her heart, to Providence, to Henry, to Wolsey, to the Emperor for his perfidy. Her prayers were answered. She was free and in a short time she would cajole Henry into letting her have her way.

"Therefore," went on Henry, "you should no longer consider yourself under contract to the Prince of Castile."

"Most joyfully," she answered.

"Do not think though that we have not your future at heart, dear sister. We have a dazzling proposition to put before you, for Monsieur de Longueville has brought us an offer from his master. What would you say if I were to tell you that within a few months you will be Queen of France?"

"Queen of France! But I do not understand . . ."

"Then let me explain. Louis XII, King of France, recently widowed, seeks a new bride. He has heard glowing accounts of your beauty and virtue and he offers you his hand and crown."

She had turned pale; her blue eyes seemed suddenly dark. "*No!*" she whispered.

Henry came and put an arm about her. "Dearest sister, you are astonished. It is indeed a dazzling prospect. Louis is our friend now; he has shown us who our enemies are. Not for you the pallid Prince of Castile with the mad mother, but the great King of France. You will be crowned in Paris. Mary, you cannot understand yet what honours are about to be laid at your feet."

Still she did not speak. She could not believe it. It was a nightmare. She had longed so fervently for her freedom, had prayed so vehemently for it, and she must wake in a moment, for this simply could not be true.

"He is driving a bargain, this King of France," went on Henry with a laugh. "Have no fear. I can provide you with a dowry rich enough to please even him. Mary, you will be the means of cementing this bond which, friend Wolsey here agrees with me, is of the utmost importance to our country."

She spoke then. "I won't do it. I won't. I have been tormented with the Prince of Castile. I'll marry where I will."

"Why, sweetheart," said Henry, "when you have heard what this means, you will be as eager for this marriage as we are. Queen of France! Think of that."

"I'll not think of it. I do not want this marriage. I do not want to leave you and England."

"There, my dearest sister, partings are sad, we know well. But you'll not be far away. I shall visit you and you shall visit us. We shall be rivals in splendour, for when you come to see us I shall have made ready for your entertainment such masques . . ."

"Stop! Stop! I cannot bear it!"

She turned and ran from the room.

She lay on her bed; she did not weep; this was a matter too tragic for tears. She stared blankly before her and refused to eat.

Lady Guildford and those of her women who loved her — and many did, for impetuous and hot tempered as she could be, she was a generous and goodhearted mistress — were afraid for her.

Henry was perplexed. He had expected a little resistance but he had not thought she would be so unreasonable. Had she not seen similar situations rising around her? Margaret had had to go to Scotland to marry a man whom she had never seen. Her own father had married her mother that the houses of York and Lancaster should be united. Did she not understand that, for all their wealth and privilege, they themselves had their duty to perform?

He went to her room and sat by her bed. Gently he talked to her, pointing out her duty. He would have saved her from this marriage if he could, but the personal desires of Princes must always be set aside for matters of state.

She burst out: "He is fifty-two and I am eighteen. He has had two wives and I have never had a husband."

Henry's eyes narrowed. "So you hold against him the fact that he has had two wives. I did not think *you* would do that."

They did not mention Brandon's name, but she understood the reference; for had not Charles himself had two wives and was he not even now contracted to a third?

"He is ancient," she cried. "He is ugly and I do not want him."

"Sister, be calm. Be reasonable."

"I hate him," she cried.

"How can you hate one whom you have never seen?"

"Because he will be the means of taking me from all I love."

And as she lay on her bed, suddenly the tears started to flow down her cheeks. She did not weep noisily, nor sob, but just lay quietly there; and the sight so unnerved Henry that he turned aside, blinking away his own tears.

I have indulged her over much, he thought. I have loved her so well. I shall miss her as she will miss me.

By God, were it not that so much was at stake, I would give her Brandon just for the sake of seeing her happy.

Then another thought occurred to him. "Why, Mary," he said, "your bridegroom, as you say, will be an old man. I hear that he suffers much from the gout."

"And for these reasons should I be doubly glad to marry him?" she cried angrily.

He put his face close to hers and whispered: "Why yes, sweetheart. He lives but quietly, retiring to bed early; he eats frugally; it is necessary for his health. When he sees his young and beautiful bride he will be excited, depend upon it. He is in a fever of impatience to see you. I hear that in his youth he lived well and was very fond of women."

"You do not make him any more attractive to me."

"Do I not? That is because you stubbornly refuse to grasp my meaning. Sister, if you become the wife of the King of France and so serve your country, I do not think it will be long before you are the widow of the King of France."

She caught her breath. "And then . . .?" she asked.

"And then . . . you will be mistress of yourself, sister."

She sat up in bed and caught at his coat with impatient fingers.

"Henry, if I marry the King of France to please you, will you, when I am a widow and free, let me marry where I please?"

He saw the hope in her face and it pleased him. He had to rouse her from her melancholy, for if he did not he would have a sick sister who would be unfit for any marriage at all.

"I promise," he said.

Her arms were about his neck. "Swear, Henry. Swear solemnly."

He stroked her hair with great tenderness. "I give you my word," he assured her.

After that interview with her brother, Mary's manner had changed. She rose from her bed; she ate a little; it was true she remained melancholy, but those about her noticed that she had become resigned.

She had realised that as a princess she had her duty and must needs perform it.

She did not see Charles, whom Henry had sent from Court for a while because he knew that to allow them to be together at such a time might be like putting flame to gunpowder.

If only Mary would continue in this state of resignation until the nuptials were completed he would feel at peace.

Charles spent the days of his absence staying at the home of his ward.

Elizabeth had heard a great deal of gossip about him and at one time had thought he would be the wife of Margaret of Savoy.

She had never greatly desired to marry him but since that day when he had rescued the child from the river she had viewed their future union without the distaste she had first felt for it. She had come to believe that since she must marry she might as well marry Charles Brandon as any.

But when she had learned that he had gone to Flanders as Lord Lisle — the title he had taken through his connection with her — and using it had attempted to woo Margaret, her pride revolted; and when he arrived at the manor she greeted him without much warmth.

Charles was too immersed in his own problems to notice this in the beginning.

He was thinking along the same lines as those which Henry had put before Mary. Louis was an old man and it might well be that he would not live long; indeed marriage to a young and beautiful and vital girl would not help him to longevity. Could it be that it was only a matter of waiting?

To imagine Mary in the bed of Louis was revolting; but he would try to think beyond it. Their position had been extremely dangerous; they could not expect to have their desires fulfilled without facing bitter trial beforehand.

In time, he thought, we shall marry. It is only a matter of waiting and enduring for a while.

Elizabeth said to him one day when they rode together: "You have been thoughtful, my lord Duke, since you came here."

He admitted he had much on his mind.

"I think I know what it is that makes you moody."

He turned to smile at her.

"Why, my lord," she said, "you are now the Duke of Suffolk and as such have no need of the title which you took from me. It was useful for a while when you paid court to the Lady of the Netherlands. Now, of course, as a noble Duke you need not concern yourself with the daughter of a viscount."

He was silent, not really paying attention to her because he could not stop thinking of Mary, going to France, being crowned there, her meeting with Louis.

Elizabeth sensed his lack of attention. She said angrily: "Have no fear, my lord Duke. I have no intention of holding you to your promise. Let me tell you this: I have no intention of marrying you. Nothing would induce me to."

He turned and looked blankly at her. Piqued and angry, for she sensed he was still not paying full attention to what she said, she whipped her horse and rode on because she was afraid he would see the tears which had started to her eyes.

Charles looked after her retreating figure. He did not pursue her.

She had spoken in childish anger, but he must accept her refusal, because he, like Mary, must be free for whatever good fortune could befall them.

He would return to Court in due course and, when an opportunity offered itself, he would tell Henry that Elizabeth Grey had rejected him and thus he was released from his contract to marry her.

The ceremony took place in the state apartments of Greenwich. Mary was solemn in her wedding robes. At her side was Louis d'Orléans, that Duc de Longueville who had played such a big part in arranging the match, and who on this occasion was acting as proxy for his master, King Louis XII of France.

As he took her cold hand and slipped on it the nuptial ring, as he put his lips on hers for the nuptial kiss, she was thinking: It will not be for long. I could not endure it if it were. What sort of a marriage is this, where the wife can only endure it because she hopes her husband cannot live long? What sort of a person have they turned me into, that I can long for the death of a man I have never seen, and that man my own husband?

She went through the ceremony mechanically, repeating words that she was asked to repeat, without thinking of their meaning; she only knew that, in place of the slack-mouthed boy, she had been given to an old man, and the only change for the better was that in the ordinary course of life the latter must die before the former.

The King of France had expressed the wish that the ceremony should be conducted with realism. "Having heard of the beauty of his bride," the Duc de Longueville had confided to the King, "he can scarce wait to receive her." Therefore he wished the marriage to be consummated symbolically.

It was a trying ordeal to be divested of her court gown by her women and put into her magnificent sleeping robes. With her golden hair falling about her shoulders, the robe about her naked body, her feet bare, she looked very appealing, particularly because she was so unnaturally subdued and there was a look of fear and resignation in her eyes.

As she lay down on what was called the nuptial couch, she saw her brother smiling at her encouragingly. Beside him was his Queen. Katharine, who understood, was trying not to weep in sympathy. And there was one other there. Suffolk had recently returned from the country, free of his engagement with Elizabeth Grey; he could not look at her, nor dared she look at him.

The Duc de Longueville approached the couch and, sitting down on it, gazed at the Princess; then he took off one of the red riding boots he was wearing; and, that all present might see, he lay down on the couch beside the Princess and touched her bare leg with his bare foot.

Symbolically the marriage had been consummated, and the Princess Mary was now the Queen of France.

The whole Court was talking of the impatience of King Louis. And who could blame him? He was an old man and he could not have many years left to him. He had a young bride, notoriously beautiful; it was natural that he should want her to be with him without delay.

Couriers were arriving at Greenwich every day, bringing gifts from the King of France. There were jewels and trinkets at which all those who knew the King marvelled, because he was not noted for his extravagance; but so eager was he to show his bride the affectionate greeting which was awaiting her, that for once he forgot to calculate the cost.

Mary declared her intention to learn French; she had, of course, studied that language but she did not feel as yet proficient enough. "I should prefer not to disappoint my husband," she said demurely. Henry knew that she was seeking to delay her departure by every possible means. She feigned great interest in a grammar which her French master, John Palsgrave — a Londoner who had graduated in Paris and spoke French like a Frenchman — was compiling for her. He must write the book for her, she said; for how could she perfect her knowledge of the French language without such a book? John Palsgrave worked too hard for her at his task, and she was not pleased when he told her delightedly that he had been writing the book for some time and would be able to present it to her in a week. This he did; it was called *Éclaircissement de la Langue Française*.

There was her trousseau to be prepared and it was decided that some of her dresses should be made in the French style out of compliment to her husband.

"My dressmakers should go to Paris to study the dressmakers there," she suggested. "They should make absolutely certain that there is no mistake."

But her brother knew, and Wolsey knew, that her great wish was to delay her departure; and, as theirs was to expedite it, her case was hopeless for they were more powerful than she.

Wolsey himself harangued the dressmakers. If they had not enough seamstresses they must find more . . . quickly. The sixteen dresses which comprised the Princess's trousseau must be made in record time even though some were in the French style, some in the Italian — in order to please Louis who, as well as being

King of France, was titular ruler of the Milanese. And some of the dresses must of course be of the English fashion, to remind all who saw the Princess that she was of that nation.

Mary would stand still in silence while the dazzling materials were tried on her, showing no interest in the clothes whatsoever, and her women, watching her, were sad because they remembered how excited she had once been over her gowns and her jewels.

As for the jewels, few of them had ever seen any collection so glorious as those which were being prepared for the Princess. Her carcanets were adorned with rubies and diamonds; there were gold bracelets set with priceless gems; there were glittering girdles and imitation flowers to be attached to her gowns — roses, marigolds (Mary's own emblem) and fleur-de-lis decorated with every precious stone that could be imagined. Her litter was a thing of beauty adorned with the arms of her parents and her grandfather, King Edward IV. There was a canopy of a delightful shade of blue embroidered with the figure of Christ sitting on a rainbow, bearing the motto of the new Queen of France: *La Volenté de Dieu me suffit*.

Mary would stand like a statue while the necklaces were placed about her neck, while the girdles encircled her waist, and her women combed out her lovely hair and set the jewelled ornaments on it.

"Oh my lady, don't you care that you have all these beautiful things? Does it mean nothing in the world to you that you have more honour done to you than any woman in England?"

She answered: "I care not."

And she thought: "I would give up all the jewels, all the silks and velvets, if I could leave the Court this day with the man I love."

During those melancholy weeks she was on several occasions ready to find her way to Charles, to say to him: let us go away from here together . . . anywhere. What does it matter if we abandon rank, wealth, everything? I have proved that all these things mean nothing without love.

They would be outlaws, but what did she care?

She smiled to think of them, living in some humble cottage. They need not starve. She would take a few jewels with her — those which were her very own — and they would sell them and live on the proceeds for the rest of their lives, humbly perhaps, but oh, how happily.

They would never be seen at Court again.

And if they were discovered?

Now came the vision which made the dream impossible of fulfilment. They would take him from her. The Tower for him . . . perhaps for them both. She would be safe though for she knew Henry would never allow his sister to be harmed.

But what of Charles? She could not bear it. They would take him to Tower Hill. She could see his beautiful head held high in the executioner's bloody hand.

"Here is the head of a traitor!"

No, not that.

She must go on with this. It was the only way. And each morning when she awoke the thought was in her mind: Louis cannot live long.

The cavalcade had come to Dover Castle. In her apartments there, Mary looked across the slaty sea. She could not see the land but beyond that strip of water lay her new home, and the man who was to be her husband was waiting for her there.

She was glad when the storm rose, because it seemed to her then that the elements were on her side and every day which passed now was a day nearer to freedom.

There was no gaiety in her apartments, although Henry, who had accompanied her, tried to make some in the Castle. She heard the sounds of the lutes but she had no wish to join the merrymakers.

Henry came to her apartment, unable to enjoy the dance because she was not there.

"Come, little sister, you'll not be so far away. Smile. Join the company."

"Leave me, Henry," she said. "Go and dance and sing. There is no reason why you should share my misery."

He stamped his foot with rage. "If you must be such a fool, be so alone," he said, and left her.

But he soon came back.

"Would we could have kept you with us, Mary."

She looked at him stonily. "You are the King," she retorted.

"It is hard for you to understand all that is involved in important State matters."

"It is as I thought," she answered. "I am of no importance. Throw me to whichever dog best pleases you at the moment. The drooling young Prince of Castile today; the old man worn out by his lechery tomorrow."

"Your tongue is too loose, sister."

"Would it were looser, that I might tell you what you have done to me."

Then she threw herself into his arms, for it grieved her to see his lips drawn down in pain.

He stroked her hair and soothed her, whispering: "It won't be for long, Mary. It can't be for long."

"Holy Mother," she said, "forgive me, for I pray for his death."

"Hush, sister."

"It's true. If I am wicked, then fate has made me so. If I could have married where I pleased I should not have had these wicked thoughts."

"Do not utter them."

"Then repeat your promise."

"What promise, Mary?"

"That if I should become a widow, I marry where I like."

He could see that only by looking far into the future could she tolerate the present; and he repeated his promise.

Then he left her. At the door of her apartment he saw a very young girl who was but a child. He called her because he thought that it would be safer for one so young rather than someone older to be with his sister at this time, for Mary was in a reckless mood.

"Come here, child," he said; and she came and curtsied prettily; then she lifted enormous, dark eyes to his face, and he was faintly amused by their lack of fear. "Are you waiting on the Queen of France?" he asked.

"Yes, Sire," was the answer.

"Go to her now. Sit beside her. Comfort her. Bathe her face with scented water. Tell her the King sent you to soothe her. She is sad because she is going to leave our Court."

"Yes, Sire."

"Stay. What is one so young doing here?"

"I am to go to France with the Queen, Sire. I am with my father."

"Who is your father?"

"Sir Thomas Boleyn, Sire."

"And you are?"

"Anne, Sire."

He patted the dark hair. "You are a good girl," he said. "Go to, and remember what I have said."

She curtsied gravely. Henry was lightly amused for a moment; then he forgot the child; his concern was all for his sister Mary.

Early in the morning of the second day of October the wind dropped, and preparations were made to sail. The ships lay in readiness; the fine garments, the precious jewels had been put on board.

Henry took his sister's hand and led her down to the shore. There he kissed her solemnly.

"My beloved sister," he said, "I give you to God, the fortune of the sea and the governance of your French husband."

"Henry," she whispered, "you have not forgotten your promise to me?

"I do not forget," he answered. "Be of good cheer. I'll swear ere long you will be back with us."

Katharine was waiting to take her fond farewell, and Mary kissed her gentle sister-in-law with tenderness.

Somewhere among those assembled was Charles; she dared not look at him; she was afraid that, if she did, she would cling to him and refuse to go aboard.

The Queen's fleet was not far out from Dover when a storm arose. Her women were terrified, but Mary remained calm.

"If this be the end," she said to Lady Guildford, "then I shall at least be spared the months to come."

"You are inviting death," scolded her lady-governess.

"Why not, when life has lost its savour?"

"This is wickedness, my lady, and tempting Providence. Do you forget there are other lives in danger beside your own?"

Then the Queen became grave; and she knelt down and prayed that they might reach the French coast in safety. The storm grew wilder, separating the ships so that many were blown in the direction of Flanders, which, had events been different, might have been their destination. Others were tossed toward Calais; and the Queen's vessel, isolated, was brought, not without much difficulty, into the harbour of Boulogne. At the entrance of this harbour it ran ashore, and for some time it seemed as though all aboard were in the greatest danger. The people of Boulogne, who had been awaiting the arrival of the Queen's fleet for days, attempted to send out small boats to take the passengers from the ship, but even these could not be brought onto the beach.

Then one of Mary's knights, a certain Sir Christopher Garnish, begged leave to carry her ashore; and he waded through the water holding her in his arms.

Thus Mary came to France.

Exhausted by her ordeal, Mary was lodged in Boulogne for several days; but messengers in the meantime had hastened to Paris to tell the King of her arrival. Delighted, Louis immediately sent the Ducs de Vendome and de la Tremouille to welcome her and to bring her by degrees to Abbeville where he himself would be waiting for her.

All along Mary had been playing a delaying action. She could not leave Boulogne; she was too weary after her sea crossing; she must wait for the rest of her fleet to arrive, for they contained her wardrobe, and her bodyguard.

She was sorry when, sooner than she had believed possible, the missing vessels arrived in Boulogne; for then there was no longer any excuse to delay.

The journey southward must begin, and Mary rode out of the town attended by her archers and horsemen, her baggage and her chariots.

It seemed to her that she heard the notes of doom in the sound of the horses' hooves for every hour now brought her nearer to the husband who could only bring her happiness by his death.

Within a few days the cavalcade would be in Abbeville; they had rested at the mansion of a nobleman who was eager to do the Queen honour as he had been commanded by the King.

Nothing must be spared in making her welcome, Louis had said; and he expected obedience.

A rich apartment had been allotted to her, the walls of which were hung with tapestries and cloth of gold; and as she was being prepared for the day's journey she heard the sounds of arrival below, and a great fear came to her. Could it be Louis, impatient to see his bride, who had ridden here? They were within a few days of Abbeville, so it was possible.

"Holy Mother," she prayed, "help me. Do not let me betray the loathing I know I shall feel. Let me forget for a while the beauty of my Charles, that I do not compare him with my husband."

"Go to the window and see who comes," she said to her women; and it was Lady Guildford who, knowing her mistress's feelings better than most, apprehensively obeyed.

She stood for some seconds at the window, and Mary, suddenly impatient, joined her there.

It was an elegant company and the centre of attraction was an extremely tall man who sat his horse as though he had lived all his life in the saddle. He was laughing and, suddenly, seeming to know that he was watched, raised his eyes and saw the two at the window.

He snatched off his hat and bowed. Mary could not take her eyes from his face because it was such an unusual one. He radiated vitality in a manner she had only seen equalled by her lover and brother; his eyes were dark as sloes, but his most arresting feature was a nose so long that it gave a humorous touch to his face.

Mary turned away from the window because she feared she had stared too long.

"It is not the King," she said to Lady Guildford.

"Some noble Duke, I'll swear," was the answer, "sent to welcome Your Grace."

The chatelaine of the mansion asked permission to enter.

She curtsied and, lifting her flushed face to Mary, said: "Your Highness, the Duc de Valois is below and asking permission to be brought to you."

"Pray bring him to me," said Mary.

When they were alone, Lady Guildford said: "Do you know who this is? The Duc de Valois is also the Duc de Bretagne and Comte d'Angoulême. Moreover he is the Dauphin."

"I have heard much of him."

Lady Guildford caught her mistress's hand. "Have a care, my dearest lady. This man could be dangerous. He will be watching you. He may well be your enemy. Do not forget the crown of France is at stake. If you give the King of France an heir, this man will no longer be the Dauphin. He stands to lose a throne."

There was no time for more, because the door was opened and in came François, the heir presumptive to the crown of France, his brilliant eyes amused, his long nose giving him a look of slyness, his senuous lips curved in a smile.

He came to Mary and knelt; then he lifted his eyes to her face and there was nothing but intense admiration in his gaze; the slightly impudent eyes, travelling over her body from head to foot, implied a knowledge of the feminine anatomy and its potentialities.

He rose to his feet, towering above her — for he was as tall as Charles, as tall as Henry — and he said: "Madame, but you are enchanting. Rumour has not lied. The King of France is the luckiest man alive."

Mary had caught something of her lady-governess's fear, but she felt suddenly alive. She did not know whether this man was going to be her bitterest enemy or not; but she did know that he had driven away her listlessness.

François the Dauphin had entered her life, and she, like any other woman, could not be indifferent to his presence there.

Part Two: The French

CHAPTER FOUR

Young François

Some sixteen years before François, the heir presumptive to the throne of France, had his first meeting with Mary Tudor, he was in the gardens surrounding the *château*, which was his home in Cognac, with his sister, Marguerite, who was two years older than himself.

François, even at four, had an air of distinction. He was tall for his age, sturdy, healthy, handsome, and in addition to his physical perfections he had already shown himself to be quick-witted. He knew he was the most important person at the *château*; yet he did not make those about him suffer the tantrums of a spoiled child. He accepted the fact of his importance as naturally as he accepted the sun and the rain.

This was partly due to his sister, herself as handsome and even more clever — but that might have been because she had two years' advantage. They did not quarrel as most children do. If she thought François needed correction, Marguerite explained gravely where he was wrong, and because he knew that everything his sister or his mother did was to his advantage, he would listen with serious attention.

Life at Cognac was quiet and well ordered, presided over by the children's mother — good-looking, energetic and twenty-two years old. She was Louise, Duchess of Savoy, some two years a widow; her hair was of a light auburn shade, her eyes blue, her skin fair; she was not tall, as her children promised to be, but petite and dainty; she was marriageable, but so far had eluded the propositions which had been made for her. All her passion and devotion were for her children and, because one of these was a boy, because it was not inconceivable that a great future might be his, she had imbued her daughter, Marguerite, with her own enthusiasms; and the little girl was learning, as her mother did, to make the boy the centre of her life.

So now in the gardens of Cognac Marguerite sat with François under a tree and read aloud to him while he leaned against her and watched her finger as it pointed out the words she read. He was contented because he knew that when he tired of the book Marguerite would tell him stories of her own invention; and the hero of these stories, who always faced great odds and overcame them, was a man of kingly bearing, of great nobility, for whom some sort of crown was waiting — but Marguerite never explained what crown — and he was dark, and saved from being effeminately beautiful by a long nose which somehow was very attractive simply because it was his. This hero had a variety of names; he might be Jean, Louis, Charles . . . but the boy knew that these names were disguises, and he was in truth François.

A pleasant occupation; lying in the hot sun, watching the peasants at work in the vineyards, thinking of his pony which he could ride when he wished, although he must take a groom with him, because his mother was afraid for him to ride alone. But that was only because as yet he was four years old and one did not remain at four forever.

Any problem, any fear he had only to take to Marguerite or his mother and they would lay aside what they were doing to put his mind at peace.

Life was good when at four years old one was the centre of it. The peasants showed their respect for him. When he went by on his little pony they shouted for Angoulême. "Now that your father is dead," his mother told him, "you are the Comte d'Angoulême and these people look to you as their master." But because he was clever he knew how much he depended on those two who were always at his side; so he listened to them and gave them love for love.

There was not a happier family in France than that one at Cognac.

From a window of the *château*, Louise watched her children. There could be no more lovely sight for her: her charming daughter, with the book in her lap and her adored one leaning against his sister. She often told herself that life had begun for her with his birth, and that while she could plan and scheme for him she would find it well worth living. His childhood should be happy in every respect; it should be quite different from that which she had suffered. Although had she suffered? Not really, because she had never been one to accept defeat. She had always believed that she had had a proud destiny; and she had learned what it was: to be the mother of François.

Now here at Cognac on a lovely spring day she thought of Amboise. There she was, a little girl walking discreetly with her governess in the grounds of the *château*. She could almost feel the heat of those stone walls against her back; she could clearly see the cylindrical towers and the great buttresses, the tall windows rising behind her; and, below the rocky plateau on which the *château* stood, the valleys of the Loire and the Amasse. She had been brought up with the Court by the eldest daughter of Louis XI, the Regent Anne of France, who ruled France until such time as her little brother Charles should be old enough to take the crown.

They had not been entirely happy days for one as proud as Louise of Savoy, because Anne had been a stern guardian. There were no fine clothes, no jewels, few pleasures. Louise had to learn to be a serious young woman who would gratefully accept the husband who had been assigned to her. It was true that Louise's aunt, Charlotte, had been the wife of Louis XI, but although she was Queen of France she had been of small account, and all knew that Louis had taken a malicious pleasure in bullying the poor woman until she almost lost her senses.

Therefore it was scarcely likely that Louis's stern daughter should consider Charlotte's niece of much account; yet, as a member of the family of Savoy, which through the marriage had been linked with the royal family, the child must be cared for.

What long days they had been, sitting quietly in one of the great chambers of the Château d'Amboise, working unobtrusively at one's tapestry, keeping one's ears open, taking in all and saying nothing. Yet Anne of France had not neglected her word; Louise must learn to play the lute, to dance in a sober fashion; she must study affairs so that she would not be a complete fool in conversation.

The husband Anne chose for Louise was Charles d'Angoulême, son of Jean d'Angoulême, who was a grandson of Charles V, and thus not without some claim to the throne.

Louise remembered, as a little girl of eleven, being betrothed to Charles, who was sixteen years older than she was and not very pleased to be given a child for his bride. His domestic affairs were a little complicated. He had a mistress, Jeanne de Polignac, who had given him a child; and he had installed her in his *château* at Cognac. Jeanne was a clever woman and had taken under her care two other illegitimate children of her lover's; it was a pleasant, easygoing household he had set up in Cognac, and Charles felt that an eleven-year-old wife would be a complication.

However the Regent Anne was insistent and the ceremony had taken place.

How well Louise remembered arriving at Cognac; a little apprehensive, eager to please her husband, determined to have a son; she could never forget her husband's connection with the royal family, and she could not help being secretly delighted that the young King, Charles VIII, was malformed and possibly would not have healthy children.

At Cognac Jeanne de Polignac was in control as the chatelaine of the establishment; and with her was her daughter Jeanne (who was also Louise's husband's daughter) and the little Souveraine and Madeleine whom he accepted as his, although Jeanne was not their mother.

It was a cozy household, efficiently managed by Jeanne, herself completely contented because she knew that a Polignac could not marry a Comte d'Angoulême. She gathered the young bride in her maternal arms and treated her as another daughter; and Louise, shrewd, wise, understanding her husband's devotion to this woman, and that as yet he had no need of herself, accepted the situation.

Later she was glad of that move, for the good-hearted Jeanne became her greatest friend and confidante and helped her to live more comfortably through those first years of marriage than she otherwise would have done.

Now, looking at her own children, she was thinking of all this. Jeanne was still in the *château*, as devoted to little Marguerite and François as she was to her own Jeanne and Souveraine and Madeleine. Jeanne was a wonderful manager, now as she had always been; and what they would have done without her, Louise could not imagine, for Charles was comparatively poor and had always found it a struggle to live as a man of his rank should. Therefore little entertaining had taken place at Cognac, and often a strict economy had been necessary; but all were ready and willing to serve the Comte for, as his men and maid servants reminded themselves often, in serving their master they were serving the great-grandson of a King of France.

Perhaps for this reason Jeanne had been happy to remain his mistress when she might have had a good marriage; it was certainly the reason why Louise was happy to be at Cognac and to be his wife; it was the reason why she dreamed of the boy she would one day have.

Eventually her triumph came; she was pregnant and she prayed for the son who, she was sure, when he was born would make her completely contented with her lot. But the first pregnancy resulted in a disappointment as the child was not the boy she longed for, but merely a girl. This child, however, was beautiful and healthy from the day of her birth and she named her Marguerite. Louise had been sixteen years old then and she came through her confinement with miraculous ease. A girl and a disappointment; but she had at least shown she could bear children.

With the coming of Marguerite there had been a subtle change in the *château*. Jeanne stepped into the background; the chatelaine was now undoubtedly Louise. Not that Jeanne resented this. No, there was another little one to take into her motherly arms, and as she said to Louise: "This one surpasses the others. I never knew a child so quick to notice what goes on around her. It was never thus with even my own little Jeanne."

Louise was exultant. Soon, she must have her boy.

Impatiently she waited for the signs of pregnancy; but at Court certain events were giving her anxiety. The young King Charles VIII had taken Anne of Brittany to wife. In his childhood little Margaret, the daughter of Maximilian, had been intended for him, and Margaret had come to Amboise to be brought up as the future Queen of France; but eventually it had been decided that it was more necessary for young Charles to bring Brittany to the crown than to forge an alliance with the Emperor; so Margaret was sent home, and Charles betrothed to Anne of Brittany. It was an insult which Maximilian would take a long time to forget.

So now that Charles and Anne were married, the fervent desire of Anne of Brittany was to get a son.

When Louise had heard that the marriage had been consummated she had shut herself in her chamber because she was afraid that she might betray her anguish. Between her husband and the throne of France stood two men: Charles VIII, a cripple who might possibly be unable to beget a son, and Louis d'Orléans, son of Charles d'Orléans, elder brother of Jean d'Angoulême, Louise's own husband's father. When she considered that Louis d'Orléans had married the daughter of Louis XI, Jeanne de France, a poor malformed creature who had been unable to give him an heir, her hopes had been high — if not for her husband, for that son she intended to have.

But if Charles VIII and Anne of Brittany should have a son, that would be the end of her hopes.

She might be only a girl herself, but she had her ambitions even then. And what sorrow was hers when the news was brought to Cognac that Anne of Brittany had been delivered of a healthy boy. How Anne would laugh, for she was well aware of Louise's hopes, and as determined that they should come to nothing as Louise herself was that they should be fulfilled.

Then Louise discovered that she was once more pregnant.

She could smile now, as she remembered journeying to Amboise that she might make a pilgrimage to the cave of François de Paule, known as the Good Man, who inhabited a cave on the banks of the Loire. It had become the custom for pregnant royal ladies to visit him, imploring him to intercede with the Saints and ensure the birth of a healthy boy. The Good Man was reputed to have lived for a hundred years; he scorned the jewels that were offered him in exchange for his services, and all he asked for was enough food to keep him alive.

He had given her holy candles to be burned in her lying-in-chamber, and she now laughed to remember the day. It was September and warm; and she had not thought her pains were near.

How like him, she thought. All impatience to be born! He did not need holy candles. Was it for that reason that he came before I was prepared?

She had been out of doors, some distance from the *château* — for Jeanne had advised her that a healthy young woman should not lie about during the months of pregnancy — when suddenly he had decided to be born. There had been no time to get back to the *château* so her attendants had helped her to a tree and there she lay back in its shade and under the September sky was born her love, her life, her François, her King, her Caesar.

And watching him now, with his sister, Marguerite, she said aloud: "And from that moment the world was a different place because he had come into it."

She had rarely allowed him out of her sight; his robust looks were a perpetual delight to her; and it had been clear from the first that he was no ordinary child. "This will be a fine man," Jeanne de Polignac had laughed, holding the boy high in the air. "I never saw such perfect limbs. See, his features are already marked. That is his father's nose."

Such joy; and it would have been complete if Anne of Brittany was not also rejoicing for the same reason.

Jeanne said to her: "I doubt the Dauphin has the looks of our young François. I doubt he can yell as loudly for *his* food." And Louise answered that there could not be another in France to compare with François. And she asked herself how stunted Charles and Anne of Brittany, who was scarcely in rude health, could have a lusty child. But she knew that although the peasantry in Cognac and Angoulême might rejoice and drink themselves silly with the wine from their grapes, the fact that there was an heir of Angoulême was making little stir elsewhere — and all because Anne of Brittany had produced the Dauphin of France!

A satisfied smile curved Louise's lips. François had leaned forward and shut the book on his sister's lap.

She knew he was saying: “Tell me a story, sister.” Marguerite’s arm was about him, and she was beginning one of her stories which were really brilliant for a child of her age. What a pair! They were incomparable; and if Marguerite had but been a boy she would have been as wonderful as little François. But what joy it gave her to see this love between them!

She laughed aloud suddenly. She could not help it; she was thinking of how Fate was on her side, and she was certain that every obstacle which stood in her way was going to be removed. For little Charles the Dauphin, son of malformed Charles and ambitious Anne of Brittany, fell suddenly sick of a fever and not even the prayers and ministrations of the Good Man could save him. His mother was prostrate with grief and Louise believed that as soon as she had recovered a little from the shock she thought of that little boy who was now sitting under the trees with his sister Marguerite, strong and healthy, never out of the loving care of his mother.

There was a hatred between the two women, which must keep them apart. Louise could not imagine what disaster might befall here if she were ever misguided enough to go to Court. She was too apprehensive of the welfare of her François to flaunt his superior beauty and strength before a sorrowing and bereaved mother.

“They will never get a healthy son,” she whispered to Charles, her husband. “And if they do not, it will soon be your turn.”

“Louis d’Orléans comes before me,” he had reminded her.

"Louis d'Orléans!" she cried scornfully. "Married to crippled Jeanne! He'll get no son to follow him. I tell you it will be you first and then François. I can see him, the crown on his head; and I'll tell you that none ever has worn it, nor ever will, with more grace."

Charles gave her his cynical smile. "Why, wife," he said, "I had thought you a shrewd woman. And so you are in all other matters. But where our son is concerned you are over-rash. Have a care what words you utter. It would not be well if they were carried to Court."

She nodded. She had her precious François to consider. She believed he must be kept away from intrigue, brought up in the quiet of Cognac, so that others less fortunate than she was might not see him and envy her. He must be kept hidden until that time when he was ready to emerge and claim his own.

"So I pray you have a care," Charles had warned her, "and do not betray your feelings when we are at Amboise."

"At Amboise!"

"My dear, it is natural that his kinsmen should follow the Dauphin to his tomb."

How disconcerted she had been. She must travel from Cognac to Amboise with her husband, to pretend to mourn; not that that perturbed her as much as being forced to leave François behind. She had been more thankful then than at any other time for the presence of Jeanne de Polignac at Cognac. "Take care of the children," she pleaded with her, "and never let the boy out of your sight."

Jeanne laid her hand on Louise's. "You may trust me as you would trust yourself."

How cold it had been that December! It was small wonder that the little Dauphin had not recovered from his fever. Yet François toddled through the great rooms of the *château*, cheeks rosy, oblivious of the cold; and Marguerite hovering, ready to catch him should he fall, also glowed with health. The bitter winds which carried off the infirm could not hurt them. It is their destiny to win great distinction in the world, Louise told Jeanne; and because she believed this, she left Cognac with an easier mind than she could otherwise have done.

But disaster coming from an unexpected direction was at hand. She and Charles set out with their attendants in that inclement weather, and when they left Cognac, Charles had seemed well. He was not an old man, being but thirty-six years of age, and the cold did not seem to trouble him; but by the time they had reached Châteauneuf he had begun to cough, and with each cough suffered such agonising pain in his side that he could not suppress his groans. It had been impossible for him to remain in the saddle, and she had ordered that he be carried into a nearby house while she sent a rider with all speed to Cognac for the best physician to be found. What energy she had displayed in those two weeks which followed; she had never left Charles's bedside; but even at that time of anxiety she had not forgotten to send messengers back for news of François. Praise be to Jeanne, François continued in good health, so that she could devote herself wholeheartedly to the fight for her husband's life. While she sat at his bedside she visualised what his death could mean to her. She, a girl not yet twenty years of age, to be left alone to fight for her son's place in society! She had the utmost confidence in her ability, yet she must remember that she was but a woman and that strong men would be ranged against her. Charles must live . . . for the sake of François.

But on that bitterly cold New Year's Day Louise had become a widow. And a widow she had remained in spite of attempts to give her a husband. No one was going to marry her off. She had made one marriage for State reasons and out of that marriage had come her François; any other marriage might not be advantageous for her son; therefore there should be no marriage; he was enough for her from now on.

And now watching him from the window she thought: and so it shall be, my little love, until I see you on the throne of France.

François had leaped to his feet and started to run; Marguerite was immediately beside him, taking his hand. Something had happened to excite them. Louise left the window and hurried down to the courtyard.

Jeanne de Polignac joined her on her way down.

"I heard the horses," she cried. "Someone has arrived, and I wondered who."

"That must have been what the children heard," answered Louise, and together they passed out of the *château*.

There was the messenger, but Louise's eyes went first to the sturdy figure of François who was standing staring up at the man on horseback. She noted with pleasure that Marguerite was beside him, never for one moment forgetting her solemn duty; her restraining hand was on the boy's shoulder, lest the bold little darling become over-rash.

François turned, saw his mother and Jeanne, and immediately ran to Louise to throw his arms about her knees. She lifted him in her arms.

"So my beloved heard the arrival of the messenger?"

"Beloved heard it," he answered. "Look! See his livery. It is different from ours."

Then she realised that the messenger wore the royal livery, and she signed to one of the grooms, who had hurried up, to take the man's horse.

"Pray come into the *château*," she said. "You bring me news from Court?"

"Yes, my lady."

He would have told her there and then, but she was never one to forget her dignity.

"Come," she said, though her heart was beating fast for it was a convention that messengers matched their expressions to the news they carried, and this one's was very grave.

In the great hall she called to one of her servants to bring wine for the messenger and he, unable to contain himself, said: "Madame, the King is dead."

"The King . . . dead!"

Instinctively she held François more firmly in her arms; the little boy did not wriggle even though the extra pressure made him uncomfortable. He always accepted the adoration of those about him with a meek resignation, as though he was aware that everything they did was for his good.

Even Louise could not now suppress her curiosity.

"Madame, his Liege had gone to watch a game of tennis with the Queen, and on his way through the *château* to the court he struck his head on a stone archway. He took little notice of this at the time and continued on his way with the Queen; but as they sat watching the game he was seized with a sudden fit. A pallet was brought for him to lie on, for it was feared to be dangerous to move him on account of his strange illness; and there he lay throughout the afternoon. He died just before midnight."

"Died . . . and he so young!" murmured Louise. "God help the Queen. How is she taking this?"

"She is stricken with grief, Madame."

Certainly she was! thought Louise. No husband! No son to follow him! It was understandable that that ambitious woman was stricken with grief.

The man stood back a few paces; then he proclaimed:

"Charles the VIII of France is dead. Long Live King Louis XII!"

"Long live the King!" said Louise; and all those about her echoed her words, so that the hall of the *château* was filled with the cry.

"Long live the King!" shouted François with the rest.

And Louise was thinking: my little love — only one now between you and the throne of France. Louis d'Orléans, thirty-six years old, yet no longer in the prime of life; he has lived his life without great care for the health of his body, and now it is said he must pay the price. Louis XII of France, married to Jeanne, the cripple. What hope have they of getting themselves a dauphin!

Very clearly could she see the crown on the head of her François.

Louis XII of France, who had been known as Louis d'Orléans until his cousin had walked into an embrasure at Amboise and died because of it, received the news of his accession with elation. He had always believed that he could give the French nation what it most needed, and naturally, since he was so near the throne, he had often visualised this possibility. Yet he had scarcely hoped that the crown would be his, for who would have believed that Charles, who was so much his junior, would have died so suddenly?

What great good fortune that the little Dauphin had died not so long ago, for a Regency was never a good thing, and how much more satisfactory it was when there was a sober, serious-minded King ready to mount the throne.

As soon as he heard the news he summoned two of his greatest friends to his side in order to discuss the future with them. One of these was Georges d'Amboise, Archbishop of Rouen; the other was Maréchal de Gié, a celebrated soldier.

They came to him and knelt, but he shrugged aside their homage.

"Come, my friends," he said, "let us dispense with the ceremony and concern ourselves with more important issues."

He bade them be seated. They could see that this was the moment for which he had longed all his life; it was a pity it had come when he was no longer in good health. He sat painfully, being troubled by the gout; he looked much older than his thirty-six years, and that was not to be wondered at considering the life he had led. Being a rebel from his youth he had gone so far as to incite the country to civil war; but he had not come through his adventures unscathed and had suffered imprisonment. But already there was a change in him. The rebel had become the King and there was a serenity in his face — that of a man who has at last achieved what he has longed for since the days of his youth. He was wise; he would never desert old friends, nor forget those who had suffered with him; it was for this reason that these two whom he had summoned to his presence should be the chief advisers to King Louis XII, since they had proved themselves good friends to Louis d'Orléans.

He had never spared himself in the days when he was strong and healthy but had revelled in all sports and had indulged himself in all carnal pleasures; but it was different now. He was wise enough to know that he could only hope to go on living if he lived with care, and he did not intend to die yet; that was why he ate little, always had his meat boiled and retired early to bed. In fact he had put his days of dissipation behind him and would be more particular to do so now that the crown was his.

His friends, looking into his bright, over-prominent eyes, at his thick lips which were dry and parched, at his enlarged Adam's apple, were concerned and they showed it.

Louis smiled. "Put your fears to rest," he said. "I am alive and that is how I intend to remain." He smiled suddenly. "I'll swear there's rejoicing at a certain *château* in Cognac this day."

"Madame d'Angoulême, I have heard, believes her boy to be already the Dauphin of France," said the Archbishop.

Louis nodded. "And we must accept the fact that, were I to die tomorrow, he would be the next to mount the throne — unless the impossible happens ere long and I get me a son."

"Sire . . ." began Georges d'Amboise; then he stopped.

"Speak on," said the King. "You need not weigh your words with me now, Georges, any more than you did in the past. You were about to say that to hope for a son is to hope for an impossibility."

"And that," put in the Maréchal, "is no fault of yours, Sire."

"I know, I know. The Queen has been a good wife to me. At least she has been a docile, affectionate and uncomplaining wife; and because she is the daughter of Louis XI it was considered I had made an excellent match."

"And so it would have been, Sire, had she been fertile."

"Alas!" sighed Louis. He was thinking of poor limping Jeanne, with her pale face and shoulder which was so much higher than the other — her only asset, her royalty. Their marriage had never been fruitful and never could be. And a king should have heirs. He said the last thought aloud: "A King should have heirs."

Georges d'Amboise hesitated, coughed and then said recklessly: "Sire, it is only possible if you find yourself a new wife."

Louis's eyes seemed more prominent than ever. "I had thought," he said, "that it would be desirable to keep Brittany for the crown."

The Maréchal caught his breath but it was the churchman to whom Louis was giving his attention.

"So recently a widow," he whispered.

"Yet she has proved that she can bear children — sons. They did not live, it is true, but Charles was a weakling . . . like his sister Jeanne. If I were not married to Jeanne, if I could marry Anne of Brittany, I could perforce bring to my country all that as King I wish to. Brittany remaining in the crown; a Dauphin in the royal nursery."

"It would be necessary first to divorce Jeanne," the Maréchal pointed out.

"That's true," answered the King, still looking at Georges.

"If she would go into a nunnery," murmured Georges. "If she would declare herself tired of life outside convent walls . . . and if Anne could be persuaded that there is nothing shameful in this divorce . . . it might be arranged."

Louis laid his hand on Georges's arm. "Think on it," he said. "I know, my friend, that if you do, you will find the solution."

* * *

In the royal apartments at Amboise, the Queen faced her husband. Louis had always found it difficult to look into her face because he was afraid that she would read there the repulsion he felt for her — and the pity. He was not a cruel man but in his youth he had been thoughtless. It had been a great shock to him when he was given this hunch-backed gnome for a wife; it had been small consolation to him that she had been the daughter of the King of France, and he later suspected that her father, the wily Louis XI, had married her to him to prevent heirs coming to the Orléans branch of the family and making trouble. It must have been a sore trial to him to see his only son, who had become Charles VIII, a malformed dwarf not much better than his daughter Jeanne.

It had not been necessary to remain at her side for long at a time, and he could never make love with her except in the dark. That was a fruitless occupation in any case for how could such a creature bear children? She had proved, as all had suspected she would, sterile.

Now she looked at him with affection for, oddly enough, she loved him. Poor Jeanne! She had been ready to love any who showed her kindness, and he had done that.

"Louis," she said, coming to him with ungainly steps and looking up at him appealingly without touching him, for she knew that he did not care for her to do that, "I have heard rumours."

"Rumours?" he repeated; and he felt a deep dismay. Had they already been talking of his proposed divorce?

Had they already been linking his name with that of Anne of Brittany? He was regretful for two reasons. First that Jeanne must be hurt; and second that the proud Anne of Brittany might be shocked at the thought of marrying another husband so soon, particularly as he was a man who had to rid himself of a wife to marry her.

"I understand," went on Jeanne mournfully. "I am of little use to you. I cannot give you a Dauphin and I see that that is what France expects of you . . . now."

"You should not distress yourself," he told her gently.

"But I do," she replied. "You have always been kind to me, Louis, and I know how I have failed you."

"There are many childless couples in France."

"They are not the King and Queen."

Then suddenly she began to weep. "Oh Louis, Louis, do not abandon me. I know I have nothing to offer you. Look at me! None would ever have married me had I not been a king's daughter. And you do not need me. The crown is yours through your own line. I have brought nothing to you. You will cast me off, Louis. They will persuade you that it is your duty . . ."

He put his arms about her. "Jeanne," he said, "set aside your fears. Why, I'd rather die without a son than hurt you."

She slid to her knees and embraced his legs, alas looking sadly repulsive crouching there. He wished she would rise; he was hating himself because he knew that Georges d'Amboise was already preparing a plan to dissolve their marriage; and that she could not long be kept in ignorance of this. Her grief would be the greater because he had tried to soothe her with false words.

Louise of Savoy set out for Paris to see the new King. Jeanne de Polignac warned her to be careful, but Louise was full of purpose.

"Forget not," she said, "that my position is different from what it was before the death of Charles. Am I not the mother of the heir presumptive?"

"All the more reason why you should act with care," replied the practical Jeanne.

Louise laughed. "Do you think I ever forget that I am *his* mother and that he needs me! Set your fears at rest, Jeanne. I am going to have him acknowledged; and the best way in which I can do this is to get him the title which is his due and which will proclaim to all that the King regards him as the heir to the throne. Why, the title falls vacant, does it not, now that Louis has given it up to take that of King? François is going to be Duc d'Orléans — that royal title belongs to him now."

"All I say is, Louise, take care."

"And you, my dear, take care of the children while I am away." She embraced her friend. "How I rely on you, Jeanne! I'd never leave him in anyone else's hands."

When François and Marguerite came to say farewell to their mother, she embraced the girl tenderly but clung to the boy as though she had almost made up her mind not to leave him.

"My precious will do what Jeanne and Marguerite tell him while I'm away?"

"Yes, dearest Maman, Precious will," answered the boy.

"That's my little love." She looked appealingly up at Jeanne and Marguerite, and although she did not speak, her eyes told them that she was placing in their hands her greatest treasure.

François stood at the gates of the castle, Jeanne on one side of him, Marguerite on the other; Jeanne the younger, with Madeleine and Souveraine, stood behind him and a short distance from this little group were some of their attendants.

Louise turned to look back again. "I shall soon be with you. Take care while I'm away."

They watched her until she and her band of attendants were out of sight.

"I should like to go to Paris," François announced.

"You will one day," Marguerite told him.

When he rode to Paris it would be in a purple robe and he would have a standard on which were the golden lilies. His mother had told him this, and the picture was clear in his mind. But it was not yet; and in the meantime he had to amuse himself.

Marguerite took his hand and they went to the nurseries where Madeleine and Souveraine were playing with their dolls.

They stood watching Madeleine who was dressing one of the dolls and talking to it as though it were a baby.

"Come along, Marguerite," said Souveraine, "here is the little Papillon. See how dirty she has made her dress! Change it and scold her, will you? Tell her she will be in trouble if she cannot keep her dresses cleaner than that."

Marguerite stared at the doll which was being thrust at her and said stonily: "How could *that* be blamed for making the dress dirty? It was Madeleine who did it."

Souveraine looked as though she was about to cry. "Why will you never play our games, Marguerite?" she demanded. "I believe you laugh at us. And we're older than you, remember?"

"You are too old to play with dolls," said six-year-old Marguerite, "and so am I."

François looked on with interest. He would have liked to join the game, only instead of being mother to the dolls, he would have been their King and they would have been his subjects.

"How silly!" said Madeleine. "*Maman* said that I was a little mother."

(Both Madeleine and Souveraine called Jeanne *Maman*.)

"I would be a little mother," said Marguerite, "if I had a real baby. But I would not play with dolls."

She took François firmly by the hand and led him away. "I will read to you," she said.

François allowed himself to be taken down to the gardens, and, when they were seated under a tree, Marguerite opened the book and began to read, but she had not read more than a few sentences when François laid his plump hand on the page and said: "Marguerite, I want you to be a little mother, and I want to be a little father."

Marguerite shut the book and looked at him. "You want to play with Madeleine and Souveraine?" she asked reproachfully.

"No," he answered vehemently. "They play with dolls. I want us to have a real baby."

Marguerite was thoughtful. He looked so earnest and so certain that she could provide him with what he wanted that her great desire was to keep his high opinion of her.

She stood up and he was beside her, putting his hand into hers.

An idea had come to Marguerite. She began to walk resolutely away from the *château* grimly holding François's hand. They were forbidden to leave the gardens but this was in a special cause; and she had only to walk to the cottage just beyond the castle gates.

François, trotting beside her, kept laughing to himself in an endearing way he had which meant that he was excited and happy. He knew he could always rely on Marguerite to make life both amusing and adventurous.

On a patch of grass before the cottage a baby was crawling.

François knew of course what was going to happen now. Marguerite had as usual provided him with what he wanted. She opened the gate and, going into the garden, picked up the baby, who was not very clean.

"And we shall not scold her," said Marguerite, "for she is too young to know that she must be clean. This is our baby, François. We are not going to play with dolls."

François skipped round his sister. "Shall I carry her, Marguerite?"

"No, you are not big enough. I'll carry her and when we've cleaned her, you shall hold her."

They entered the *château* without being observed and went up to the nurseries.

There they undressed the child and washed her; then Marguerite found some of François's discarded garments and dressed the baby in them. It was a wonderful game, for the child had to be soothed when she whimpered; then it occurred to Marguerite that she was hungry, so they fed her with sweetmeats.

"Now you see, François," said Marguerite, "how different it is to be a real father and mother from playing with dolls!"

"Dolls!" cried François contemptuously. "Who wants dolls!"

When they had dressed and fed the child they decided that it was time she was put to bed. So they put her in Marguerite's bed, where she lay serenely laughing at them and kicking her legs as though she enjoyed the game as much as they did.

Madeleine came in and discovered them, and when she saw that they had a real baby she gave a gasp of wonderment.

"You go and play with Papillon," commanded Marguerite. "This is our baby — mine and François's."

It was impossible to keep their secret. Madeleine told Souveraine and Souveraine told little Jeanne who told big Jeanne. Moreover the baby had been missed and her parents were distractedly searching for her.

Jeanne de Polignac came into the nursery where François and Marguerite, one on each side of the bed, watched the baby who was crowing contently at them.

"But what is this?" she asked.

"My brother wanted a real baby. He did not wish to play with dolls," explained Marguerite.

"So you took her from the cottage! Her mother is searching for her."

"She cannot have her," cried François. "She is our baby . . . mine and Marguerite's. We have to have her because we do not play with dolls."

Jeanne went out and shortly afterward came back with the child's mother.

"The young Compte and his sister have taken a fancy to the child," she explained. "They want to keep her in the *château* for a while."

The mother was relieved to see her child, and delighted at the interest of the children, because she saw advantages for her little daughter in this interest. She had several other children and if her daughter could be clothed and fed at the *château* she would be a fool to protest.

"It is a charming picture," she said.

Jeanne laid a hand on her arm. "We will see that the little one comes to no harm in the nurseries."

Marguerite spoke with grave dignity. "We will see that she is kept clean," she said.

With one of his sudden impulses François knelt on the bed and kissed the baby as his mother kissed him.

The matter was settled. The children should have the baby for as long as they wanted her.

"What is her name?" asked Marguerite. "We could name her ourselves, but perhaps she has a name already."

"It is Françoise, Mademoiselle," said the child's mother.

François solemnly got down from the bed and began to jump as high as he could. This was an expression of great pleasure.

He was François; the child was Françoise. She was truly his.

Louise returned to Cognac in dismay.

Once she had assured herself that her children were safe and well she shut herself up with Jeanne.

"I do not like what I discovered."

"The King was gracious to you?"

"Hm. I know Louis. He is all soft words, but there are plans afoot."

"He would not give François Orléans?"

"No, he would not. I think I know what goes on in his mind. He was evasive. François is too young yet, he says. He bids me wait a while. François is not too young to be the heir presumptive, I hinted; therefore he is not too young to bear the title. Jeanne, I am alarmed. I see that I have my enemies. I am but a weak woman . . . and I am the only one to protect my little King from all those who would work against him."

"You're no weak woman," laughed Jeanne. "François couldn't have a better protector, even if his father lived."

"But listen. Louis is determined to get an heir."

"He never will. Jeanne is incapable of bearing a child. She proved that when she was Duchesse d'Orléans; she can't become fruitful merely because she's Queen."

"That's the point, Jeanne. Louis doesn't intend that she shall remain his Queen. He's determined to have an heir, and he's going to rid himself of her in order to do so."

Jeanne was startled now, seeing the threat to François's hopes as clearly as Louise did.

"Still," she temporised, "Louis is scarcely a strong man."

"Strong enough to get a son if he had a healthy bride. I've heard rumours, Jeanne. He wants something else besides a son, and he's looking to a new bride to give it to him . . . Brittany!"

"*No!*"

"'Tis so."

"Anne of Brittany will never marry a divorced man."

"Not if he is King of France? You don't know Anne. I understand her well, and I'll tell you why. She and I share an ambition. We want to be the mother of the King of France. She is a determined woman, and so am I. And you know as well as I do that if I realise my ambition she cannot, and if she gets what she wants that is enough to make me lose everything I hope for. We're rivals, Jeanne. We're enemies. And if this divorce takes place, I shall not know a moment's peace for years . . . not until Anne is too old to bear a son — and she is but a young woman. Do you wonder that I am uneasy?"

They were silent, thinking of all that this meant.

At last Louise spoke. "Louis, I am sure, is certain of ridding himself of Jeanne and getting Anne. He's certain that she will give him a boy."

"Anne wasn't very successful with Charles — three boys all dead."

"But *boys*, Jeanne. And Charles was a dwarf . . . little better than his sister whom Louis is now trying to discard. No. I am sure his hopes are high. That is why he would not give François the Orléans title. He suggested he should become Duc de Valois instead."

The two women stared into space as though they were trying to peer into the future.

The King came to Cognac. He had a fancy to see the boy who, unless he could get a son, would follow him as King of France.

There was a bustle in the castle and throughout the countryside, All along the route the people lined the roadside to cheer the new King.

Louise greeted the sovereign while on either side of her were two of the most beautiful children Louis had ever seen. The girl with the clear, intelligent eyes was very charming; as for the boy, he was as robust as any parent could wish.

Louis took them in his arms and embraced them warmly. He was impressed with the girl, but his eyes kept straying to the boy, who greeted him without a trace of shyness.

"I have a dog," the boy told him.

"Have you?" asked the King.

"Yes, and I have a pony. I ride on their backs. My dog is big." The plump arms were outstretched as far as they would go. "And we have a baby, Marguerite and I. Her name is Françoise. She is a very good baby."

Louis noticed that the little boy was allowed to take the stage. Well, he could understand the mother's fondness.

I'd give half my kingdom, he thought, for a son like that.

François had put his hand confidently in that of the King.

"Are you a king?"

Louis admitted that he was.

"I shall be one when I grow up."

"Is that so?" said Louis with a smile; and he thought: not if I can prevent it, my little man.

"Yes, a great king," prattled François. "And I shall have two queens — Marguerite and my mother."

Louis looked at Louise, who was faintly embarrassed.

"I see," he said, "that your son already displays excellent judgment."

He was conducted to his apartments and when he was alone with his own attendants he was very thoughtful. He could not get that boy out of his mind. What vitality! Why had they not married him to Louise of Savoy instead of poor tragic Jeanne!

He was unhappy every time he thought of his wife, so he tried to thrust her from his mind and look ahead to the days when he would be married to Anne. He was thinking a great deal about Anne. There was something about that woman. It was true she limped a little and was somewhat pale and certainly severe; but she was a Queen in truth, born to rule; and once they had dispensed with this awkward business of freeing him from one who was useless to him, she would be a good wife.

He could trust Georges to arrange things. Before he had come to the throne he used to say, when he was in a difficulty: "Let Georges do it." He said that now. There was no one quite so wily, when dealing with delicate matters, as a man of the Church. Georges would find a reason, which would satisfy even Anne, why his marriage should be dissolved. He did not anticipate a great deal of trouble, because he was so sure of help from that quarter from which it was most essential. The Holy Father would be ready to grant the divorce in exchange for certain favours to his son. It was easy to deal with a Borgia, and Pope Alexander VI loved his son Cesare so deeply that it should not be impossible to strike a bargain. Trust Georges to arrange this matter.

In the meantime he had the importunity of people such as Louise of Savoy to contend with. She would not be quite so complacent about this merry little fellow on whom she doted when he and Anne, safely married, presented the country with their son. That would put that somewhat long though enchanting nose of Monsieur François out of joint. Not that he was aware of that yet — with his dogs, ponies and babies.

Louis enjoyed his sojourn at the *château* and spent most of his leisure with the children. He would go alone unannounced to the nursery, and he thought how delightful Louise's two looked, bending over a chess board; he would sit beside them and watch the little fingers — the boy's still showing signs of baby fat — moving the pieces with a skill extraordinary in players so young. There was a real baby, he discovered; and he was very amused to hear that François had demanded it and that his sister, Marguerite, had promptly left the *château* and found her imperious brother that for which he'd asked.

The boy will be spoiled, he thought, left to the care of women. And women who dote on him to such an extent! He would consult with Georges at an early opportunity, for they must remember that, as yet, he was not even married to Anne, and that while this state of affairs persisted young François could be King of France. He should not therefore be tied to women's apron strings, but brought up as a man.

During his visit he broached the subject with Louise.

"You are justly proud of two such children," he told her. "I'll swear that you will wish to put such a boy in the care of a great soldier, and that soon."

Louise was startled. "I had no such plans, Sire."

"He is so advanced for his age that one forgets how young he is. Such a one needs to be brought up with boys of his own age and under stern discipline. He must learn how to become a knight — to use a sword, how to conduct himself in combat. Remember, he could one day hold a very important position in this land."

"'Tis true, Sire. But I would wish to remain in charge of his education. He must learn all that a man should learn, but that will come later."

"You have too much sense," said Louis with a smile, "to wish to leave it too long. I will speak to de Gié of our François. As you know he is one of the greatest soldiers in France, and I am sure, Madame, you will agree with me when I say that none but the best is good enough for François."

Louise was trembling with apprehension but the King noticed the firm set of her lips, and he said to himself: there is a woman who will fight for her boy like a tigress for her cub. She is determined that one day he shall be King of France. Alas, Madame, you are doomed to disappointment.

He felt sorry for her and spoke gently to her when he took his farewell, complimenting her once more on her children, and adding that he believed she would never allow them to leave her care.

But when François knelt before him, looking so dignified that he brought tears to his mother's eyes as she watched him, Louis stooped and picked the boy up in his arms.

"What a big fellow you are!" he said. "I'll swear that when next we meet you'll be showing me how well you can handle a sword."

François's eyes gleamed with pleasure. "A sword . . . for me!"

"Well, you'll be a man one day," said the King. "You may need one."

François was delighted. Now he wanted a sword.

The *château* seemed quiet after the King had left. Jeanne de Polignac sensed Louise's concern and tried to soothe her.

"One thing is certain," she said. "Louis does not believe he will ever get a son because he would not concern himself with the upbringing of François if he did not consider him to be the Dauphin."

There was comfort in that thought.

"But I shall not allow anyone to take him from me," said Louise fiercely.

When Georges d'Amboise sought an audience with the King there was triumph in every line of the Archbishop's plump body.

"Alexander is willing, Sire," Georges explained. "He is concerned at the moment for his son Cesare, and Cesare needs your help. Alexander says — most diplomatically and in that veiled language of which he is a past master — that if you will please him, you shall have your divorce."

"What are his terms?" Louis asked.

"Cesare is tired of his Cardinal's robes. He fancies himself as a conqueror. There is no doubt that he arranged the murder of his brother, the Duke of Gandia. You will remember, my Liege, that that young man's body was found in the Tiber; he had been stabbed to death. Alexander loved that boy, but he has given up grieving now. He has another son, and so besottedly does he love his children that he now gives all his devotion to Cesare and his daughter Lucrezia. He seems to have forgotten poor Gandia now that he is dead — at least he forgives Cesare for murdering his brother."

"It may be that he wishes to see the Borgias triumphant. Tell me what he asks for Cesare."

"You will remember, Sire, that when Cesare became a Cardinal Alexander prepared documents which proclaimed him to have been born in wedlock. Now he has prepared further documents. Cesare is his bastard and therefore, being of illegitimate birth, cannot be accepted as a Cardinal. Cesare will leave the Church, and he plans to come to the Court of France; he wants you to help him to marry Carlotta of Aragon, and he would be pleased to accept a French dukedom. He wishes to make an alliance with you so that you may join forces in attacking Italy."

"Alexander knows how to drive a bargain."

"He does, Sire. But you have always greatly desired Milan and have had a claim to it. Cesare would come with the dispensation which will dissolve your marriage; and all we should have to do is have the case tried here before judges whom you would select."

Louis was thoughtful. "You are an able man, Georges. You should have your reward too."

Georges smiled. "I understand that Cesare will bring, in addition to the dispensation for you, a Cardinal's hat for me."

"The Borgia knows how to make a bargain irresistible."

"'Tis so, Sire. And you need the divorce, unless we are prepared to sit back and see young François mount the throne of France."

Louis nodded. "Have you put the case before Queen Anne?"

He waited nervously for the reply.

Georges was frowning. "She is reluctant. She feels that to marry so soon after the death of her husband would be a little unseemly."

Louis beat his fist on his knee. "I am in no mind to wait."

"You should have no fear on that account, Sire. There is one thing for which she longs and that is to be the mother of the King of France. I mentioned Louise and her François, and that was adding fuel to the flame. I am sure that Louise — and young François — are scarcely ever out of her thoughts. She sees Louise as her greatest rival. She cannot endure the thought of her triumph. I do not think we shall have trouble with Queen Anne, Sire, once you are free of Queen Jeanne."

"I am sorry that I have to do this, Georges."

Georges lifted his shoulders. "It is the fate of royal personages, Sire. I am sure she will understand."

"Well, let us hasten on the affair. Have you prepared the case?"

"I have, Sire. You will swear that the marriage is impossible of consummation. The Queen is unfit to be a wife and a mother. That is good enough reason for a king to put his wife away."

"Poor Jeanne, I fear she will take this sadly."

"She will recover."

"It is not strictly true to say that she is unfit to be a wife."

"It is in this case, Sire."

"There are times when I almost wish . . ." Louis did not finish his sentence. It was quite untrue of course. He was longing to be rid of Jeanne; he dreamed nightly of Anne who was becoming more and more desirable to him. He was certain that in the first weeks of their marriage she would conceive. But it was true to say that he wished he did not have to hurt Jeanne.

"It will be over very quickly, Sire. The physicians will ask to examine Queen Jeanne."

"To examine her!"

"To ascertain her unfitness for marriage."

"But she will never submit to such indignity."

"Then all is well, Sire," smiled Georges, "for then it will be assumed that she is indeed unfit, for if she were not, it will be said, why should she refuse the examination?"

Louis gazed at his friend; then he rose and going to the window looked out.

Yet it must be, he thought. There were demands of kingship to be served.

Jeanne could not believe it. Louis had always been so kind. It was true that he found her repulsive, but she had loved him dearly because he had always made such an effort to pretend this was not the case. He had been unfaithful to her; she had expected that. It was his kindness which had always made her feel so safe. He was also so genial, so logical — except when he was ill or anxious. Then he was inclined to be irritable, but that was natural.

And now he was assuring the Court of Enquiry that it was impossible to consummate the marriage, and on those grounds he was asking for a divorce.

She had wept the night before until she slept from exhaustion. Now her eyes were swollen and she looked uglier than ever.

"If only my brother Charles had not died!" she murmured. "Then Louis would not have been King. He would not have cared that I could not give him a son. And Anne of Brittany would not be free to marry him."

The bishops came to her — one of them was the brother of Georges d'Amboise who she knew worked wholeheartedly for the King and had arranged this matter for him. They were determined, she knew, to give Louis the verdict for which he was asking.

Gently they told her that she was judged unfit for marriage.

"It is not true," she answered. "Except that my back is crooked, my head set awry, my arms too long, my person unprepossessing."

"Madame, you have but to submit to an examination. The royal physicians are ready to wait on you."

Her thick lips, which did not meet, were twisted in a bitter smile.

"I'll swear they know the answer to what they seek before they begin their examinations," she answered. "Nay, messieurs, I will not submit to this further indignity. You — and others — forget, it seems, that, unwanted as I am, I am yet the daughter of a king."

"Madame, it would be wise . . ."

"Messieurs, you have my leave to depart."

When they left her she covered her face with her hands and rocked to and fro.

This was the end of life as she had known it. The answer would be to go into a convent where she must devote herself to the good life and forget that she ever tried to be a wife to Louis.

She rose and picked up her lute. She had been a good lutist, and when she played men and women had been apt to pause and listen. They forgot then that she was deformed and ugly; they only heard the sweet music she made. Often she had found great comfort in her music and when she felt sad and neglected she had told herself: "There is always my lute."

But one did not play the lute in a convent.

Deliberately she threw it to the floor and stamped on it; and looking down at what she had once loved she thought: like the lute my life is broken and finished.

Louise, eager yet apprehensive, had moved with her family from Cognac to Chinon. Each day she was watching at her turret for messengers from the Court; and she would start up every time she heard the sound of riders approaching the *château*.

Jeanne comforted her as best she could. It was quite impossible, she pointed out, for the King to put away his wife. The Pope would never agree to a divorce. Jeanne, a king's daughter, would never submit to such treatment; and Anne of Brittany would not marry until at least a year had elapsed since the death of her husband, for she would consider it quite indecent to do so.

"I know Anne of Brittany," said Louise. "She wants to give birth to the heir of France. There is only one way in which she can do that, and that is by marrying Louis. She'll take him if she has the chance. She is as jealous of me on account of my son as any woman could be."

Louis travelled to Chinon with a great retinue and Louise's anxiety increased, for there were plans to welcome a visitor to France, and this important personage was shortly to arrive in Chinon. His name was Cesare Borgia.

Why was the King so eager to do honours to the illegitimate son of the Pope? Louise anxiously asked herself.

François was untouched by her apprehension. From the window of the *château*, his mother beside him and Marguerite close by, he watched the Borgia's entry into Chinon.

The little boy could not stand still but leaped up and down in his excitement.

"But look, look," he kept crying, for he had never seen such dazzling colour. The Pope's son had determined to impress the French with his worldly possessions. His attendants were clad in crimson livery; his pages rode on the finest horses; his baggage, covered with satin in dazzling colours, was carried on mules brilliantly caparisoned. Thirty noblemen attended him, all magnificently attired and behind them, accompanied by Georges d'Amboise who had ridden out from the *château* to meet him, was the Borgia himself, lithe, dark and sinister, sitting his horse whose accoutrements glittered with pearls and precious stones of all colours, himself more dazzling than anything which had gone before. His person appeared to be covered in jewels, with rubies — such a foil for his dark lean looks! — in predominance.

Louise, catching at her son's hand, wondered whether in one of those coffers with which the jewel-decorated mules were laden, was the dispensation which would enable Louis to marry Anne of Brittany.

She was soon to learn.

Louise was in despair. The King had obtained his divorce and Anne of Brittany had overcome her scruples. They were now married.

Louise lay awake at night thinking of them, indefatigably pursuing their efforts to get a child. They were both so eager. Could they fail?

"Holy Mother," she prayed, "hear me. My little François was born to be a king. I beg of you let nothing stand in the way of his coming to the throne."

Yet, she thought, Anne is offering her prayer to the Virgin with the same vehemence. But surely all must see that it is my François who should be King of France.

There was further cause for anxiety. Louis was growing more and more delighted with his bride, and consequently giving way to all her wishes. He knew that he had a wife on whose fidelity he could rely absolutely; Anne of Brittany might not be a beauty; she might walk with a limp; she might be pale and severe; but she was regal, intelligent, a Queen of whom a King — not very young himself, not very robust — could be proud. It was clear that Anne was going to have a great influence on the King's actions.

Above all, she would not forget Louise and François. Although, no doubt, she prayed every night that she might be fruitful, that prayer had not yet been answered, so she wanted Louise where she could keep an eye on her.

Thus she persuaded the King that as, until they had a son, they must, though reluctantly, regard François as the heir to the throne, they should keep him under surveillance.

Consequently Louise received orders from Court. She was to leave Chinon for Blois.

There was no help for it. The command must be obeyed, and Louise moved her household to Blois. But she hated the place with its nearby tanneries giving off foul odours which she feared might be harmful to the children. The great *château*, built on a rock, supported by buttresses, with its many underground dungeons in which deeds too horrible to be contemplated had been committed, seemed no place for her gay little François, for her beautiful Marguerite.

She felt as though she were a prisoner at Blois; and she never ceased to deplore the King's marriage to one who, she knew, through envy of her François, was a rival and an enemy.

She wrote pleadingly to Louis, hoping to reach him without his wife's knowledge. It was impossible. Anne was determined to rule with her husband; and he was so indulgent that he allowed this to happen.

So Louise of Savoy felt that Blois was like a prison, did she? Let it be. It was necessary to keep a sharp watch on that woman who was ambitious beyond reason.

But as the weeks passed Anne of Brittany softened toward Louise. If the woman hated Blois so much, let her go to Amboise. Louise was delighted when she received permission to leave Blois, for Amboise would be more salubrious, and she was happier than she had been since she had left Chinon when, surrounded by her family and household, she rode into the little town and saw the conical towers of the old *château* which dominated it.

A royal *château*, she thought, a fitting place to house her little King.

But before many weeks had passed she lost her complacence. News came to her from the Court. The miracle had happened. The Queen had conceived. She was taking every precaution regarding her pregnancy, consulting the holy men, making all the necessary pilgrimages, carrying many holy relics; she was doing everything possible to ensure the birth of a healthy boy.

There followed some of the most anxious months of Louise's life. She questioned everyone who came from the Court as to the Queen's health, until Jeanne trembled for her and begged her to desist. She remained for long periods on her knees, night and morning, beseeching the saints and the Virgin for their help. It did not occur to her that to plead for the death of an unborn child was unseemly, for she was incapable of seeing anything as evil which furthered the future of her darling.

Naturally François was unaware of his mother's anguish. He liked Amboise; and when he passed through the town the people cheered him. Marguerite was his constant companion, and they had little Françoise with them. There had been talk of a sword though; he had not received that yet; and when he mentioned it, his mother — usually so eager to give way to his whims — shook her head and said that was for later.

When plague came to certain cities Louise left Amboise in haste for Romorantin, a quiet retreat in the heart of woodland country. Amboise had been unaffected but there was much coming and going there, and she could not allow François to run the slightest risk.

Louis had gone off to Italy to carry out his treaty with the Pope, while his Queen was patiently waiting for the end of her pregnancy at Blois.

When Louise sat with Jeanne one day while they worked on their tapestry, Jeanne tried to reason with her. "You are unlike yourself, Louise. You are over-wrought."

"Once Anne has given birth to a girl or a still-born child I shall regain my composure. Although there could well be other pregnancies. But Louis is away at the wars. Long may he stay there. And if this child she is bearing should prove to be . . ."

Jeanne shook her head. "You must be more at peace. If the worst should happen . . ." She shrugged her shoulders. "Well then, François would still have a great future, I am sure."

"A great future! There is no future great enough for him but that of kingship. He is a king from the top of his lovely head to his dear little toes. God bless him, my King, my Caesar."

"Louise, forgive me, for I love the boy dearly, but I think that you could allow your devotion to him to drive you mad."

"Mad! Then mad I would be. He is my life and my love. I would die tomorrow if I lost him. And I think that if another took the crown from him I should begin to die from that moment."

It was no use talking to her. She was a woman besotted with love and ambition for the loved one.

"I hear the approach of horses," said Jeanne, rising. "I wonder who comes this way."

She went to the window and, looking out, exclaimed in such astonishment that Louise came hurrying to her side.

When she saw the litter which was being carried she caught her breath in wonder. There was no mistaking that litter. It was decorated with the golden lilies of France.

"Anne herself!" whispered Louise. "But what can this mean?"

"You should go and find out," Jeanne told her.

Louise hurried down to greet the party. Anne of Brittany, Queen of France, noticeably advanced in pregnancy, was helped from her litter.

Louise knelt before her till Anne bade her rise.

The Queen looked down somewhat cynically at the little woman with the fierce blue eyes and the firm jaw.

"We are greatly honoured at Romorantin," said Louise.

"There is plague at Blois," answered the Queen. "I dared stay no longer."

"Madame, if we had but had warning . . ."

"There was no time to give it, but we knew that we could rely on Madame d'Angoulême."

Louise's sharp eyes swept over the Queen's body. She looked tired. She was pale. The journey must have exhausted her. So there was plague in Blois. What if some of the party already carried it? My King, my Caesar! What if . . . It was unthinkable. But if the Queen herself were suffering, if the child . . .

She must banish her wild thoughts and give her attention to entertaining the Queen at Romorantin.

How ironic! So the Queen was to give birth to that all-important child under that very roof where Louise was living with her cherished heir presumptive.

What strange days they were! Anne kept to the apartments which had been hastily prepared for her. The Queen was in a dilemma; she longed to summon holy men to her, but she feared they might be carriers of the plague. She wanted to make her pilgrimages; but she felt exhausted and was afraid that a journey might harm the precious child she carried.

She was fully aware of the watchful eyes of Louise — blue, cold and calculating.

She hated the woman; she knew what was going on in her mind, and when she caught glimpses of that boisterous boy who seemed to run everywhere and take sudden leaps into the air in an excess of good health and high spirits she was overcome with envy. "Holy Mother," she prayed, "give me a boy such as that one and I will spend the rest of my life in good works."

"How is the Queen today?" Louise asked Anne's attendants.

"A little tired, Madame."

"The saints preserve her."

When the Queen's women told her of the solicitude of Madame d'Angoulême Anne smiled graciously, but inwardly she was sardonic. She wishes me as much good will as I wish her, she thought. How I long for the day when my son is born!

It was a pleasant pastime, planning how she would summon Louise to her bedchamber and proudly display the heir to the throne, how she would thank her for all she had done to make her confinement comfortable.

Every night Louise paced up and down her own apartments. Jeanne was with her, attempting to comfort her.

"It cannot be long now, Jeanne. It must be soon. If it should be a boy . . ."

"Calm yourself, Louise. She may have her spies close at hand. If she knew what harm you wished her child it might amount to a charge of treason."

"How she would like to see me and my little King in the dungeons at Blois! Praise be to the saints, we have a good King on the throne. He is her dupe, I know, but he would never be persuaded to murder us."

"You are growing distraught and it is not like you."

"Distraught! How can I sleep? How can I eat . . . until I know that she has failed."

There was much running to and fro in the Queen's apartments. The pains had started. The Queen had ordered her attendants to pray constantly, all through her labour, for a boy.

Louise sat calm, waiting. The tension was relaxed because now she soon must know.

Then from the royal apartments came the cry of a child.

Louise clenched her hands in an ecstasy of pain. "Why don't they tell me!" she demanded. And yet she dreaded to be told.

Jeanne brought her the news, but as Louise looked into the face of her faithful friend she did not need to be told. Rarely had she seen such shining happiness in that well-loved face.

"A girl!" cried Louise.

Jeanne was laughing on the edge of hysteria.

"A girl, Louise!"

"Oh praise be to the saints. All glory to my King, my Caesar."

"A sickly girl . . . I heard. But it may be false. I heard that she was deformed and may not live."

The two women fell weeping and laughing into each other's arms.

CHAPTER FIVE

François in Jeopardy

The child was christened Claude and when Louise saw her she realised that rumour had not lied. The little girl was unhealthy and as far as could be seen had a squint.

Louise brought François and Marguerite to see the child, and from her bed Anne watched them at the cradle with narrowed eyes; she could have wept at the sight of the boy's sturdy limbs, his glowing dark eyes, the vitality which, on instructions from his mother, he was trying to suppress.

"What a *little* baby!" That was the boy's shrill voice.

"She is but a few days old, my love."

"Was I a little baby like that once?"

"You were never a *little* baby. You were always a *big* one."

The boy had started to jump, and his sister laid a restraining hand on his shoulder. Spoiled monster! thought Anne. He thinks the whole world was made for him. But if only I had one like him . . .

"I like our Françoise better," declared François. "*She* is pretty."

Louise had taken his hand and turned to smile at Anne. Such high spirits! And how can one so young and innocent be expected not to say what comes into his mind? You have to admit, the baby *is* sickly.

Would that I could call the guards, thought Anne, and have her taken down to one of the dungeons and kept there with her precious son.

She looks ill, Louise was thinking. She cannot take confinements lightly. She will have to take care of her health, and in view of the failure she has had with Charles, and now this weak little infant by Louis, it seems she may well continue to fail.

Louise stooped to François. "You will love the little Princess when she is old enough to run about." That's if she's ever able to, she thought. It wouldn't surprise me if she took sick and died.

Louise had come to the bed. "He loves playing with little children," she said, her expression soft again. "Madame, you should see him with the little Françoise, this child whom he and his sister brought into the *château* because they wanted a baby to care for."

Besotted fool, thought Anne. Does she think everyone is going into ecstasies of admiration at the childish doings of that boy?

"He is five years old, is he not? The Princess Claude will mayhap prefer to play with children of her own age."

The Queen closed her eyes; it was the sign of dismissal. Through lowered lids she watched the little party leave. If she thought that boy was going to marry Claude, Louise was mistaken. If she could marry Claude to a foreign Prince, if her next child were a son — Madame Louise was going to find herself and her adored François very much less significantly placed than they were at this time.

Louis had returned from the war. He was not the most successful of generals and, although he had longed to bring Milan back to France, he knew that his real genius was for home government. He was never extravagant on his own account; but he was eager to see his people living in greater comfort, and during the first years of his reign, France prospered. His subjects were aware of his virtue and conceived a great affection for him. He became known as the Father of his People.

Genial, approachable, shrewd, he was loved by those who surrounded him; he was capable of moments of irascibility, but these all knew were only when he suffered pain or was anxious over some danger threatening the country. He was, however, deeply respectful to his wife and apt to give her her way in everything; and as Anne of Brittany was a forceful woman, France was governed as much by her as by Louis.

It was a source of great disappointment that they had only one child — little Claude, who was undersized, walked with a limp and was clearly never going to be strong.

Reluctantly he told Anne they must face the fact that François had a very fair chance of following him to the throne.

"In that case," said Anne tartly, "he should be brought up as a man and untied from a woman's apron strings."

Louis agreed that this was so and, sending for Maréchal de Gié, told him that he was to go to Amboise and become Governor of the household of Angoulême, his special charge being the boy François who was to be brought up in all manly activities.

De Gié recognised the importance of this task and set off with a will.

Louise received him with great apprehension, although she realised that now François was seven years old he could no longer be regarded as a baby. As for the boy himself, as long as he was not separated from his mother and sister, he was happy enough to have a chance to fence and learn how to joust.

On the day before de Gié was due to arrive at the *château* Louise was alone with her son and daughter. She sat with one on either side of her and put an arm about each.

"My children," she said, "you are growing up and you will find that we cannot go on in the way we have. Soon life in the *château* will change. They are going to make our François into a man — and they do not think his mother, being a woman, is capable of doing that."

"But you will be here with us, dearest Maman?" asked Marguerite anxiously.

"Do you think that I should allow anyone to part me from you? Nay, my children. We are as one — we three. We are a trinity. Let us remember it forever."

"I shall never forget," said Marguerite.

"Bless you, my daughter. I know you love your brother."

"And I love my sister," cried François.

"You love each other; and I love you both; and you love me. My dear ones, there was never such love in the world as we have for each other. Let us remember it. And one day when you, my son, are King of France, you will know that there is none whom you can trust as you trust your mother and sister — because we are as three in one: a trinity."

François liked the new life. Maréchal de Gié was determined to ingratiate himself with one who might well be a King of France, but at the same time he laid down rules which must not be broken. He explained to the boy that these were necessary; to acquire manhood one must never ignore discipline.

François was a good pupil. Being strong and healthy he loved the outdoor life; being quick-witted, and for so long under the surveillance of his brilliant sister, he was fond of learning. He was good-natured and strangely unspoiled by the devotion of his family; he loved his mother and sister almost as devotedly as they loved him and was anxious never to displease them nor cause them anxiety.

De Gié's first act had been to replace François's pony with a horse. Louise came out to the courtyard to see him mounted, and tears of emotion temporarily blinded her at the sight of that upright little figure perched on the tall horse.

She had a whip made for him of gold decorated with fleur-de-lis in enamel; he was delighted with the gift and would not abandon it even when he was not riding.

One of the charms of François was that, indulged as he was, he could always feel enthusiasm for small delights.

It had been necessary now to send the little Françoise back to her parents. It was no task for an embryo knight to care for a child; and as Marguerite was growing too old for such pastimes and had to increase her studies, they must say goodbye to their little protégée.

They both had plenty with which to occupy themselves, and life at Amboise seemed to François like one adventure after another.

One day Louise was at the window watching his equestrian exercises under the surveillance of de Gié. François was mounted on a new horse and he sat it boldly, brandishing his whip.

She watched him taking a jump. What a horseman the boy was becoming! He excelled in everything he undertook.

"I verily believe," she said to Jeanne who was with her, "that he is a god in earthly guise."

Then she caught her breath in dismay. The horse had started to rear; it had the bit between its teeth and was galloping blindly over the fields, while François was clinging to it with all his might. De Gié, who was talking to some of the attendants, had not seen what was happening, and for some seconds Louise was unable to move. She saw her life in ruins; she saw them bringing in his mangled body — her beautiful one, her beloved . . . dead. She would die with him. There would no longer be any purpose in life.

"Holy Mother, help me," she prayed; and she dared not look at that madly galloping animal with the small figure still managing to stay in the saddle.

She rushed down the great staircase and out of the *château*, shouting to all who could hear as she did so: "The Comte's horse is running away with him. Quick! All of you. Monsieur le Maréchal! Everyone! Help! The Comte is in danger."

By the time she had reached the field in which François had been exercising his horse, de Gié had seen what was happening and, galloping after the boy, had brought the runaway horse to a standstill. Louise, watching, felt her knees tremble so violently that she thought they would not support her. The relief was almost unbearable; for there was François, laughing as though the whole affair had been something of a joke, being led back to the spot where his mother was waiting.

He took one look at her and saw the distress still in her face.

"It is unharmed, Maman," he called reassuringly. "See, I have not broken it."

He held up the whip for her to see; and the fact that he had believed she was concerned for the thing brought home to her that he was after all but a child.

She laughed, but the tears were very near.

It was fitting, said the Maréchal, that François should have friends of his own age. They should live at Amboise as his equals, because it was not good that a boy should believe himself to be superior to others until he had proved himself to be so.

Therefore he proposed to bring to Amboise certain boys, and they should play and fight together, as young boys will.

Louise did not raise any objection; she knew that it would be useless to do so; in any case she agreed with this decision and, as long as she was allowed to remain under the same roof as her darling, she was happy that the Maréchal should undertake part of his education.

Thus to Amboise came some boys of François's age — all of noble birth, all willingly placed under the control of the Maréchal. François made friends with them, played games with them, learned to fence, hunt, joust and fight with them. They were Montmorency, Chabot, Montchenu, and Fleurange; they would sit together after the mock combat, talking of the real war, and longing for the days when they themselves would go into action. Although they knew that François would most probably one day be their King, they did not allow this to influence their attitude toward him; in fact they forgot it for days at a time; and François did not remind them. He was too intent on enjoying life as a growing boy to worry about the crown which was somewhat precariously held over him.

He would sleep deeply and dreamlessly each night, delightfully fatigued after his exercise. He would rise fresh in the morning, and drag his comrades out of their beds if they showed any desire to remain in them.

"Come on," he would shout. "The sun is already up. I'll race you to the stables."

He was growing up.

Louise watched him often with delight, often in anguish. He was so like those other boys and yet so different, because he never forgot for one moment that he was part of that trinity; and friendly as he might be with Fleurange, dearly as he loved to tilt against Montmorency, his love for his sister and his mother was never dimmed in the slightest way.

De Gié, determined as he was to remain on good terms with Louise, yet tried to wean the boy from her. He would have preferred to have complete charge of François, to let him live entirely with male company; but he quickly realised that, short of a command from the King, he could not separate Louise from her son.

He tried means of persuasion.

Once he said to her: "It seems a sad thing that a lady — young and beautiful as you are — should remain alone."

"Alone? I am not alone. I have my children."

"You should have a husband."

"I am content."

"The King would arrange a match for you with Alfonso d'Este. It would be a good match."

"Leave France! Leave François! Nay, Monsieur le Maréchal. That is something I shall never do."

He looked at her sadly.

"Clever women can combine wifeliness with motherhood."

"With the father of their children, yes. Alas, I lost my husband, and I am in no mind to take another."

Later there was a rumour that Henry VII of England, recently widowed, was urgently looking for a wife and liked much what he had heard of Louise of Savoy.

"I have no mind to go to England," was her retort to that. "My home is where my children are, and that happens to be in Amboise. There I shall remain."

Such a woman! thought the Maréchal. And there were times when he felt almost tender toward her.

Who would take to wife a woman whose affections were exclusively occupied by another — even though that other were her own son?

So Louise clung to her widowhood; and François grew in stature so that he was taller than all his companions; he could almost always beat them at their sports. Each day, thought Louise, he grows more and more like a king.

Anne was pregnant once more, and there followed months of anxiety, until one day the news was brought from Court that she had given birth to a stillborn child. And that child had been a boy.

Then Louise went on her knees and cried: "I see, O Lord, that You are with me."

And after that she was more certain than ever that the next King of France would be her son.

Louis despaired of getting a male heir.

His health was deteriorating rapidly and he was beginning to be exhausted at the least exertion. Moreover the Queen's last confinement, which had resulted in the birth of a stillborn boy, had made her very ill and she showed little sign of regaining her former strength. He was afraid of what another pregnancy might do to her.

"We must perforce resign ourselves," he said. "François will follow me. There is no help for it."

Anne clenched her fists and her face was set in determined lines.

"And give Louise of Savoy what she has been dreaming of ever since she gave birth to that boy?"

"There's no help for it. He is the next in the line of succession; and I suppose we should be thankful that he is so robust. He is being brought up as a king. Let us face it. We should accept him as the Dauphin."

"While there is life in my body I never shall."

Louis laid his arm about her shoulders. He admired her so much. She was so strong-minded, so intelligent; but her hatred of Louise of Savoy was almost unreasonable. It was surely natural that the mother of François should be ambitious for him; nor were her ambitions misplaced; when all was said and done the boy was the heir.

"We should affiance him without delay to our daughter."

"Claude . . . to marry that . . . lout!"

"She is our daughter; we can at least make sure that she is Queen of France."

"I am determined to have a son."

"My dearest wife, I could not allow you to endanger your life."

"It is my duty to bear a son."

"No, no. Not when we have an heir in François. He is healthy enough to please anyone. The people are already interested in him. He has all the gifts that will appeal most to them. It is our fate and we must accept it."

"He shall not have my delicate Claude."

"If he is to be King she could not make a better match."

"Could she not? I have decided that she shall have the grandson of Maximilian. Little Charles of Castile shall be for our Claude. I should like to see Louise's face when she hears of that. Claude married to the Archduke Charles; and I to have a son. Where would Monsieur François be then . . . for all his mother's ambitions?"

"Have you decided then?" he asked sadly.

"I have decided. François shall not have Claude."

Louise laughed aloud when she heard.

"Does she think I shall mourn! Does she think I want that poor little insect for Caesar? It would be like mating a donkey with an Arab steed. Let the Archduke have her. Let him be promised to her. It won't be the first time he has been promised in marriage."

Yet she was annoyed, because the people would have been pleased by the match. And when a king is not a king's son it was better that he married the daughter of a king.

Had Louis suggested the match she would have been pleased. She would have told François: "Marry the poor creature. It is your destiny."

And François would have married her and, because he was François, would have provided France with heirs. She smiled thinking of the beautiful women who would count themselves honoured to be his mistresses.

But she snapped her fingers. "Caesar shall have a princess for a bride — she will have beauty as well as rank."

The King was ill and the news spread throughout the country that he was dying.

Louise was exultant. There would be none between François and the throne. He was not quite twelve years old, so there would have to be a Regency. Her mind was busy. She would impress upon him the need to keep his mother at his side.

She could scarcely contain herself. She paced up and down her room. Once again Jeanne de Polignac implored her to hide her exultation; if it were carried to Court that she had exulted because the King was dying she might be accused of sorcery, or at least treason. Had she thought of the consequences of that? She must not forget that Anne of Brittany was the Queen and her enemy.

"They'll not dare harm the King's mother. François loves me as he loves no other. He would not allow it."

"François is yet a boy."

"François will be King. Perhaps at this moment he *is* King. They will cry *Le roi est mort, Vive le Roi* — and they will mean *Vive le Roi François Premier*."

"It is too soon to triumph."

Louise embraced her good friend. "How wise you are to warn me. But I am so happy I cannot contain my happiness."

Louise was downcast when the King recovered.

In the streets of Paris the people rejoiced because the "Father of his People" was still with them. But he was very weak, and it seemed that he could not live long.

Louise's spirits were soon rising again. The King an invalid. The Queen an invalid. It seemed unlikely that they could produce a healthy heir, yet Anne would insist that they go on trying as long as there was life left in them both.

Anne, desperately afraid that she was going to lose her husband, decided that she would go on a pilgrimage to her native Brittany; and she left the King in the care of his physicians.

Louis lay limply in his bed and, when his Queen had been absent for some days, he sent for his old friend, Georges d'Amboise.

"Georges," he said, "I fear my end is not far off."

Georges was too wise a man to deny this, because he knew the King would not respect untruthfulness.

"At Amboise Louise of Savoy will be waiting for the moment when that boy of hers will mount the throne. It is coming, Georges, and the Queen and I shall not be able to prevent it. François Premier will follow me."

"Sire, you are a little better. I had it from your physicians. There may be some time left to you."

"I may get up from this sick bed, yes. But methinks I shall soon be back in it. I am worried about my daughter. I should like to see her Queen of France."

"A match with François would be appropriate, Sire."

"The Queen is against it."

Georges looked at his master shrewdly. He saw the command in his eyes. It was the old cry of "Let Georges do it." Georges d'Amboise must find a way in which a match between the heir presumptive to the throne of France and the King's daughter should be made without delay.

Georges went away and considered the matter. The Queen was in Brittany. The affair should be concluded in her absence. Louis would have to answer to her when she returned and, as he hated to ignore her wishes, if one did not wish to displease the King there must be a very good reason.

Georges went back to his master.

"It is the will of the people," he said, "that the Princess Claude should be betrothed to François."

Once again, Georges had done it.

The two enemies watched the ceremony. Anne was sullen, but she knew there was nothing she could do to prevent it, because the people of Paris had sent a deputation to the King begging that their Princess be married to their Dauphin.

Louise was not, in truth, displeased, although determined to hide this fact from Anne. But she could not prevent her eyes shining with contentment as they rested on twelve-year-old François, so tall, so handsome, so bright-eyed, every glorious inch of him a Dauphin, and turned to poor sickly seven-year-old Claude who looked as though she would not live long enough to consummate the marriage.

Louis was well pleased. He did not suffer from the same envy as Anne did, and could not help eyeing the boy with satisfaction. It was good that a branch of the royal family could produce a boy so worthy in every way of his destiny.

The King recovered his health in some degree; but his physicians warned him that he must take care. He should eat frugally, always have his meat boiled, and retire early, making sure that he did not tax his strength in any way.

He consulted with Georges d'Amboise and they decided that, now François was the King's prospective son-in-law as well as his heir, he should be at Court under the eye of the King.

De Gié had disgraced himself when Louis had been dangerously ill by presuming that the King was as good as dead. He had made an effort to seize control, that he might have charge of the young Dauphin and guide him in all matters.

Louis had understood the Maréchal's action and thought it not unwise in the circumstances. There was always danger to a country when a king died and his successor was a minor. But de Gié had attempted to restrain Anne of Brittany, and for that reason she insisted that he be punished.

Louis had to face his wife's anger, and that was something he never cared to do. However he did save de Gié from execution, but the Maréchal lost his post and was sent into exile.

This was another reason why François, deprived of his governor, should come to Court.

"It is not fitting," said Anne, "that wherever the boy is his mother should be. He must learn to stand on his own feet."

Louis agreed with her; and as a result François was summoned to Chinon where the Court was in residence.

When he had left, Louise was desolate.

"For the first time in our lives we are apart," she wailed.

Jeanne reminded her that it was because her son was accepted as Dauphin that he must go to Court; and was that not what she wanted more than anything else?

"But how dismal it is without him. There is no joy left in the place."

François was an immediate success at Court. The King could not help being amused by his high spirits, nor admiring his energy. In addition he was already witty, so that he found friends, not only among the sportsmen, but among those who were interested in ideas.

Although but a boy he was already drawing about him his own little court.

"That is as it should be," said the tolerant Louis. "As the old King grows more infirm it is natural that men and women should turn to him who will next wear the crown."

Anne transferred her hatred of the mother to the son.

"Brash! Conceited! Altogether too sure of himself and his future," was her verdict.

"Louis," she insisted, "we *must* get a son."

The King was weary. He would have preferred to let matters rest; but Anne was indefatigable. She herself was as weak as he was; she had never recovered from the birth of her stillborn son, and had never ceased to look back with great bitterness on that event.

When Anne triumphantly announced that she was pregnant, this news brought little pleasure to anyone but herself. Louis was alarmed, because he was aware of her state of health and wondered whether she would survive another ordeal like the last. He was so much older than she was that he had always believed she would be with him to the end; and the thought of losing her now that he was so infirm depressed him. He wished that she could have accepted François as placidly as he did. As for Louise, she was beside herself with anxiety. She had lulled herself to a sense of security of late, because she had been certain that Anne could not produce a boy. Yet she was capable of becoming pregnant, and Louise recognised in the woman a spirit as indomitable as her own. Such women had a habit of getting their own way; and when two such were fighting each other, Fate could take a hand and give the victory to either.

François himself was now old enough to feel apprehension. Life at Court suited him well. He was the darling of his set; and he accepted their adulation as gracefully as he had accepted that of his mother and sister. Not only had he good looks and charm but he was the Dauphin — the most important man at Court next to the King, and the King was old and ailing.

He had discovered too what he believed from now on would be the greatest of all pleasures: making love to women.

He did not want any change. To be Dauphin at the Court of France was a wonderful life.

One bright day Louise's anxieties were miraculously swept away. The Queen had given birth to a child who lived, but the child was a girl and little Princess Renée could present no threat to François the Dauphin.

"And this *must* be the last," Louise told Jeanne. "She can never manage it again."

François pursued his way at Court, charming all. Marguerite was now married to the Duc d'Alençon. Poor Marguerite, she was a most reluctant bride; but she had been brought up to do her duty and, although she suffered so intensely that it was feared she might die of melancholy, she went through with the marriage.

François, to whom she confided all things, wept with her, for her sorrows would always be his. She was seventeen, François fifteen; and he was angry with himself because he was powerless to help her.

There was little point, he said, in being Dauphin if one could not have one's way. He wanted to go out and kill Alençon so that the man could not marry his sister.

Marguerite, who had declared that she would rather be dead than have to live with the man whom they had chosen for her husband, forgot her own grief when she saw how upset her brother was.

"Why, my dearest," she said, "I would marry ten such men rather than that you should be unhappy on my account. Smile, François. What does it matter whom I marry? I shall love one man until I die, and that is you, my brother."

They embraced; they kissed; they mingled their tears.

"And you know, Marguerite, my pearl of pearls, I shall never love a woman as I love you."

"I know it, for we are as one, beloved. We are part of that trinity to which I am honoured to belong, while feeling myself unworthy."

François assured her that she and their mother were the most wonderful of women, and when he was King of France he would do all in his power to make her the happiest woman alive. She should leave her husband; she should come to Court; they would be together always.

Marguerite was comforted. "No world could ever be desolate which contained my beloved brother," she told him.

The Court was at Blois and François was in love.

He had seen the girl on her way to church; she was demure, keeping her eyes downcast and he had followed her. He did not want her to know that he was Dauphin; he wanted her to love him for himself alone, and he had come to suspect that many of the women at Court showed a preference for him partly because of his rank.

This girl was different. She was not of the Court. He did not know who she was, but he suspected she was the daughter of some not very prominent citizen.

After church he followed her to a house in the town; it was a humble enough dwelling from his viewpoint and he was only the more enchanted by this; it seemed incredible that one so fair and dainty could live in such a place.

For days he watched for the girl. He hung about near the house; and one day when she was going to church he waylaid her as she crossed the churchyard.

"I beg of you," he said humbly, "stay awhile. I would speak with you."

She turned and faced him. She was very young, and more beautiful seen closely than from afar. He was filled with happiness because he noticed that her gown, though tastefully made, was of simple material, and very different from the garments worn by Court ladies.

"What have you to say to me?" she asked.

"That you are beautiful and I have long desired to tell you so."

She sighed. "Well, now 'tis done," she said, and turned away.

He laid a hand on her arm, but she shook her head. "I know that you are the Dauphin," she said. "It is not fitting that you should be my friend."

"How did you know who I am? And I tell you it seems very fitting to me, because I am eager to be *your* friend."

"I should always know you," she replied. "You have changed very little. You don't remember me though."

"Pray tell me your name."

"It is Françoise," she said.

"Françoise!" He took her by the shoulders and peered into her face. Then he laughed aloud with pleasure. "Little Françoise! Our baby . . . grown into a beautiful girl . . . the most beautiful girl in France."

Françoise lowered her eyes. He thought he had discovered her afresh; but she had seen him many times when he rode with the King or members of the royal party. She had thought him the most handsome, charming creature in the world, and when she had seen the women clustering round him, a great sadness had touched her. She had longed then to be young again — a baby whom he held in his arms. She had felt it was the greatest sadness in her life that he should be the Dauphin of France and she a humble maiden. If he had been a shepherd, or a lackey of the Court, how happy she could have been!

"Look at me, Françoise," he commanded, and she obeyed. She saw the desire in his eyes, as he took her hands in his and pressed burning kisses on them.

But Françoise was frightened; she withdrew her hands and ran away.

François stood looking after her. He was smiling in a dazed fashion.

He was in love for the first time in his life.

He sought out Marguerite; he was so excited because he had found their little Françoise again.

"Dearest, do you remember our baby?" he cried. "Do you remember little Françoise? I have met her again and she is beautiful . . . the most beautiful girl in the world, except yourself. I am in love with her."

Marguerite smiled at him indulgently. "I am glad, beloved, that you are in love. It is so good for you. Lust without love is a poor pastime. And you have found Françoise. I knew that she was here, because one of my servants is married to her sister. She lives with her family in the town. It is rather charming that you should love our baby."

"Marguerite, tell me what I should do. She was a little afraid of me, I think. I spoke to her in the churchyard and she ran away."

"Next time do not allow her to run away. Tell her of your feelings. She will be your mistress, and it is good for you to have a mistress. And Françoise is a good girl . . . a virgin, I promise you. I am delighted that this has happened."

"You think that she will be my mistress?"

Marguerite laughed aloud. "Any woman in France would be honoured to be your mistress."

"You say that, who loves me."

"Beloved, you have all the gifts. You are young; you are charming, witty, and handsome. And you are the Dauphin of France. My love, you look to me like a king already. No woman would resist you."

But Françoise, it seemed, was the one woman in France who would not become his mistress.

She avoided him, and again and again he was disappointed. She no longer walked across the churchyard, and it took him some time to discover that she now went to another church. When he had traced her, he told how hurt he was, but to his consternation Françoise implored him to leave her alone.

Disconcerted, he once more consulted Marguerite who herself went to Françoise to find out the real cause of her reluctance.

Françoise broke into bitter weeping when questioned by Marguerite. Indeed she loved François; she had loved him since she was a baby. Through her life she had gathered all the news she could about him. She would always love François.

"And he loves you too. How happy you will be," said Marguerite.

But Françoise shook her head. "I cannot meet the Dauphin," she said. "We are too far apart, and I would die rather than commit the sin of becoming a man's mistress, whoever that man might be."

Marguerite pointed out that this was folly. It was good to be virtuous, but to be the mistress of a king — and the Dauphin would one day be King — was not a disgrace but an honour.

"Madame," answered Françoise, "to me it seems a sin whether it be a dauphin or a beggar."

Marguerite shrugged her shoulders and went back to François.

"The girl adores you," she told him, "and so she should. She talks of sin. You must have her abducted, seduce her, and then I'll swear she will forget all about sin and you will both be as happy as you were intended to be."

François was happy again. He could trust Marguerite to find the solution to all his problems.

They had brought her to him; she was pale and trembling. François was afraid they had hurt her. He had ordered them to be gentle, but she had obviously struggled.

She looked at him, and he felt that he would never be able to forget the reproach in those brown eyes.

"So," she said, "you have trapped me."

"But Françoise," he replied, "it is only because I love you so much."

She shook her head, and he saw the tears on her lashes.

He went to her then and took her roughly in his arms. She was small and he was so strong. He knew that he could subdue her.

"Now," he demanded, "are you not happy because they brought you to me?"

"François," she answered earnestly, "if you harm me, this will be something which your conscience will never let you forget."

"Oh come, Françoise. You have been brought up too simply. At the Court people make love and do not call it a sin."

"I know what is in my heart, François."

"Do you hate me then?"

"I have confessed to your sister that I love you."

"Why then . . ."

But she covered her face with her hands.

He put his hand on her breast and felt the tremor run through her body. She stood rigid, and he thought suddenly: But she means it. She calls it sin.

"Françoise," he said. "Little Françoise, you must not be afraid of me. When we are lovers in truth you will understand that I would not hurt you for the world. Please, Françoise, smile and be happy."

"I am in your power," she said, and shivered.

He was angry and an impulse came to him to force her to do his will. Was he not the Dauphin? Had not Marguerite said that any woman would be honoured to be his mistress? Any woman . . . except Françoise, the one he wanted.

He caught at the bodice of her dress. In a second he would have ripped it from her shoulders. But he did not do so. He thought of little Françoise, the helpless baby; she was as helpless now.

He loved her — not as he loved his sister and mother, for he would never love any with that deep abiding emotion. But he wanted to protect her, never to hurt her, and he could not bear to see her frightened and to know that he was the cause of her fear.

"Oh Françoise," he said, "do not tremble. I would not harm you. I love you too well. You shall go to your home now. Have no fear. You will be safe."

She knelt down suddenly and kissed his hand; her tears were warm and they moved him deeply.

He laid his hand on her hair, and he felt grown up . . . no longer a boy, but a man.

And although he had lost Françoise, because he knew that to see her again would be to put a temptation in his way which he might not be able to resist, he was happier than he would have been if he had seduced her.

"I shall never forget you, Monsieur le Dauphin," she said. "I shall never forget you . . . my King."

"Nor shall I forget you, Françoise," he told her.

She left him and, true to his word, he did not see her for some years, although he never forgot her and often made inquiries as to her well-being.

When he told Marguerite what had happened she was as pleased as he was by the outcome and said that he had acted with his usual wisdom. She had believed that Françoise would have been delighted by her seduction; but Françoise, it seemed, was an unusually virtuous girl; and by renouncing her he had acted like the perfect knight he was.

She was proud of her darling, as always.

Christmas at Court lacked its usual gaiety. There had been a humiliating skirmish with the English and, although the French had not taken the boastful Henry VIII and his army seriously, the result had been the Battle of the Spurs, and the border towns of Thérouanne and Tournay had been lost. The King of England had taken a few prisoners, among them the Duc de Longueville. It was rather depressing, particularly as Louis was in great pain with his gout, and his Queen was in an even more sorry state.

Anne had suffered a great deal since her confinements, and the fact that they had brought her but two girls made her very melancholy. She now had to accept the fact that she could not prevent Louise's boy ascending the throne, and when she recalled that he was betrothed to her own Claude she was apprehensive.

"What sort of life will our delicate child have with him?" she demanded of Louis. "Already one hears constant talk of his conquests. And he affianced to the daughter of the King! My poor Claude! I fear for her. Would that I had my way and she had married the Archduke Charles who is, by all accounts, a gentle person. But this François has too much energy. He is too lusty. He is horribly spoiled. And this is the Dauphin! This is the husband-to-be of my poor Claude!"

Louis tried to soothe her. "He is a fascinating young fellow. Claude will be the envy of all the women. He'll be a good husband."

"A good and faithful husband," said Anne sardonically.

"He's too young for fidelity, but when he mellows he'll be a good King, never fear."

"But I *do* fear," insisted Anne. "I fear for my delicate daughter."

She persisted in her melancholy; and since the King retired to bed early and could eat nothing but boiled meat, it fell to the lot of the Dauphin to make a merry Christmas.

This he did with little effort, and already men and women of the Court were beginning to look forward to the day when the King of France would be young François Premier instead of old Louis the Twelfth.

Shortly after the New Year the Queen took to her bed; she suffered great pain and Louis, summoning the best physicians to her bedside, found that instead she needed the priests.

When, on a cold January day, Anne of Brittany died, Louis was distraught. He had been in awe of her; there had been times when he had had to resort to subterfuge in order to go against her wishes; but he had loved her and respected her. She had been such a contrast to poor Jeanne, his first wife; and because, when he had married her he had been past his youth and in far from good health, he had counted himself fortunate, in an age of profligacy, to have a faithful wife on whose honour he could absolutely rely.

He wept bitterly at her bedside.

"Soon," he said, "I shall be lying beside her in the tomb."

But the bereaved husband was still the King of France. He sent for his ministers. "The marriage of my daughter to the Dauphin must take place without delay," he said. "Even the fact that we are in mourning for the Queen must not delay that. I do not think I am long for this world; I must see my daughter married before I leave it."

So François was to prepare himself for marriage, and Louise, hearing the news, made ready to join her son.

"Ah, Jeanne," she cried, "what happiness! My enemy is no more and I have heard that, by the looks of the King, he will not be long in following her. Then the glorious day will be with us. Caesar will come into his own."

Even Jeanne de Polignac believed now that no more obstacles could stand in their way.

The two women embraced. Anne of Brittany could no longer produce an heir. The way to the throne was wide open and no one stood in the way of François.

Louise laughed in her glee. "All these years I have feared and suffered such agonies! Why, Jeanne, I need never have worried. All her efforts came to naught; and now my beloved is at Court and no one dares dispute his claim. How long has Louis left, do you think? I hear that the death of Anne upset him so much that he had to keep to his bed for a week. Well, Louis has had his day."

They were joyful as they prepared to go to Court.

"But," Jeanne warned her friend, "be careful not to show your elation. Remember we are supposed to be mourning for the Queen."

"Louis knows too well how matters stood between us to expect much mourning from me. Louis is no fool, Jeanne."

"Still, for the sake of appearances . . ."

"I will play my part. What care I? All our anxieties are over. The crown is safe for Caesar."

François stood beside his bride, and all who had gathered to witness this royal marriage were struck by the contrast between them. François, tall, glowing with health, handsome and upright. Poor little Claude, who dragged one foot slightly as she walked, who was short, and now that she was in her adolescence beginning to be over-fat in an unhealthy way. François was gay; Claude, who had been brought up by her mother, was deeply religious. An incongruous marriage in some ways; but in others so suitable. It was understandable that the King, seeing another man's son ready to take his crown, should want his daughter to share it.

François played his part well, and if he regarded his bride with repugnance, none noticed it; he smiled at her, took her hand, did all that was required of him as though he believed her to be the most beautiful lady in the land.

Claude adored him; and it was pathetic to note the way her eyes followed him.

All who had gathered in those apartments at Saint-Germain-en-Laye for the Royal wedding wondered what the future would hold for those two. Would Claude be able to give France heirs? There was no doubt that François would; but it took two to make a child.

There was an atmosphere of foreboding in that chamber hung with cloth of gold and silver, with the golden lilies of France prominently displayed. But then the Court was still in mourning — and the bride particularly — for the recently dead Queen.

Louis felt a great relief once the marriage ceremony was over; and much as he mourned Anne he found life more restful without her. He was living very quietly and was discovering that he felt better than he had for some time.

The Dauphin was becoming more and more important at the Court. Often Louis from a window would watch the young man with his companions. Claude was never one of them. François was showing a certain ostentation. For so many years he had lived in the shadow of doubt and now that it was removed he had become almost hilariously gay, which was scarcely becoming while the King still lived. He was most elegantly attired and wore many jewels.

On trust? Louis wondered. Is he borrowing against the time when he inherits what I have? Who would not be ready to let the future King have all the credit he asked for?

Louis liked his heir's robust looks but he would have preferred him to be less high-spirited, less gorgeously attired, less obviously enjoying his position, more serious.

He thought of all the benefits he had brought to France, and he said to his ministers: "It may be that we have laboured in vain. That big boy will spoil everything for us."

His ministers replied: "Sire, he may not come to the throne yet, for you might marry again. And if your bride were young and healthy, why should you not give France an heir?"

Louis was thoughtful. He had been receiving information from his kinsman, the Duc de Longueville, whom Henry VIII had taken as a prisoner into England. The King had a sister — a vivacious and lovely girl. If France made an alliance with England, why should there not be a marriage between the two countries? Circumstances were auspicious. The King of France had become a widower; the King of England had a marriageable sister. Moreover, Henry of England was disgusted with the Emperor, to whose grandson his sister had been betrothed for years. Henry was hot tempered; he was young enough to enjoy acting rashly. He wanted now to show the Emperor and Ferdinand of Aragon that he was snapping his fingers at their grandson. Nothing could do that more effectively than a French alliance.

The more Louis thought of the idea, the more he liked it. A young girl, and an exceptionally beautiful one. If she were malleable — and she should be, for she was so young — he could perhaps delude himself that he was young again . . . for the time that was left to him.

The thought of having a son was exhilarating.

Louis rose from his bed and called for a mirror.

I am not so old that I am finished with life, he told himself.

He thought of his first wife, Jeanne — poor crippled ugly Jeanne! What sort of a marriage had that been? And Anne? He had loved Anne, admired her greatly and had been desolate when she died. But she had been a dominating woman. Why should he not start afresh with this gay young foreign girl? That would be an entirely different sort of marriage.

Besides, it was politically wise.

He called his ministers and his secretaries, and in a few days a message was dispatched to the Court of England.

* * *

Louise was in despair; Marguerite was horrified; as for François, for once he was completely bewildered.

The future was no longer secure. The King, who had appeared to be on his deathbed, had now revived; he was almost young in his enthusiasm for a new marriage. And a young girl was coming from England to share the throne with him.

Louise, tight-lipped, white-faced, shut herself in her apartments with Jeanne de Polignac because she dared not risk betraying her feelings outside those walls.

"So it is to begin again. And I thought it was over. Louis . . . to marry again, and this young girl who, by all accounts is strong and marriageable! Jeanne, if aught should go wrong now . . ."

Jeanne once more tried to soothe her as she had over the last twenty years. But it was not easy. Louis was fifty-two, still able to beget children; and a young girl was coming from England.

François was aware of the sympathy of his friends; the certainty had become a grave doubt. If he should fail to reach the throne now it would be the greatest tragedy of his life, and how near he was to that tragedy!

The King was looking younger every day; and a few months previously people were prophesying that he would be dead before the year was out.

Fate was cruel. To hold out the glittering prize so close and, when he felt his fingers touching it, to snatch it away!

"He'll never get a son," said François vehemently.

And how he wished he could believe it!

Louis was sending gifts to the Court of England every day. He could scarcely wait to see his bride. He was like a young man again as he listened delightedly to reports of the young woman's charm and beauty.

The treaties were signed; a marriage ceremony had taken place at Greenwich with the Duc de Longueville acting as proxy for Louis; and the Earl of Worcester had arrived in France that a marriage by proxy should take place there. This had been celebrated in the Church of the Celestines and, although the Earl of Worcester spoke the bridal vows for Mary, Louis looked almost like a young bridegroom as he made his responses.

Marguerite, only less distracted than her mother because of her natural serenity, whispered that the bride had yet to cross the Channel. That stormy strip of water could present many hazards.

How they clutched at fragile hopes! Suppose her fleet was wrecked. Suppose she perished in a gale.

"It would kill Louis," said Louise, her eyes glistening with hope.

But in spite of bad weather Mary reached Boulogne, and the King had had new clothes made, less sombre than he usually wore. All who saw him declared that he looked younger than he had for many years.

He summoned François to his presence.

"It is fitting," he said, "that my bride, the Queen of France, should be greeted by the highest in the land. I have already sent off Vendôme and de la Tremouille.

Alençon will be following. But you, François, must be the one who brings my bride to me."

Thus it was that François rode off to Abbeville to greet Mary Tudor.

CHAPTER SIX

The Unwilling Bride

Dressed in a gown of white cloth of silver, her coif set with jewels, the Queen of France rode toward Abbeville. She sat on her white palfrey, which was magnificently caparisoned, looking like a figure from some fairy legend, and Lady Guildford, who had looked after her since her babyhood, thought she seemed like a different person from that gay, laughing girl whom she had known at the English Court. Mary Tudor had become a tragedienne in the drama which was going on around them; yet the change of role had not detracted from her beauty.

Such glittering magnificence to be the background for such sorrow! thought Lady Guildford. But she will get over it. Would she? Was that not rather a glib solution inspired by hope?

Had there ever been a young woman as single-minded as Mary Tudor? And had she not for years decided that the only man she could happily accept as her husband was Charles Brandon?

Her ladies — there were thirty of them — presented a contrast to their mistress. They were looking forward eagerly to life at the Court of France. Pretty creatures in their crimson velvet and jewels — ay and merry, a colourful foil for the white-clad Queen.

Several hundred English horsemen and archers rode on ahead of them, for although they came in friendship, Henry had declared that it was well to let the French know the mettle of English warriors. Following these were English noblemen, and side by side with them rode Frenchmen of similar rank. A pleasant sight for the people who had come out to watch the cavalcade and were more accustomed to seeing men march to war.

Lady Guildford felt a little uneasy when the young man on his spirited charger drew in close to Mary's palfrey. This man had made her uneasy from the moment she had set eyes on him. One could not deny his undoubted attractions. He sat his horse as though he were part of it; and it was splendid enough to be. He was elegantly dressed; his was the type of face that impressed itself on the memory; it might have been the alert, humorous eyes, or that extremely long nose, which for some reason added to his charm.

What was going on behind that elegant and quite fascinating exterior? What *could* be going on in the mind of a man who must be ambitious, who had believed himself to be within a step of the throne and now saw, in the person of this exquisite, though somewhat melancholy girl, the frustration of all his hopes?

He must hate her.

If he did, he certainly managed to disguise his feelings; his dark eyes caressed her in a manner which, according to Lady Guildford, was most unseemly. He was reckless; that much was obvious. It would be interesting to see how far he dared go when the King arrived on the scene.

François, holding his horse in check, smiled at Mary. "I could not resist the pleasure of riding beside you."

"How good you are to me!"

"I would I had an opportunity to show you how good I could be to you."

"I have been learning to speak the French language and to understand the ways of the French," Mary replied with meaning.

She saw the smile curve his lips. He knew she was telling him that she was prepared for extravagant compliments and would give them only the attention they deserved.

"I will tell you a secret," he said. "Since I heard we were to have an English Princess for our Queen *I* have been thinking a great deal about the English."

"Then we do not meet as strangers," she replied.

"That makes me happy. I should be desolate if I were anything but a dear friend to one who is surely the loveliest lady in the world."

"You have travelled throughout the world?"

"One does not need to travel to recognise perfection."

"Nor to flatter, it seems."

"Madame la Reine, it would be impossible to flatter you, for if you were addressed in what appeared to be the limit of hyperbole, it would still not exaggerate your charms."

Mary laughed for the first time since she had arrived in France.

"It is well that I am prepared," she said. "Tell me, when shall I meet the King?"

"It has been planned that you shall do so in his town of Abbeville, but I'll swear he will be too impatient to wait for you to arrive. Do you know, it would not surprise me if suddenly we saw a group of horsemen riding toward us, headed by an impatient bridegroom who could no longer wait for a glimpse of his bride."

"If you should see such a party, I pray you give me warning."

"You would not need it. You would hear the people cheering themselves hoarse for the Father of his People."

"The King is well loved in France?"

"Well loved he is," said François. "He has had a great many years in which to win his people's affection."

She looked at him sharply. His tone was bitter. Small wonder. He was certainly an ambitious man. Holy Mother, thought Mary, how he must hate *me* when my very presence here threatens his hopes.

To be hated by such a man would be stimulating; and for all his flattering talk he must hate her.

It was strange that contemplating his feelings for her made her feel more interested in life than she had since she had known she could not escape this French marriage.

At least, she thought, I should be thankful to him for adding a little zest to my melancholy existence.

François was not hating her; far from it. He was too gallant to hate a woman who was so beautiful; and she had spirit too; he sensed that; and she was far from happy at the prospect of marriage with old Louis. That was not surprising. How different it would have been had she arrived in France to marry another king. A king of her own age! What an ironic fate which had given this lovely, vital girl to sickly old Louis, and himself the weakling Claude.

What a pair we should have made! thought François. Life was a mischievous old sprite who loved to taunt and tease.

He continued to talk to her, telling her about the manners and customs of the French Court, asking her questions about those of England. His gaiety was infectious, and Lady Guildford was a little disturbed to hear Mary laughing again. She had wanted to hear that sound, but that it should be inspired by this dangerous young man could be significant. Not that Mary would be affected by his charm. There was some good coming out of her devotion to Charles Brandon. She would be faithful to her love for him, which meant that no Frenchman, however charming, however gallant, would be able to wean her from her duty to the King.

François, sensing her underlying melancholy, had managed to infuse the same quality into his own demeanor. He was implying that although it gave him the utmost pleasure to be in her company he could not forget that she was the bride of another man.

Lady Guildford made up her mind that at the first opportunity she must warn Mary that the French had a way of implying that their emotions were deeply engaged, when they were only mildly so.

The party was within two kilometres of Abbeville when, as François had prophesied, a party of horsemen came galloping toward them.

Mary felt her body numb with apprehension, for she knew that the moment had come when she was to be brought face-to-face with her husband.

"The King!" She heard the cry about her, and the horses were immediately brought to a standstill while Louis rode ahead of his friends and came to his bride.

Fearfully she shot her first quick glance and discovered a face that was not unkindly, although its eagerness at this moment alarmed her. The eyes were too prominent, the lips thick and dry; and she noticed with repulsion the swollen neck.

She prayed silently for courage, coupled with the ability to hide her feelings, and prepared to dismount that she might kneel before the King of France.

"No, no," he cried, "it is I who should do homage to so much beauty." He left his horse and came to her side, walking rather stiffly. The Dauphin had dismounted and was standing at attention; and Mary knew that the young man was watching them, aware of every emotion which showed itself in their faces.

"God help me," prayed Mary. "Do not let me betray my feelings."

The King had taken her hand in his; she felt his kisses on her skin and steeled herself not to shrink. Now those prominent eyes were studying her face beneath the coif of jewels, her young yet voluptuous figure in the cloth of silver.

"So young," murmured Louis. "So beautiful. They did not lie to me then."

He seemed to sense the fear in her, for he pressed her hand firmly and said: "Be at peace, my little bride. There is nothing to fear, you know."

"I know, Sire."

"The people are lining the road between here and Abbeville," he told her, "so eager are they to see their Queen."

"The people have been kind," she answered, "since I set foot in France."

"Who could be anything else to one so lovely?" The King seemed to be suddenly aware of François. "And the Duc de Valois, I trust, looks after you in my name?"

"None could have cared more for my comfort."

For a moment Louis turned his eyes on that tall, elegant figure, and he felt that he would willingly have given half his kingdom if he could have borrowed his youth and vigour. It was only now, when he was face-to-face with this beautiful girl, that he longed so desperately for his youth. And François, standing there, too sly, too clever, might well interpret his thoughts.

"That is well," said Louis briskly. "I left Abbeville this day, telling my friends that I wanted to hunt. That was not true. My intention was to catch a glimpse of my bride, so great was my impatience. So I rode this way. But this is an informal meeting and I am going to leave you now because, when you ride on your way, I do not want my people to think they must cheer the King. I want their cheers to be for you alone."

"You are so kind to me," she murmured.

"Know that it shall be my chief task in the future to look to your comfort and pleasure."

He mounted, then took off his hat and bowed his head; he seemed loth to turn away because that would mean taking his eyes from her.

The King and his horsemen rode off with a clatter of hooves; the Dauphin had leaped in the saddle and the cavalcade was ready to go forward.

"The King is enchanted," murmured François, "as he could not fail to be."

Mary was silent; her limbs were trembling so much that she feared it would be noticeable. She wanted to cry out: How much happier I should be if he had shown me indifference.

She could not forget those prominent eyes alight with desire for her. How far off was the marriage ceremony with the shadow of the nuptial bed hanging over it? One day? Two days? Could some miracle happen to save her even now?

In that moment she could almost wish that she had gone to Flanders, because she had heard that Charles was rather a simple-minded boy, a boy whom she might have been able to command; he would have been shy and inexperienced. But this old man who was her husband would never be shy; he was far from inexperienced; and his intentions regarding her had been apparent in his looks and gestures; even in that short time they had been together.

He looked ill. What was the swelling at his neck? She shivered. When he had ridden up he had not looked as though he were near death, decrepit and diseased as he was. Holy Mother, she thought, he could live for years. Years with those dry hot hands making free with her body . . . years of longing for the handsome virility of Charles.

She wanted to cry out her defiance; and she believed that she was saved from doing so by the sight of that tall figure beside her, whose alert eyes missed little and who, she was sure, knew exactly how she was feeling now. What was it he was attempting to offer? Commiseration? Consolation?

The town of Abbeville lay ahead. Mary felt exhausted, not with the physical exertion of the ride but with mental agitation.

The Dauphin was still talking; he did not wait for her answers; it was as though he understood her feelings perfectly — and was telling her: I chatter merely to give those about us the impression that all is well with you.

He explained how the King was waiting for her in the Hôtel de la Gruthuse which would be his residence during his stay in that town. The people of Abbeville were so honoured that the official meeting between the King and his bride should take place in their town that they had decorated the streets and were preparing to show her their pleasure in the union.

"You have ridden far," he said tenderly, "and this has been a great ordeal for you. Would you care to enter the town in your litter?"

Mary was grateful for the suggestion. In the litter she would feel less exposed; and it was true that she was tired.

"I will ride beside the litter," François told her with a smile. "So you will not have lost your . . . protector."

"Why, Monsieur le Dauphin," she replied, "the people of France have shown me such courtesy that I do not feel in need of a protector."

He grimaced in a manner which was charming. "I pray you do not rob me of my role for I have rarely found one more to my taste."

He turned away to call a halt, when the litter was brought forward and Mary entered it. She made a charming picture sitting there, for the litter was a thing of beauty, being covered with cloth of gold on which was embroidered the golden lilies.

"We must have it open," François pointed out. "The people will want to see their Queen."

So, riding in the open litter, Mary came into Abbeville, and when those watching from the city walls witnessed the approach of the party, the order was given for a hundred trumpets and clarions to sound, that their joyous greeting might fill the air. But to Mary they sounded like the notes of doom.

She saw the excited people who called out to her that she was beautiful. Long life to her, the Queen of France. She looked so young sitting there, the cloth of silver falling gracefully about her, her golden hair showing under the jewelled coif. She was more than a beautiful Queen. Recently there had been war with her people; but that was done with, and this lovely young girl was a symbol of the peaceful days ahead.

Through the triumphal arches they went, Mary turning this way and that to acknowledge the greetings, to express wonder at the tableau which the people of Abbeville had erected for her pleasure.

At last they came to the Church of St Wulfran, where the Queen was helped from her litter that she might be led to the altar in order to adore the host.

She lingered; there was panic within her which forced her to make everything that preceded her meeting with the King to last as long as she could make it.

François was close.

"The King will be impatient," he whispered. "He is awaiting your coming at the Hôtel de la Gruthuse."

She nodded pathetically and allowed herself to be led back to her litter, and the journey continued.

The Duke of Norfolk had now taken the place of the Dauphin; he it was whose duty it was to lead her to the King and make the formal introduction. Mary did not like Norfolk because she believed he was no friend of Charles's. He was a man who was so proud of his rank that he resented it when other men were lifted up to be set on an equal footing with him. He was Norfolk. Why should a man who had nothing — except a handsome face and skill in sport — be given honours so that he could stand as an equal against men who had been born to dignity? Moreover he knew that the Princess Mary had fancied Suffolk, and he believed the fellow had entertained a secret hope that he might marry her.

It gave Norfolk grim pleasure that both the Princess and Suffolk had been robbed of that satisfaction.

He would conduct this girl, who had so far forgotten the dignity of her position, to the King of France with the utmost pleasure.

Mary was aware of his sentiments and she felt more desolate than ever. She must face the truth that no one or no thing could save her from her imminent marriage.

Into the great reception hall of the Hôtel de la Gruthuse Norfolk led the Princess to the King who was waiting to receive her.

With Louis were the highest ranking nobles of France, the Dauphin prominent among them.

Louis embraced his bride and welcomed her to France. He wanted her to know that all those assembled wished to pay her the homage due to her.

He then presented the Dukes of Alençon, Albany and Longueville, with, among others, the Prince of Naples and de la Roche-sur-Ion.

The next stage of the ceremony was a banquet followed by a ball. Louis kept his bride beside him during the former, and when the dancing began he said that he knew she was longing to dance and he was eager to see her do so. It was a matter of chagrin that he himself was unable to do more than open the ball with her and dance a few steps. François was hovering, ready to do his duty as Dauphin; and Louis sadly watched the young pair dancing together. They were a little apart from the others — the most distinguished pair in the ballroom. Never had

François looked so kingly; never had Louis felt so envious of the one whom he had come to think of as the Big Boy.

When the ball was over, Mary was taken to the apartment which had been prepared for her; and as, until she had actually undergone the ceremony, it was deemed unfitting that she should sleep under the same roof as the King, she was conducted along a gallery — erected for this purpose — to a house which had been made ready for her and which was on the corner of the street leading to the Rue St Gilles.

Here Lady Guildford helped her to disrobe. When the jewelled coif was taken from her head, she shook her golden curls about her shoulders, and the robe of cloth of silver fell at her feet; she looked so young and desolate that Lady Guildford had to turn away to hide her emotion.

"So it is to be tomorrow," said Mary.

"You did not think it could be very long delayed?"

"But tomorrow . . . it seems so near! Oh, Guildford, what can happen between now and tomorrow?"

"You can get a good night's sleep, which is what you will need. You will be exhausted if you do not. You cannot hide anything from me, you know; and you have been sleeping badly since this journey began."

"I want to feel exhausted. I want to be so tired that when I lie down I shall sleep. You see, then I do not have to lie and think."

"All this honour for you and yet . . ."

"And yet I am not satisfied. No, I am not. I am most dissatisfied, Guildford. How much do all these jewels cost . . . all this feasting . . . all these ceremonies? They are extravagant, are they not? And they are all to honour me, perforce to give me pleasure. Yet how happy I could have been with none of them. What I asked would have cost them so little. Guildford, it makes me laugh."

"No, no, my dearest. Be calm. We are here, and tomorrow you will marry the King. He seemed to be so kindly, and he loves you already."

"He loves this face, this body, because it is young and he is old. Yet what does he know of me, Guildford? If he could look into my heart he would hate me, for I . . ."

Lady Guildford had put her hand over Mary's lips.

"Hush! You do not know who listens."

Mary laughed bitterly. "I am guilty of treason," she whispered. "Treason to the King of France. What then? Shall I be thrown into a dungeon? Let it be. I'd as lief find myself in one of his dungeons as in his bed."

She covered her face with her hands.

"Oh Guildford, I had hoped . . . I had never thought it would come to this. How can I bear it? You understand, do you not? There is Charles in England, you see, and here am I in France."

"Others have borne it before you, my dearest."

"Others have not loved Charles. If I had never seen him, if I had never known him . . . then perhaps it would have been easier to face this. But I have seen him. I love him, Guildford, and tomorrow night . . ."

"Hush, my lady. Hush!"

"Hush! Hush!" cried Mary. "That is all you can say? How can I expect comfort from you! What do you know of love? If you understood, you would find some way of helping me. I hate everyone and everything that keeps me from Charles. I should be going to *him* tomorrow. Do you not understand? Are you so blind, so deaf, so stupid, that you cannot comprehend one little bit of what it means to love as I love him . . . and to be given to this old man?"

"Come to bed. You need your strength for the morrow."

"My strength." She was laughing again, wildly, alarmingly. "I need my strength to face . . . that. You are right, Guildford."

"Come, say your prayers. You should be asleep by now."

"I'll say my prayers, Guildford. And do you know for what I pray? I pray for a miracle which will prevent my having to go through that ceremony tomorrow, or when I have gone through it, will prevent my being with him through the night. That is what I shall pray for, Guildford. Now you are looking shocked . . . frightened too. I am weary of pretense and subterfuge. Guildford, you fool, do not pretend you do not know what I pray for is to be made a widow."

It was Lady Guildford's turn to cover her face with her hands, to stop up her ears, suddenly to run to the door to make sure none lurked outside, to ask herself in desperation if ever a woman had undertaken such a delicate and dangerous task as conducting this Princess to her husband.

Her terror sobered Mary.

"Be still, Guildford," she said; "it would seem it is I who must care for you. Come, help me to my bed. I am fainting with weariness."

"It is for this reason that you talk so wildly. You are over-wrought. It has been such a long day."

"Stop talking nonsense. I am not weary of the saddle, or the litter. I am weary of my fate. That is very different, Guildford. It is not physical weariness that exhausts me. I love and I hate and so fiercely do I both love and hate that I am weary. Come to bed."

"And to sleep, my love."

She lay in the bed, and Lady Guildford drew the coverlet over her. She herself would sleep in the same chamber. She was glad that she had dismissed the other attendants; it would have been dangerous for any of them to have witnessed such a scene. Fortunately she, who knew her Princess so well, had seen that coming; that was why she had dismissed them.

Poor sad little Princess — jewels without price were hers; lavish entertainments had been devised in her honour; few could have been feted as she was; but few could have been more unhappy than she was that night. Yet a simple ceremony in an English church, with no jewels, no brilliant company, no crown, could have made her the happiest woman in the world, providing the right man had shared that ceremony with her.

But she asks the impossible, mused Lady Guildford, which was characteristic of her. She knew that Mary had gone on believing — in the face of circumstances — that this marriage would not take place; that a miracle would happen and that the man who stood beside her and spoke his marriage vows would be Charles Brandon.

Mary had preserved a childlike faith in her destiny; she knew what she wanted; and Lady Guildford was aware that when she achieved it she would be content. But how could she achieve the impossible? How could a royal Princess hope to marry the man of her choice when he was not of royal blood?

And because Mary had believed it possible, because she was capable of enjoying great happiness and knew so unswervingly what she wanted, tomorrow's wedding would be all the more tragic.

Lady Guildford lay in her bed at the foot of the Princess's, thinking of these things.

And when she rose to take a look at her charge who lay very still, she saw that she was asleep and that there was a solitary tear on her cheek.

Poor sad little Princess, thought Lady Guildford, so tragically sad, on this night before her wedding.

She was composed on the morrow. She had awakened to the melancholy knowledge that no miracle could happen now; and because she was a princess she must do her duty.

Lady Guildford was greatly relieved by her demeanor; she had had alarming dreams during the night that the Princess stubbornly refused to go through with the ceremony. Now here was the girl, subdued but resigned; and so young and lovely that sorrow had not set its mark on her; it merely seemed to change her personality, and as the King of France had never seen the gay young girl who had lived at her brother's Court he would not marvel at the difference in this quiet young beauty who was preparing to take her vows with him.

In spite of her sadness, rarely had Mary looked as beautiful as she did in her wedding gown, which was cut in the French fashion and made of cloth of gold edged with ermine. Diamonds had been chosen to decorate it and she seemed ablaze with their fire and sparkle. Her long golden curls had been released from restriction and hung about her shoulders reaching past her waist, and on her head was a coronet made entirely of jewels.

Her attendants who clustered around her, themselves splendidly clad, could not take their eyes from her. Only Mary herself, when she was implored to look at her reflection, did so with blank indifference.

"The time has come," said Lady Guildford apprehensively, scarcely daring to look at Mary lest she saw the resentment flaring up again.

But Mary only said quietly: "Then we should go."

From her apartments she walked to the temporary gallery where her white palfrey was waiting for her; and with it were the Duke of Norfolk and the Marquis of Dorset.

She mounted the palfrey and Norfolk and Dorset walked, one on each side of her, as she rode along the gallery to the door of the Hôtel de la Gruthuse. There she dismounted and was led into the hôtel by the two English noblemen.

The ceremony was to take place in the great hall of the Hôtel de la Gruthuse, an impressive chamber made even more so for this occasion. Tapestries had been hung on the walls and the hangings were of cloth of gold; costly furniture had been brought in for the ceremony; and there was a lovely light which came from the coloured windows on which were depicted the exploits of the town's patron saint, Wulfran.

Slowly Mary made her way across the mosaic floor to where Louis awaited her. He looked well; there was a faint colour in his face which was unusual with him, and her first thought was: He will live for years.

Then she was ashamed of the thought, for he was smiling so kindly and she was aware that he had great tenderness for her.

The Cardinal de Brie was waiting to perform the ceremony and two brilliantly attired French nobles advanced with the royal canopy, which they proceeded to hold over Louis and his bride. One of these was the Duc d'Alençon, and the other was François the Dauphin.

The vows were made; Louis had put the nuptial ring on her finger and the nuptial kiss on her lips. She was now his wife and Queen of France.

It was time to celebrate Mass and make their offering, but the King and Queen could not do this last in person; and it was the duty of the first nobleman of the land and the first lady — next to the King and Mary — to perform this on their behalf.

François made the King's offering. Mary watched him on his knees, and she felt a faint pleasure that he was there because he seemed like a friend. Then her attention was drawn to the lady who made the offering on her behalf — a pale woman, who limped a little and appeared to be slightly deformed. Surely not the Dauphin's wife! The woman rose, in somewhat ungainly fashion, and as she did so she looked at the new Queen of France. It was not exactly hatred that Mary saw in that face; it was too mild for that. Was it resentment?

Doubtless, thought Mary, married to that gay young man she has cause to be resentful. It is unlikely that he is a faithful husband. But that was no reason why she should resent Mary.

Mary had too many anxieties of her own to consider for very long those of Claude, Princess of France and wife of the Dauphin.

The sounds of trumpets rang through the halls of Hôtel de la Gruthuse. The solemnity was over; and the King was now ready to lead his bride to the banquet.

He took her hand gently, almost as though he believed she was a precious piece of porcelain that would break with rough handling. Seated beside him at the centre table she partook very moderately of the food which was offered, and the King was concerned about her lack of appetite.

It was clear to all those present that the King was delighted with his bride. They had not for years seen him looking so young or so full of vigour.

There was the long day to live through, for the marriage had been performed at nine in the morning; and in accordance with the etiquette of France Mary retired after the banquet to apartments which had been prepared for her personal use, and there she entertained the Princesses of France, and ladies of the nobility.

Now she had an opportunity of making closer acquaintance with Claude and her young sister, Renée. The latter was pleasant enough and inclined to be excited by all the pageantry which had taken place; but the melancholy of Claude, which held a hint of reproach, was disturbing.

"It is my Father's command," Claude told her, "That I discover your needs and supply them."

"There is nothing I need ask for," Mary replied, "though I thank you."

And in that moment Mary forgot her own troubles because she was suddenly overwhelmed with pity for this poor, plain girl, who was married to that extremely attractive young man.

She smiled, wanting to show this girl that she was ready to be friendly with her, and laying a hand on her arm said: "I am your mother now. It may be that we can be friends."

Claude drew back as though she had been struck. "My mother is dead. It is not a year since they laid her in her tomb. No one else could ever take her place."

She limped away, ugly colour in her face and neck.

Someone else was at Mary's side — a very beautiful, composed young woman a few years older than herself.

"Madame Claude still mourns her mother," said the newcomer in a low and charming voice. "I also have tried to comfort her. At this stage it is useless."

"They were devoted to one another?"

"They were. And the Princess is so like her mother in many ways. Queen Anne thought it was sinful to enjoy life, and brought her daughter up to think the same. A sad philosophy, do you not think so, Madame; and an unwise one?"

"I agree."

"I knew you would. My brother has already told me of your conversations during the journey from Abbeville."

"Your brother?"

"The Dauphin, Madame. I am Marguerite de Valois, Duchesse d'Alencon. You will remember my brother."

Mary smiled. "Having met him I could never forget him."

"There is no one like him at the Court . . . nor anywhere in the world, I am sure. François is unique."

"I can see that you are proud of him."

"Can you marvel at that? Madame, may I present you to my mother?"

Mary was looking into a pair of lively blue eyes, and meeting the intent gaze of a short but vivacious woman.

"The Comtesse d'Angoulême," Marguerite explained.

"I pray you rise," said Mary warmly. "It gives me great pleasure to greet you. I have already made the acquaintance of your son, the Dauphin, and now Madame la Duchesse d'Alençon."

"We are honoured by your notice," Louise replied, and her bright smile belied her inner feelings. She felt sick with apprehension. This girl was beautiful beyond the glowing reports she had heard. If ever a woman could have an aphrodisiacal effect on Louis's flagging desires it must be this one. Perfectly formed in every way, healthy, and with a look about her which suggested she would be fertile. At least that was how it seemed to Louise's imagination.

She had seen her from a distance at the wedding ceremony, and of course she had looked exquisite. But who wouldn't, Louise had asked herself, covered in diamonds and cloth of gold? Even Claude had looked tolerably handsome on her wedding day. But seen close at hand, that fine glowing skin which proclaimed good health, those clear eyes, added to her anxiety.

Marguerite, being fully aware of her mother's chagrin, told her that the Queen had been enlivened with the company of François during her journey and Louise's smile illuminated her face as she said: "He is at the right hand of the King. So occupied that his mother sees little of him nowadays. Not that I do not hear his name constantly mentioned. Who can be surprised at that?"

"I am sure," said Mary, "that he is successful in all he undertakes."

Other ladies were waiting to be presented to the Queen, and Marguerite and her mother moved away.

Keeping her hand on her mother's elbow, Marguerite piloted Louise out of the main *salon* into a small room. There she shut the door and said: "Maman, I fear you may betray your feelings."

"That girl!" said Louise.

Marguerite looked over her shoulder significantly.

“That girl!” whispered Louise. “She is so young . . . and she’s beautiful too. They say Louis can scarce wait for the night and the blessing of the nuptial bed. How can you look so calm, Marguerite, when this very night our hopes may be blighted?”

“Louis is old, Maman.”

“He has taken a new lease on life.”

“It only appears so. The flush on his cheeks is not good health but excitement.” Marguerite took her mother by the shoulder, drew her close and whispered in her ear: “And excitement could be harmful to him.”

“He could die tonight . . . and the damage could already be done.”

“Dearest Maman, we have to be careful, not only of our words but our looks. Infatuated as Louis is becoming, he could be very susceptible to our slightest mood.”

“Oh, Marguerite,” sighed Louise, “you who have suffered so much with me must understand my feelings this night.”

“I understand absolutely, Maman, and my feelings are yours. We must pray and hope . . .”

“And watch. Watch the girl, Marguerite, and see that, when we cannot do so, those whom we can trust carry out our wishes. An alarming thought has occurred to me.”

“Yes, Maman?”

“Louis, as you suggest, may be incapable of getting her with child . . .”

Marguerite’s eyes were full of warning.

Louise hissed: "She is very desirable, that girl. She seems full of dignity but there is a smoldering fire within her."

"I noticed it," said Marguerite.

"So if Louis should fail, there might be others to . . . to . . ."

Marguerite closed her eyes; there was an expression of fear in her face, and Louise's own fears were but increased to know that Marguerite shared them.

The King might be too old to provide the heir to France; but what if the young Queen took a lover, and what if he were young enough . . . virile enough . . . ? A bastard could inherit the throne, and none be sure that he was a bastard. A bastard to appear at the eleventh hour and oust François from what should be his!

It was unbearable, the greatest of tragedies.

I never suffered quite so much through all the years of anxiety as I do at this moment, thought Louise.

The beautiful young Mary Tudor could cause her greater concern than Anne of Brittany had ever done.

The nuptial bed was being blessed, and the night which Mary had dreaded for so long was about to begin. She listened to the words of benediction. They were sprinkling holy water on the bed while they prayed that she might be fruitful.

She looked at the great bed with its canopy of velvet embroidered with the gold lilies of France. The silken counterpane had been drawn back; her women had undressed her and she was naked beneath the robe which enveloped her.

She thought of that other ceremony when she had lain on a couch and the Duc de Longueville had removed his boot and touched her bare leg with his bare foot. This would be very different.

Louis in his disarray looked older than he had at the marriage ceremony; she could see how swollen his neck was; it hung over the collar of his gown; there was still a faint colour in his cheeks and his eyes were bright as they met hers.

In what a different mood from hers did he approach this nuptial bed; it was clear that he was growing impatient of the ceremony while she wished it would go on and on through the night. He was longing for that moment which she so dreaded.

And now it had come. They were in the bed together and one by one those who assisted at the ceremony departed from the room.

Mary lay in the nuptial bed. It was over, and it had been less horrifying than she had believed it would be. Louis was no monster. He had begged her not to be afraid of him; he told her that she enchanted him; that he had never seen anyone as beautiful; he loved her dearly already and it would be his pleasure to show her how deep went his devotion.

He must seem very old to her; he understood that. It was inevitable since she was so young. He could imagine how sad she must be to leave her brother's Court and come to a strange land to be with strangers. But she would find here the best friend she had ever had in her life — her husband.

It was a comfort to discover that he was so kind. Had she been of a meek nature she would have been very grateful to him, and could have given him some mild affection. But Charles's image never left her. She longed for Charles; she was capable of strong passion, but only for Charles. He did not know, this kind old man, how he was making her suffer. If he would be good to her there was only one course of action he could take: Leave her alone and then, as soon as possible, die and make her a widow.

But this was something which even she, who sometimes thought that she could endure her lot better if she could be perfectly honest and say what was in her mind, could not betray. She must be submissive; she must pretend that she was shocked by the consummation of the marriage because of her innocence and not because she longed for another man.

She could rejoice at the King's infirmity when he lay beside her, exhausted.

"You are delightful," he told her. "Would that you had come to me twenty years ago."

That was an apology for his weakness. He need not have apologised. She loved his weakness.

And now he slept, and she lay wide awake, saying to herself: If it does not last too long, I can bear it.

CHAPTER SEVEN

The Queen and the Dauphin

The next morning when the King had risen and she was with her attendants, she thought of Charles and wondered if he were thinking of her this day. Then it seemed to her that she was defiled, and a great melancholy came over her.

She whispered to Lady Guildford: "Send the others away."

Lady Guildford did so, and when they had gone she took Mary into her arms and rocked her to and fro as she used to when Mary was a child and had needed comfort.

"My dearest Princess," she murmured. "Tell Guildford."

"Guildford, it is over."

"And you are very unhappy?"

Mary nodded. "Because of Charles."

"Tush!" said Lady Guildford. "And do you think he is weeping at this moment because of you?"

"He is very sad because of me, Guildford."

"But the King was kind?"

"He is kind. If he were not I should doubtless kill him. And he is very old. He was soon asleep. But *I* did not sleep, Guildford. I lay there, thinking . . ."

"And you are reconciled. I can sense it, dearest. I know you so well."

"It won't last, Guildford. That's why."

Then suddenly she threw her arms about Lady Guildford's neck. It was the first time she had given way to such tempestuous weeping.

The King came in. He saw the tears; he saw the embrace.

Mary started to her feet, while Guildford rose and curtsied deeply.

Louis was smiling. "Leave us," he said to Lady Guildford; and she went.

Mary, her cheeks wet, stood waiting for her husband to ask the reason for her tears; but he did not. She was to learn that it was a point of etiquette at the French Court to avoid seeing or talking of anything that might prove embarrassing.

"My love," said Louis, taking her hands and kissing them, "I came to give you this."

He took from his pocket a ring in which was set one of the largest rubies Mary had ever seen.

"Thank you," she said. "It is very beautiful."

"Let us try it on your finger."

He put it on and held her hand admiringly.

"You do not like jewels, my little Queen?" he asked.

"They are very beautiful," she answered.

"You must learn to love jewels. They become you so."

He took her cheek between his fingers and pinched it affectionately.

"They are planning a ball for this day," he told her. "I shall enjoy seeing you dance. Why, you are as light as thistledown and as lovely as a spring day."

The morning was over when Lady Guildford was able to visit her mistress. Mary took one look at her faithful governess and was alarmed, for Lady Guildford was no longer her calm self; her eyes were wild and there was a hot flush in her cheeks.

She embraced Mary as though she would never let her go.

"Guildford, what is it?" demanded Mary.

"It is goodbye, my dearest."

"Goodbye!"

"I have had orders to leave for England at once."

"But you cannot. I need you here."

"The King does not think so."

"You mean he has told you that you must go!"

"Not the King in person. But his wishes have been made clear to me."

"I don't understand."

"He feels I have too much influence over you. He wants you to become wholly French. He saw you with me this morning, dearest. He did not like to see you crying in my arms."

"I must speak to him. I won't let you go."

"He has made up his mind."

"But we have been together since . . ."

"Since you were a baby, yes. But you are in no need of a governess now. You are a queen and a wife."

"I won't have it, Guildford. I tell you I won't."

Mary hurried to the door.

"Where are you going?" Lady Guildford cried in alarm.

Mary turned, her eyes blazing. "I am going to tell the King that I shall choose my own attendants."

"Dearest, I beg of you, have a care. You will do no good to either of us."

Mary ignored her and, with blazing eyes and flaming cheeks, ran from the room.

It seemed accidental, but it might not have been, that Marguerite, Duchesse d'Alençon, was in the anteroom through which Mary had to pass on her way to the King's apartments.

"Madame," cried Marguerite in alarm, "something is amiss?"

"My attendants are being dismissed," cried Mary. "Lady Guildford, who has been with me all my life, is being sent back to England."

"I am so sorry."

Mary would have passed on, but Marguerite said: "Madame, I should like to help you if you would allow me."

"Help me?"

"Yes. You are going to the King, are you not?"

"Certainly I am going to the King."

"I beg of you, do not act rashly. The King appears to be mild but, when he has made up his mind, is very determined."

"If he has made up his mind on this matter he must unmake it."

"Madame, forgive me, but you have little experience of our Court. The King has already given orders that your retinue is to be reduced. If you asked him to allow your attendants to remain, he could not grant your wishes because he has already given this order. It would grieve all your friends that your first request to the King should be refused — but refused it would be."

"I have found the King kind," retorted Mary; and she went on her way.

The Dauphin and the Duc d'Alençon were with the King when Mary burst in on them. The three men looked surprised, for it seemed that the Queen was ignorant of French etiquette, since she came in thus, unannounced.

François was secretly amused and delighted to see her, as he told himself he always would be. She would have to learn the importance of etiquette at the French Court; doubtless in her brother's, gracious manners were not of such importance as they were here.

Louis came to her and gently took her hand.

"I want Lady Guildford to remain with me," she said.

"Lady Guildford?" Louis repeated gently.

"She has been my governess since I was a child. And now she is being sent away, and she tells me that others are going back to England with her."

"Ah, yes," said Louis quietly. "I live simply here, and you must perforce do the same. You will not need all the attendants and servants whom you have brought with you. So they must go back to their native land."

"But . . ."

She looked from Louis to François, who had raised his eyebrows and was shaking his head almost imperceptibly.

She wanted to tell them that she cared nothing for their French manners. She was angry; she was desolate and she would let them know it.

"The arrangements have been made," went on Louis, and although he smiled and spoke with the utmost gentleness she saw the purpose in his eyes.

"I was not consulted," Mary complained.

"My dear little Queen, we did not wish to disturb you with such matters, and it is my custom to decide who shall remain at my Court."

"Lady Guildford . . ."

The King said to François, "Have my daughter and your sister brought here. They will look after the Queen and show her that she has new friends to replace those who are going."

"But I want . . ."

"You want these ladies to be brought to you? It shall be done."

Mary suddenly felt gauche, young and helpless. She saw that Marguerite d'Alençon was right. She had been foolish to rush in in this way. She should have waited until she was alone with the King and then tried to persuade him. Now she had spoiled everything.

François, who had returned to the King's side, was giving her a look which was both tender and a warning;

and she warmed toward him because she believed that he was trying to help her.

Almost immediately the page was announcing the arrival of Claude and Marguerite. Claude looked sullen, Marguerite lovely and eager.

"My dears," said Louis affably, "the Queen is feeling a little unhappy because some of her English friends have to leave for their home. I want you two to look after her, to take their places."

"Yes, Sire," said Marguerite, while Claude mumbled inaudibly.

"Go with the Queen back to her apartments and explain to her how useful you intend to make yourselves."

Feeling foolish and frustrated, Mary left the King's presence with her two new attendants.

Louis's delight in his bride grew stronger, and, because he wished to compensate her for the loss of her English attendants, the next day he gave her a tablet covered in diamonds and a pendant of pearls.

Mary accepted the gifts with thanks but inward indifference. She had written at once to Henry and Wolsey telling them of her indignation over the dismissal of her friends, and imploring them to take up this matter with her husband.

But as those days passed she became slightly reconciled for two reasons. The first was that Marguerite had become her friend, and Marguerite was, in truth, much more interesting and entertaining than dear old Lady Guildford could ever be.

Marguerite's mother, Louise of Savoy, was also making herself agreeable and, as the Dauphin sought every opportunity of being in her company, she found that this fascinating trio were helping her through the difficult days.

The other reason was that the excitement of his wedding and the days and nights which followed had been too much for Louis. His gout had become worse and was alarming his doctors.

Louis called Mary to his couch one day and, when they were alone together, he took her hand and smiled at her regretfully.

"My dear," he said, "I greatly desire to see you crowned and make your ceremonial entry into Paris, but as you see, I am confined to my couch, and my physicians tell me that it would be unwise for me to leave Abbeville for some days."

"I fancy," said Mary, "that you have been departing from your quiet life during the last days and this is not good for you. You must rest more."

"But, my dear, I want you to know how pleased we all are to have you with us, and it is only fitting that we should make merry. It is my wish that the balls and banquets should go on."

"But you should rest more," said Mary. "I am your wife and I shall insist that you do."

He was touched that she could be so concerned for his health, and Mary was quick to seize the advantage. She took on the role of a charming little nurse and gave orders in the King's apartment.

"This afternoon you shall rest on your couch and I will sit beside you and talk to you if you wish. Or I can be silent."

What an enchanting creature she was — so young and yet willing to forgo the pleasures of the hunt or the banquet for the sake of her husband.

He told her this, taking her hand and kissing it as he did so; and when she sensed that he was inclined to become amorous she raised a finger and put on a stern expression.

"*I* am going to command you in this matter. You are to rest; and there must be no excitements."

He allowed her to take charge. He found it very pleasant to lie back on his couch, the delightful creature beside him, listening to her quaint accent which he found quite fascinating, while she occasionally soothed his hot brow with sweet unguents; and although she allowed him to stroke her arms she was very insistent that caresses should stop there.

"I have to consider what is good for you," said the charming child.

It was so comforting to realise that she was young and inexperienced, that she accepted his shortcomings as a lover; indeed insisted that he should not exert himself.

Each day he gave her a jewel. He had put several trinkets aside for her, and he doled them out one by one — partly because he was a man who always liked to get the utmost return for what he paid out; partly because she expressed as much pleasure over one small jewel as she would have done over twenty.

He contemplated that rarely had he been so contented in his life, and his greatest regret was that when he had married Mary Tudor he was fifty-two instead of twenty-two.

He did not wish, of course, to allow life to become dull for her. He had dismissed her English attendants because he believed they had too much influence over her, and when she was upset he did not want her to cry in the arms of Lady Guildford but in his. That little disturbance was now settled, thanks to Marguerite de Valois who was as scintillating a companion as anyone could have.

He sent for the Dauphin. François came at once to his couch. Louis was not so pleased with François; there was something sly about the Big Boy. Outwardly he was too gay, and he could not be feeling gay. If Mary gave birth to a son — not an impossibility — that would be the end of François's hopes; so what had he to be gay about?

Definitely the boy was sly. Now he was doubtless amused because an old man had become too excited over his marriage to a beautiful young girl and consequently had to take to his couch for a few days.

"My boy," he said, "I have decided to delay leaving Abbeville for a few days. The gout is troubling me and my physicians say I need rest. I cannot therefore escort the Queen as I would like to, and I do not wish that all the balls and banquets should be cancelled. As the nobleman of highest rank you should take my place at the Queen's side."

"Yes, Sire."

"The Queen understands. In fact she is most charmingly solicitous of my health. I shall be present at the festivities, but you must lead the Queen in the dance and talk to her when I am weary."

François bowed his head. It was duty he could contemplate with the utmost pleasure.

François was in love. This was not an infrequent occurrence, but in this case the situation held a certain piquancy.

He loved her golden hair and her perfectly formed body; he loved her English accent; but what appealed to him more than anything was that latent fire which he sensed within her. When aroused she would be a passionate creature, and François longed to be the one to arouse her. The fact that she was recently married to the King brought such an element of danger into the relationship as to make it absolutely irresistible to one of François's temperament.

He had received no greater blow to his hopes than when the King had married; he had even felt — rare for him — depressed. He needed some glorious adventure to give life a new zest. A love affair in itself would not have been enough — he had had so many of them already; but a love affair with the recently married Queen, which could place them both in jeopardy, would give life the excitement which at this time he greatly needed.

He was constantly at the Queen's side. A little touch of the hand, a burning intensity in the eyes, the caressing note in his voice, the words which were full of a hidden meaning . . . surely they were enough to tell Mary the state of his feelings?

She pretended not to understand these indications; and he was sure it *was* pretense. She was not as innocent as she would have them all believe. And the fact that he was not quite sure what was going on behind those beautiful blue eyes only added to her fascination.

He became angry if anyone else attempted to dance with her; he made it clear that, while the King was indisposed, it was the task and privilege of the Dauphin to entertain the Queen.

Mary was fully aware of his feelings, and she was grateful to him as she was finding these days at Abbeville so wretched on account of her longing for Charles; François's attempt to involve her in an intrigue enlivened the days, particularly as she had no intention of becoming involved, while at the same time it was amusing not to let him know this.

She enjoyed showing wide-eyed innocence, as though his innuendoes passed over her head. She did not for one moment believe that the Dauphin's feelings were deeply involved. They both needed excitement at this time; she because she was an unwilling bride; he because the marriage which had proved such a tragedy for her was one for him also. She could see that ambition was strong behind the insouciant manner and witty frivolity. François wanted to take revenge on Louis for marrying again, by making love to Louis's wife.

Thus she was being caught up in an intrigue which amused her; and desperately she needed to be amused.

Louise sought out Marguerite. Louise was very apprehensive, and Marguerite mildly so.

"Marguerite," cried Louise, "François is constantly with the Queen."

"The King being indisposed, it is the place of the Dauphin to look after her."

"I know my son well. He is becoming enamoured of that English girl."

"She is very beautiful," Marguerite agreed.

"Have you considered what might come out of this?"

"Thoughts have entered my head."

"Louis will never get a healthy son. But if those two were lovers . . . why, Marguerite, can you doubt what the result would be? It would be inevitable. And she would pass it off as Louis's."

"You mean your grandson and my nephew would take the throne from his father."

"Unacknowledged! It would be a tragedy."

"Maman, this is wildest imagination."

"It could be fact. Admit it, Marguerite. François, bless him, is virile, as he should be. He is in love with the Queen, and can you doubt the Queen's feelings for him! She pretends that she is unmoved. My dear Marguerite, could any woman remain unmoved by François? I tell you our beloved is in danger of losing the throne . . . not through Louis — poor impotent old man . . . but by his own actions."

"Our François is no fool, Maman."

"He is brilliant, I grant you. His wit sparkles and makes the Court a gay place. But his emotions are strong, as is natural in all young men. Let the Queen succumb . . . and how can she help it? . . . and we shall be hearing that she is pregnant. Louis, the old fool, will be beside himself with glee and within a year there will be a little dauphin in the royal nurseries. I tell you we are in danger . . . the utmost danger."

"What do you propose to do, Maman? Point out the danger to François?"

"François has realised the danger. He must have. Do you remember how he always courted danger? He is daring — and I would not have him otherwise — but daring in this case could be fatal to his future. I remember the time when as a boy he let a bull loose in the courtyards of Amboise. He himself slew it . . . but he was risking his life and knew it. He loves risks. They are the salt of life to him. And now he is ready to take this one. I see it in his face. I know my François."

"Maman, should we speak to him?"

"I am uncertain, daughter. He is no longer a boy. I know that he likes to make his own decisions and, although he would listen to us courteously as he always has, yet by pointing out the hazards we might increase the enchantment."

"We must watch this affair closely," Marguerite murmured.

"And you are near the Queen. You must take an opportunity of pointing out the dangers to her."

Marguerite was thoughtful. But there was no denying that she was as anxious as her mother.

* * *

Mary had been riding and as she went up to her apartment Marguerite intimated that she wished to be alone with her, and the other attendants were dismissed.

"My poor little sister-in-law is not very happy," Marguerite began. "It is sad for her that she is so different from my brother. They are not well matched. Do you agree, Madame?"

"They are not alike in temperament, but I have heard that people of different types are often attracted to each other."

"Poor Claude! I fear it is inevitable that she should be a little jealous."

"Is she of a jealous nature?"

"I believe that, like most of us, if she thought she had reason to be jealous, she could be so."

"And has she reason?"

"Having recently acquired such a beautiful stepmother, only a year or so older than herself, must necessarily accentuate her own ungainliness, particularly when . . ." Marguerite hesitated and Mary raised her eyebrows enquiringly, ". . . when her husband seems so very much aware of that stepmother's charm."

"You are telling me that Claude is jealous . . . on my account!" Mary's surprise was clearly feigned, and she meant Marguerite to know that it was.

"François is so clearly attracted to you."

"Then should you not speak to *him*? I can assure you that *I* have done nothing to make Claude jealous."

"He is impetuous and reckless."

"I see." Mary turned her clear gaze on Marguerite. "I certainly think you should warn him in that case."

Marguerite laid a hand on Mary's arm. "If the King were to be aware of this . . ."

Mary said coolly: "I can set your mind at rest. There is nothing in the matter that I am aware of which could give the King the slightest cause for displeasure."

She was reminding Marguerite that she was the Queen of France, and that she had no wish to discuss the matter further; but secretly she was amused because she had learned a great deal about the relationships of that family. Louise of Savoy had been tortured all through her life by fear that a son of Louis might follow his father to the throne. And now they had actually gone so far as to believe that she might be François's lover and have a child which she would pretend was Louis's.

In her present position it was good to have something to laugh at. François greatly desired the crown and yet the need to satisfy his sexual impulses was so demanding that he was prepared to risk the first in order to assuage the second! And the devoted mother and sister were fearfully looking on.

She might have said to them: François shall never be my lover. There is only one who could be that, and he is in England.

But the knowledge of intrigue around her was helping her through these melancholy days.

The royal party had been at Abbeville for almost a fortnight, and Louis was showing signs of recovery.

Mary, still acting as nurse, watched him uneasily as she sat by his couch.

He took her hand and said: "Thanks to our ministrations I am beginning to recover."

"You must be very careful not to exert yourself too much," said Mary quickly.

"Have no fear. I think we shall be able to leave here within a few days, and our first stop shall be at Beauvais. I have a surprise for you."

Mary opened her eyes wide in an endeavour to express excitement. A ruby? A diamond? She knew what his surprises usually were and she was beginning to dread them because she must pretend to show enthusiasm which she could not possibly feel.

"We shall have a joust to celebrate your coronation, and I thought that it would please you if we made it a contest between the country of your birth and your adopted one. It would be a symbol of the friendship between us. The people will remember that not long ago we were fighting each other in a real war. Now we will have a mock-battle and see who is the more skilled in the joust."

"There are few Englishmen here who would be able to give a good account of themselves."

"I know, and this must be a fair contest. So I thought it would please you if I wrote to your brother and asked him to send over some of his most skilled knights to challenge ours. This I have done."

For a moment she found speech impossible. She was asking herself: Whom will Henry send?

"I can see that the thought of this match between the two countries pleases you more than jewels. I am content."

"You are very good to me," murmured Mary.

He laughed. "Remember though that you are a Frenchwoman now. You must support *us*, you know."

"We shall see," she answered.

They left Abbeville for Beauvais and as she rode beside the King, acknowledging the cheers of the people, Mary was asking herself the question: Is it possible? Would Henry send Charles?

Louis had said that he was asking that the most skilled men might be sent. In that case Charles *must* come. For the honour of England he must come. Henry would see to that. Yet, knowing the state of her feelings, would Henry consider it unwise to send Charles?

Rarely had she looked so beautiful as she did then; there was a suppressed excitement in her eyes which did not pass unnoticed by Marguerite.

The Queen is in love? she thought. Has it gone as far as that? Oh, François, beloved, have a care.

It was a golden October day when they rode into Beauvais; and as they reached the mansion where they were to stay for the night, Mary was alert for a sign of the English party.

A banquet had been prepared in the great hall, and she had taken her place at the centre table, when the news was brought to the King that the English knights had arrived.

"Have them brought in at once," was Louis's answer. "We must give them a good welcome, for they come on behalf of my good brother, the King of England."

And so the doors were thrown open and as the Englishmen came in, Mary caught her breath with wonder; for they were led — as was only natural that they should be — by Charles Brandon. And there he was coming to the centre table, his eyes on the King, betraying only by a twitch of a muscle that all his thoughts were for the young woman who sat silently there, her cheeks aflame, her eyes sparkling as no one in France had seen them sparkle yet.

She must see him. Who would help her now? If only Lady Guildford were with her! But Louis had artfully removed all her English attendants except little Anne Boleyn who, he considered, was too young to influence her.

She dared confide in no one. Marguerite was a friend — up to a point — but only when by being so she could do no harm to her brother. And if she told Marguerite that the man she loved was in Beauvais and she must have an interview with him alone, Marguerite would immediately suspect that Charles might take the place of François in that wild drama she and her mother had conjured up. Therefore, Marguerite would never help her arrange a meeting with her lover — in fact, for the sake of François, might even betray her to Louis.

Perhaps it was natural that she should wish to receive the party from her brother's Court. If they came to her she could flash a message to Charles who would be ready for it.

This was what she did when, headed by Charles, the Englishmen came to her apartment. Of course her French attendants were present. Nevertheless she must do the best she could.

How happy she was to see him kneeling before her, taking her hand in his, putting his lips to it. She was trying to communicate all her feelings to him, and she knew by the pressure of his hand that he understood.

"It pleases me to see you here," she said.

He told her that her brother sent her affectionate messages and there were letters which he would bring to her. "Yes . . . yes," she answered.

She must receive the others; she must murmur platitudes to them. She must tell them how excited she was at the thought of the coming joust, and she hoped they would conduct themselves with honour for England.

Oh Charles, she thought, stay near me.

He understood. He was by her side. He said quietly: "Are you happy?"

"What do you think?" Her voice was sharp and bitter.

"You are more beautiful than ever."

"I must see you alone," she said. Then added hastily: "Come back in five minutes' time after the party have gone. I will endeavour to be alone except for young Anne Boleyn."

He bowed his head and she turned away lest Norfolk, who was with the party, should be suspicious.

Now she was impatient for them to be gone, and afraid that if they lingered much longer the King would come to her apartments.

But at last they went, and she dismissed her attendants, saying that she was going to rest for an hour; and to avoid suspicion kept little Anne with her.

He came back, as they had arranged; and she commanded little Anne to sit on the stool near the door of the main apartment while she drew Charles into a small adjoining chamber. If anyone came to the door, Anne was to tell them her mistress was resting.

It was dangerous, but Mary was ready to take risks. An interview alone with Charles was worth anything she might be asked to pay for it.

They embraced hungrily.

"My love," said Charles, "I have lived it all with you."

"Oh, Charles!" She was half laughing, half crying, as she touched his face with her fingers. "I can't believe it, you see. I have to keep assuring myself that you are here."

He kissed her urgently.

"We must be careful," he said at length. "Did you notice Norfolk's watchful eyes? That fellow hates me."

"A curse on Norfolk."

"I agree, my dearest, but he could do us much harm."

"You mean he could tell Louis that I love you."

"He could have me sent back to England."

That sobered her. "Oh, Charles, we must be careful."

"I should not be here. At any moment we might be discovered."

"The little Boleyn will give the warning."

"That child would not protect us. Mary . . . Mary . . . what shall we do?"

"When Louis dies and I am free I shall marry where I wish. You know where that will be."

"But to talk of the King's death . . ."

"Is treason, and we should die for it. Then I should not have to spend any more nights in his bed."

"Hush, Mary. Was it . . . terrible?"

She shivered. "I lay awake all that first night thanking God and his saints that he was an old man. He apologised for his breathlessness, for his inability. I wanted to shout, 'Do not apologise to me, Louis. I want to sing Glory to God because of it.' "

"And so . . .?"

"Do not ask me to speak of it. But he has been ill since. Alas, he tells me he is getting rapidly better. It will begin again. But it won't be for long, Charles. I feel it won't be for long. I am certain of it, and that is why I can endure it, because, Charles, I have Henry's promise that when it is over I shall marry where it pleases me to do so."

"You grow too excited."

"Can I help that? The one I love is here and I am in his arms. Who would not be excited?"

"I must not stay. You may depend upon it we shall be watched. I don't trust Norfolk."

"But you are here . . . in France. Oh, this is the happiest day I have known since I came to this land. Stay near me, Charles."

"I shall as long as it is in my power. But, dearest, let us be cautious . . . for the sake of the future."

"The future, Charles. I live for it."

Once more they were in a close embrace. Then he slipped out of the small chamber into the main apartment where the little Boleyn sat, her great dark eyes filled with dreamy speculation.

The royal cavalcade was now journeying across Picardy toward the capital. Louis no longer suffered so acutely and could take pleasure in his bride. Mary's moods were variable. Sometimes she felt rebellious and there were occasions when she told herself that she could not endure her husband's embraces; at others she was resigned, for afterward the poor man always seemed so exhausted. Then Charles's presence in the party made her feel recklessly gay. Life was never dull because all the time she felt as though she were living on the edge of disaster, for with the man she loved so near, she believed she could not continue to control her feelings.

Those about her noticed the change in her. Her beauty had become more vital.

Marguerite, watching her closely, thought: There is a woman in love.

And because it was inconceivable to Marguerite that any woman could be indifferent to François, she naturally thought that Mary was in love with her brother.

François thought so too; and so did Louise. They all felt themselves to be on the verge of an inflammable situation, disastrous from the point of view of them all while it was yet irresistible to François.

Mary became more aware of those two women and, understanding the reason for their apprehension, an innate streak of mischief made her long to mislead them. After all *they* had first conceived the myth.

There was more than mischief in it; there was sound common sense, because presumably she had been unable to hide the fact that she was in love. No one could think it was with Louis, and they must not guess it was with Charles Brandon. Therefore they must believe it was with François.

Her manner toward the Dauphin was changing; she showed quite frankly how she delighted in his company.

The more nervous Louise and Marguerite became, the more hopeful was François.

And Mary was diverted enough to laugh secretly as she amused herself at their expense.

Louis would not be content until Mary was crowned Queen of France; and as he did not wish to enter Paris until she could do so as crowned Queen he was anxious for the ceremony to take place as soon as possible. He continued to present her almost daily with some jewel; and he told her that he hoped very much to regain his health so that he could be more like the husband she deserved.

She told him — fervently truthful — that she preferred him as he was; which he thought charmingly tactful. He discussed the coming celebrations with her, adding that he thought that tall Englishman would be a good match for the Dauphin.

"I look forward to see them in combat," he added; "I hear that man is something of a champion at your brother's Court."

"I believe the Duke of Suffolk to be second only to my brother in the joust."

Louis laughed. "A diplomat into the bargain, eh?"

Mary thought then that the French were often a little too subtle; perhaps that was why she enjoyed leading Marguerite and Louise a merry little dance.

"Now, my dear," said Louis, "I shall be forced to leave you at St Dennis for a few days, because I must go to Paris. There are matters of state to which I have to give my attention. Your coronation will take place here and then there will be your triumphant journey into the capital. The people of Paris are eagerly waiting to welcome you."

"I trust they will be pleased with me."

"They will love you as we all do. I have only one regret and that is that I must leave you."

Mary kissed him gently on the brow. She did not want him to see the relief which she feared might show in her face.

The King had gone on ahead to Paris, and the coronation was to take place in a few days.

François joined the Queen as she rode out with her attendants.

"It is the only way in which I can have a word with you in private," he complained.

"You deceive yourself. We are being watched now. Do you not know that we are always being watched?"

"What an evil fate is this? You come to marry the King of France, and I might so easily have been that King!"

"You are rash."

"Driven to it by your beauty."

"Do you forget that ears are straining at this moment to hear what you say to me?"

"Surely they do not need to strain. They must guess. What could I be expected to say to the most beautiful woman I have ever seen?"

"You might be expected to be a faithful husband and remember that I am the wife of your King."

"That would be asking too much of me."

"I do not think the King would be pleased if he knew that you speak such words to me."

"It is not my wish to please the King."

"François, you are very reckless."

"You shall discover that I can be more so."

"To what purpose?"

"When can I see you alone that I may explain to you?"

"I am listening now."

"This needs more than words. If you would come to an apartment I know . . ."

"I . . . come to an apartment! I do not think I have heard aright."

"Disguised of course. We should both be disguised. It can be done. It is always amusing to be incognito. Do you not agree?"

"I have had no experience of that."

"There are so many delightful experiences waiting for you."

"And you propose to be my tutor?"

"I should be the happiest man alive if I were that."

She laughed and slackened her pace so that she was close to those attendants who had fallen back.

François was disappointed, but he was certain he had made some progress. He had met opposition only once, and that was with poor simple little Françoise. The only woman who had ever refused him! But she was a virtuous woman; there had been no fire in Françoise.

How different was this lovely, vital girl.

Passion was strong in her; and he was certain that she was in love.

In the Cathedral of St Dennis, François, the Dauphin, took the hand of the Queen and led her to the altar. As she knelt on a cushion which had been put there for that purpose, from a quiet corner of the cathedral Louis watched her. He had not wanted the people to know that he was present, because this was her day and he had no wish to distract attention from her.

His eyes were a little misty as he watched her. Tears came easily in age as they had in extreme youth, and he was deeply moved by her beauty. She looked so young in her dazzling robes with that wonderful hair, which he loved to caress, falling about her shoulders. There could never have been a more beautiful Queen of France, and he would never cease to regret that she had come to him in the days of his infirmity.

Cardinal de Brie was anointing her, and she remained still as a statue while the sacred oil was poured on her head. Now the sceptre was being placed in her right hand, the rod of justice in her left, the ring on her finger. De Brie held the crown matrimonial over her head; it seemed too massive for that feminine fragility and Louis trusted it would not cause a headache.

The ceremony of crowning her Queen of France was almost over, and she was moving toward the chair of state on the left side of the high altar. It was the duty of the Dauphin to lead her to it; and she in her splendour, he in his elegance, must surely make all consider how well matched they were.

Poor François! Poor Mary! Fate could so easily have given them to each other. If I had died a few months ago, mused Louis, there would still have been a need to make an English marriage. If my poor Claude had not married François, and he had been free . . .

But it was not so. Life did not work out as smoothly as that. And now this beautiful young girl was his wife, and poor misshapen Claude was united with François.

Louis shrugged his shoulders. When one was old one realised that all glories, all sorrows, passed away in time. In time, yes. For time was always the victor.

They were singing Mass and François had taken his stand behind the chair of state that he might hold the heavy crown over the Queen's head to relieve her of its weight.

And afterward, to the sound of trumpets the party, accompanied by the leading noblemen and women of France, left the cathedral.

In the royal apartments Louis embraced his Queen.

"You are now truly Queen of France, my dear," he said. "And it gave me great pleasure to witness your coronation."

"It was an impressive ceremony, and I trust I did all that was expected of me."

"You acted with perfect composure as you always do."

She was momentarily moved because of his pride in her; and she was ashamed because of the many times she had wished him dead. She still did, but she was sorry that it had to be; and she had an impulse then to throw herself on to her knees before him and beg him to understand the motive behind her desires. She wanted to explain: It is not you personally, Louis, for you have shown me nothing but goodness; it is simply that, having been forced to marry when I love elsewhere, I cannot live without hope that I may one day be free.

He was shrewd, she knew; and often she wondered whether he understood more than he let her believe. Had he noticed the change in her since the arrival of the English party? Others had — Marguerite for instance. Marguerite was clever, yet like most people had her blind spot, and that was where her brother was concerned. She thought that every woman must be in love with him and ready to follow when he beckoned; and he had certainly beckoned to Mary.

Life was too complicated; and she was simple in her desires. She knew what she wanted — so few people did that — and when one knew so certainly, it was possible to make a straight path toward it. She was as certain of this as she was of being alive: one day she would marry Charles, because Louis must die sooner or later and, when he did so, she had her brother's permission to marry where she would. It was this knowledge which helped her to live through these days.

She wished it were possible to explain all this to this kind, tired old man; but of course it was not. Louis was tolerant and indulgent — but not to the extent he would need to be to accept such a situation.

When they retired she said: "I am so tired tonight."

"My dear," he replied, stroking the long golden curls, "it has been an exhausting day for you."

She lay down and closed her eyes, feigning sleep. He bent over her and kissed her forehead gently before lying down beside her.

Perhaps he was relieved; for he too was very tired. He was asleep almost at once. She was not. She lay breathing as quietly as she could, trying to propel herself into the future, reminding herself that every hour that passed was bringing her nearer and nearer to her heart's desire.

And in the morning Louis left for Paris. He wanted to be there to receive her when she made her ceremonial entry into his capital.

* * *

The grand procession was moving toward Paris, led by a guard of Swiss archers, the heralds of France and England, and the peers of France. The noblemen themselves followed with the Princes of the Blood Royal leading; and it seemed that each had endeavoured to outdo all others by the splendour of his equipage.

Mary herself rode in her litter; she was dressed in cloth of gold and on her head was her glittering crown; with her hair falling about her shoulders she looked like a fairy queen. Beside the litter, mounted on a magnificent charger, himself a-glitter with jewels, rode the Dauphin.

He chatted lightly with her as they rode along, but behind his conversation was the urgency of his desire. He told her that there had never been a queen or a woman in the world to compare with her; and she listened complacently, all the time wondering whether she would see Charles at the banquet and whether she could arrange to have him beside her.

"Since you have come to France you are more beautiful than ever," he told her. "I ask myself why this should be."

She smiled absentmindedly and he went on: "I think I know. You have become happier, since you have been in France, than you were when you arrived."

"That may be so."

"And that is due to some of us . . . or one of us?"

She smiled at the group of people who were calling greetings to her.

"When we are in Paris," went on François, "it will be easier for us to meet."

"In Paris?" she repeated idly.

"You shall see."

"I shall see," she echoed, and the Dauphin was satisfied.

They had reached the Porte St Dennis on which a tableau had been set up, and there was a halt to admire it. It represented a ship in which were sailors who chanted a welcome to the beautiful Queen.

This was the first of the tableaux and what were called mysteries; at several points in the city they had been set up and at each of them the cavalcade must stop while praises were sung to the Queen. Thus the journey to Notre Dame was punctuated by many halts; and when the cathedral was reached and Mary was received there, and had attended the service in her honour, she was beginning to feel tired because it was nearly six o'clock. But the long day was by no means over. She would have supper at the Palais de la Cité, but this she must do in public and during the meal she would be the centre of attention. She dared not show how weary she was. She must continue to smile; and all the time she was watchful because she knew that somewhere among the crowds who stared at her was Charles Brandon, and she would certainly see him at the joust, which would take place within a few days' time, to celebrate her coronation.

Always the Dauphin was at her side; continually he whispered to her, waiting for her to give him that encouragement for which he sought and which he was certain he would soon be given.

Louis had taken up his residence at the Hôtel des Tournelles so that, he had said, all the attention should be concentrated on the Queen. Mary wondered whether he was glad to escape the ceremonies. At the Tournelles he would be resting in his apartment, eating simple food which had been specially prepared for him, and going to bed early, so that when she joined him he would be ready, as he said and as she dreaded, to be a good husband to her.

In the meantime she had some respite, and she strove to forget what the future held for her. Tonight she would be alone.

In the *grande salle* of the Palais de la Cité, Mary took her seat which had been placed on that tablet of marble from which proclamations were made. The room — which was two hundred and twenty-two feet in length — was hung with rich tapestry; and round the walls were effigies of the Kings of France, from Pharamond, that Knight of the Round Table who was said to have been the first King of France and reigned in the fifth century, to Louis XII himself.

Mary's attendants were headed by Claude and Marguerite, and she was conscious of their watchful eyes, particularly when François was near. She felt sorry for poor Claude and wanted to tell her that she need have no fear, and that she herself had no intention of becoming François's mistress. Not that that would prevent him from giving the poor creature cause for jealousy.

How different it will be when Charles and I are married! sighed Mary.

She was thankful on account of her good health that day, for it had been a long and trying ordeal; and as she sat in that magnificent hall she suddenly saw the English party among the diners, and with them Charles.

Across the assembly their eyes met, conveying messages of love and longing.

Mary was no longer weary; and none who had not witnessed the day's pageantry would have guessed that she had been the centre of it; she was gay, fresh and sparkling.

Many people watching her said to themselves: "The Queen is in love." And because the Dauphin was never far from her side, because he too was unable to hide his feelings, it was whispered that a delicate *contretemps* was brewing.

"Watch the Dauphin and the Queen!" was the whisper that passed round the hall.

CHAPTER EIGHT

Death of a King

A high stage had been erected in the park of the Hôtel des Tournelles and on this had been put a couch, for the King's gout was troubling him again and he was too indisposed to be able to sit in one position for long at a time. Yet he must be present on this occasion, because the English had come over specially to test their skill in the joust against the French champions, and already the excited people of Paris were crowding into the Rue St Antoine which adjoined the Park of Les Tournelles where the lists had been set up.

The noise was great as people wagered as to who would be the victor. The fame of the English Duke of Suffolk had been discussed and it was believed that he would challenge the Dauphin himself.

The people were jubilantly sure of the outcome for they did not believe there was an Englishman living who could rival the Dauphin.

The sound of trumpets announced the arrival of the royal party, and the King, looking very ill, mounted the stage with great difficulty. It was pleasing to see how solicitous the lovely young Queen could be with her husband. She was attended by the most noble of the ladies; and what a contrast she made with poor insignificant Claude. Marguerite, the Dauphin's sister, was a real beauty, but it was the Queen with her wonderful golden hair and bright complexion who attracted the attention of everyone.

Louis lay on his couch smiling rather wanly as he acknowledged the acclaim of his people. The more sober ones were depressed by the sick looks of the Father of his People, reminding themselves that he had been a good King to them and life in France had been the better for his rule. The young ones, though, could not take their eyes from François, who was every man's ideal.

Some studied the Queen's trim yet voluptuous figure. It was too early yet to show any signs of pregnancy, but it was possible that she was in that state. Then the dazzling François would never reach the throne. It was an intriguing situation; and because of it the people's interest in the royal family was even greater than usual.

Louis wanted to close his eyes. The shouting of the people, the blare of the trumpets tired him. What would he not have given for the quiet apartment, the hangings shutting out the light, the comfort of his bed . . . sleep.

But he must be present on this occasion; so he took pleasure in watching the excitement of his Queen.

He had come to believe that there was much he had to learn of her. He did not really know his Mary. She had been shy and shrinking as one must expect a virgin to be and she had remained so. He had thought that in time he might rouse her to passion for he sensed passion in her, latent, unawakened. Yet recently he had been aware of a change in her. There had been a suppressed excitement and she had seemed a different girl from the one he had known in the first days of their marriage.

He was not unaware of François's greedy eyes which rested too frequently on her. Could it be? He could not be surprised if it were, nor could he blame Mary. He knew François's reputation. But François would not be so foolish. The Big Boy might philander when and wherever he had a chance, but he would not be such a fool as to engage in a love affair with the Queen.

And yet . . . there had been that change.

Now the English party were riding into the arena, led by their champions, the Duke of Suffolk and the Marquis of Dorset. Suffolk was a fine figure of a man — as tall as François and broader. To see those two together would be worth a little discomfort.

The Queen had clasped her hands and was watching the riders who bowed on their horses as they passed the royal gallery, the plumes in their helmets touching their horses' heads as they did so.

Her gaze was on the Duke of Suffolk; the King noticed how her eyes followed him round the arena.

Now it was the turn of the French who had been challenged, and they rode in, led by the Dauphin.

To be as young as that! thought Louis. To hear the applause of the people in one's ears and to know it was because one was young and strong, a dashing, reckless hero. François doubtless had his trials to come, but

Louis would have given a great deal to be the man in that glittering armour on that day.

And the Queen; she was applauded with the rest. It was strange that her eyes did not follow the French knights as they did the English.

She is hoping that her own countrymen are going to win the championship, thought Louis indulgently. It is natural.

Yet if she were attracted by François she must admire him more than ever in such a role as he now played.

Unless of course she was being cautious. But one did not connect caution with Mary.

She is young and innocent, he thought. She is unaware of François and, like a child, she wants her own countrymen to win.

Loudly the crowd applauded. They had to concede that the English were very skillful and even François could not quite match the tall Englishman who jousted as though he were inspired.

The Queen sat forward watching, the colour in her cheeks heightened.

Of all the pageants I have had arranged for her, thought Louis, whose eyes rarely left her, none has pleased as this has.

She caught her breath with the thrill of the joust; once, when it seemed the tall Englishman was about to be thrown from his horse, she shut her eyes and shuddered. But all was well; it was only a feint and the man was once more victorious.

It was inevitable that the Duke of Suffolk should challenge the Dauphin, and when these two tilted against each other, Mary was clearly apprehensive.

There was, indeed, an atmosphere of tension not only on the royal stage but throughout the crowd, because thousands of Frenchmen wanted to see the Dauphin win.

Louis watched the Dauphin's mother and sister and saw them craning forward, watched their apprehension — which was no greater than the Queen's.

Sardonically Louis thought of the years when Louise had suffered every time his late wife had promised to bring an heir to the throne of France. What anxiety those ambitious women had endured on the Big Boy's account; and still did. He could not take part in a game without their making a drama of it.

There was a sudden murmur of horror; Mary had risen to her feet and Marguerite and Louise were staring at the arena in dismay.

Louis wished his eyes were better. "What has happened?" he demanded, and for a few seconds those about him ignored him, forgetting that it was the King who had spoken, so intent were they on what was happening in the arena.

"François," cried Louise. "My son . . . my son!"

François had been wounded in the hand and this was a blow to French hopes. Suffolk was about to prove himself the champion, and the honours were going to the English. That was the result of the first day's joust. But there were more to come.

François appeared at the banquet which followed, with his hand in a bandage; ruefully he confessed that he would be unable to hold a lance, so was out of the tournament.

He talked to the Queen as they supped in the *grande salle*.

"Your Englishman took me off my guard," he told her.

"Was that not what you would have expected him to do?"

"So you favour the English?"

"I lived all but the last few weeks of my life among them, remember."

"Shame! I thought you had become one of us." He leaned toward her. "'Twas my own fault. I was thinking of you when I should have been concentrating on my opponent."

"Confess," she retaliated, "your opponent was too good for you."

"Nay, I'll challenge him yet and defeat him."

"I fancy he will be judged the victor of this tourney."

"It was my devotion to you, not his skill, that gives him that victory."

"It is not a good enough excuse! You went in to win and you found him a better man."

"You are vehement in your praise of him. I grow jealous of this man . . . Suffolk, is it?"

"Charles Brandon" — she said his name slowly, loving every syllable — "Duke of Suffolk."

"Something of an adventurer, I have heard. Do you know he tried to marry the Archduchess Margaret? The Emperor put a stop to that little game."

"I do not think he played that little game as well as he jousted today."

"I will tell you a secret," said François. "Monsieur Suffolk is not going to be declared the champion."

"How can you be sure of that, Monsieur le Dauphin?"

"Because I must avenge this." He touched his bandaged hand.

"How so when you cannot hold a lance? And if you could not beat him before you were injured, how can you hope to now?"

"Madame, you are too triumphant. There is a German fellow in my service. He is even taller than I; he is the strongest man in France. He is unbeatable. I am going to put him up against Monsieur Suffolk, and he'll have the fellow out of the saddle. You will see. It will be more than a bloody hand he'll be nursing tomorrow."

Mary turned away. She was afraid that in seeking his revenge François would do Charles some harm.

The Queen spent a sleepless night and her restlessness awakened the King.

"What ails you, my love?" he asked.

"I am well enough," she answered.

"Yet you do not sleep. Perhaps you are overtired. It was an exhausting day."

"And there will be another tomorrow. Louis, I heard that a German who has never yet been beaten is going into the joust. Is it true?"

"Oh, I know the man. One of the Dauphin's servants, a great burly fellow. I've seen him turn men out of their saddles as though they were sacks of corn. Yes, it is true, none can stand against him."

"Then he is the champion of France?"

"My love, he is not of the nobility so we do not often see him joust."

"Then he should not joust tomorrow."

"Ha," said Louis. "Your Englishmen are too good. We have to throw in what we have in the hope of defeating them."

"Yet it should not be."

"How vehement you are! I promise you, you will see good sport."

She was betraying herself; she knew it. She must be silent. Charles will not be harmed, she assured herself. Charles is invincible. He could always have triumphed over Henry, had he tried to.

Yet she was frightened; and when she slept she dreamed of disaster. She did not know what it was; but when she awoke it seemed to be hanging over her.

François was seated with the royal party on the stage — a spectator now that he could no longer be a participant. He was all eagerness for the moment when the German should ride into the arena to challenge the Duke of Suffolk in the name of France.

François felt a little sullen. It so rarely happened that he was not the hero of such occasions. That Englishman had been too quick for him. It was true that he had been thinking of Mary, eager to shine in her eyes, tilting for show rather than with intelligence; and the Englishman had seized his opportunity and incapacitated him.

A poor showing for the Dauphin! He had disappointed everyone — his mother, his sister, the people — and most of all himself.

Mary? He could not be sure of Mary.

He looked at her, and in doing so caught Claude's glance. She was looking affectionately maternal, trying to tell him that she did not care whether he was a champion or not; her feelings for him would not change. She herself had insisted on dressing the wound.

It was depressing to be so adored by someone who bored, to be so uncertain of another whom one longed to make one's mistress.

Not a very auspicious day this, for François.

Mary was leaning forward in her seat. And now there was the German. What bulk! What strength! He was invincible. The Englishman would not have a chance.

The crowd was silent. It was like two giants meeting, as the pale November sunshine touched their armour when they rode toward each other.

Everyone was watching them intently, except two people on the royal stage — one of whom was the King, the other the Dauphin; and they could not take their eyes from the Queen, who sat upright, pale and tense, her hands clasped in her lap; and so absorbed was she in those two glittering figures that she was quite unaware that the eyes of both King and Dauphin were on her and that she was betraying herself.

Louis's emotions were mixed and it was a long time since he had been deeply moved by them. Sorrow, regret and pity for her as well as for himself tormented him. So she loved the Englishman and, because she was vehement in everything she did, she could not hide that love. This was why she had changed since the English party had come to Court. It was obvious. Why had he been so blind as not to see it before?

Pictures came into his mind of their nights together. Poor child, he thought. Being vehement in love, vehement in hate, she would suffer deeply. Did she hate me? Sick old man — obscene, disgusting. And her thoughts all for that blond giant!

It was a tragedy which befell most royal people; they suffered; but they learned resignation. He remembered his first marriage, to Jeanne of France. He had been a young man then. But he could not compare the repugnance he had felt for his bride with the sufferings of Mary Tudor.

She was clenching her hands together, and had moved forward slightly, breathing quickly. My poor little one, he thought. If you stood up and shouted, I love Suffolk, you could not tell me more clearly what is in your mind. It is time I was dead.

And he had never loved her so dearly as he did at that moment.

François's face had hardened. He too had read the secret. He was angry, for never had she seemed more desirable than she did now that he knew she was in love with another man. She had never taken his courtship seriously, but had fooled him as she had old Louis.

Beaten in the joust! Beaten in love! And possibly the Queen pregnant with the child who would oust him from the throne. Never had the Dauphin's fortunes been so low.

"*Foi de gentilhomme*," he swore, "what if she gets with child by Suffolk! Here's a pretty state of affairs. Had it been my own son who robbed me of my rights, that would have been one thing — but that it should be an English bastard!"

Louis, the old fool, drooling over a beautiful girl, must be made to understand the significance of the danger which threatened.

In the meantime Suffolk must be defeated in the arena.

But it was not to be so. Suffolk was inspired. Never had he jousted in all his life as he did in the Park of Les Tournelles, and even the most partial of judges must declare him the victor.

The Queen had risen; she clasped her hands with joy. She could not wait to greet the champion; and all the time she was watched by the sad eyes of the King, the lowering ones of the Dauphin.

François was in the King's apartment and they were alone together.

The Dauphin was decidedly uneasy and Louis made a shrewd guess as to why he had come to him. It was not easy to hint — for he would not dare say outright

— what was in his mind; yet he had to convey to Louis the dangers of this delicate situation.

"And the hand?" asked the King.

"Almost healed, Sire."

"You have healthy blood."

"It was unfortunate that it happened so early in the joust, Sire. I regret losing the pleasure of unseating the Englishman."

"Ah, my big François, he was too good for us, let us admit it."

"The English method, Sire, is less polished than our own."

"And more effective."

François hesitated and then said: "The English — and in particular the Duke of Suffolk — seem to be highly favoured at our Court."

"It is necessary to entertain our guests."

"True, Sire. Yet methinks there are some members of the Court who would be glad to see the English return to their own land."

"The Queen delights to entertain her countrymen."

"She has had many opportunities of doing so, Sire."

That was as far as he dared go. He was right of course, mused Louis. The fellow should not be allowed to come and go as he wished. It was putting too great a temptation in the way of the Queen. He did not wish for trouble.

"The Court will be moving soon to St Germain," said Louis quietly. "We shall not expect the English to accompany us there."

Poor child, he was thinking. But it is better so.

* * *

Charles had left for England and there had been no opportunity for a private interview. Mary was desolate, and desperately tried to hide this.

When shall I see my Charles again? she asked herself, and could provide no satisfactory answer.

The Dauphin seemed secretly amused; he had renewed his attentions which, she remembered then, had ceased for a while. Charles was going home covered in glory. Henry would be pleased with him. She pictured them together talking of her.

What would I not give to be sitting in Greenwich Palace between them as I used to!

The King came to her and put her lute into her hands.

"Play for me," he said. "I am in the mood for sweet music."

So she played the songs she had played for Henry, and the King, watching her, shared her melancholy. Her golden curls were held from her face by a band set with pearls, but they fell over her shoulders; her gown of violet velvet was cut away in the front to show a petticoat of amber satin which was decorated with a gold fringe, and about her white throat was a necklace of pearls.

This was folly, thought the King. She must forget England and her Englishman. She is the Queen of France now — a proud destiny which should be enough to satisfy anyone. If they could beget a child she would be contented.

A child? Why not? He was not so very old, and on his good days he felt almost young again.

He loved her; he did not see why they should not live together in amity. If there was a little dauphin she would care for the boy so much that she might come to love his father.

He came to her and laid a hand on her shoulder. The lute was silent.

"It does me good to watch you," he said. "I feel young again." She tried to repress the shiver which ran through her, and almost succeeded.

He pitied her but told himself he must harden his heart. She was his wife; he had given her the crown of France; and in exchange she must give him a dauphin.

Louis refused to accept age. At St Germain he hunted with his old enthusiasm. The Queen rode out with him, and he was at her side during the banquets. He partook of the rich dishes, forsook his boiled meat; and even tried a measure now and then; and when he retired with the Queen he assured himself that having a young wife had made him young again. Gone was the old man of France.

He knew that the Dauphin with his mother and sister looked on sourly; inwardly he laughed at their discomfiture.

The most beautiful girl at the Court was his Queen, and he was man enough to rejoice in her.

The Court had returned to the Palais des Tournelles in order to celebrate Christmas and the New Year.

The Queen was feverishly gay. If the King wanted to prove that he was not an old man, let him. He must join her in the revels; and she would show them how

Christmas and the New Year was celebrated at her brother's Court.

The weather had turned bitterly cold; deep snow was in the streets and biting winds swept through the Palace. The Queen did not seem to be affected by the weather. Her mood became more hilariously gay as the days passed.

This is how she was meant to be, Louis told himself. She is getting over her infatuation with the Englishman. She is ready to enjoy her new status; it is a glorious thing to be Queen of France even if one must take the old man with it.

When she was with him Louis strove to be gay; he was constantly attempting to prove that he had regained his health and strength. He wanted to make that sly speculation on the face of the Dauphin a certainty. He wanted to send Louise's hopes diving down to disaster. He was using all the means he could lay his hands on to give his old body a semblance of youth.

He opened the Christmas revels with the Queen beside him; he danced with her; he supped with her, and it was his wit which provoked her to laughter.

As for her, she seemed inexhaustible; it was as though she danced a wild dance and bewitched the King into sharing it with her.

On New Year's Eve her gaiety seemed to reach its climax. The King never left her side.

When she rose to dance she held out her arms to him and François watching with his mother and sister had never felt his hopes so low.

"She is a witch," hissed Louise. "She has breathed new life into him. He looks ten years younger than he did before his marriage. He was never so besotted with Anne as he is with this one, and Anne could lead him by the nose."

"Oh, Mother," sighed Marguerite, "who would have thought it would have come to this? Each night she is in his bed. There can be one outcome."

"All our hopes . . . all our plans . . . ," moaned Louise.

"And at that time," muttered François, "when the crown seemed about to be placed on my head!"

The trinity was in despair.

The Queen was aware of this. Mischief would lighten her eyes every time she met one of the family. Yet behind her gaiety there was a certain brooding, a watchfulness.

The heat of the ballroom had been excessive; outside the temperature was at freezing point.

They had danced and retired late to their apartments; the Queen lay in her royal bed, rejoicing. There could be no love-making tonight. He was too ill. He could not pretend to her as glibly as he did to others.

She had comforted him. "My poor Louis, you are so tired. You shall sleep. I shall be close to you . . . thus . . . and when you have rested you will feel well again."

She bent over him and, looking up into her round young face, he longed to caress her; but she was right, he was too tired.

So he lay still and she lay beside him, keeping her fingers laced in his.

And she thought: It cannot be long now. Something tells me. She was sorry and yet exulting. She wanted to throw herself into his arms and ask his pardon. She wanted to say: I wish you dead, Louis, and I hate myself for wishing it; but I cannot stop this wish.

It was long before she slept. She kept thinking of the heated ballroom, and she fancied she could still hear the sound of music mingling with the howling wind outside. Faces flashed in and out of her mind. François, lean and hungry . . . hungry for her body, half loving her, half hating her, since the tournament in which Charles had beaten him. Louise, alert and fearful, those glances which covered the whole of her body, speculatively fearful; and Marguerite so anxious that her brother's way to the throne should not be blocked. The King . . . whose spirit yearned toward a greater amorousness than his body would allow.

She thought of Charles in the arena — the dreadful moment when she thought the German would unseat him and perhaps inflict some injury. Then she remembered him, victorious, receiving the prize from her hands.

How long? How long? she asked herself.

She did not have to wait for the answer.

She would never forget waking on the morning of New Year's Day when the wintry light filtered into the bedchamber and on to the gray face of the man in the bed. She leaned over him in deep compassion and said: "Louis . . . you are very sick today?"

He did not answer her. He did not even know it was his beautiful Queen who had spoken.

Then she knew that the day for which she had prayed and yearned had come.

The door of the cage was opening; she would soon be free.

Yet when she looked down at that withered face, at the bleak, unseeing eyes, she could only murmur: “The pity of it!”

CHAPTER NINE

Is the Queen Enceinte?

Dressed completely in white, Mary sat alone in that room in the Hôtel de Clugny which was known as *la chambre de la reine blanche*. Here she was to remain, in accordance with custom, for six weeks while she mourned her husband.

Mary was relieved to be able to shut herself away in this manner. Her husband was dead but she knew that she was not yet free to make another marriage, and that there would be all sorts of opposition to her choice possibly not only from England but from France. She had come to understand that the English and the French would be wrangling over her dowry, her jewels, and all the costly appurtenances with which they had thought it necessary to load her before making her Queen of France. The fight was not yet over; therefore it was a pleasure to be shut away from the Court and be alone with a few of her attendants: six whole weeks in which to review the new life which lay ahead and to plan that she should not again be deprived of her heart's desire.

The Hôtel de Clugny was situated in the Rue des Mathurins and had once been the home of Cluniac monks. It was small compared with Les Tournelles, but her own apartments were adequate; and somberly fitted out as a mourning chamber and lighted only by wax tapers, they gave her the feeling that she was shut away from the world; in such intimate surroundings she could think clearly.

Strangely enough she did mourn Louis, for she could not forget his gentleness and many kindnesses; and in spite of her relief she was a little sad because she had longed for his death; so while she exulted in her freedom she was a little melancholy; and now that he was dead she knew that she was not yet out of danger.

This was made clear to her during her interview with François; for although she was shut away from the Court her close relations were allowed to visit her; and of course these included François.

They faced each other and neither was able to suppress the excitement which burned beneath that solemn facade which convention demanded they should show the world. His future was in the balance, no less than hers, for whether or not he was to be King of France would be decided in a few weeks. Perhaps she could tell him now.

"My dearest *belle-mère*," he murmured, using that name which he had always spoken with tenderness and an implication that it was ridiculously amusing that, through his marriage with her stepdaughter, one so young and beautiful should bear such a relationship to him. "These are sad days for you and I have been waiting impatiently to come to you and tell you that I am thinking of you every hour."

A smile was upon her lips. Indeed you are! she thought. For on me depends whether or not you will be, in a few short weeks, crowned King of France.

"You have always been so thoughtful," she murmured.

"I trust you are in good health . . . ?" His eyes strayed about her body.

"In excellent health," she answered.

"And not indisposed in any way?"

"I am as well as can be expected . . . in the circumstances."

She saw the lights of alarm shoot up in his eyes, and a tremor of laughter ran through her. Serve you right, François, she thought. Did you not bring out the big German in the hope that you would unseat Charles? You might have harmed him . . . if he had not been so much better than your German.

"The circumstances . . . ?" he began.

"Have you forgotten that I have recently become a widow?"

His relief was obvious. Where was his old subtlety? It had deserted him, so anxious was he.

"I feared the King's health was growing steadily worse in the weeks before his death."

"Yet there were times when he was so gay . . . almost like a young man. Why, only just before his death . . ."

François clenched his fists. He was longing to ask her outright: Are you *enceinte?* Yet it would be unseemly to do so, and if he could only curb his patience for a few weeks he would know.

He left her, no wiser about this important matter than before.

Louise and Marguerite embraced François when he came to them direct from the Hôtel de Clugny.

Louise looked earnestly into his face.

"Did you discover?"

François shook his head mournfully.

"She might not know yet," suggested Marguerite.

"Surely if there were already signs she would have told you!" protested Louise.

"She would have been only too ready to make it known," mused Marguerite. "She would be so proud to be mother of the King of France."

Louise covered her face with her hands. "Do not say that." She shivered. "If it were true I think I should die of melancholy."

François went to his mother and put his arm about her shoulder. She gave him the smile which was kept for him alone.

"Dearest, we should still be together," he said.

"And while the world held you, my King, there would be a reason for living. But that another should have that which is yours! I think I should be ready to strangle the brat at birth."

"I doubt they would allow you to be present at the birth," retorted Marguerite grimly.

"You must not despair," said François. "I do not think Louis was capable."

Marguerite looked at her brother steadily. "And others?" she asked.

"I think the Queen was . . . entirely virtuous."

Mother and daughter showed their relief. At least François had not shared her bed, and they were inclined to think that Louis, who was even weaker than they had realised, must have been incapable of begetting a child.

"The point is," said Marguerite precisely, "is it possible for the Queen to be *enceinte*?"

"It is certainly possible," François said.

"But if she is a virtuous woman, unlikely," went on Marguerite.

"In a few weeks we should know," put in Louise.

"And even if we should learn that the Queen is *enceinte*," added Marguerite, "we should not utterly despair, because it is just as likely that she might give birth to a girl as a boy."

"Even you do not understand," cried Louise. "For years I have been in torment. I have seen the crown so near and suffered the frustration. And now I know I am near the end of that dreaded uncertainty, but it might prove that all my worst fears will be realised. It has been too long . . ."

"Mother dear," said François, "we shall soon be out of our misery. Let us remember that."

She slipped her hand through his arm and laid her cheek against his sleeve while she looked up at him adoringly.

"Trust my King to soothe me," she murmured.

"Whatever happens," François reminded her, "we have each other. Remember . . . the trinity."

"Yes," said Louise fiercely, "but it must be a trinity with the King of France at the apex."

"I have a feeling it will be," said Marguerite calmly.

François smiled at her. "I share your view, my pearl. So much so that I am already thinking as though I am King of France. We must find a husband for Mary Tudor . . . in France."

"You have discussed this with her?" asked Marguerite. "It is as yet too soon. She is, after all, making a pretense of mourning Louis. But I have heard that her brother is already sounding Charles of Castile. Such an alliance would not be good for France. Moreover it would mean that we should have to return her dowry, and there would be the question of her jewels. Louis was constantly giving her trinkets and, as these by right belong to the crown of France, I should not want to see them leave the country. Therefore I have been thinking of a possible match for her."

"In France, of course," said Louise. "Oh for the day when Mary Tudor is safely married and no longer a threat to François!"

"I have two suitors in mind for her. There is the Duc de Lorraine, and the Duc de Savoy."

"My beloved," cried Louise, "what a King you will make! What a happy day it will be for France when you mount the throne!"

Marguerite, her eyes shining, knelt before him and taking his hand kissed it. The gesture meant that she was paying homage to the King of France.

"It must be so," murmured Louise. Then her eyes narrowed and she added: "It *shall* be so."

* * *

Mary was filled with despair. The walls of her mourning chamber seemed to her like a prison, and within them she felt herself to be doomed.

For six weeks she must remain here. She could have borne that if when she emerged it was to be to freedom. But there were plans to prevent this. To ambitious kings she was not so much a woman as a bargaining counter. François forgot his gallantry when he considered her future; was Henry going to forget his promise?

Fear was her companion. Little Anne Boleyn who, in spite of her youth, knew how to keep her ears and eyes open, had told her that there was gossip among the French attendants and that they were wagering who would have his way over the next marriage of Mary — François or the King of England.

Henry was in negotiation to renew the match between Mary and Charles of Castile which had been broken when she was affianced to Louis. François had other plans for her.

"I could not bear it!" Mary murmured into her pillows. "I will not endure it. Henry *shall* keep his promise to me."

She became so melancholy that her attendants were alarmed for her health. She complained of toothache and headaches; and on one or two occasion she burst into loud laughter which turned into weeping.

"The Queen realises that she has lost a good husband," said her attendants.

Each day she arose, fretting against her incarceration in the Hôtel de Clugny, while at the same time she rejoiced in her seclusion because it gave her time to think. She would feel suddenly gay because she had gained her freedom from Louis; then the gaiety would be replaced by melancholy when she asked herself how long this freedom would last.

Marguerite, hearing of the Queen's state of health, came to visit her in some concern. Her moods, reasoned Marguerite, could be due to her condition, and Marguerite was a woman who believed that it was better to know the worst and plan accordingly. In the mourning chamber, Marguerite embraced her. "You are looking pale," she said anxiously.

"Are you surprised?"

"Indeed no. You have had a great shock. And, even though the King's death was expected, when these things happen they shock nonetheless. Tell me about your health. I hear that you have headaches and toothache."

"I have never had them before."

"Have you any idea why you should feel thus . . . apart from your melancholy over the King's death?"

Mary lowered her eyes. They were too insistent. In spite of her alarm for her future she felt the laughter bubbling up inside her. Had François or Louise sent Marguerite to question her? They had all three lost their subtlety in their great anxiety.

"I feel at such a time it is natural for me to be in delicate health."

"Are there any other symptoms?"

"I felt a little sick this morning."

Mary reproached herself on seeing the look of despair which Marguerite could not suppress. Poor Marguerite! She had always been very kind to Mary. It was a shame to tease her.

Mary went on quickly: "I think it was because I was upset. I had heard that my brother was already planning a new marriage for me."

"And you do not favour such a marriage?"

"I was affianced to Charles of Castile before I came to France. He was not eager for the match then; I am not eager for it now. Then I was a Princess of England; now I am a Queen of France."

"I'll swear you have grown to love France during your stay here and have no wish to leave it."

Mary stared dreamily ahead of her and Marguerite went on: "My brother is anxious on your behalf. He wants to see you happy. He would make a very good match for you here in France. Then you need never leave us."

"I do love France, it is true," answered Mary. "But do you not think that it is somewhat unseemly to think of marriage for me when . . ."

"When?" asked Marguerite, alarmed.

"When I have so recently lost my husband?"

"Marriages for royal people are invariably arranged with little consideration for their personal feelings."

"Alas," sighed Mary.

"And my brother would not wish to force you into anything that was not congenial to you."

"At this time it is congenial to me to remain as I am."

"That he understands, but he puts forward certain propositions to you that you may bear them in mind; and if your brother should become insistent, you can tell him that you have plans of your own."

Mary smiled, secretively and in a manner which increased Marguerite's despair. "I *have* plans of my own," she murmured.

"The Duc de Lorraine, whom my brother had in mind for you, is affianced to the daughter of the Duc de Bourbon; but Charles, Duc de Savoy, would be an excellent match. Oh, Mary, please stay with us."

With a gesture of affection Marguerite had thrown her arms about Mary. Were those caressing hands trying to discover whether there was any thickening of the girlish figure?

Mary returned the embrace but continued to look mysterious.

"I can decide nothing . . . yet," she said.

"But your brother, I have heard, is sending an embassy to France. I think his wish is that you should return to England with it."

"An English embassy! I wonder whom he will send."

"I do know that it will be led by the Duke of Suffolk."

All melancholy was replaced by joy. If Henry was sending Charles, it could mean that he remembered his promise. Was Henry saying: Now it is up to you?

This changed everything. Charles was coming. Nothing in the world could have made her happier.

She must hide her joy. Marguerite was too watchful; and a little sly, she had to admit, for Marguerite, while posing as her friend, was in truth her brother's spy.

She knew full well that although Marguerite expressed her friendship and François constantly hinted that a closer relationship would please him, they were her enemies — in so much as they would not help her to marry Charles Brandon.

She was not so simple that she did not know the reason for François's desire for a French marriage. He wanted to keep her dowry.

But Charles was coming! And this time she would not be cheated.

She walked to her couch and lay down on it.

"I feel a little tired," she told Marguerite. "I think I shall have to rest a little more frequently . . . now."

"You mean . . .?"

"Just that I do seem to be in need of this rest, my dear Marguerite. Thank you for coming to see me."

She turned her face away and Marguerite must leave her, bewildered, frustrated, as deep in that dreadful uncertainty as she had been before her visit.

It was unseemly for a widow to be so happy. She could not help it. When she rose she wanted to sing: "Charles is coming to France." It was her last thought before retiring each night.

Every day she waited for news of the English embassy. She would say to herself, "This very day he may come walking into the apartment." She knew what she would say to him when he did come. "Charles, Charles, now. No delay. We must take no more chances. I have waited too long and will wait no longer. Take me now, for I am yours and you are mine for as long as we both shall live."

Still he did not come. But she was not in despair. Perhaps he was waiting at Dover now. Perhaps the gales were too fierce. Oh, the perils of the sea! They alarmed her; they frightened her. But he would come through them safely. She was certain.

"Soon, my love. Soon I shall be in your arms," she murmured. And meanwhile the trinity were watching for signs of her pregnancy, and they would try to prevent her marriage to Charles Brandon, she knew, because their plan was to force her into marriage with Charles of Savoy.

I'd die rather, Mary told herself.

She was burning with impatience. She could scarcely endure the days, and life was so dull and dreary in the mourning chamber while she was waiting for Charles that she had to try to infuse a little gaiety into her life.

She kept little Anne Boleyn at her side. The girl was discreet, she was sure; moreover she was English.

"Soon," Mary told Anne, "we shall be going to England. I shall never marry here."

Then she was afraid that she had been indiscreet and, taking the girl by her long black hair, warned her of the horrors which would befall her if she ever repeated what she had heard.

The serene black eyes were untroubled; Mary knew she could rely on the child, who was wise beyond her years.

She would have only Anne to help her dress and insisted that together they spoke English. And if Anne was astonished at the petticoats Mary insisted on wearing she gave no sign.

"There!" cried Mary. "How do I look?"

Anne put her head on one side, her black eyes disapproving. She was already fastidious about her dress, and a very fashionable young lady who could always be relied on to bring out the ornaments which looked best on certain gowns.

"Too fat, Madame," said Anne.

Then Mary laughed and taking the girl by the hands danced round the room with her.

"So I look fat, do I? So would you, Mistress Anne, if you were as petticoated as I am. And I will tell you something; tomorrow I shall wear yet another petticoat; and I want you to find some quilting."

"Quilting, Madame?"

"I said quilting. Those black eyes are very inquisitive. Never mind, little Anne. You shall discover. In the meantime not a word . . . not a word to anyone of petticoats or quilting. You understand me?"

"Yes, Madame." The black eyes were demure, the lips turned up at the corners. The girl had wit enough to enjoy the joke.

Each day Mary was visited at the Hôtel de Clugny by Louise, Marguerite or François.

Daily her body seemed to grow thicker and each day as they left her they were in greater despair.

Mary's eyes, sparkling with excitement, would be watchful. They knew that she guarded some secret, which gave her the utmost pleasure.

"There can be no doubt about it," said Louise in despair. "Louis has left her pregnant."

François beat his fist against his knee. "Months of waiting . . . then the birth. And if it is a boy . . . *Foi de gentilhomme*, why is Fate so cruel!"

Louise paced up and down her apartment.

"That it should have come to this. All the years and now . . . *this*. Who would have thought Louis capable!"

Only Marguerite had comfort to offer. "It may be a girl," she said.

But even so there would be the months of uncertainty.

Mary had shut the door of her chamber and taken little Anne by the hands. She danced with her round and round until they were both breathless.

"Anne, did you see her face? Marguerite's, I mean. Poor Marguerite! It is a shame. She has been a good friend to me."

"She has been a better one to her brother, Madame."

"Well, Anne, that is natural. As for Louise, I believe she would like to kill me."

"And would do, Madame, if it were possible for the deed not to be discovered."

"I know it well. That is perhaps why I enjoy my little joke."

"The quilting has slipped, Madame."

"I find it rather hot, Anne. Perhaps I will wear fewer petticoats tomorrow."

"You must not grow smaller, Madame."

"Not until the time is ripe," was the answer. "Have you heard any rumours about the embassy from England?"

"No, Madame, only that the King has chosen the Duke of Suffolk to lead it."

Mary clasped her hands together.

"My Charles, soon he will be with me." She began to dance once more round the room, her arms held out as though to a partner. She stopped suddenly. "I should be mourning Louis. Poor Louis who was always kind to me. But I cannot pretend, Anne. How can I mourn when Charles is coming to me? And when he comes, this time I shall never let him go."

Anne had run to her and was picking up the quilting which had fallen from her skirts.

Mary snatched it from her and threw it high into the air. "When he is here, the joke will be over. I would not have him see me ungainly, I do assure you."

Then she laughed and wept a little while Anne watched her with solemn eyes.

Marguerite, her eyes wide, her face pale, burst into her mother's apartment.

"What is it, my dear?" demanded Louise, and François, who was with his mother, came swiftly to his sister's side.

"I have just left the Queen," stammered Margaret.

"And she has told you . . ." began François.

Marguerite shook her head. "I can't believe it, and yet . . ."

"My dearest, it is unlike you to be incoherent," François murmured.

"Come, come," put in Louise impatiently. "What is it?"

"I was studying her figure and thinking that it had thickened even since yesterday. She was seated and suddenly rose; I am sure my eyes did not deceive me, but it seemed that something beneath her gown moved."

"Is it so far gone then!" cried Louise in panic. She began counting on her fingers. "They were married in October. Could it have happened then? Impossible. Old Louis would have been so proud, he would never have kept the secret."

"Not a child," said Marguerite slowly, "definitely not a child. It was as though something . . . slipped." The three looked at each other.

Louise spoke first. "It's impossible. Would she attempt to trick us? For what purpose? What can she hope to gain from it?"

"Some amusement," suggested François, and he began to laugh, partly with relief. For if what had entered his mind were indeed true then he would be a very happy man.

"We must find out," declared Louise.

"How?" asked Marguerite.

"How, my dear! I shall go to her apartments. I shall see what it is she wears beneath her garments."

"You cannot mean, Maman," protested Marguerite, "that you will go to the Queen's chamber and ask to see what she wears beneath her gown! Remember she is still the Queen of France."

"My dear Marguerite, if your eyes have not deceived you as that girl is trying to deceive us, I am — at this moment — the mother of the King of France. I fancy my son would allow no one to criticise *my* actions. Is that not so, Sire?"

"Mother, if I ever forget what I owe to you I should never deserve to wear the crown."

"Then I shall take this chance. Come with me, Marguerite. But wait awhile. We will prepare her for our meeting. Go, my dear, and send one of the pages to the Hôtel de Clugny to tell the Queen that we beg leave to call on her."

Mary patted her body affectionately. A visit from Louise and Marguerite! When the former came she could always be sure of some amusement; she never felt ashamed of duping her, as she did Marguerite.

"How do I look, Anne?"

"Very *enceinte*, Madame."

"What would you say, my child? Three months?"

Laughter bubbled to Anne's lips. "It would seem, Madame, that you carry a large and healthy boy and have been doing so for more than three months."

"And if I look larger than other women that is natural, Mistress Anne. Do I not carry a little king? Do I carry him high? They tell me that that is a sign of a boy."

"Oh *yes*, Madame. But you are far too large."

"We will leave it now, Anne. I shall remain thus until the English embassy arrives. See who is at the door."

Anne came back, her eyes sparkling. "Madame d'Alençon with her mother, Madame."

Mary went to her couch and reclined there, looking wan.

"How is that, Anne?"

"Excellent, Madame."

"Bring them in. And then go discreetly into the corner and sit there with your needlework. You must look very serious. Remember that you are in a chamber of mourning."

Mary might have been warned by the militant glare in Louise's eyes, but she scarcely looked at her.

She smiled wanly and held out her hand.

"Welcome," she said in a quiet voice. "It does me so much good to see you here. And Marguerite also. Welcome too, my dear."

"We have been hearing accounts of your health which give us some concern," Marguerite told her.

"My health? You must not be so anxious on my behalf. It is all so natural."

"And how are you feeling, now, Madame?"

"A little tired. A little sick now and then. With diminished appetite, and now and then a fancy for some odd thing."

"I trust your servants are taking good care of you."

"The utmost care. The little Boleyn is a treasure."

"I would," said Marguerite, "that you would allow me to be with you more frequently."

"At such a time I am happy to be with little Boleyn. I am in no mood even for your sparkling conversation."

Louise had spoken little, but her sharp eyes never left the Queen's reclining figure for one moment.

She came close to the couch and two spots of colour burned in her cheeks, as she said: "I trust, Madame, that you did not catch the King's complaint when you nursed him so carefully."

"The King's complaint?"

"Gout!" hissed Louise, as with a swift movement she leaned over the couch and touched that spot where the padding beneath Mary's gown was thickest.

"Madame!" Mary began indignantly, leaping from the couch as she spoke.

Louise, so triumphant, so conscious of the fact that as privileged mother of the King she was in a position to act as familiarly as she cared to with the Dowager Queen, jerked up the Queens gown, exposing the layers of petticoats; and not content with that she probed further until she was able to pull at the padding. Mary shrieked her protest but Louise was in command now. "A new fashion perchance from England?" asked Marguerite, and there was laughter in her voice.

"Exactly so," answered Mary. "Did you not like it?"

"It gave you the appearance of a pregnant woman," went on Marguerite, for she saw that her mother was struck speechless by the mingling of delight and fury.

"Is that so?" replied Mary calmly. "Then that must have pleased some, while it displeased others."

"Your royal body is more charming in its natural state," went on Marguerite.

Mary sighed and put her hands on her hips. "I feel you may be right."

By this time Louise had recovered her speech, and all the anxiety of years was slipping from her. But she had to make sure. She took Mary by the arm and shook her.

"You will tell me," she said, "that you are *not* with child."

Mary's mischievous eyes looked straight into Louises. The little game was over. She had to tell them the truth.

"Madame," she said, "I am not with child. I trust that ere long I may have the pleasure of greeting the King and saying, as all his subjects will wish to: '*Vive François Premier.*' "

CHAPTER TEN

Triumph of the Queen

He sat opposite her in the mourning chamber. He was at his most handsome and insouciant. The anxiety was over; moreover it was a thing of the past because it had gone forever.

He was jaunty, sitting there, his long, elegant legs crossed, studying her with smiling eyes.

"I am honoured," she told him demurely, "to be visited by the King of France."

"It is a marvellous thing," he replied, "that I should have been a King before I was aware of it."

"Stranger things have happened."

He laughed suddenly. Then he said: "I trust you enjoyed the game."

"It was the greatest fun," she answered frankly.

"It gave my mother and sister much anxiety."

"And you, I fear."

"It would seem to me that you are a little *méchant, ma bellemère*."

"It is why I have always felt drawn toward you, *mon beau-fils*. We are alike in some ways."

"All those weeks of uncertainty! I should have been crowned at Rheims by now."

"But that is to come, Sire."

"You should be trembling, so to have duped the King and his family."

"So should I, did I not know that the King loves a joke — even against himself — as well as I do."

"Nevertheless, this was beyond a joke."

"Then, Sire, you are indeed angry. But I do not believe it. You still look at me with such friendship."

François began to laugh and she joined in; she was thinking of young Anne, carefully padding her, and the expression on Louise's face when she had studied her thickened figure.

"'Twas a good joke, Sire," she said between her gusts of laughter. "You will admit that."

"It did not seem so then," he said, trying to look solemn; but he could not set his face into severe lines, and he was thinking: Why was I not given this girl instead of Claude? He was speculating too. He would marry her to Savoy and she and her husband should be at Court. He would carry on his flirtation with her and, when he was King and she was Duchess of Savoy, there was every hope of their little affair reaching its culmination. He might come to an arrangement with Savoy that the marriage should be one of convenience. Savoy need never be a husband to her and she could be the *maîtresse-entitre* of the King of France. It was not difficult for a king to arrange such matters.

He could see a very pleasant future ahead of them, so how could he be angry with her?

"If you were not so beautiful," he said, "I might decide you should be punished in some way."

"Then I thank the saints for giving me a face that pleases the King of France — and a body too . . . although that did not once please him so well."

"So," went on François, "instead of sending my guards to arrest you and take you to some dark dungeon, I will tell you of the future I have planned for you. I shall never allow you to leave France, you know."

All the gaiety left her face; she was alert now.

"My home is in England," she began. "Now that I no longer have a French husband I should return to my native land."

"My dearest *belle-mère*, we will find you a husband who will please you. In fact I have someone in mind for you."

"The Duke of Savoy by any chance?"

"So you already had your eye on him. He will be a good husband to you."

"When I marry, Sire, I should like to be the one who had decided on my partner."

François slowly uncrossed his legs. He rose and came to her chair. There he stood smiling down at her.

"You are fully aware of my feelings toward you."

"Oh yes. You forgive me my follies because you like my face and now my figure."

He took her hands and pulled her up, standing very close to her.

"I have thought a great deal about our future," he told her.

"Ours?"

"Yours and mine."

"Yours is a great destiny."

"I should like you to have a share in it. I think that together we should find great . . . contentment."

"I to share your life? And your Queen?"

"Poor little Claude. She will do her duty in a docile manner, but she will not expect to share my life."

"But she shares your throne."

"Here in France it is the woman the King loves who is in truth Queen of France — not the one he marries."

"You are suggesting that I become your mistress!"

"Do not look horrified. You have forgotten that I am now the King. Everything you wish will be yours. Savoy shall understand the position so that he will be no encumbrance to you."

"I see. Is that how matters are arranged in France?"

"It is how I intend matters shall be arranged in France."

He had his arms about her and she placed her hands on his chest, holding him off. He could see now that she was in truth afraid of him.

"François," she said urgently, "you have always been my friend."

"And always will be, I hope."

"From the moment I saw you, although my coming could well have meant the death of all your hopes, you were good to me. More than anyone you made me feel welcome and comfortable in a new land."

"That was my endeavour."

"So now I am going to be frank with you. I am going to ask you to help me. I am fond of you, François. You see I speak to you as my friend — not as the King of France. But I shall never willingly be your mistress. Oh, it is not that I hate you, or find you repulsive. That would be foolish. Everyone knows you are the most attractive man in France. But François, before I came to France I loved, and I do not change. I shall love one man forever."

"Suffolk?" said François.

"You know."

"You betrayed your feelings at the tournament, when he tilted against the German."

She had clasped her hands across her breast and was looking at him appealingly. François turned away. This was too much. After having played her tricks on him and his family she was asking him to help her make a secret marriage with Suffolk, so that the dowry and the jewels should not after all remain in France.

The impudence of this girl was past belief.

She was catching at his arm and there were tears in her beautiful eyes. "Oh, François, you who are so gallant, so wise, will understand. I shall tell you everything because you are as a brother to me . . . the dearest, kindest brother any girl ever had. I thought I should die of a broken heart when they told me I should have to marry Louis. And my brother promised me that if I did, on his death I should marry whom I pleased. That time has come, and I shall look to my brother to keep his promise."

François walked away from her and pulled thoughtfully at the hangings.

He said, without turning to look at her: "I can tell you this. Your brother has no intention of keeping his promise to you. He is negotiating for the Prince of Castile as your second husband."

"When I see my brother I can persuade him."

"As you hope to persuade me?"

"I know that you are kind at heart and would always want to help a woman in distress."

"You ask too much," said François. And indeed she did, she who refused his embraces and had the effrontery to ask him to help her to enjoy a rival's!

"Not of you . . . the King . . . the all powerful King."

"The marriage of Princesses cannot be settled at the whim of one King."

"Not even when the King proposes to make a princess his mistress after marrying her to a complaisant husband?"

François muttered: "It is the wish of my ministers that you remain in France."

"But you will not allow your ministers to rule France, surely?"

She came to stand demurely at his elbow and when he looked down into her lovely young face and saw the purpose there, when he remembered how moved she had been at the tournament, he was touched. He admired women who knew what they wanted and determined wholeheartedly to get it. He believed — and he knew he would continue to do so all his life — that the two most wonderful people in the world were his mother and sister. They had always known what they wanted and would always be bold enough to fight for it. Mary Tudor was another such. So he had to admire her while deploring what might have been called her insolence. François was deeply affected by women; having been brought up by such a mother and sister, women had been his chief companions during the formative years of his life. He idealised them, preferred their company to that of his own sex, and could not bear to disappoint those for whom he had some affection. Women aroused all his chivalry, and as he had been ready to sacrifice his desire for Françoise, he was now ready to do so for Mary Tudor.

He took her hand and kissed it.

"I envy Suffolk," he said.

She threw back her head and laughed, showing her perfect white teeth and plump, rounded throat. What I am losing! thought François regretfully.

"*You!*" she cried. "You envy none. You are the King of France which is what you have always longed to be — and you will be beloved by your subjects, particularly the females, so you should envy none."

"None but Suffolk," he answered.

"François, you are going to help me? You are going to allow me to see Charles when he comes? You are going to put nothing in the way of our marriage?" She leaped up and threw her arms about his neck. "François, how I love my *beau-fils*."

He smiled down his long, humorous nose. "But not as you love Suffolk?" he asked plaintively.

She shook her head sadly and kissed his cheek. Then she knelt demurely before him and, taking his hand, kissed it.

"I shall remember you all my life," she said, "as one of the best friends I ever had."

* * *

Mary paced up and down her chamber. In that adjoining, the English embassy was dining, and among them was Charles. She had not seen him yet, but she knew he was there.

The six weeks since the death of Louis were not quite at an end, but the Duke of Suffolk, as emissary of her own brother, would be allowed to visit her.

Burning with impatience she had plagued young Anne and all her attendants. How weary she was of her white mourning! How she longed to put on something gay. They assured her that nothing could have been more becoming than her white garments, but she was uncertain and so eager to appear at her best before her lover.

François, who on the 28th of January had been crowned at Rheims, clearly intended to keep his promise to her, for he raised no objection to Suffolk's enjoying a private interview with Mary; and it was for this that she was now waiting.

It seemed hours before he came to her; she studied him intently for a few seconds and then threw herself into his embrace.

"I thought I should never be free," she told him.

He kissed her with both tenderness and passion but she sensed his disquiet.

"Why, Charles," she said, "are you not happy?"

"I could be happy only if there was nothing between us two."

"But we are both free now. Think of that, Charles! And François is my friend. He will help us. There must be no delay. I shall not allow you to leave me again."

He took her face in his hands and shook his head.

"There is the King," he said.

"Henry? But I have his promise."

"He is making plans for your marriage, and they do not include me."

"Then he must change his plans. You forget that he has given me his word. Why, dearest Charles, you must not be unhappy now. I have been so excited . . . waiting for this moment. And now it is here, I do not intend to be cheated again."

"I had a long talk with your brother before I left England."

"But Henry knows what will happen. He would not have sent you here to me if he had not approved of our marriage, for he must know that I intend to marry you."

"I must tell you something, my dearest. Before I left England, Henry made me take a solemn oath."

Mary stared at her lover with tragic eyes.

"And there was naught I could do but take it."

"And what was this oath?"

"That I would not induce you to plight your troth to me, nor seize the opportunity which my presence here might give me."

"Henry made you promise that! And you did?"

"My beloved, you know your brother. What else could I do? I should not have been allowed to come here if I had not made it."

Mary stared ahead with narrowed eyes. Her lips were firmly set. "I'll not be cheated again," she declared. "I tell you, I will not."

Then she was twining her arms about his neck, giving him kiss after fierce kiss.

"I'll not let you go," she insisted. "I kept my side of the bargain, and Henry shall keep his. Charles, if you love me you will not allow a miserable promise to keep us apart. Do you love me, Charles? Do you love me one tenth as much as I love you?"

"I love you infinitely."

"Then why so sad?"

"Because, my beloved, I fear our love will destroy us."

They could not remain alone for long. That they should have been given this short time together was a great concession. He must return to his embassy, she to her mockery of mourning.

But before he left she had shown him her determination. She was a Tudor and she would have her way.

She talked to Anne Boleyn of her suspicions. She was certain that many were jealous of her Charles.

"Why, look," she cried, "he is handsome, so clever, so skilled in everything he does. He is my brother's best friend. So they are jealous of him — men, such as Norfolk, seek to spoil the friendship between him and Henry. They have whispered poison into my brother's ear so that he forgets his promise to me. But I do not forget."

She liked to talk to Anne because the child never attempted to soothe her. She merely sat and listened, and now and then added a shrewd remark of her own.

"It is for this reason that Henry extracted a promise from Charles before he left England. But my brother also gave me a promise, and I have no intention of forgetting that, I tell you. The King of France will help. So I shall insist on Henry's keeping his promise to me. For if my brother did not wish me to have Charles, why did he send him over here with the embassy?"

"It is said that he sent the Duke of Suffolk in order to lure you back to England, Madame."

"So they are chitty-chatting about me and Charles, are they?"

"It is said that the Duke is a very ambitious man, Madame, and that, having failed to win an Archduchess, he will try for a queen."

Mary pulled Anne's long black hair sharply. "Do not speak of the Archduchess to me. Charles never had any fancy for her."

"No, Madame."

"And understand this, little Boleyn, that my Charles would never lure me back that my brother might marry me to that slack-mouthed idiot of Castile."

The Queen's confessor came to her apartments and asked that he might speak to her alone; and when Mary signed to Anne to go, the young girl went quietly from the room.

The friar was an Englishman — and that she should have a confessor from her own country was another concession from François.

"Madame," he said, "I wish to speak to you on a most urgent matter."

"Speak on," Mary commanded.

"It concerns one of our countrymen who is here on a mission."

Mary studied him through narrowing eyes. "Which man?" she demanded.

"His Grace of Suffolk."

"And what of his Grace of Suffolk?"

"A most ambitious gentleman, Madame."

"Is that so? I see nothing wrong with ambition. I doubt not that you have some of that tucked away behind that holy expression you show me and the world."

"Madame, I come to warn you."

"Of what and whom?"

"Of this ambitious man."

The colour was high in her cheeks but the friar ignored the danger signals.

He went on blithely: "It is said that Your Highness is inclined to favour this man, and I have been warned that I should make known to you the type of man he is. Beware of Suffolk, Madame. He traffics with the devil."

"Who told you this?"

"It is well known that Sir William Compton has an ulcer on his leg which will not heal. Your brother, the King himself, has made an ointment which has cured other ulcers. Nothing cures Compton's. And do you know why?"

"Yes," Mary replied. "Compton has led too merry a life, and the ulcer is an outward sign of all his gaiety."

"Your Highness misjudges him. Suffolk laid a spell on the man out of jealousy of the King's friendship for him. Suffolk is a friend of Wolsey who, it is well known, is one of the devil's servants."

"They are my friends, also, sir friar. And you are not. You fool, do you not think I shall treat your lies with anything but what they deserve? If there is one grain of sense left in your addled pate, you would remove yourself from my presence without delay, for the sight of you so sickens me that I wish never to look on your silly face again. And I tell you this: If you repeat to anyone the lies you have told me, you will ere long have no tongue with which to tell even the truth, if so be you have a mind to it — which I doubt."

"My lady Mary . . ."

She went toward him, her hand uplifted to strike him. The friar hurried from her presence.

When he was gone, she threw herself onto her couch. So many enemies, she thought. Powerful men against us. Where will it all end?

But not for more than a moment would she allow her confidence to desert her.

There was another interview with Charles.

She faced him triumphantly.

"I have the answer," she told him. "Henry made you swear not to influence me. Well, you have kept that promise. You did not influence me. My mind has long been made up. He made you promise not to induce me to plight my troth to you. Well, have I? Did I need any inducement? Now, Charles, you have kept your promise. But I insist that you plight your troth to me. I command that you marry me."

Charles shook his head sadly. "I fear it will not do."

"But it shall do," she insisted.

"And afterward?"

"Oh, let us not think of afterward. I will deal with that if need be. I will make known to Henry that I was determined to marry you and commanded that you should obey me. Oh Charles, why do you hesitate? Do you not want to marry me?"

"More than anything on earth. But I want to live with you in peace and comfort for the rest of our lives. I want us to be able to watch our children growing up. I do not want a few short nights and then a dungeon for us both."

She took his hands and laughed up at him. "I would not think beyond those few short nights," she answered.

Then his emotions seemed to catch fire from hers. He seized her hungrily and they remained close.

Then she said: "If you do not marry me, Charles, I shall go into a convent. I'll not be thrown to that other Charles. Oh my dearest, have no fear. I will face Henry. He will never harm us. He loves me too dearly and has often said that you are his greatest friend. What do you say, Charles?"

"When shall it be?" he asked, his lips close to her ear.

"As soon as it can be arranged. François will help us."

"Then," said Charles, "we will marry. And when it is done, together we will face whatever has to be faced."

"I promise you this, my love," she told him solemnly. "There will be no regrets. As long as I live there shall be none."

* * *

In the oratory chapel of the Hôtel de Clugny a marriage ceremony took place in great secrecy.

Only ten people were present, and the priest was a humble one who had no notion, when he had been summoned, of the people whom he was to marry.

And there Mary stood, blissfully content, for this was the ceremony of which she had dreamed over many years.

The nuptial ring, the nuptial kiss — how different this occasion from that other in the Hôtel de la Gruthuse — how simple this, how elaborate that!

She smiled to think of the cloth of gold she had worn, and all the glittering jewels; they served their purpose for they did hide some of the bitter dejection, the melancholy which was then in her heart.

Now there were no jewels and the ceremony was simple; yet she wore her exultation, her supreme happiness more proudly than she had worn the costly treasures of France and England.

And as she stood beside her bridegroom, one of the spectators, smiling down his long nose at the bridal pair, cynically told himself that he was a fool to pass over this radiant girl to a rival. Yet it gave him pleasure to contemplate his own chivalry, and he would always remember the grateful glances of the bride.

The ceremony was over, and Mary Tudor was married to Charles Brandon.

The King of England might be furious, but at least they had the blessing of the King of France.

Part Three: The English

CHAPTER ELEVEN

The Return

The countryside was at its most beautiful when Mary and her husband returned to England, for the spring was well advanced. What a joy to be riding once more through the country lanes of her native land with the man of her choice beside her.

Charles was the perfect lover, the perfect husband, as she had always known he would be, simply because she had long ago decided that he was the only man for her. He was more uneasy than she was, particularly since they had crossed the sea. He was apprehensive, thinking of facing the King.

As they came near to London, she said: "Charles, whatever happens now, it was worth it."

He turned to smile at her. Her recklessness amused and delighted him while it often startled him; and when he thought of the honeymoon and the singleminded passion of his wife, he could say honestly that it was worthwhile and he would do the same again.

"But," he added, "having tasted bliss, I could not bear to give it up now."

"Nor shall you," she retorted. "I know Henry well. He wants us back at Court. He will speak sternly to us but that is not to be taken seriously. At heart he is rejoicing because we are coming home."

Charles did not deny this. But he could not forget those noblemen who were his enemies and who would be ready to poison the King's mind against him. If Wolsey had not been on his side, he felt, it would almost certainly be a cell in the Tower of London which would be awaiting him.

Wolsey had indeed been his friend, and it was he who had warned the Duke how to act. The King, Wolsey had told him, was extremely displeased with both his sister and her husband. It was a foolish — one might say treasonable — act to marry without the King's consent, and so quickly after the Queen had become a widow. Wolsey trembled at the thought of the King's anger, but knowing the great love he bore his sister he believed that His Grace might be slightly placated if Mary made over to him her French rents, which amounted to some twenty-four thousand pounds. Then there was the matter of the Queen's dowry which François had promised to pay back to her. This was some two hundred thousand crowns. If the King was asked graciously to accept these monies, together with the Queen's plate and jewels, he might show a little leniency.

Mary had laughed when she heard this. She had waved her hand airily:

"Let him have all my possessions. What do I care? All that matters is that we are together, Charles."

"I doubt we shall be able to afford to live at Court."

"I believe, sir, you have estates in Suffolk?"

"You will find them somewhat humble after all the splendour you have known."

"I was never more unhappy than when I lived most splendidly, Charles. I shall be happy, if need be, in Suffolk. Not that I believe Henry will allow us to leave Court. Did he not always love to have us with him? Why, when he was about to plan a joust his first thought was: 'Where is Mary? Where is Suffolk?' "

"That was before we had so offended him."

"Nonsense! Henry is only offended with those he dislikes. He loves us both. We shall be forgiven."

"At a great cost."

"Who cares for the cost?"

"Twenty-four thousand pounds? Two hundred thousand crowns?"

"Oh come, Charles, am I not worth that?"

He laughed at her. She was worth all the riches of France and England . . . and indeed the world, he told her.

Now as they rode along she was remembering how she had left Paris accompanied by the nobility of the Court. François himself had ridden with her, a little sad at parting, she fancied.

She would miss him, she assured him. Evidently not as he would miss her, he replied.

"Why, François," she told him on parting, "if there had not been such a paragon of many virtues in the world as Charles Brandon, then I think I might have loved you."

François grimaced and when he kissed her in parting at St Dennis he was very loth to let her go.

She had embraced Marguerite tenderly; she would always remember their friendship with pleasure, she told her.

Louise was affectionate, bearing no malice, because she was now a completely contented woman. Her blue eyes sparkled with delight and she seemed years younger, for she was a woman with a dream at last come true. Even Claude said goodbye as though she were a friend; but that might have been due to relief at the parting.

Then on to Calais, leaving that phase of her life behind her forever.

They stayed some weeks in Calais, and it was then that she had been aware of Charles's fear. They dared not cross to England until they had Henry's permission to return, and each day Charles had eagerly hoped for a messenger from his King.

Mary had been content to remain in Calais, for anywhere was a good place as long as Charles was in it; and she could not completely share his anxieties because she was certain that she would be able to win Henry to her side as easily as she had François.

And at last the message had come. Henry would receive them; but with his invitation, carefully couched, was Wolsey's more explanatory letter. The King was displeased; it was necessary to placate him; the pair must come to England not as a married couple, but they might call themselves affianced and there should be a ceremony of marriage in England; but in the meantime Henry would receive them.

Thus they rode on to Greenwich.

* * *

Henry stood, legs apart, hands clasped behind his back, studying the pair who stood before him. His eyes were narrowed, his little mouth was tight. Secretly he was glad to see them but he was not going to let them know it yet.

A pace or so behind him, her face set in lines of anxiety, stood Katharine, his wife. She would have liked to offer them a warm welcome, but she dared not until Henry gave her a sign that she might.

Mary smiled at her brother, but he was not looking at her. That is because we are not yet alone, she assured herself. When we are, he will be quite different. She glanced at Katharine. Poor Katharine! Her appearance had not improved in the last months and she was looking her age which was several years more than Henry's.

Mary knelt and kissed her brother's hand; she then paid homage to the Queen.

"I am so happy to be home," she said.

Henry's mouth slackened a little, as he took her hand and led her into the Palace, while Katharine followed with Charles.

"Henry," whispered Mary as they walked together, "how well you look! You are taller than ever. I had forgotten how truly magnificent you are."

"I hear that the King of France is tall."

"Very tall, but lean, Henry."

"I like not lean men."

"And 'tis not to be wondered at. I have been longing to see my brother."

He was softening visibly.

"You have behaved in a manner which I find truly shocking."

"Dearest Henry, how can you, who have never had to leave your home, your country, your beloved brother, understand the desire to return to all that you love!"

"So you preferred the King of England to the King of France?"

"There can be no comparison."

"I have heard he is a clever fellow, this François."

"Not clever enough to see through my little joke. Oh, Henry, I must tell you how I duped them all. As soon as possible let us be alone, you, Charles and I . . . and perhaps Katharine. I could tell this only then, and you will laugh so much. You will tell me I am *méchant* . . . as the King of France did."

"Now you are in England we shall expect you to speak in English."

"A little wicked then, Henry."

His mouth was already beginning to turn up at the corners. How good it was to have her home! How lovely she was — even more so than when she went away — with her French clothes and her way of wearing them. She made poor Katharine look a little dull. It was to be expected, he supposed. This was a Tudor girl, his own sister. They were so alike. It was small wonder that she glowed and sparkled as none other could.

She was looking at him slyly. "Henry, confess something."

"You forget to whom you speak."

"Forget I am speaking to my dearest brother, when I have thought of doing little else for so many months!"

"Well, what is it?"

"You are as glad to have me with you as I am to be here."

"I am displeased . . ." began Henry; but his eyes were shining. "Well," he said, "I'll not deny it. It pleases me to see you back here at Court."

She was smiling.

Charles dearest, she was thinking, it is easy, as I knew it would be.

Henry had laughed uproariously at the farce of keeping the royal family of France guessing. The tears were on his cheeks. He had not laughed so much since Mary had gone to France.

"How I should have liked to see you prancing about with your skirts padded. I'll warrant that long-nosed Frenchman was beside himself with anxiety."

"*And* his mother, *and* his sister. And then they caught me, Henry. The little Boleyn had not padded me carefully enough. The padding slipped . . ."

Henry slapped his thigh and rolled on his chair. Katharine looked on a little primly; she did not entirely approve of such ribald clowning. Poor Kate! thought Mary fleetingly. She does not amuse him as she should.

"I would I had been there," declared Henry.

"Oh that you had!" sighed his sister. "But now we are home and all is well."

"Is all well?" Henry scowled at Charles. "You should not think, Brandon . . . nor you, Mary, that you can flout my wishes and not suffer for it."

Mary went behind her brother's chair and wound her arms about his neck.

"Suffer for it?" she said. "You would not hurt your little sister, Henry?"

"Now, sister," said Henry. "Do not think to cajole me."

"You promised me that if I married Louis I myself should choose my next husband."

"And would have kept that promise had you trusted me. I meant you to have him, but you should have asked my consent. And to marry as quickly as you did was unseemly."

"'Twas not Charles's fault. 'Twas mine. I insisted, Henry."

"Then Charles is a bigger fool than I thought him, if he allows himself to be forced into marriage."

"There are ways of forcing, Henry. We loved so much. But he did not want to offend you. The fault was mine. I was so much afraid of losing him. Katharine is shocked, because I tell the truth, but it is something I am not ashamed of."

Henry scowled at his wife. "You should not be shocked because a woman loves her husband, Kate," he said.

"Not that a woman should love her husband, Henry, but that before they were married . . . it is not usual for a woman to insist on marriage."

Henry laughed suddenly. He pointed at Mary. "That girl's a Tudor. She knows what she wants, and she makes certain she gets it."

"'Tis true, I fear," agreed Mary. "Oh Henry, have done. Charles and I are married."

"You have not been married in England."

"But you cannot say we are not married. What if I should be with child — which I can tell you may well be the case. Now I have shocked Katharine again. But I am blatant, Katharine." She went to Charles and put her arms about him. She sighed. "You must send us to the Tower if you will, Henry, but one boon I ask of you. Let us share a cell, for I never want to be parted from this man as long as I shall live."

Watching them, Henry's face softened. They were such a handsome pair and there was much love between them. Henry felt a little envious. Katharine would never be a wife as Mary was. Mary was a woman of passion and he felt more alive since she had come back. Let them pay him vast sums. That should suffice.

He laughed suddenly. "Well, you will have to be married in my presence," he said. "It shall take place soon and we'll have a tourney to celebrate it. Charles, I'll challenge you. Perhaps we'll ride into the arena disguised as knights from a foreign land . . ."

Mary threw herself into her brother's arms.

"Oh, it is wonderful to be home," she said.

Henry was constantly in the company of his sister and brother-in-law; and it was useless for Norfolk and his supporters to attempt to poison the King's mind against them — they were home and he was happy. Moreover he had gained financially from their exploit, and if they were now not as wealthy as might befit their rank, Henry was secretly pleased at that because his sister would be all the more delighted with the gifts he intended to bestow on her.

Mary was his beloved sister, the person whom, at heart, he loved best in the world; Charles Brandon was his greatest friend. At the joust Charles was his most worthy opponent, brilliant enough to arouse the applause of the spectators, but never quite equalling the King. Mary's laughter was more frequent even than in the days of her childhood. Never before had she been so merry; never before had she been so contented.

He took them Maying with him and Katharine on Shooters Hill, where they were intercepted by men disguised as outlaws who turned out to be gentlemen of the Court, and who had prepared a magnificent picnic for them in the woods — an entertainment after Henry's own heart, made more amusing, more hilariously gay, because his sister and her husband were present.

Our of love for her he decided that she should launch the latest ship he was having built. Wherever she went, the people cheered her; they said she looked more like the King than ever, and there was not a more beautiful girl in England than Mary Tudor, Dowager Queen of France, nor a more handsome man than Henry VIII of England.

Glowing health and glowing spirits added to their natural beauty, and Henry, making merry in the new vessel which would hold a thousand men, dressed in cloth of gold, his great golden whistle hanging round his neck, was an expansive host; and his sister Mary in green velvet, cut away in the front to show an amber satin petticoat, her golden hair flowing freely about her shoulders, gave the ship the name *La Pucelle Marie*.

Those were happy days. There was no longer any fear of the King's displeasure.

When they returned to Greenwich after the launching of the ship, Mary noticed that Charles was thoughtful, and because she was susceptible to all his moods was certain that something was disturbing him.

As soon as they were alone in their apartments she asked him what ailed him. "For it is no use your trying to keep secrets from me, Charles."

He sighed. "I preceive that to be so," he answered, and went on: "Now that the King demands such payments from us we are much poorer than others at Court. I have been wondering whether Court life is too expensive for our pockets."

Mary smiled. "Well, then, Charles, if we cannot afford to live at Court we must perforce live elsewhere."

"But you are a king's daughter."

"King's daughter second. First I am the wife of a country gentleman with estates in Suffolk who cannot afford to live at Court."

"How would you like to live in the country?"

"The country . . . the Court . . . what care I? If we are together one place will suit me as well as the other."

"You have never lived away from a Court."

"Then it will be interesting to do so. Charles, I have been thinking that perhaps I should enjoy life in the country. They say Suffolk is very beautiful."

"You would find it very dull, I fear."

"I have a craving for a quiet life. I did not mean to tell you . . . until I was sure."

"Mary!"

"I think it may well be so. Oh Charles, I thought my happiness was complete, but when I hold our child in my arms I shall have reached the peak of content."

"If it is a boy . . ."

"Nay." She shook her head. "I shall not pray for a boy, Charles. I think of poor Katharine who constantly asks for a boy, and I am saddened by her disappointments. If my child is a girl I shall be quite happy. Yours and mine Charles — that is all I ask the child to be."

He took her face in his hands. "You are an extraordinary woman," he said.

"I am a woman in love. Is there anything so extraordinary in that?"

They sat on the window seat; his arm was about her as they talked of the future. Perhaps, when she was certain, he suggested, it would be advisable to retire to the country, where they could live without great cost in his mansion of Westhorpe. There she would be the Lady of the Manor and the people would love her.

"I should like the child to be brought up there," she reflected.

"What would Henry say?"

"I shall tell my brother that we cannot afford to live at Court. He will know why."

"We were fortunate to escape his anger. When I think of what we did . . . I tremble still."

"Did I not tell you that all would be well? I know Henry. We shall see him often. He will insist on our coming to Court, so we shall not be entirely cut off. It would not surprise me if he travelled to Westhorpe to see us."

"To entertain the Court would be costly."

"Never fear, Charles. I shall make Henry understand how poor we are. And there is something I wish to ask you, Charles. You have two daughters."

"Yes; Anne and Mary."

"They should live with their father."

He looked at her in surprise.

"I am their mother now," she went on. "Indeed I must be pregnant for I have a great longing for a large family. Yes, Charles, I want to leave Court. I am tired of all the masques and balls. I never want to disguise myself as an Egyptian or a Greek again. I never want to stand on the floor of the ballroom listening to the gasps of amazement when we unmask. I am tired of flattery and deception. I want to be in the country; I want to visit the poor and the sick and the sorry. I want to make them laugh and to show them that the world is a wonderful place. That's what I want, Charles, with you and my large family of children growing up round me. What are you thinking? You look solemn,"

"I was thinking that you are a woman who has always achieved what she desired."

She laughed. "This is the good life," she said.

"And we are in our prime to enjoy it."

"Well, Charles, I shall always be in my prime while you are beside me to love me."

Then she embraced him, and laughing, talked of the baby which she was sure she would soon be holding in her arms. She was certain of her happiness; the only thing she was not sure of was the child's sex; and that was a matter of indifference to her.

"Your thoughts run on too far," Charles told her. "You are not even sure that you are pregnant."

"And if I am not, I surely soon shall be," she retorted. "And when I go to the country I want all my children there. Your two girls and my own little one. A large family you will admit, considering I have been married barely two months."

"You can always be trusted to do everything on a grand scale."

"And the girls will come to Westhorpe?"

"If that is what you wish."

He then told her how he had rescued a child from the river and was bringing her up with his daughters.

She listened with shining eyes. "So I have three daughters already. I would that it were time for my own little one to be born."

It was impossible, living with her, not to share her zest, her love of life.

CHAPTER TWELVE

The Family at Westhorpe

Henry came to the Suffolks' London residence in Bath Place, and went at once to his sister's bedchamber, where he found her lying back on her pillows, flushed and triumphant, looking as though the ordeal had meant little to her. Her blue eyes sparkled although there were lines of exhaustion about them and her golden hair fell in a tangle of curls about her shoulders.

Henry came to the bed and stood looking down at her.

"Well done, sister."

"Oh, Henry, beloved brother, it adds to my joy that you should come to my bedside."

"Certainly I came. You've acquitted yourself with honours. Suffolk's a lucky man."

She called to her woman to bring the baby to the King, and as Henry held the child in his arms his face darkened.

"He looks to be a bonny boy," he said; and watching her brother, Mary read his thoughts. Why should others have bonny boys when he could not?

Poor Henry. Katharine had at last given birth to a healthy child, but it was unfortunate that it had to be a girl. Katharine adored the little Princess Mary who had recently come into the world and the King was fond of her too, yet he could not hide his chagrin that after all their efforts they had failed to get a boy.

"They tell me he has the look of a Tudor already," Mary said. "Some say they see you in him."

"Is that so?" Henry's scowl was replaced by a smile as he peered into the baby's face.

"In any case," Mary went on, "we have decided to call him after his uncle. That is if you raise no objection, brother."

"Ha!" cried the King. "Young Henry seems to have a fancy for his uncle. See! He is smiling at me."

He would not relinquish the child to his nurse but walked up and down the chamber holding him. The look of sorrow had come back into his face. Lately his thoughts had been more and more occupied with the desire for a son.

In the hall of the mansion in Bath Place stood gentlemen holding lighted torches which set a soft glow on the faces of the illustrious personages gathered there for a great occasion.

At the font, which had been set up for the purpose of christening the son of the Dowager Queen of France and the Duke of Suffolk, stood the King with Wolsey and the King's aunt, the Lady Catherine, Countess of Devon, daughter of Edward IV. These were the baby's godparents.

Henry watched the procession through half closed eyes, telling himself that he rejoiced because his sister's marriage was fruitful; but what would he not have given if that young male child were his son instead of his nephew?

"Why do I not get a son?" Henry asked himself peevishly as he watched the child being carried by Lady Anne Grey while Lady Elizabeth Grey bore the chrysom, preceded by the bearers of the basin and tapers; and for the moment his resentment of his fate was so overwhelming that instead of the red and white roses of his House which adorned the crimson of font and canopy, he saw the pale, apologetic face of his wife, Katharine, and his rage threatened to choke him. What was wrong with Kate that she could not get a healthy boy? Mary had not been married long before she had one. His sister Margaret had a healthy son. Why should *he* be victimised? There was nothing wrong with the Tudor stock. Where could three such healthy people as himself and his two sisters be found? No, if there was a flaw in his union with Katharine it did not come from the Tudor side.

His lips jutted out angrily, and several of those who watched read his thoughts.

Now the ceremony was being performed and the blue eyes of the baby were wide and wondering. He did not cry. Wise little fellow. All Tudor, thought Henry.

"I name this boy Henry," said the King; but the fact that he gave the child his name did not ease his sorrow.

Mary, fully aware of her brother's resentment, was suddenly fearful that he might dislike the boy because he could not get one of his own. But this could not be so. Henry would never hate a little child. He was as fond of children as she was.

While spice and wine were served she stood beside her brother and thanked him for his gifts to her child, which included a gold cup.

"He will treasure it always because of the donor," she told him. "I shall bring up my son, Henry, to serve you well."

Henry took her hand and pressed it.

"The child has received many beautiful gifts," he said.

"But none to be compared with yours."

"You are fortunate," he burst out suddenly. "Your firstborn . . . a son!"

"You will be fortunate too, Henry."

His mouth was grim. "I see little sign of that good fortune as yet. You have your son; Margaret has hers, and I . . . who need one more than either of you, am disappointed time after time."

"But you have your lovely Mary."

"A girl."

"But the next will be a boy."

His expression startled her, because it betrayed more than resentment. Was it cruelty?

In that moment Mary had a longing for the peace of Westhorpe. She wanted to be in the heart of the country with her husband, her stepdaughters and her own little son.

She thought: When a woman has much to love she has also much to lose.

She remembered how, when Charles took part in the jousts against Henry, she was always afraid that he might be going to win. Now there was another to fear for.

Yes, she was certainly longing for the quiet of the country.

Westhorpe, which was close to the town of Botesdale, was a commodious mansion and Mary had loved it from the moment she saw it.

Here she and Charles lived in retirement with their little son. It had not been difficult to slip away from Court because Henry was short of money, and Wolsey had decided to call in certain debts. Since the marriage of Mary and Charles they were two of the King's biggest debtors and, explaining to Wolsey that if they were to meet their commitments they must economise without delay, they took the opportunity of slipping away to the country.

As Henry was making a tour of some of his towns he did not immediately miss them, so no obstacle was put in the way of their leaving. As soon as Mary entered Westhorpe she brought an atmosphere of gaiety with her, and Charles was surprised, for the mansion seemed a different place from the one he had known before.

He had been afraid that Mary would quickly tire of the quietness, but he had a great deal to learn about his wife. She had always known that she desired to live in peace with her husband and family, and wanted nothing to threaten that peace; while she was at Court — much as she loved Henry — she would always be afraid that her husband might in some way anger him. There were too many people at Court jealous of Charles, and bold as Mary was, she could be nervous where her husband was concerned. She wanted to keep him safe from harm, and where better could she do that than far away from the Court, in his country house in Suffolk?

She declared herself delighted with the house. As soon as they arrived she made the acquaintance of the resident servants as though she were a squire's lady instead of a Queen; and they who had prepared to be overawed were immediately captivated by her free and easy manner. Mary and Charles had brought with them a very small party from Court consisting of two knights, one esquire, forty men and seven female servants — a small retinue for a Queen. But she had insisted on it and had estimated that the wages which would be paid out at Westhorpe were no more than three hundred and twenty-seven pounds a year.

"This," she had said, "we can afford; and, Charles, I intend that we shall live within our means."

It was a great delight to her to play the chatelaine; there was so much to learn, she explained to the governor of the household, and when one was brought up to be a Queen, one's education was neglected in many other ways.

She insisted that her little son sleep in her chamber; and she herself often attended to him. She was delighted with the new life — so different from everything she had known before, so much more intimate, so much more domestic.

"I do not envy Kings and Queens," she told Charles. "They see so little of their husbands and wives, they might as well not be married!"

Her contentment spread throughout the manor, and this was a very happy household.

But she was already planning for the future.

"Your daughters must come to Westhorpe, Charles, as we arranged," she said. "Also the little one you rescued from the river. I hope young Henry will soon have a little brother or sister. I told you I want a large family."

"Mary," said Charles soberly, "you know Henry will soon be back at Greenwich."

Her face clouded.

"You think he will command our return?"

"He said the Court was not the same when we were away."

He saw the fear in her eyes, and he went on quickly: "At the moment you do not wish to leave Westhorpe, but when the novelty has gone you will grow a little tired of our home where nothing much happens."

"Something happens all the time. I am happy here, and that is the best thing that could happen to anyone. I shall never grow tired of it. I don't want to go to Court. I am afraid . . ."

"Since when have *you* been afraid?"

She put her arms about him and held him close to her.

"Since I had so much to lose," she said.

"Why should you lose that which you treasure?"

"Treasures can be easily lost in my brother's Court, Charles. I want to stay here forever . . . because here I feel safe."

He understood. But he did not believe she would be allowed to have her wish this time.

It was a happy day for Westhorpe when the little girls arrived. Mary and Charles watched them from the battlements — three somewhat bewildered children, the eldest not more than six years old.

Mary's heart was immediately touched as she watched them dismount from their ponies, when the eldest took the two younger ones by the hand as though she would defend them from all the perils that might be waiting for them.

"Come," cried Mary. "Let us go down to them."

She ran down the staircases to the courtyard, for she had not yet grown accustomed to being able to act without ceremony, and still found it one of the most enjoyable advantages of her new existence.

She went to the little girls, and kneeling, embraced the three of them at once.

"My dear little daughters, welcome home!" she cried.

Anne, the eldest, who was the spokeswoman of the party, had been rehearsing what she would say when she was confronted by her stepmother who, she had had impressed upon her, was a queen.

She tried to kneel and glanced sternly at the others to remind them of their duty.

"Your Highness," she began.

Mary laughed.

"Call me your mother not Your Highness," she said. "I think it is difficult for a mother to be a Highness. Now which is Mary and which the little water nymph?"

The smaller child, who had already seen Charles and could not take her eyes from him, was pushed forward by Anne.

"She was nearly drowned," said Mary.

"But my father saved her," added Anne.

Mary lifted up the child and kissed her. "And how glad I am that he did, my little nymph."

"Nymph is not her name," Anne protested.

"But it shall be my name for her," replied Mary, who was delighted with this child because of her obvious devotion to Charles.

"You do not look like a queen," said Anne. "You have no crown."

"I did wear one . . . once," Mary told them.

"And you have lost it?"

Mary nodded and the faces of the young children puckered with sympathy.

"But I am not sorry," Mary went on quickly. "It was very heavy, and very uncomfortable to wear, so methinks I am happier without it."

The three little faces showed incredulity.

"It's true," said Mary. She turned to Charles and slipped her arm through his. "Is it not so?"

"I believe your mother to be speaking the truth," he said.

"Is she indeed our mother?" asked Anne.

"I am indeed," answered Mary.

"Mine too," said the youngest child.

"Yours too, my little nymph. And now I want you to see your brother. He is young yet and may not appreciate so many new sisters, but he will in time."

Thus Mary gathered her new family to Westhorpe and settled down to enjoy the golden days.

Before long distinguished visitors came to Westhorpe. The children, who were playing in the nurseries, were the first to see the approach of the party and ran down into the gardens to tell their parents.

Mary was in the enclosed rose garden gathering the blooms which she herself would arrange later; Charles sat on a wooden bench near the fish pond which was a feature of this garden, marvelling at the enthusiasm with which his wife still performed all these simple tasks. He could not believe that she would continue to do so. He often felt that he wanted to live every minute of his new life to the full, because he was certain it must change. They would not be long left in peace.

Anne led the two little girls into the rose garden crying: "Dearest Father and Mother, there is a crowd of people riding on the road."

The little one who had been given the name of the Water Nymph, usually shortened to Nymph, ran to Charles and was lifted up and placed on his shoulder.

"A party of riders," said Mary placidly. "I wonder if they are coming to Westhorpe."

"They look as if they are coming to Westhorpe," said Anne.

"Then mayhap we had better go and see who our visitors are," Charles said.

Mary held one of the roses to her nose. She had no wish for visitors. Visitors could mean the disruption of the peaceful routine, and this was the last thing she wanted.

"The scent of these roses is delicious." She made them all smell in turn; and because the children were most contented when they were with Charles and Mary, they were as ready to forget about the visitors as she was.

But they could not ignore the sounds of excitement; and soon a servant, flushed of face and bright of eye, came to break the peace of the rose garden.

"My lord, my lady, the Queen's party is here."

"The Queen!" cried Mary. "And the King?"

The servant looked aghast, as though that would be too much to be borne. It was enough that the Queen alone was here.

Mary and Charles, the children following, made their way to the courtyard where, looking exhausted and weary with the long journey, was Katharine.

Mary embraced her and Charles knelt. Katharine was smiling. "I am so glad to be here," she said. "The journey has been tedious."

"And you are in need of refreshment and rest," Mary said. "We are delighted that you should so honour us."

With Charles on one side, Mary on the other, Katharine was conducted into the hall of Westhorpe.

"So this is where you are hiding yourself away," said Katharine.

Then she saw the children who had run up, the Nymph clutching at Charles's doublet, his daughters keeping behind their stepmother.

"Your Grace has seen my large family?"

"Your family! I had thought there was but the boy."

"I always wanted a large family," laughed Mary. "And you know my impatience. Well, I have four children already. Who could do better than that in such a short time?"

The children were presented to Katharine, who patted their heads tenderly.

She sighed and turning to Mary said: "I have just been on a pilgrimage to the shrine of Our Lady of Walsingham."

Mary knew for what reason; Katharine was praying that she might bear the King a son.

When Katharine had rested in the apartments which had been made ready for her as soon as she entered the house, she wanted to see the nursery; and as Mary watched her bending over the cradle of her son, she felt a deep pity for her sister-in-law. Never, since her great happiness had come to her, had she felt as grateful as she did at that moment. How easy it was for the lives of royal people to go awry.

"Mine never shall," she told herself fiercely.

Katharine, returning to Court, talked to Henry of the household at Westhorpe. Henry was amused; he laughed heartily.

"So she has become a simple country woman, has she? How long will she be contented with that life?

Depend upon it, ere long she will be requesting to come back to Court."

Katharine was not so sure, but she rarely disagreed with the King's opinion; and when Henry heard of the nurseries of Westhorpe containing three little girls and a bonny boy — Mary's own son at that — he became glum.

He wanted to hear all about the boy, and Katharine was not sure which would have distressed him more, to have learned that his nephew was ailing or, the truth, that he was a healthy boy.

When Katharine told him: "Little Henry is growing so like you," he was pleased but almost immediately disgruntled because he had not a boy to whom he could give his name.

"I feel so much much better since my pilgrimage to Our Lady of Walsingham," Katharine told him. "I am certain that she will soon answer my prayers."

But of course she would, thought Henry. There was his good and pious wife. As for himself, did he not hear Mass regularly? Was he not as devout as God could wish?

He was suddenly good-humoured. "We will have a merry masque," he declared. "My sister Margaret will soon be with us. We must show her how we amuse ourselves here in England, for I believe the Scots to be a dour race. Now if we should have a tourney our champions must be there. Suffolk must come back to Court and Mary must greet her own sister."

Katharine remembered, a little sadly, the country idyll she had disturbed, and imagined the messengers arriving there with the King's orders.

Moreover she thought of Mary, the mother of a son, being at Court with Margaret who also had a boy. Henry would be delighted to have his sisters at his Court, but he was going to be very envious of them.

CHAPTER THIRTEEN

The Birth of Frances

When the king commanded, there was nothing to do but obey.

Reluctantly Mary said goodbye to the peace of the country. She left governesses and nurses in charge of the children with her own special instructions as to the care which was to be taken of them. Then sadly she rode away from Westhorpe.

Charles laughed at her melancholy.

"Once you are back you will realise how much you miss the pageantry and splendour at dull old Westhorpe."

"Do you know me so little then?"

"But you used to love to dance, and did so more tirelessly than any."

"That was when I thought it was an accomplishment to dance. If it is, I no longer care."

"Do not grieve. You will soon be back again."

"There is Margaret to entertain. And Henry may refuse to let us go. Oh, Charles, in the joust, you must take care . . ."

"I can face any who rides against me, you know."

"The one I fear most is my brother. Never unhorse him, Charles. Always remember . . . he must be the victor."

Charles laughed. "Dearest, you seek to teach me a lesson which I mastered years ago."

She was silent. "I am growing a little afraid of Henry," she said after a while. "He is changing. I loved him dearly . . . I still do. When he was a boy, and I seemed so much younger, I thought him perfect. But since he has come to power . . ."

"Ah. Power is not always good for a man."

"And supreme power, Charles . . ." She shivered. "There are times when I am so sorry for Katharine. She was pathetic, Charles, when she looked at our little Henry and I fancy that my brother has not been kind to her, and has implied that it is her fault they have no son."

"They'll get a son in time."

"They have been unlucky so far."

"Well, they have Mary. Katharine can produce healthy children, it seems."

"You understand now why I do not wish to leave Westhorpe. It contains all my treasures when you are there, and I want to keep them safe."

"Safe! We're safe enough. Henry is our friend."

She shook her head. "He was Katharine's friend once. Sometimes I doubt whether he still is. And when I remember her bending over our Henry's cradle, when I remember the look of longing in her face . . . yes and fear, Charles, I am afraid too . . . afraid for you. So, dearest, as you love me, while we are at Court, have a care.

He leaned toward her and touched her hand.

"You talk as though I were going into a den of lions."

"Sometimes I think you are."

"But you will be there, my love, to protect me."

He might laugh, but she was serious. She would not be really at peace until they had done a turnabout and, instead of riding toward London, were on the journey back to Suffolk.

During that visit there was cause for uneasiness. Henry had been determined to show his sister Margaret the splendours of his Court, and had appointed Charles to select twelve gentlemen while he himself did the same. They were to make the opposing teams who would joust in honour of the ladies.

Mary had sat with Katharine and her sister Margaret watching Charles ride out in white velvet, with crimson satin, shaped like lozenges, making a splash of colour on the white, his entire costume decorated with gold letters — M and C entwined; the King's party were as dazzlingly attired and their letters were H and K.

Charles had been as clever as usual, arranging that his side should joust brilliantly and be only that fraction less skillful than the King's. But there were times when some spirit of mischief would make him seem as though he were going to beat Henry; then Mary believed he remembered her and resisted the temptation.

She had sat with her sister and sister-in-law — both rather sad women at that time: Margaret because, having lost her first husband, the King of Scotland, she had recklessly married the handsome young Angus and was beginning to find him unsatisfactory. Katharine because, on account of her inability to bear a male child, she had begun to glimpse the cruelty of her husband. Only Mary was content with her state. Yet she must be fearful too, for Henry was changing, and no one was completely safe at his Court.

How delighted she was when she was able to return to Westhorpe; but it was not long before the summons to Court was repeated because Henry enjoyed the company of his youngest sister and her husband more than that of any others, and was not pleased that they should wish to live in retirement. Back to Court they went, and back again. Mary was in London at the time of the Evil May Day when she with Katharine and Margaret, who was preparing to return to Scotland, pleaded for those unhappy apprentices and secured their pardon. But the episode was an ugly one and gave her a further glimpse of the manner in which her brother's anger could be aroused.

She was more urgently reminded that she, who had so much to love, had a great deal to lose, and she longed for the peaceful security of Westhorpe.

Henry was loth to let her go, but this time she had a good reason.

She told him about it as they walked in the gardens of Greenwich and he reproached her for wishing to leave him and his Court.

"I have indulged you much," grumbled Henry. "You disobeyed me when you took Brandon to your bed. It was scarce decent. I might have had you both in the Tower. But I forgave you."

"Like the beloved brother you have always been."

"So beloved that you constantly wish to leave us."

"Not constantly, only now, because Henry, I am in a certain state of health . . ."

"What! You are with child?"

"Yes, Henry, and I believe I should live quietly in the country while awaiting its birth."

Henry turned to look at her, his lip jutting out. "You already have a healthy boy."

"And you have a bonny girl."

"I want boys."

"They'll come."

"They're being uncommonly shy about making their appearance."

"You are too impatient, Henry."

"Impatient! I am the most patient of men. You have a boy and another coming, like as not. Margaret has a boy and a girl. And I . . . the King . . . who must give my kingdom an heir . . . am frustrated. Why do you think it is so?"

"Because, brother, you are impatient. Kate will bear you many fine boys, I am sure."

"I would to God that I were. Sometimes I think there's a blight on my union with Katharine, Mary."

"Nay, Henry. But you understand that I must leave the Court. I want the fresh air of the country and the quiet life at Westhorpe. In the circumstances you will let me go."

Henry lifted his shoulders. "I like it not when you leave us. But I would not have your health suffer."

Mary lost no time in leaving Court lest he should change his mind.

Mary did not stay at Westhorpe but took up her residence in another of her husband's country mansions — Bishops Hatfield — while she awaited the birth of her second child; and here little Frances was born.

Looking down at the little one, Mary rejoiced that she was a girl.

"The child one has, always seems exactly what one wanted," she told Charles. "That is the miracle of childbirth."

"I know at least one child who disappointed her parents at birth," Charles reminded her.

"My niece Mary. But Henry has an obsession for boys. Perhaps I should have said it is the miracle of contentment."

"Strange," said Charles; "you are his sister and in some ways not unlike him, in others so different."

"Perhaps I was luckier than Henry. I knew what I wanted and I did not ask for what was impossible. I wanted you, Charles, and any child of yours would please me. Henry wanted sons — and that is for Providence to decide. You see I was wise in my desires."

"We could so easily have lost this life together," Charles told her, "and methinks Henry, in his desire for sons, was more reasonable."

She laughed. "You'd forgotten I always get what I want."

"And Henry?"

"I pray he will too." She was sober suddenly. "For if he does not," she added, "he will be very angry, and I believe, Charles, that when Henry is angry he can be very cruel."

The christening ceremony of little Frances Brandon was less grand than that of her brother, Henry, although tapestries were hung in the church of Bishops Hatfield for the occasion, and the chancel was decorated with cloth of gold. Henry the King was not represented but Katharine had sent two ladies to represent her and the young Princess Mary. One of these was Anne Boleyn who had been Mary's maid of honour when she was Queen of France.

Mary was pleased to see the girl again. She had always been interested in Anne. Such a composed little creature she had been and always so elegant. She was growing up to be a very distinguished young lady who had profited from her stay in France and wore clothes which must have been self-designed as they were so original; and she contrived to make the other royal representative, Lady Elizabeth Grey, look most insignificant.

But Mary's thoughts that day were all for her daughter. It would be wonderful to have another child in the nursery. Perhaps their next would be a boy. Even if it were a girl she would not mind. She adored her little Frances already, being certain that she could detect in her — as she certainly could in little Henry — some resemblance to Charles.

How good the child was during the trying ceremony.

She lay blandly staring up at the canopy of crimson satin on which roses and fleurs-de-lis had been embroidered.

Dear innocent little baby, thought her mother. One day you will have to go to Court because, after all, my precious one, you are the niece of the King.

Christening was a time for good wishes.

May she find happiness in her husband as I have found it in mine, prayed Mary.

CHAPTER FOURTEEN

Danger at the King's Court

The years were passing and the love between Mary and her husband was strengthened. She had always believed that theirs would be an ideal marriage; he had been too cynical to accept this view, but she had weaned him from his cynicism, and he substituted her creed for his.

He had begun by being mildly astonished; and now he had accepted his happiness as a natural state.

She was different from other women; she was unique. It was in her capacity for happiness and her genius for choosing those gifts from life which could give her true contentment.

Little Eleanor had been born. Another daughter. But it seemed that Mary had wanted a daughter. And as she said to Charles once, the fact that from time to time they must show themselves at Court only increased their appreciation of a quiet life in the country.

Rarely had Lords of the Manor been loved as they were loved. It was a strange situation, Charles often said: A Queen who longed to be a simple country lady;

a Duke and Duchess who sought to retire from Court instead of making their way there.

He had watched her when Charles of Castile had come to England. Perhaps that was one of her most enjoyable visits to Court. Then she had seemed like the young Mary who had loved to dance and flaunt her charm. Charles of Castile had been betrothed to her and had sought another match; and how she delighted in letting him know what he had missed! She had set out to charm him and she had succeeded. Poor Charles of Castile had watched her open-mouthed, had sought every opportunity to be at her side, and was clearly furious with those who had advised him against marrying her.

Henry was amused at his sister. He laughed with his friends to see the poor young Prince of Castile fascinated by the girl who had once not seemed a good enough match for him.

"By God," said Henry, "where Mary is, there is good sport. She should be at Court more often."

Later they accompanied Henry to France for his extravagant meeting with François; and François, while his eyes followed the radiant woman who had taken the place of the beautiful girl he had known, was as regretful as Prince Charles.

It was as the King said — where Mary was there was amusement.

"You should be more often at Court," he constantly repeated.

"Your Highness," was Charles's answer, "since I married your sister I have become a poor man. I cannot afford to live at Court, and my wife and I must needs retire to the country from time to time when we can live most cheaply."

Henry scowled at his brother-in-law. If he thought he was going to be excused his debts he was mistaken.

But later he conferred with Wolsey, and one day summoned Mary and Charles to his presence; and as he greeted them his blue eyes were shining with pleasure.

"It grieves me to see you two so poor that you must needs leave us from time to time," he said. "But do not think I shall excuse you your debts. I have been lenient with you, and it is not meet and fitting that my subjects should disobey me and be forgiven."

Mary smiled at her brother. "Nay, Henry, we do not ask to be forgiven our debts. We are content to pay our debts."

"Then you admit they are your debts."

Mary smiled demurely. "I forced Charles to marry me, and you thought we acted without consideration of our duty to you. You therefore imposed fines upon us which have made us poor. You were kind to us, brother. You might have sent us to the Tower. So we do not complain although we do at times have to retire to the country."

"I miss you when you are away," said Henry. "But I'll not let you off your debts for all that."

"Most right and proper," Mary agreed.

He dismissed them soon afterward, and as they were leaving he thrust some documents into Charles's hand.

"Look at these and let me have your opinion," he said.

Charles, surprised, bowed his head and Henry waved them away. When they were in their apartments Charles unrolled the documents while Mary watched him.

"What is this?" asked Mary.

Charles stared at the papers. "Buckingham had estates in Suffolk," he murmured.

"Buckingham!" Mary's face was set in lines of horror. She was thinking of the Duke of Buckingham whose claim to be as royal as the King had angered Henry. Poor Buckingham, one of the leading noblemen in the country, had been unlucky enough or unwise enough, to offend Wolsey. The result was that he had been sent to the Tower to be tried by his peers who dared do nothing but obey the King, and the proud Duke had been taken out to Tower Hill where his head was severed from his body.

Mary shivered when she thought of Buckingham, because his death was symbolic. In commanding it Henry had shown himself in truth to be a King whom his subjects must fear.

"Yes," Charles was saying, "your brother gives to us estates in Suffolk which belonged to Buckingham. You understand?"

Mary nodded. "We were too poor to stay at Court, and it is his wish that we should be there more often. We can no longer speak of our poverty, Charles."

She laughed suddenly, but it was not her old happy laugh. There was a hint of bitterness in it.

"So now we are rich, when we would rather be poor."

She threw her arms about him and held him tightly to her. She was fanciful that day; she could imagine that the axe which killed Buckingham threw a shadow over Charles's head.

For, she told herself, any who live near the King must live in that shadow.

Peace had fled from Westhorpe as Mary had known it would when Henry presented them with the Suffolk manors. There was no longer the excuse of poverty. It was no use for two people in so prominent a position to plead the need for retirement. Henry wanted them near him, and near him they must be.

It was always sad to leave the children, and one of Mary's nightmares was that she was riding away from Westhorpe to London, looking back, waving farewell to the children who watched them, their faces puckered, holding back the tears which would be shed when their parents were out of sight.

To love was the greatest adventure life had to offer; but to love was to suffer.

At this time her anxiety was great, because England was at war with France and Henry had decided that the skill and experience of the Duke of Suffolk could be used to England's advantage. Henry had no wish to lead his men to France so he would honour his friend Suffolk by allowing him to go in his place.

Mary remembered now that moment when Henry had made his wishes clear, how he had beamed on them both — his dear sister and his great friend whom he loved to honour.

They were expected to hear this news and fall on their knees and thank him for it. How little he understood! How impossible it was to explain! Mary had tried to.

"Henry," she had said, "I am a woman who likes to keep her husband with her."

Henry had smiled at her fondly. "I know you well," he told her. "You made up your mind to have Suffolk and none other would do. And you continue in love with him, which pleases me. Having great respect for the married state, I like not unfaithful wives and husbands. And because I have your interests at heart I am giving this man of yours an opportunity to win great honours. Let him make conquests for me in France and you will see how I am ready to reward him."

Impossible to say they did not want great honours, but only to be together. That would offend Henry, because when he gave he liked the utmost appreciation; and it was growing more and more dangerous to offend Henry.

So Charles had gone overseas, and so disconsolate had Mary become that she, being ill and longing for the quiet of the country and the children's company, had at length gained Henry's permission to leave Court.

But even at Westhorpe her anxiety did not fade. Each day she was at the turret watching for a messenger from London, for she had given instructions that as soon as there was news it should be brought to her.

The children were continually asking when their father would be with them, and it had been sad explaining to them that he was in a strange country fighting the King's war.

"Soon he will come," she promised them; and often they would run to her and say: "Will he come today?"

News came that he and his men had captured several castles, and that the King was delighted with his progress; but there had been no news for some time and winter was approaching.

One misty day while she was with the children she heard sounds of arrival and she could not suppress the elation which came to her because she was constantly hoping that one day Charles would ride unexpectedly to Westhorpe, although this was what he would call her wild optimism, since it was scarcely likely that if the army had returned to England she would not have had some news of this before Charles had time to reach her.

It was a messenger from London and as she could see by his face that the news was not good, she sent the children back to their nurseries before she demanded to hear it.

The news was alarming. The armies had been disbanded; the Duke of Suffolk was at Calais, and among the dispatches which he had sent to the King was a letter which, he had instructed, was to be carried immediately to his wife.

"My dearest wife," he had written:

> This finds me in dire straits. Our position was untenable; the weather was such that to remain in

camp would be disastrous. I asked the King's permission to disband the army, but I had no reply to my request, and perforce was driven to act without that permission. I disbanded the army and started on my way home when a command to hold the army together and stay where I was reached me. It was, as you will understand, impossible for me to do this, and I greatly fear that I have incurred your royal brother's displeasure by seeming to disobey his orders. You know full well what happened to Dorset. I now find myself in a similar case. Therefore I have gone to Calais because I feel that to return to England would be to place myself in jeopardy . . .

Mary let the letter fall from her hands.

She was remembering Dorset, returning to England after his campaign, a sick man who had been unable to walk ashore. She remembered her brother's fury against him and how he had almost lost his life.

Now she feared that his hatred would be directed against Charles. Henry had changed since Dorset had failed abroad; he had become more aware of his power, and that awareness had awakened in him a latent cruelty. In the old days she had never been afraid of her brother; she was now . . . desperately afraid for Charles.

The little girls and their brother came running to her; they had escaped from their nursery, sensing that something important was about to happen. Little Eleanor came toddling in after them to catch her skirts.

She thrust the letter into the neck of her gown and picked up the baby, while the others made a circle about her.

It was Anne who spoke. "My father is coming back?" she asked.

"Yes," replied Mary firmly. "In time he will . . . but not yet."

"When . . . when . . .?" They were all shouting together and she tried to smile at them.

"As soon as possible," she answered. Then: "First I must go to see your uncle."

"Uncle King?" asked Henry.

"Yes," Mary told him. "And when I come back I hope to bring you news of your father."

"Don't go away," said little Frances, catching at her mother's skirts.

"Never, fear, little one," Mary reassured her. "I shall soon be back . . . with your father."

Henry glowered at his sister.

"So you thought fit to come to see us."

"I would, Henry, that you could come to see *us* now and then."

"I have matters of state to attend to and those on whom I should rely do not always serve me well."

"Never was a king blessed with more faithful servants. If they could command even the weather to work for him they would do so."

"I thought as much. You have come to talk to me about that husband of yours."

"Who is your great friend and servant, Henry."

"It does not seem so, Madam."

"That is because you are not being reasonable."

His eyes narrowed; his scowl deepened. "I pray you do not bring your rustic manners to Court, sister."

She laughed and, going to him, boldly put her arms about his neck and kissed his cheek.

"All your scowls and harsh words cannot make you other than my big brother whom I have adored since I was a baby."

It was easy to soften him. She was his little sister again.

"I was ever over-indulgent to you."

"How could you be otherwise toward one who had so great a regard for *you*?"

"Methinks you are about to ask some boon, sister."

"And you, being the wisest man in Christendom, know what it is."

"I like it not when my orders are disobeyed."

"But Henry, your orders would have been obeyed had he received them."

"He did not wait to receive them. He has made me look a fool in the eyes of Francis."

"Oh no, Henry. You could never look a fool. Dear brother, the men would not stay together. The weather, the conditions, everything was too bad."

"So he has been whining to you. And now cowers in Calais, afraid to come home until his wife has pleaded with me to forgive him. By God, sister, you should have married a man, not a poltroon."

Mary's face flushed scarlet and she looked remarkably like her brother in that moment. "I married the finest man in England . . ." She added slyly: "Except one." But Henry did not see the irony.

"So he is now skulking in Calais, eh?"

"Awaiting your invitation to return."

"A pretty state of affairs when my generals take it upon themselves to disband my armies."

"Henry, you have fought in France. You know the difficulties . . ."

His brow darkened; he was thinking of his exploits abroad when he had been fooled by wily Ferdinand and the Emperor Maximilian.

"So," went on Mary quickly, "you will understand how Charles had to make this decision without your help. He made it too early, as we know; but he made it because he thought it the best way to serve you."

"And what do you want me to say?"

"I want you to tell me to write to him . . . to bring him home. You know how you enjoy jousting with him beyond all others."

It was true. He did miss Suffolk.

"You ever knew how to cajole me, you witch," he said.

She waited for no more; again her arms were about his neck and again she kissed him; and as she did so she wondered how much longer she would be able to wheedle what she wanted from this brother of hers.

Henry had lost some of his enthusiasm for the joust. He would often be shut away with his ministers; his bad temper was very easily aroused, and when he was in certain moods even his dogs would sense it and keep their distance. Wise courtiers did the same.

Mary and Charles remained in the country and were delighted that they were not summoned to Court. Mary decided that the change in Henry was due to the fact that he was growing older and had naturally lost his zest for boyish games.

One day there came a summons to Court. Henry wished to honour his young nephew and namesake by bestowing a title upon him, and he had chosen the Earldom of Lincoln.

Mary was uneasy when she heard this and called to Charles to walk with her alone in the gardens of Westhorpe that she might discuss this new development.

"He is nine years old," said Charles, "and therefore it is time that some honour was his. We should rejoice that your brother remembers him."

"I do not welcome Henry's interest in the boy," replied Mary. "He will want him to be brought up at Court and that means we shall lose him. Perhaps it was a mistake to call him Henry."

"But, Mary, we should not be displeased because the King honours our son."

"I am beginning to be fearful of Henry."

"You fear too much for your children, my love."

"I would that I could keep you all safe at Westhorpe. You see it is so easy to offend Henry now, and when he is offended one cannot be sure what he will do. He is brooding on some matter, I feel sure, and it has changed him."

"Let him brood," smiled Charles. "Now we should call the boy and prepare him for what is about to happen to him."

Young Henry was delighted at the prospect of going to Court, and the girls were envious. When the party rode out of Westhorpe for London the boy was beside his father and they chattered gaily of what was in store for him. Mary, watching them, delighted in their health and spirits, yet her very pleasure in them frightened her.

Her fears were not dispersed when she reached Greenwich, for there she discovered that the honour bestowed on her little son was not the main reason for the great festivities which had been arranged.

Henry Brandon was only one of the boys to be honoured on this occasion; a matter of much greater significance was being settled. Henry Fitzroy, the King's son by Elizabeth Blount, was to be given the royal title of Duke of Richmond, and Mary understood too well what this meant.

The King, despairing of getting a legitimate son, had decided to acknowledge his illegitimate one. Did this mean that he was prepared to make Henry Fitzroy the heir to the crown?

There must be feasting, balls and masques to celebrate the elevation of this boy who, the King would have his people know, was very close to his heart.

This was understandable, thought Mary; but what seemed to her so grossly cruel was that Katharine should be commanded to attend these celebrations. What must she feel to see her husband's bastard so honoured, and herself, unable to give him a son, forced to honour him? Where was the sentimental Henry of her childhood? thought Mary. He had certainly changed.

Poor Katharine, what would her fate eventually be?

What, wondered Mary, might be the fate of any of us who cease to please him — as she has ceased to?

They were riding into the arena — two giants who were the tallest men at Court. Mary sat beneath the canopy on which were embroidered her own symbol, the marigold together with the golden lilies of France. Beside her was Katharine, on her canopy the emblem of the pomegranate. Poor sad Katharine, how ironic that her emblem should be the Arabic sign of fertility!

But Mary had no thought for her sad sister-in-law now, for Charles and Henry had been the champions and it was time for them to meet.

She knew her Charles. He loved to joust and show his skill. There was a temptation every time he faced an opponent to do his utmost to win. And he could win easily. She knew it and she trembled.

"How well matched they are," said Katharine, forcing a smile to her pale lips. "There is no one else who can match the King."

"And Charles must not either," murmured Mary.

Katharine had glanced at her clenched hands and understood. In that moment there was a deep sympathy between them; they were two frightened women.

Suddenly there was a shout. Katharine and Mary simultaneously rose in their seats.

"The King has not lowered his visor . . . ," cried Katharine.

Mary stared in horror, for Charles was riding toward Henry, his lance in his hand pointing toward the King's forehead; and Charles, whose headpiece prevented him from seeing how vulnerable was the King, was advancing at speed.

"Charles! Stop!" cried Mary.

The crowd of spectators were shouting but Charles thinking they were applauding the King and himself, did not understand the warning.

His lance struck Henry's helmet, a matter of inches away from his exposed forehead; it was shattered and only then did Charles realise how near he had come to killing the King.

Katharine put an arm about Mary. "All is well," she whispered. "The King is unharmed."

Henry came into the banquet hall, his arm about Charles's shoulder. The trumpets sounded; the company rose and cheered.

Henry was happy. This was a scene such as he loved: The drama which had a happy ending, with himself as the hero!

He took his place at the table and cried: "This fellow all but killed his King this afternoon. He tells me he will never joust against me again. Methinks he suffered from the affair more than I!"

How bland he was, how blue the little eyes, asparkle with good humour, but ready at any moment to send forth the fire of anger; the thin lips were smiling but everyone was beginning to learn that they could curl in sudden anger.

"Nay, my brother," he said, smiling at Charles. "We know that, had your lance entered this head, you would have been the most unhappy man in England this day. We know our friends. And I say to you, I hold this not against my brother, for the fault was mine. So eager was I to ride against him that I forgot to lower my visor. I could not have his head for that, could I, my friends?"

There were cheers and laughter.

Charles was shaken; yet not more so than Mary.

The King's eyes might glisten while the suckling pig was piped to the table, he might command that one of his own songs be sung, he might smile benignly at the company when they applauded his music; but there were three very uneasy people at the banquet that night, and they were his nearest — his wife, his sister and his brother-in-law.

CHAPTER FIFTEEN

The Last Farewell

Gossip was rife, not only at Court but throughout the country. Even in the village of Suffolk there was whispering of the King's Secret Matter.

Those days seemed too short for Mary; she wanted to catch them and make them twice as long. She had lost some of her health recently and had discovered a tendency to catch cold, leaving her with an ague and a cough which would not go. Charles was anxious because of her health and to relieve his fears she pretended that she felt as well as ever.

She often wondered what was happening at Court. At least there were not the same demands for her and Charles's attendance there. There was a new set about the King — bright young people, clever young people who devised plays and masques of much wit for the King's amusement. The leaders of this set were, strangely enough, her one-time maid of honour, Anne Boleyn, Anne's brother George, and Thomas Wyatt.

It was pleasant to be left in peace.

Mary felt more and more remote from the Court, but she knew now that Henry was trying to cast off

Katharine, and there were rumours that he was so enamoured of Anne Boleyn that he wished to make her his Queen.

Mary was angry; she had been so fond of Katharine, although often irritated by her mildness; she believed that if she went to Court she would be unable to avoid quarrelling with her brother; and he was in no mood for opposition.

Had she felt well she might have gone to Court, because she did want to comfort Katharine and tell her that she would always support her against that upstart maid of honour.

Yet when she considered her growing family, when she thought of Charles, she knew that they were all safer at Westhorpe. She had her own secret to keep too; she wanted none of them to know that she suffered often from mysterious pains; that she was often breathless; she had warned her maids that they were not to mention that her kerchiefs were sometimes stained with blood.

One day Charles came to her in some dismay.

"A summons?" she asked fearfully.

He nodded gravely. "The Papal Legate Campeggio is in London and I am summoned to the Court."

"So it has gone as far as that. My poor Katharine!"

Charles took her hands and was alarmed because they were trembling.

"Your brother has determined to be rid of her," he said.

"I know. And marry that sly wench. Marry her, Charles. How can he so demean himself . . . his throne . . . his name . . . by marrying one so far beneath him!"

Charles laughed and gently touched her cheek. "These Tudors have a way of forgetting what they owe their rank when they take a fancy to some low man or woman."

"We were quite different."

"Oh no, my love. And it seems that Henry is as determined to have this girl as you were to marry me."

"Then . . . God help Katharine!" cried Mary. She clung to Charles. "Charles, have a care."

"You may trust me."

"Remember how precious you are to us all."

"I will never forget, my love," he answered.

So Charles went to London.

She was restless; she could not sleep; and when she did she would awake startled, her body bathed in cold sweat.

She had grown thinner and paler, more thoughtful, nervous, ready to be startled by a sudden sound.

One morning she awoke in great distress. If Henry could declare his marriage to Katharine invalid, because of Katharine's previous marriage with his brother Arthur, what of Charles's marriage to Lady Mortymer? She was still living. What if she herself were to die and her children be declared illegitimate?

She could not rest. There must be a dispensation from the Pope. She must make sure that her children were safe, when she was no longer there to protect them.

The case of the King versus the Queen of England dragged on, but Mary had no difficulty in receiving a confirmation of her marriage to Charles Brandon from the Papal Court.

When she knew that she had succeeded, Mary wept with happiness; and suddenly remembered that for the first time in her life she had thought of herself . . . dead.

That moment seemed significant, for in it she knew that each day she could spend with her children and husband would be even more precious, that she must live each one as though it might be the last.

She was her gay self and refused to be alarmed even when the people of Suffolk rose against the Duke. Henry, who was in need of money, had levied taxes which he commanded Charles to collect on his behalf, at which the people had risen and threatened Charles's life. But Mary knew that Charles would know how to handle the people. And she was right; by good fortune and gentle persuasion he quelled the rising; in this he was helped by their immediate neighbours who had benefited from their residence at Westhorpe and the other Suffolk manors and were ready to defend them against those who did not know them so well. Mary had once more been obliged to lay the facts before her brother and plead for clemency; and at her request Henry decided he would not demand the tax and would pardon those who had risen against her husband, who was acting as his representative.

That danger had passed and Mary was determined that the troubles which had been set in motion by the King's desire to rid himself of Katharine should not come to Westhorpe.

But it was impossible to hold them back. As well try to hold back the sea . . . or death.

Death? She thought of it now and then. Sometimes she fancied it was like a grey shadow at her elbow; and her great desire was that none should recognise it but herself.

She would not go to Court, and Henry did not insist. He did not need his sister to amuse him now. He had one far more amusing, far more beautiful, one whom he was determined to make his Queen.

"I'll not go to Court," declared Mary, "and take second place to my maid of honour. I can see her now, sitting on her little stool, staring into the future with those great brooding witch's eyes."

But it was not Anne Boleyn who kept her from the Court, so much as her own failing strength.

She would not be able to keep her secret much longer.

Only yesterday Frances had said to her: "Mother, are you ill?"

That was when they were in the garden and she had felt faint.

She had roused herself. "Nay, my love. I was falling asleep."

It was easy to deceive a child; not so easy to fool Charles. There were times when she saw his brow furrowed as though with fear.

"My love," said Charles, "a summons."

"To Court?"

"Henry is taking Anne to Calais. He wants the approval of François for his marriage."

"And he asks us to go?"

"He feels it is necessary to have us with him."

She closed her eyes. How could she endure the crossing, the masques, the banquets? She felt dizzy at the thought.

"I shall not go," she said.

Charles took her by the shoulders. "You do not deceive me, my dearest," he said. "You are ill."

"I am well enough, Charles. It is merely that I grow old."

"Think how much older I am!"

"But you are as a god, Charles. You are immortal."

"Do not suggest that I should go on living without you."

She threw herself against him that he might not see the tears in her eyes.

"I'll not go to Court, Charles. I'll not take second place to Henry's concubine. Why, if I went I should show my hatred of her. They say he grants her every wish. You must not make an enemy of her."

"Mary," he said, "I shall make your excuses to Henry. And while I am gone you must be the invalid. You must see the physicians."

She nodded. She knew she could not much longer go on playing her game of make-believe.

The hot June sun shone on the rose garden of Westhorpe, and as Mary sat by the pond watching the fishes, she could hear the shouts of the children at play.

What happiness I have known, she thought, here in this house . . . in this garden. The children are growing up now. They will not need me as they did. And Charles? Where was he now? On the way to Calais? Was he paying homage to the Concubine? Oh, Charles, be careful.

He would be careful for her sake . . . as she would be for his. He had learned to love as she loved; and this garden, this house, was encircled by their love.

God keep them all, she prayed. And if in mourning me they should be sad, then teach them not to mourn.

She closed her eyes and when the children came running into the garden they thought she was asleep.

Charles came into the room as she lay in her bed. "Charles," she whispered. He was kneeling by the bed. "My beloved."

"So you came back . . .?"

"As soon as I heard that you needed me."

"I needed you, did I not? Oh, how I needed you!"

"Mary . . ."

"Oh, Charles, you are weeping."

"Stay, Mary. Do not leave me. We cannot be apart . . . you and I. You always said it."

"This had to come, Charles. Take care of my little ones."

"You cannot leave us."

She shook her head and smiled at him.

"Charles, do you remember the chapel at Clugny?"

"For as long as I live I shall remember."

"Do you remember how I told you that there would be no regretting . . . as long as we two should live?"

"I remember."

"Charles, kiss me . . . for the last time, kiss me."

He did so.

"There are no regrets, my love," she said.

He stood up and stared disbelievingly down at her. He could not believe that the vital, beautiful Mary Tudor had left him forever.

Bibliography

Aubrey, William Hickman Smith, *The National and Domestic History of England*

Batiffol, Louis (translated by Elsie Finnimore Buckley), *National History of France*

Chamberlin, Frederick, *The Private Character of Henry the Eighth*

Fisher, H.A.L., *The Political History of England (1485–1587)*

Froude, James Anthony, *History of England*

Gairdner, James (editor), *Memorials of Henry VII*

Green, Mary Anne Everett, *Lives of the Princesses of England*

— , *Letters of Royal and Illustrious Ladies of Great Britain*

Guizot, M. (translated by Robert Black), *History of France*

Hackett, Francis, *Henry the Eighth*

— , *Francis the First*

Herbert, Edward, Lord, *History of England under Henry VIII*

Hudson, Henry William, *France*

Jackson, Catherine Charlotte, Lady, *The Court of France in the 16th Century*

Salzman, L. E, *England in Tudor Times*

Stephens, Sir Leslie, and Sir Sidney Lee (editors), *The Dictionary of National Biography*
Strickland, Agnes, *Lives of the Queens of England*
Wade, John, *British History*